"Come here," Michael said quietly. "We need each other for body heat."

Katherine crawled hesitantly toward him. She sat next to him, and he put his arm around her, tightly wrapping the blanket around them. Katherine stared into the fire, trying to deny the excitement that was building inside her. The attraction she felt for him was overshadowing all of her other instincts.

Michael slipped his other arm around her and began rubbing her arm to warm her. He too felt a sense of excitement, along with a sense of peace and contentment. He knew that he felt more than lust for this unusual woman.

Katherine instinctively rested her head on his shoulder. She couldn't remember the last time she felt this safe and happy.

He kissed her forehead softly. Katherine pulled back. She knew that if she didn't resist him now, she would quickly lose her willpower.

"We can't," she said, turning her face away. "I work for you!"

Michael gently eased her face back toward him. His intoxicating desire mixed with the brandy had created an aching need that begged to be satisfied. He wanted her. Damn the consequences.

"All right," he replied with a sexy grin. "Have it your way. You're fired." He drowned her protest with a long, deep kiss.

Margaret Allison

Indiscretion

POCKET BOOKS

New York   London   Toronto   Sydney   Tokyo   Singapore

This book is a work of fiction. Names, characters, places and inci-
dents are products of the author's imagination or are used ficti-
tiously. Any resemblance to actual events or locales or persons,
living or dead, is entirely coincidental.

An *Original* Publication of POCKET BOOKS

POCKET BOOKS, a division of Simon & Schuster Inc.
1230 Avenue of the Americas, New York, NY 10020

ISBN: 0-671-56328-9

First Pocket Books printing July 1996

10 9 8 7 6 5 4 3 2 1

Cover art by Matthew Rotunda

Printed in the U.S.A.

For Brian

INDISCRETION

1

Katherine stepped out of the taxicab and into the warm, pouring rain. Her eyes scanned the two-story wood structure in front of her. A small, red neon sign in the window conservatively confirmed it was "The Tavern."

Katherine opened the heavy door to the bar. She awkwardly struggled to close her umbrella as she tried to suppress her reluctance about venturing out in an unknown city the night before she began her new job. She would have preferred to spend the evening unpacking the rest of her things and getting organized, but her friend Cyndi had insisted that Katherine meet her at the Tavern. They were celebrating, Cyndi had announced, and they had to celebrate at the most popular bar in town. Still, Katherine had acquiesced only because she felt indebted to Cyndi. After all, if it wasn't for her old college friend, she never would have heard about the opening at the Benson Corporation.

It was Cyndi who had religiously scanned the classified sections of the *Baltimore Sun* and the *Washington Post*, hoping to find a job that might tempt her old college roommate to move from Michigan to the East Coast. Originally, Katherine held little hope of landing such a high-level job, especially at a well-respected manufacturing giant like Benson. But, to satisfy Cyndi, she sent in her résumé. To her surprise, Benson's vice president of personnel contacted her a few weeks later and offered to fly her to Baltimore.

Katherine had impressed the vice president and was asked to fly back the following weekend to present her ideas on a campaign to increase sales in the A-14 division, the favorite division of the president and chairman of the board, Michael Benson.

Michael Benson was well known in the aeronautical world. He was young, handsome, and ruthlessly ambitious. His dream was to develop an affordable engine that would double a jet's speed, revolutionizing air traffic. And most people believed he would succeed. But despite the creation of an engine that had increased the speed of small commercial planes, the A-14 division had been losing money.

Katherine felt she knew how to save the division. She created a unique advertising campaign that appealed to the actual end user: the consumer. And despite the fact that she was only twenty-eight, younger than any other director in Benson's history, she was offered the job of marketing director at a salary that was double the amount she had been earning at Aerotech. After accepting, she had only two weeks to resign her old job, pack her bags, and say good-bye to her friends.

And now here she was. In Baltimore. She squinted her eyes and peered through the air-conditioned smoke-filled room as the door slammed shut behind her. The bar was packed full of men and women, many still in their business attire even though it was almost eight o'clock.

Keeping an eye out for Cyndi, she squeezed through the crowd around the mirrored bar, trying to ignore the obvious lusty looks from the men she passed. Her long, silky, light brown hair fell loosely to her shoulders. Her faded denim jacket barely hid the rain-dampened silk blouse which clung seductively to her round and firm breasts. The rain had also had an impact on her jeans, encasing her slender hips as though sewn on by hand. The glances from the admiring crowd did not flatter her. Instead, they made her uncomfortable. Although she was aware that people considered her beautiful, her looks were not something she allowed herself to take pleasure in. In her professional life, she was constantly being pegged as "the pretty one" and had to work twice as hard to prove that she was intelligent as well. It was a source of pride for her that she had always been hired by women, not by men looking for a pretty accessory. And in her personal life, her beauty typically attracted the egotistical man who was looking for a prize instead of a person.

"Hey!" said a large, burly man as he blocked her path. "Where are you off to?" He was sweating profusely as his tortoiseshell glasses slid down his nose. Katherine could smell the scotch on his breath.

"I'm meeting someone. Excuse me," she said, ignoring his leer as she squeezed past him.

Katherine reached the end of the bar and looked back. No Cyndi. Cyndi was known for her flightiness, but she had talked to her only an hour before she left to confirm their meeting spot. Katherine took a deep breath. She tried to relax as she paused at an empty bar stool.

The bartender interrupted his conversation with two women a few seats over. "What can I get you?" he called out boisterously.

Katherine hesitated. She had to get up early tomorrow. "I'll have a glass of white wine," she said, still a bit indecisive.

"Chablis?" he asked.

"That'll be fine." She sat down on the wooden stool as she watched the bartender unscrew the cap on a wine bottle.

"Where you from?" he asked kindly as he poured some wine into a long-stemmed goblet.

"How could you tell I'm not from here?"

Before the bartender could respond, a deep, throaty voice interrupted. "Because you're too beautiful for Harry not to have noticed you before." The owner of the voice flashed her a toothy smile as he slid onto a stool beside her. In addition to a black designer trench coat, slicked-back hair, and a dimpled chin, she couldn't help but note he moved with the confident swagger of a man whose biggest fan is himself. "Isn't that right, Harry?" he added, staring at her with an intense yet casual air, as though he believed she was his if he wanted her.

Katherine rolled her eyes as she rested her chin on her hand. She leaned away from the man, ignoring the canned pickup lines. She refused to dignify his presence by acknowledging his compliment.

The bartender grinned at her snub. Although the man was a regular, it was nice to see a woman who was not taken in by his persuasive lines. "What can I get ya?"

"I think I'll try something a little . . . different," the man said, oblivious to Katherine's rebuff. He leaned forward, spreading out his arms and resting his hands on the bar, intentionally brushing his arm against hers. "Bring me a rum and soda." He focused his cold, empty brown eyes on Katherine once again. "You never did say where you're from."

"That'll be three-fifty," the bartender interrupted, pointing to the drink he had put down in front of her.

"It's on my tab," the man ordered.

"No. No thanks," she stuttered. She certainly didn't want to feel obligated to this arrogant intruder. She bent down to pick up her purse and looked up at the bartender. To her dismay, he had already given the man beside her his drink and was at the other end of the bar ringing up their tab.

The man smiled mischievously as he ran a hand through his perfectly cut hair.

"Thanks," she said meekly. She decided that if Cyndi didn't arrive immediately, she was going home.

"Here's to a solitary rose in a field of common daisies ..." He raised his glass as he gazed at her, slowly savoring her beauty. "You were saying ... ?"

The bartender suddenly reappeared. "Hey, um, Mike said *he's* paying for the lady's drink," he said, embarrassed.

The man next to Katherine abruptly turned his head toward her. His eyes grew large before tightening into suspicious little slits. "You didn't say you were with ..."

"You probably never gave her a chance," interrupted a tall, dark-haired man suddenly appearing behind Katherine. Katherine spun around cautiously. Like her, he was dressed casually. He wore a flannel shirt open at the neck, loosely tucked into faded jeans. His tousled, coal-black hair was accentuated by the black-framed glasses that sheltered his blue-gray eyes. He smiled slightly at the annoying drudge beside her.

"Hey, I'm sorry. Didn't mean to cut in," her harasser mumbled unintelligibly as he grabbed his drink. Within seconds, he was gone.

Katherine wasn't sure whether to be grateful or angry. What was she? Something to be bargained off to the highest bidder?

"This whole thing is really ridiculous," Katherine protested. "I'm just waiting to meet a friend . . . a girlfriend," she added before she could stop herself. Why did she have to make it clear that it was not a strong, jealous boyfriend she was awaiting?

"Do you mind if I stay here while you wait?" the

man asked rather harmlessly. Katherine hesitated. "I'll hold a seat for your friend," he added.

Katherine glanced angrily toward the door. Where was Cyndi, anyway? "All right, but you don't have to pay for my drink."

"Okay," the stranger replied, shrugging his shoulders nonchalantly. "I think the total was three-fifty—plus tax and tip, of course."

Katherine couldn't stop her lips from curling up into a half-smile. She hadn't expected him to cave so easily. She picked up her purse and opened her wallet. It wasn't hard to spot the solitary hundred-dollar bill in the soft leather folds. She hadn't had time to set up a new bank account yet, and all she had were large bills left over from her car trip.

"Can you change a hundred?" she asked, somewhat embarrassed.

The stranger appeared a little taken aback. "You don't have anything smaller?"

Katherine shook her head. "Sorry."

"Just forget it," the stranger said.

"No, really," she replied indignantly. "I insist."

She held the bill out to him. He glanced at her fiery, stubborn eyes. "I don't have enough change," he said. "You can buy the next round or get change from the bartender."

A moment was spent in silence as Katherine pretended to study the group at the end of the bar while waiting for the bartender. She preferred to get change. If Cyndi didn't show up, she'd need it for the cab ride, anyway. Finally, the stranger spoke.

"Do you live near here?"

"No. I mean, yes, now I do. I just moved here this past weekend."

"Really," the stranger replied, intrigued. "From?"

"Albion. Albion, Michigan."

"Albion? Oh, right," he said, as though looking at

a map. "Albion is a little town between Chicago and Detroit, right?"

Katherine rolled her eyes. She could guess what he was thinking. She was some innocent, small-town girl who comes into the big city waving around hundred-dollar bills to impress people. What did she care what he thought, anyway? She'd never see him again after tonight. She nodded curtly. "Right."

He looked at her quizzically, trying to read her reaction. He smiled warmly, as though he understood. "The great Midwest."

"There you go, boss," the bartender said, placing the drink down in front of the stranger.

"My friend needs change so she can pay me back," the stranger said, pointing toward the money.

"You got it, Mike," the bartender said with a smile that didn't escape Katherine's attention. They watched in silence as the bartender reached into his pocket and pulled out a wad of bills. He counted her change out loud.

"Thanks very much," Katherine said, accepting the bills. She knew this man was teasing her, and she didn't find it funny. She turned toward the stranger and handed him a five.

"I think you've got change coming," he said, reaching into his pocket.

"It's not necessary," Katherine replied.

The man checked his wallet and frowned. "I don't have anything smaller than a five. Now *I'll* have to get change."

"Please don't," Katherine said, inadvertently placing her hand on top of his. She pulled it away immediately, as if burned by the touch.

The man turned back toward Katherine. "Okay, thanks," he said with a hint of a smile as Katherine turned away, embarrassed by her reaction to an innocent touch. "Well . . . cheers," he said definitively, raising his glass.

She picked up her glass and quickly swallowed a large portion. Something about this casual interlude was making her nervous.

She set the glass down and peered at him suspiciously. "What did you mean by that last comment . . . about the Midwest?" she asked.

"Nothing bad," he said with a twinkle of a smile. "You seem . . . let's just say that I've found that Midwesterners in general tend to be more open and friendly than those . . . indigenous to this area," he said, rather carefully.

"Thanks, I think," she said, accepting his awkward compliment. Was he being sarcastic? "So, why was that man so intimidated by you? Do you own this place or something?"

"No." He sounded as if he found her question amusing. He glanced at her and smiled. "Perhaps he was just being a gentleman."

"I doubt that," Katherine replied, the alcohol adding assurance to her words.

"You doubt what?"

"I doubt he was being a gentleman. He didn't seem like the gentleman type," she added. The stranger smiled.

"And how can you tell?"

"I guess I just know," she replied, shrugging her shoulders.

"Expensive clothes, styled hair, polished fingernails, a polite yet commanding presence . . . those things don't make a gentleman?" he asked, raising one eyebrow curiously.

"No. At least, not in my opinion—unless, of course, your name happens to be Scarlett."

The stranger laughed. "I see. Well, I guess that's

good news for guys like me. But it seems like women prefer that type of man."

"The superficial ones, maybe. Or the very young. The smart ones have already learned their lessons," Katherine said pensively. She was still hurt by the breakup of her relationship with Ross. He had been the stereotypical heartthrob—tall, dark, and handsome, not to mention a powerful director in her old company. She had been completely infatuated with him, ignoring her friends' warnings about his wandering eye and reputation for casual affairs. She had foolishly thought that she could change him. Ha! She had learned the hard way, and the pain of his infidelities still stung.

"You speak as though you have firsthand knowledge," the stranger said, watching her carefully. His gentle gaze silently urged her on.

"An old boyfriend. I made the mistake of becoming involved with somebody at work ... a real snake, so to speak," she replied, blushing slightly. One glass of wine, and her tongue was already becoming loose.

"I'm sorry," he said quickly. He distractedly ran a finger around the tip of his beer bottle. "That's a cardinal rule of mine. Never get involved with anyone from work. There's no escape."

"Unless you find another job," she added.

"Is that why you moved here?" he asked, staring at her with a searing intensity. "Because of your breakup?"

"No," she replied quickly. "I came here to work at ..."

"How're we doing here?" the bartender interrupted. "Ready for another?" he asked Katherine.

The stranger reached toward Katherine's glass. "Let me buy you this one."

"No. I mean, I have to go," she said suddenly.

"What about your friend?"

"Maybe I misunderstood where we were supposed to meet. Anyway, I'm starting a new job tomorrow..." Katherine reached for her purse.

"Do you need a ride home? It's really raining hard outside," he asked, concerned.

"No, thanks. I can take a taxi. See you around." She stood up abruptly and turned away from him.

"A taxi might be hard to get around here..." he said as she started walking away. "Wait. I don't even know your name," he called out. But Katherine was already caught in the midst of the crowd.

She elbowed her way toward the door. The man had seemed nice enough, but she didn't need to be meeting any new men right now. And anyway, no matter how nice a guy seemed at first, she knew the routine. If she had learned anything at all from Ross, it was that. He loves her, can't live without her, and the minute she lets down her defenses and gets involved, he stops returning phone calls. No thanks. She didn't need any distractions from her new job.

Katherine had the door in sight when the big, heavyset man in tortoiseshell glasses shot up his arm, blocking her path.

"What's the magic word, princess?" he asked sloppily. His friends turned from the bar to watch.

"Let me by," Katherine replied through clenched teeth. She was cognizant of the attention they were attracting. The man pushed his glasses up on his nose with his free hand.

"What's your hurry?" he asked, licking his lips for effect.

"Please," Katherine said.

Before Katherine realized what was happening, the man leaned forward as though trying to kiss her. Horrified, Katherine grabbed his drink off the bar and threw it in his face.

"Hey!" he yelled, attracting even more attention to

the scene. The spectators burst out in peals of laughter.

"Pardon me," Katherine replied politely, gliding past him as he wiped his eyes.

Katherine opened the door and escaped outside, welcoming the warm blast of air as she fumbled with her umbrella. The incident had unsettled her. She felt embarrassed and somewhat violated. After all, he had basically tried to assault her. She had had every reason to throw the drink in his face. And anyway, she was in a new city. She didn't know those people. She'd probably never see them again.

Katherine snapped her umbrella open. She lifted it over her head and looked down the street. Baltimore was a commuter town, and although she had been in the bar only a short while, the street had cleared out. The cars that were jamming the street when she entered the bar were now on the expressway or pulling into their garages in the suburbs.

She walked toward the corner. The warm rain continued to fall. Warm rain. She had thought that a contradiction in terms until she had stepped out of her apartment that evening. But Baltimore was known for its long, hot, humid summers. Even the rain didn't break this late-August heat. She stopped to pull off her denim jacket as she pondered her situation. There were no cabs in sight, nor could she see any pay phones where she could call for one. She found herself wishing that she had driven her own car, but she had been unsure about parking near the bar, and Cyndi had suggested she take a taxi instead. The light changed colors, flashing the white "walk" sign at Katherine. She stood where she was, holding her umbrella over her head like a swordsman ready to fight. If she looked like she wasn't one to mess with, she might be left alone.

Alone. The word was even more poignant in the

dreary, foreign city. For a split second, she questioned her decision to move away from a town where strangers were virtually unheard of.

The wind began to pick up, causing pellets of rain to seep through the tiny tears in her small, beat-up umbrella. Urged on by the melancholy evening around her, a thick fog of loneliness enveloped her. It wasn't just her hometown she was missing. Ever since her mother died, she had been acutely aware of her status in the world. Perhaps that was what made Ross so appealing. She had needed someone, and he had been there. At least for the first few months. Long enough to allow her to be hurt.

She wondered what her mother would have thought of Ross. She had always been so perceptive. She probably would have seen through his smooth veneer. But then, she too had made a mistake when she was young. Katherine's father had died when she was just a year old, and although her mother had never breathed a negative word about him, Albion was a small town with few secrets. Her mother had told her that her dad had died while driving home drunk from the bar, but Katherine had known for as long as she could remember that her father did not die alone, nor was he on his way home.

Katherine sighed. She must not allow herself to dwell on the past. She had a new life now. A life far removed from memories.

The sound of footsteps behind her snapped her back to the present. Suddenly nervous, she quickly decided that despite her embarrassment, she would go back to the bar and call a cab. She didn't have any choice.

She turned around. The fat man who had just harassed her in the bar was standing in front of her, just inches away.

"Confused, princess?"

Katherine held her breath as she clenched her purse

defensively. Fear tingled down her spine as she backed away.

"Leave me alone."

"You embarrassed me back there," he spat, stepping toward her threateningly. "I don't like to be embarrassed!"

"I'll scream!" she warned.

"Like hell." He grabbed her, abruptly knocking the umbrella out of her hand as he twisted her arm behind her. His other hand was clamped tightly against her mouth, making it difficult for her to breathe. The blood rushed to her head as she struggled blindly against the fat man's dead weight. She bit down on his fingers.

"You think you're too good for me, do you?" he growled menacingly. He twisted her arm even tighter as his iron grip on her mouth threatened to cut off all oxygen.

Suddenly, the man who had offered to drive her home from the bar was there.

"I said, *let her go,*" he repeated threateningly.

The fat man pushed Katherine away, knocking her to the ground.

The stranger didn't miss a beat. He threw a punch so powerful it sent the fat man sprawling to the wet pavement.

A flash of lightning bolted across the sky, illuminating the violent scene. The storm had soaked the stranger's clothes, revealing the strong, taut muscles of an athlete. He reached down and grabbed the fat man by his lapels.

"Please. No more," the fat man whined in a whisper. "I was only joking around here. That's all."

Still holding on to the fat man's lapels, the stranger glanced back at Katherine. His blue eyes, free from the glasses he had been wearing when they met, bore down on her with a steely glare. "Did he hurt you?"

Katherine shook her head as she pushed herself up off the ground.

"Do you want to press charges?"

Katherine hesitated, her mind in a thick haze. "No," she said softly. She hardly felt like spending the night before her first day at work at the police station.

Not releasing his grip, he yanked the fat man to his feet.

"I better never see you again. *Got it?*" he snarled through gritted teeth.

The fat man nodded his head quickly. Tears were dripping down his swollen face.

"Give this woman an apology!" the stranger ordered.

"Sorry," the fat man squeaked. The stranger loosened his grip.

"Now, move it!" he commanded with disgust, practically throwing the fat man toward the street. The fat man gulped anxiously before turning and running down the street.

Katherine rubbed her sore arm.

"Thanks," she mumbled.

"Are you all right?" he asked, looking worriedly at the way she was rubbing her arm.

Katherine nodded, fighting back the tears that threatened. "Is he a friend of yours?" she asked.

"Hardly. But I know who he is," he said. "I'll make sure he pays for this."

Katherine glanced at the stranger. His eyes were strong and menacing. She could tell it was not an empty threat.

"Let's get out of here," he said. He picked up her umbrella and jacket and glanced up at her. She was staring motionless at the puddle where her purse lay open, its contents scattered haphazardly about. A calm, numbing shock had set in, leaving her oblivious to the rain beating down on her.

"I got it," he said, quickly picking up her wet bag and shoving the loose items back inside. "This way," he said, standing up. "I'm driving you home."

He gently took her arm. Still holding her belongings with his other hand, he steered her around a large puddle. "I'm parked behind the bar."

They walked through the rain quickly and silently. Only when they had reached the neon light of the bar again did Katherine speak.

"Thank you again ... I ... it was stupid of me to ... well, how did you know ... ?"

"I saw the incident in the bar. And I saw him tear out after you."

"Good thing you were there," she said, half under her breath.

"Even if he hadn't followed you out, you never should have been walking around here by yourself. You're not in Oz anymore, Dorothy."

"I realize that," she replied, stung by the sudden admonishment. "I couldn't find a cab ..."

"And your pride wouldn't let you accept a ride from me."

"I don't even know you," she said, her voice angrily rising above the storm. "I had to pick the lesser of two evils, and I did."

The man stopped suddenly. "I don't even know your name," she added defensively as she continued walking. At this point, she wasn't about to be bullied by him or anyone else.

"By the way ..." he called out.

"What?" she replied impatiently, turning around to face him.

"My name is Mike. And this is my car," he said simply, unlocking the passenger door of a medium-size sedan.

Katherine quickly retraced her steps and slipped inside the vehicle, stubbornly avoiding his eyes. She folded her arms in front of her, as though she was cold. But the cold she was feeling was coming from internal sources.

He grabbed a beat-up trench coat from the back-seat. "Here," he said. "Use this as a blanket."

He walked around the front of the car, jumped in beside her, and turned the ignition key. He paused before speaking. "I'm sorry. I didn't mean to patronize you back there. Sometimes I'm a little gruff . . ." His voice trailed off.

Katherine stared at the strong hands grasping the steering wheel. "Do you have a last name, Mike?" she asked, still a bit defensive.

The man tensed. He was enjoying his anonymity with this woman. "I do," he said, and paused. "Why, don't you?" he asked with a smile.

She rolled her eyes. He was obviously enjoying his own weak sense of humor. Unfortunately for him, however, she was not in the mood for flirtatious banter. "So, you knew that guy," she stated, trying to take command of the situation.

"Not really. I guess I know a lot of people without really knowing them."

"Oh?" Katherine asked with an air of mock sarcasm.

The stranger's eyes sparkled, as though he secretly found her response very funny.

"Now," he said, pulling out of the parking space. "Let's get you home. Where do you live?"

"At the Warren," she replied quietly. "It's a big apartment building on the other side of Fells Point."

The stranger drove silently. Katherine glanced at his sturdy, hard profile, still glistening from the rain. She felt a sudden sense of déjà vu. It was almost as though she had seen him somewhere before. In fact, she was practically certain that she had.

"Have you spent much time in Chicago?" she asked.

"Not really," he said.

"Detroit?"

He smiled as he glanced over at her. "Now, Detroit's a different story. I like to go there every January for a nice, long vacation. It's beautiful there that time of year."

She flashed him a sarcastic smile. "Gee, how original. Making fun of Detroit." She crossed her arms in front of her. "I'm from Detroit. And I'm happy to inform you there are certain parts of the city that are very nice. Besides, I only asked because you look so familiar."

"Detroit is one of the few places I don't often visit," he replied quickly. "Anyway, I thought you told me you were from Albion."

"Albion, Detroit, same area," she said defiantly.

"Ever been to Baltimore before now?" he asked as he skillfully maneuvered the car along the narrow streets.

"Only for my interview . . ."

"New York, LA."

Katherine continued to shake her head.

"Monaco, Paris, Tokyo, Japan?" He smiled at his own sense of humor. "Speaking of which, Little Italy is to your right."

Katherine glanced down a narrow cobblestone street lined with row houses. "It looks like it would be a fun place to walk around."

"It is. It's a great place to go hang out on a Sunday afternoon. I have a favorite restaurant where I like to go have wine and spaghetti with meatballs. It's as good as anything I've had in Italy." He hesitated. "Sorry. I guess that sounded kind of pretentious. I didn't mean it to be."

"What?" Katherine asked innocently. "I wasn't paying attention." She handled arrogance with ignorance. Another tip she learned from going out with Ross.

She leaned back in the seat and snuggled comfortably under the weight of the stranger's coat. She liked being able to put arrogant men off their guard and make them feel nervous. Although she didn't really think this man was arrogant. As a matter of fact, she liked the way he talked. Down-to-earth yet sophisticated. She breathed in the musky smell of the material as she watched the windshield wipers move in a comforting, steady rhythm. She sneaked another glance at her driver. She had to admit she was almost enjoying herself. It was refreshing to be with someone who was a real man, not one who put on airs, using fast lines and a health-club membership to pick up women. She squinted her eyes, unsuccessfully trying to read the apartment building numbers on the right side of the road.

"If you're trying to figure out where we are, don't worry," he said. "I know exactly where you live. It's this building up here on the right."

Katherine picked up her purse. She had tucked her keys into the outside pocket so she would know exactly where they were. She felt around for them without success. Trying not to panic, she opened the pocket and peered inside. It was empty.

"I don't believe it," she groaned. "My keys are gone."

"Are you sure?" he asked. "I threw everything inside ..."

"I'm sure," she replied with a tinge of despair. What else could go wrong?

"They must have fallen out during the scuffle in the alley. I thought I grabbed everything ..." he said apologetically, pulling up in front of her building. "Won't the front desk attendant be able to let you in? You can get a new set made tomorrow."

"I have an extra set in my apartment," she replied. "But they won't loan out keys to anyone past ten at night. And it's already eleven." She must calm down.

She would simply have to spend the night at Cyndi's house. Wherever that was.

"We'll see. Maybe I can talk them into bending the rules. Wait here."

Katherine wondered who this man was, what he did. He certainly seemed to have a lot of confidence. Yet he didn't seem overbearing or superficial. Still, there was an edge to him. A definite edge. But she kind of liked that.

In what seemed like a split second, he was back, a set of keys dangling from his hand. He opened the door for her.

Katherine stepped out of the car, flashing a quick, polite smile in appreciation. She felt uncomfortable. This man was being so nice to her. He was almost being too nice.

"Thank you . . ." she began.

"I'll see you in," he replied, handing her the keys.

Rather than answer either way, she simply neglected to say anything as the panic swelled in her throat. Perhaps he expected her to invite him in. After all, he had rescued her from a particularly unsavory situation. A cup of coffee might be in order. But if she invited him up, he might expect . . . something.

"I'll get it," he said, pulling the building's outer door open for her. Katherine stepped into the lobby and smiled weakly at the man behind the front desk. The stranger followed her inside the inner lobby, hurrying to open up the second set of doors for her.

"Good night," he said as she passed through the doorway. She paused. The eyes that had mirrored emotions ranging from passionate hatred to sensitive concern now appeared kind and gentle. Obviously, she had been a little presumptuous in assuming he would desire an invitation to her apartment. Or perhaps he had just anticipated or sensed her apprehension.

Embarrassed, she glanced down at the coat she held in her hands.

"Your coat," she said. She held it out to him.

He accepted the offering slowly, studying her as if waiting for his cue.

"Thanks for . . . everything." She swallowed, glancing away.

"You're welcome." He paused. "Can I call you?" he asked softly.

Katherine felt her heart skip a beat. She wanted to see him again, but the last time she had been so excited about a man, she had paid miserably. Besides, she had promised herself she would spend some time focused on her career. Despite her hesitation, she was almost surprised to hear herself say, "It's a bad time for me right now."

"Okay," he said. "Then I guess . . . well." He shrugged his shoulders. "Good-bye." The glass door swung shut as he turned back toward the outer door.

"Wait," Katherine called out, opening the door. "Could I get your phone number? Then maybe I could call you when—when things lighten up a bit." Katherine looked away, embarrassed by her sudden outburst. She had never turned the tables like that.

The stranger smiled. "Sure. Got anything to write with?"

Katherine shook her head.

"Here's something," the front desk attendant said, waving a pen and a piece of paper. He had obviously been listening to their every word. Katherine and the stranger exchanged an amused glance.

The stranger accepted the offering, and Katherine watched as he scribbled down the information. "Here's my work phone and my home," he said, pointing toward the second number. "Give me a call . . . anytime."

He grinned sexily. His black, rumpled, wet hair and

unassuming yet commanding manner were causing a tickle of excitement to purr at the base of Katherine's spine. He leaned up against the door, holding the paper between his fingers.

Katherine stepped forward, her eyes meeting his. She reached out and gently pulled the paper from his fingers. His free hand swooped down and cupped her chin, his gaze lingering over her.

"What's your name?" he asked softly.

"Katherine," she managed to reply.

He smiled gently. "Good-bye ... Katherine." He turned and walked out the door.

Katherine stood still, watching him get into his car. It wasn't until he was pulling out of the driveway that she glanced at the paper she held in her hand. The information was simple, just a name and some numbers, but it was enough to make her feel suddenly ill.

No wonder he had looked familiar. She had seen him in glossy photographs in *Newsweek* and *Time*. Wearing designer suits and grinning toward the camera. Smiling as he shook hands with the leaders of industry.

The seemingly down-to-earth, unassuming man who had just left was much more than just a stranger. He was Michael Benson, the president and chairman of the board of the Benson Corporation. And as of tomorrow, he was her new boss.

2

Good morning." The receptionist stood behind a black marble podium. She smiled at Katherine pleasantly.

Katherine returned her smile, attempting to hide her nervousness. "I'm Katherine Wells. I have a nine-thirty appointment with Diane Sisson. I'm afraid I'm a little bit early," she added, glancing at her watch. It was nine o'clock exactly.

"You're the new marketing director?" the woman asked perkily.

"Yes."

The receptionist efficiently picked up the phone and pressed a button, speaking in hushed tones into the receiver.

Katherine looked around her. Although she had been here once before, the structural magnificence of the lobby was still impressive.

The Benson Corporation was located in a sprawling building that took up a block of the priciest real estate in Baltimore. The central part of the building had once been an old schoolhouse, and although the exterior was designed to reflect its historic past, the interior was almost futuristic. The second floor had been knocked out to create a massive cathedral ceiling in the lobby. Glass elevators ran up and down both sides of a court lined with palm trees. A black-and-white marble floor beckoned to visitors.

"She'll meet you on the fourth floor. Good luck," the receptionist added sweetly. Katherine smiled appreciatively. The woman had no idea how much luck she needed right now.

Katherine rode the elevator in silence, feeling her heart drop to her stomach as the elevator rose. She had a hard time believing that she had actually succeeded in landing this lucrative position. After all, only twenty-five résumés had been chosen for interviews out of more than two hundred fifty applicants. Katherine had landed an interview not only because she had once worked for several years as an account executive at a prestigious Chicago advertising agency but also because she had been working at the time as the manager of advertising for Aerotech, a company outside Detroit that manufactured parts for airplanes.

The initial interview had been held over a weekend. The following Monday, five applicants were called back and asked to present a marketing plan for the A-14 division. Katherine's presentation emphasized research. She spent the week before her presentation immersed in background documents and related articles, often reading until two or three in the morning, still getting up at six for work. She read everything she could find on the A-14 engine—background, development, even the parts that were involved. She pulled some strings and got safety records on the engines. She compared them to competitors, looking for an angle that would help her.

What she found was astounding. The decrease in sales of the A-14 engine appeared to be the result of a rumor.

She had spoken to some fairly high-ranking industry executives, and almost all had agreed that the A-14 engine was unsafe.

All of the research and data proved otherwise, but perceptions could be deadly. And she knew that in order for Benson to increase its sales, it had to not only challenge this perception but change it. Fortunately, the engineer who supervised the development of the A-14 engine was a fifty-five-year-old man with graying hair and a friendly smile. He looked like a wise old grandfather. A man you could trust and believe. Katherine knew how to solve the problem. She would give the division a face and a personality that would sell. And consumer advertising, if effective, would force the industry to pay attention. A well-directed public relations blitz could even spark a media debate.

The airlines may have ignored the A-14 engine, but they would not ignore their customers. If the campaign was successful, they would have to pay attention.

Katherine turned her back to the view as she waited for the doors behind her to open.

Diane Sisson, Benson's vice president of sales, was waiting outside the doors as promised. "Hello," she said, greeting Katherine warmly. "And welcome." She shook the younger woman's hand. "How was your move? Did everything go all right?"

"Yes, thanks," Katherine responded. The office floor was no less impressive than the lobby. Soft-focus chrome lights were placed strategically on the cream-colored walls which blended perfectly with the plush, expensive-looking mauve carpet. Although the company was known for its fast-paced working environment, the room's tranquil colors and dim lighting created an almost soothing ambiance

"Why don't I show you to your office so you can get settled? We've got a few minutes before our meeting with the old man himself."

Katherine followed Diane down a spacious hall.

"Nervous?" Diane asked sympathetically, walking past a row of offices.

"You have no idea," Katherine replied. "Do you think I'll be . . . meeting Mr. Benson today?"

"Don't tell me you're nervous about meeting him?" she said.

"It's just that I've heard so much about him," Katherine replied quickly. "It seems he's always being mentioned in the papers and magazines."

"Don't worry about him," Diane said, leading her down a long hallway lined with cubicles. "He may act a little gruff, but he's very good to his employees, although most of them are a little intimidated by him. I think that's just because not many people have a lot of contact with him. Of course, I do. And eventually you'll report directly to him as well."

Katherine couldn't help but smile. Even during her interview, Diane had referred to him as "the old man."

"Didn't he inherit this company from his father?" Katherine asked. From her research, she knew that Michael Benson had grown up in luxury, surrounded by power and wealth. His father was a millionaire businessman who had turned a political hobby into a career when he became a senator in 1964. He retired from political life after losing a bid for the presidency in 1972.

"Not exactly," Diane said, stepping into the elevator as Katherine followed. "Michael was only ten when his father stopped running the company to concentrate on being a senator. Mr. Benson senior was wiped out financially during his campaign for the presidency and was forced to sell the majority of his stock in the company to his brother, Alan, who then took control. When Michael graduated from Harvard with his MBA, he went to work at a rival aeronautics company. He organized a group of investors and managed to buy the company in 1980."

"And in 1982, he bought this company back from his uncle and merged the two," Katherine said.

Diane smiled at her warmly. "Very good. You've

obviously been doing your homework." Katherine blushed and nodded.

"It's been rumored Alan's regretted it ever since," Diane said, picking up where she left off. "Although I can't imagine why. Michael's turned this company around and increased his uncle's wealth considerably." She stopped outside a closed office door. "Anyway, to make a long story even longer, his uncle is still on the board and one of his advisers. And, of course, his father is still very active in the company. But nobody disputes the fact that the company's success is due to Michael. You could say he's got his father's flair for politics and business . . . and then some," she added, opening the door behind her and stepping aside.

"I think you'll like your office. Michael asked me to see that it was redecorated for you. I did my best, but if you're not happy with it, feel free . . ."

Katherine entered the room and drew in a breath of delight.

"Do you like it?"

Katherine walked over to the window and admired her view of the bustling city. She could even see the harbor off to her left.

"Like it? It's great!" Katherine said excitedly.

"Michael felt it was important for you to have a nice office. He said you'll be conducting quite a few meetings in here—when you're in town."

"Thank you." Katherine smiled gratefully. She set her briefcase down behind her desk. "So," she said hesitantly, "What should I call him? Mike? Michael? Mr. Benson?"

"Michael. Everyone calls him Michael," Diane replied.

"No one calls him Mike?" Katherine asked.

"No," Diane said slowly, looking at her curiously. "Why?"

"I don't know," Katherine said quickly, flashing a friendly smile, "just curious."

Diane nodded. "I want to introduce you to Louise Trehorn, your assistant. She's very anxious to meet you."

Diane walked over to Katherine's desk and pressed the intercom button on the phone. "Louise? It's Diane. We're in Katherine's office. Why don't you come on in?"

Diane smiled at Katherine. "She's a little ... different, but she's apparently very efficient." Katherine didn't have time to respond. A petite woman in her mid-twenties with frizzy red hair and large, black horn-rimmed glasses hobbled in on crutches. She was wearing what appeared to be a tie-dyed blouse with a red miniskirt and striped tights.

"Louise, I'd like you to meet Katherine Wells," Diane said.

Louise smiled and extended her hand. "Nice to meet you."

Diane looked at the crutches. "What happened?"

Louise smiled. "Skydiving. It's just a sprained ankle."

"You had a skydiving accident? Sounds dangerous," Katherine said.

"Louise is our office adventurer. Louise, I'd love to hear what happened, but I've got to make a phone call before Katherine and I meet with Michael. You'll have to fill me in on the details later. Katherine, why don't you meet me in my office in ten minutes? I'm on the sixth floor."

"I remember," Katherine said, smiling. She turned back toward Louise. "So what happened?"

"Oh, it's a long story," she said, sitting on Katherine's desk. "I'm getting ready to jump out of the plane, right? So some idiot, some macho guy, comes up to me and says, 'Don't forget to pull the string for your chute to open.' So, all of a sudden, I start freaking out. Like I'm going to forget or something. You know, the power of suggestion and all that. So then— *boom!* It's my turn to jump. I throw myself out of the plane, I'm hurling though the clouds, and I can't find the damn string.''

Katherine watched Louise carefully, horrified by what she was hearing.

"I start grabbing my vest, I'm grabbing the air around me, I'm screaming for help," Louise continued, acting out the scenario as she clutched the desk.

"You fell?" Katherine asked, astonished.

Louise raised her eyebrows and shook her head. She paused. "No. I found the string and pulled. It was great. I landed on my feet and everything. But it just shows you what can happen if somebody tries to psych you out. It's all up here," she said, pointing to her head.

Katherine looked at her, confused. "But how did you hurt your ankle?"

"I tripped carrying my parachute back to the bus."

Katherine nodded silently. She was beginning to understand what Diane meant when she referred to Louise as "different."

"Oh, well. I'll let you get ready for your meeting with Michael. Let me know if you need anything," Louise said cheerfully, hoisting herself up and hobbling out.

Katherine smiled as Louise left the room. She certainly seemed like a character. But she didn't mind that. As long as she was competent, and she trusted Diane's opinion on that. Just because Louise seemed a little flighty, didn't mean she wasn't intelligent. Katherine had a lot of flighty, talented friends. Friends like Cyndi.

When Katherine had arrived home the previous night, she wasn't surprised to find that Cyndi had left several messages on her answering machine. Apparently, the Tavern had two locations. Although Cyndi gave Katherine the address of the one that she went to, apparently Cyndi had the other one in mind. When Katherine called Cyndi back, the two old friends finally connected, if only by phone. Cyndi felt terrible about Katherine's wreck of an evening and blamed herself. She was taking Katherine out to dinner tonight to try to make up for it.

Katherine sat down behind her desk and ran her fingers over the polished wood. She turned on her computer and, restless, stood back up again, taking in her surroundings. There was a maroon overstuffed couch against the opposite wall with a brass floor lamp beside it. A perfect place to lounge when she had to stay late reading research. Next to the couch was an end table with a plump, overstuffed chair on the other side.

All in all, it was a pretty intimate gathering place. With an office like this, who needed an apartment? But she knew that there was a price for everything. She had no doubt that despite the perks of a beautiful office, the hours she would put in would more than make up for it.

Katherine turned to face the window and looked at the scene below her. The thunderstorm from the previous night had left the day warm and full of sunshine. Despite the fact that it was almost ninety degrees, people of all types were strolling around the Inner Harbor, some even attempting to escape the heat by riding paddle boats into the harbor.

If the previous night had never happened, if Katherine had stayed home instead of venturing out, she might actually be cheerful and excited at that moment. But, instead, she was filled with dread at the thought of meeting Michael, dread that was made worse by the fact that she was secretly excited to see him again.

She smoothed out the static from her short, black skirt. She pulled down the white oversize cuffs of her figure-fitting black wrap blazer as she glanced down at her black T-strap heels, complemented by black silk stockings. She knew how important first impressions were, and she knew that it would be in her best interest to appear professional, adventurous, and in tune with the times. She had hesitated to wear a short skirt, but the fact of the matter was that her wardrobe contained either short skirts or long, almost-to-the-ground skirts. And she didn't feel pants were appropriate on her first day of work.

Katherine tightened her long, sleek ponytail and made sure that both of her gold button earrings were in place. She felt like a soldier about to face inspection.

An inspection she had every reason to fail. And not because of her outfit. Katherine's forehead wrinkled as she thought about the coincidence. Who would have thought that the unassuming guy she had met in the bar would turn out to be Michael Benson? She should have known by the way he came after the guy who assaulted her that he was not just a regular barfly. And the way he said good-bye . . . thank God he hadn't kissed her. And thank God she hadn't invited him up for that cup of coffee. Who knows what might have happened? As it was, of course, nothing had happened. She had to keep reminding herself of that.

She picked up her purse and pulled out her antique-gold-framed Calvin Klein glasses. She put them on and glanced at the phone. Perhaps she should call Michael before their meeting and explain the odd coincidence before she just barged in on him. Who knows? Perhaps he would find it all very funny. Just a wacky coincidence.

Katherine looked up his extension, took a deep breath, and dialed his number. Busy.

3

Katherine knocked quietly on Diane's open office door.

"Perfect timing!" Diane said, standing up. "That was Millie, Michael's secretary. He's ready for us."

Katherine followed Diane down a long hall and up an ornate circular staircase.

"Michael had these stairs built for those of us who wanted to get our exercise in," Diane joked, rapidly climbing the stairs. "Easy access or not, he rarely ventures onto any floor but the floor his office is on. I hope you don't mind the climb," she added. "It's only four flights."

"No," Katherine replied as cheerfully as she could.

"Of course, there's always the elevators, but they take too long for my taste. Katherine," Diane said, pausing slightly as she stopped walking. "There's one thing I should, well, warn you about." Katherine glanced at her nervously. It was obvious that whatever she had to tell her was important. "Michael has gotten where he is because of his business nature and intelligence," Diane continued. "He keeps all his associates at arm's length. No one really knows anything about him or his personal life, besides what they may catch in the papers. I just don't want you to interpret his distance as him not appreciating your work."

"Thanks for the warning," Katherine said carefully

as she studied the tall, handsome woman in front of her.

"He's also, well," Diane continued awkwardly, beginning to climb again, "very attractive. And ... you're going to be spending a lot of time with him on the road."

"What are you getting at, Diane?" Katherine asked quietly.

"Just be careful. I didn't hire you thinking you'd be anything else."

Katherine grimaced behind Diane's back. Should she say that she had met Michael last night? Katherine hesitated. Perhaps she should keep quiet. After all, Diane might not believe her interaction with Michael had been innocent. Katherine had to admit, the truth did sound a bit absurd. And who knows? Michael might find it embarrassing. No, Katherine thought, better to keep her mouth shut. If Michael did say anything about last night in front of Diane, Katherine would pretend that ... well, she would just have to take that risk.

They climbed the last stairs in an awkward silence and entered the president's abode. Unlike the other office floors, there were no narrow hallways or dim lighting. The inner walls had been knocked out, creating a wide open space with the quiet, refined air of a library. Rays of sun from a skylight fell on large marble pillars. Some expensive-looking leather chairs and a couch were grouped in the center of the chamber, giving Katherine the impression she had just walked into a deserted hotel lobby.

"Looks more like an expensive living room, doesn't it?" Diane asked, leading the way. "This space was originally designed solely for receptions. Michael likes to keep his office up here because it's quiet." She walked toward the middle-aged woman sitting behind the desk at the end of the room. There was a closed door behind her.

"Good morning, Diane," the woman said coldly. She had the low, gravelly voice that comes after decades of smoking.

"Hi, Millie," Diane responded, flashing the woman a sedate smile. "I'd like you to meet the new director of marketing, Katherine Wells."

Millie looked Katherine over carefully, clearly surprised to see someone so young and attractive in this position.

"Hello, Katherine," she acknowledged warily.

"Should we knock?" Diane asked hurriedly.

"He's on the phone. Go on in and have a seat," the older woman ordered. "He won't be long."

"This way," Diane said, holding the door open for Katherine. Michael Benson was sitting behind an antique mahogany desk, swiveled around in his chair so that his back was to them. He spoke on the phone, his gaze directed out the floor-length circular window directly behind his desk.

"Have a seat," Diane whispered, pointing to a couple of chairs that were placed strategically in front of his desk.

"I don't care if that's not what you understood . . ." Michael Benson shouted into the phone, ignoring his visitors. Katherine felt a wisp of panic in her chest.

"I spoke with Alan this morning . . ." he continued.

Diane looked over and smiled at Katherine reassuringly. Katherine grinned back, doing her best to breathe evenly.

"I've got a meeting," the man behind the desk stated authoritatively. "Work on it, and get back to me within the half hour." He hung up the phone and turned toward Diane.

"Michael, I'd like to introduce Katherine Wells," she said. He stood up and put out his hand to Katherine. Katherine swallowed nervously before accepting the outstretched hand of the man she had last seen less than twelve hours before. She attempted to avoid his eyes as she shook his hand.

"Nice to meet you, Mr. Benson," she said quietly.

"Michael, please," he replied, his blue eyes revealing nothing as they acknowledged her. There were no glasses to shade the intensity of his eyes. His curly, slightly unruly hair now stylishly framed his handsome, square-jawed face. His muscular body was perfectly fitted with a dark Armani suit.

"Katherine is our new marketing director. I told you about her. I recruited her from Aerotech in Albion, Michigan," Diane said.

"Really?" Michael said politely, almost coldly. "And how do you like the city so far?"

"Fine," Katherine said, straining to retain her composure. She felt a sudden and rather desperate need to get some fresh air.

Diane looked at Katherine curiously. She attributed Katherine's quietness to Michael's obvious charms.

"Diane has told me about you—your qualifications, to be specific. I hear your presentation was quite impressive." He picked up a video from his desk. "Diane taped it for me, but, unfortunately, I haven't gotten around to watching it yet. Personally, I was concerned you might be a little . . . inexperienced for this position. But they've assured me that you'll bring some new ideas and a fresh approach here."

Katherine forced a smile. She did not find Michael charming. Instead, she found him slightly patronizing. Of all people, she hardly thought he would be the one to view age as a deterrent. After all, he bought the company when he was twenty-eight.

Although he was not giving any sign of ever having laid eyes on her before, she couldn't help but wonder if some of this harshness was because of embarrassment on his part. True, this time, she was the one wearing glasses, and her hair was pulled back, but was it possible she looked so different?

"Do you have any questions for me?" he asked.

Yes! she felt like saying. *Why didn't you tell me your name in the first place? This whole uncomfortable scene could have been avoided.* "No," she responded meekly.

"Very good, then," he said, sitting back down behind his desk. "I look forward to working with you."

"Likewise," she replied softly, still avoiding his eyes.

"I'll see you at noon for the meeting about the expansion," Diane said to Michael, aware that he was dismissing them.

"Right," Michael said as he nonchalantly looked back down at his work. Diane followed Katherine out, closing the door behind her.

Unbeknownst to Katherine, Michael sighed deeply with relief after the door closed. It had taken a significant amount of self-control not to demonstrate his recognition of Katherine. He could tell by the crimson color of her face that she was embarrassed herself.

"Damn," he said softly. Until she walked in, he had found himself preoccupied by the thought of her. Wondering if she would call, hoping that he would see her again . . . soon. But he had not counted on seeing her as soon as he turned around.

Michael leaned forward on his desk. He realized that if he was going to build a successful working relationship with her, he was going to have to utilize quite a bit of restraint.

It shouldn't be difficult, he consoled himself. After all, a relationship with her was now out of the question. An affair with someone who worked for him would be disastrous. And anyway, even if she didn't work for him, it probably wouldn't have worked out. He had no desire to get married, and the women in his life right now could at best serve only as temporary companions. The thought of having to see an old girl-friend day in and day out made him cringe. Of course, there was Carly, he reminded himself. But she was a vendor, not an employee. That was different. A potential liaison with an employee opened up all sorts of legal implications. After all, he was the boss.

"Millie," he said, pressing the intercom button on his phone. "Ask Miss Wells to come back here, will you?"

Katherine excused herself to Diane, quickly escaping into the ladies room. She ran some cold water and rinsed her face. She cursed herself, Cyndi for not showing up last night, the stars, and anything else she could think of to blame for her awkward predicament. Who would have thought that Michael Benson would be hanging out at a neighborhood bar?

She folded the towel neatly and grabbed her folder. She had to pull herself together.

Millie stood outside the ladies room, chewing gum waiting for Katherine.

"Miss Wells," she growled in a husky voice. "Mr. Benson would like to see you in his office."

"Now?" Katherine asked.

"Now," she replied.

Katherine winced. Obviously, he had recognized her. She walked resolutely toward his closed office door. She knocked quietly.

"Come in!" a voice barked from the other side.

Katherine opened the door and stepped inside. Michael stood behind his desk, looking out the window. His hands were crossed behind his back.

"Close the door, please, Miss Wells," Michael said, still not facing her.

Katherine swallowed as she turned around and closed the door.

"Have a seat," he said.

Katherine sat stiffly in the chair.

"I'm not going to beat around the bush," he said, turning around to face her. "I have never gotten involved with anyone who worked for me—as an employee in this company," he added quickly. Katherine caught the distinction. "I have every intention of keeping it that way. Am I making myself clear?"

"Yes," Katherine responded. She didn't like the tone of his voice. It was almost as though he was accusing her of something. The reason for his warning suddenly dawned on her. She had stupidly alluded to her affair with Ross. And now he was throwing her own words back at her. She was the "type" of woman who would mix business and pleasure. And he was not that kind of guy. But if he was so innocent, why had Diane told her to be careful? "If I had known who you were, I never would've, well." Katherine stopped herself. She had not behaved improperly last night. She had nothing to apologize for.

"You're well qualified for the position, and Diane thinks you have a lot of potential . . . but look, I don't want any rumors floating around about a supposed relationship . . . between you and me . . . understand? Has any damage been done so far? What did you tell Diane?"

Katherine stared at him coldly. How dare he insinuate that she would gossip about having an affair with him!

"I didn't mention it. I was concerned that she might read something into an . . . obviously innocent situation."

"That was wise," he said, leaning forward.

Katherine sat stiffly in the chair, her slender hands clasped in her lap. Michael stared at her. He was impressed by the way she was standing up to him. He could feel his strict, professional facade slipping away.

"How are you feeling today?" he asked.

"Fine," Katherine replied nonchalantly.

"You're not hurt?"

Katherine shook her head.

"I haven't forgotten about the idiot who attacked you. I'll deal with him."

"There's no need," Katherine said quickly. "Like you, I prefer that we forget about the entire incident."

"All right," he said, shrugging his shoulders. "That's enough of that." He sat behind his desk, swiftly changing subjects. "Benson's commercial sales have not been very good in the past few years. As I'm sure you're aware, most of our revenue comes from defense contracts. I want that to change. And eventually, I want to hear your thoughts on how to do it. But before we can start dealing with that, I want you to focus on the A-14 division. Carry out that marketing plan you developed. I'm meeting with members from the board in two weeks. I want you to present it to them. You can bring creative if you want, but they're going to be looking for raw numbers. You should work closely with our advertising agency on this."

"You use Bresser and Tenner, right?" she asked.

"You've heard of them?"

"Sure. They do a lot of business-to-business." Although the firm was based in downtown Baltimore, there was a New York office as well.

"I want you to meet with Carly Wentworth. She's our account executive. She'll bring you up to speed on what we've done in the past, what we're currently doing. I know Roy enjoyed working with her. I'm sure you will too," he said, referring to Roy Collins, the man who had been the director of marketing before Katherine. He had left the company to go into business with his wife.

"If you have any other questions, talk to Diane. She'll be going with us in a month."

"Where is the meeting?"

"Miami."

Katherine nodded. "I'll be ready." She stood up. She hesitated. "Again, about last night. I assure you, had I known . . ."

"I thought we agreed it was forgotten."

"Right," she said, biting her tongue. They were no longer equals. He was the one who would call the shots. He was her employer. And her new employer at that.

"I don't know how much you know about the background of the A-14 division, but it's very important to me," he continued. "I'm counting on you to help me convince them that we can make this work."

She managed a cool, professional smile.

"Thanks for your time. That'll be all," he said, dismissing her.

Michael waited until she was gone before buzzing Millie.

"Millie, make reservations for Katherine, Diane, and myself at the Four Seasons in Miami. We'll be there the fifth through the seventh," he said, and took his finger off the buzzer. His mind drifted back to the previous evening. He remembered the surge of excitement he had felt as he held Katherine's chin in his hand, the overwhelming desire to take her in his arms and kiss her. He forced himself to focus back on the present. He couldn't allow himself to think of her like that anymore. Michael picked up the pitcher of water on his desk and poured himself a glass of the frigid liquid.

Katherine took the stairs back down to her office. She felt a bevy of emotions, ranging from anger to embarrassment. She cursed fate for the unlikely coincidence.

She stepped into her office and shut the door. She leaned back against it. She looked around suspiciously as though Big Brother might be monitoring her reactions. She took a deep breath and stepped away from the door, sinking into a convenient chair.

Despite Michael's assurance that last night would be forgotten, she felt he planned on holding it against her. Intellectually, she realized she had done nothing wrong—with the possible exception of showing a little naïveté. But emotionally, she was mortified. Not only had she alluded to her previous office romance, but he had staved off her attacker. It was obvious he viewed her as a wayward little girl, someone who needed protection. How could he possibly take her seriously now?

Katherine walked behind her desk. She would just have to work twice as hard, she thought resolutely.

She sat at her desk and flattened her hands against the heavy, shiny wood. She had to stop berating herself for not recognizing him when she first saw him. After all, who would have thought she would run into Michael Benson at a local watering hole? And with his tousled hair and casual attire—not to mention nondescript car—he certainly hadn't fit the description of a business czar. But today—today he did. He was cool, polished, and professional. Smooth and slick. Just like . . . Ross, she realized with a shudder. Naturally, she thought miserably. She was a magnet for men like that.

She looked around her clean and empty office. It was difficult to believe that she could ever feel she belonged here. Time, she thought. She just needed a little time to get acclimated. And she would. After all, she had a lot of work to do. In only four weeks, she would be giving her first presentation.

Katherine picked up her purse. She reached inside

for her lipstick, and her fingers brushed the tip of a piece of paper. She pulled it out and glanced at it quickly. It was the paper Michael had written his name and phone number on.

Like a guilty child, she crumpled up the paper and tossed it in the basket. She wished she could just forget about last night. She had more pressing things on her mind right now. Like how to convince an advertising agency that they should change their trade campaign to one directed at consumers.

She hoped she would like her account executive at the agency. She knew the woman was probably a little nervous to meet her. They would be working closely together. And if Katherine didn't like her, as the director of advertising and marketing, she had the power to change agencies. And the Benson account was worth twelve million dollars.

Her intercom buzzed, causing Katherine to almost jump out of her chair. "Yes Louise?" she said breathlessly.

"It's Diane on line one for you."

"Thanks, put her through," she answered. "Hi Diane."

"Katherine, listen. Michael just called. He wants me to give you some background. Believe it or not, you've got to make a presentation to the board in Miami in a month."

"Great," Katherine said, trying to muster some enthusiasm. She had distinctly heard Michael state that Diane would be there as well.

"Aren't you going to be there?" Katherine asked hopefully.

"I'll help you put it together, but I'm afraid I'm going to have to throw you to the wolves alone. At least you'll be someplace exotic."

"What do you mean?" Katherine asked nervously.

"Unfortunately, I've got a meeting here, and it's

imperative I attend. Otherwise, I wouldn't mind going. We've gone to meetings there before, and it's absolutely beautiful. Right on the ocean. You and Michael will just have to send me a postcard." Diane laughed pleasantly, unmindful of the tension crackling though the wire.

4

The woman walked out of the World Trade Center building and into the midday heat, pausing for a moment to straighten her crisp, hot-pink linen blazer and adjust her silk scarf. It was important that she look her best. And her best was perfect.

She stepped into the black limousine waiting at the curb. "The Benson Building, please," she said.

Even though the Benson Building was only five blocks away, she had no intention of walking. Why should she when she had access to a limousine through her job? Besides, she never exercised. Whenever anyone asked her how she stayed so thin, she would laugh and say, "My job is the only exercise I need."

And it was true. As vice president of account management at Bresser and Tenner, she rarely had a dull moment. She supervised four major accounts, including Benson. She was quick on her feet and a practiced charmer. She had experienced little trouble in rising to the position of vice president. Of course, her wealthy background and connections hadn't hurt. And she had brought in the Benson account.

INDISCRETION

She had known Michael Benson and his family for years. She and Michael had dated in college for a while, although their relationship was never really serious. Their families had been close, and it was in part because of them that they had become involved. When she and Michael ended up at the same undergraduate school, her parents, who adored Michael, had called him and asked him to take Carly out to dinner. Their parents had been excited by the possibility of a marriage between the families, but by the end of three months, Michael had claimed that he was too young to be seriously involved. It wasn't her, he had assured her, but the timing. And she believed him. They had stayed in touch, and after Michael got out of grad school, they had run into each other at a mutual friend's party. By that time, she was an account supervisor at a small Baltimore agency, having a not-so-secret affair with her boss. She persuaded Michael to sign with her agency, and she had represented his firm ever since. Of course, her affair had soured, and she had switched agencies to Bresser and Tenner, but she had taken Michael's account with her. She was secure with it. But not necessarily with him.

Her relationship with Michael was far from business as usual. She was his official date for functions where he had to bring a date. Every now and then, he would make an exception and take her out to dinner or to the theater, but these occurrences had become less and less frequent. It wasn't that he was seeing anyone else. Oh, he dated, she knew that. But not seriously. He simply couldn't commit, and, ironically, it was his fear of commitment that kept them together. He knew she was aware of his limitations and accepted them. They could spend an evening in bed together and then not talk for three months. When he finally did call, there would be no confrontations, no questions asked. That was their unspoken understanding.

She could afford to be patient. She felt that they were destined to be together eventually. And Michael Benson was a man worth waiting for. She knew it was just a matter of time before he realized that she was the woman for him. Perhaps he realized it already. But, until he proposed, she had no trouble mixing a little sex with business. She was thirty-five years old. She had quite a bit of experience controlling her emotions, if not her passions.

She glanced down at her diamond-encrusted watch. She would arrive exactly on time. In most cases, the hiring of a new director of marketing and advertising at a company would mean the end of an agency's tenure. The new director usually wanted a new agency or even the agency he or she had worked with previously—an agency that was loyal, that the director knew he or she could work with. But this situation was different. She had a relationship with Michael. She wasn't threatened by the thought of a new director. Besides, she had heard that the woman they had hired was extremely young. Of course, it was ridiculous giving that much power and responsibility to someone so inexperienced. But, then again, it wasn't unusual. Most companies had cut back on expenses, and advertising budgets were one of the first things cut. More and more companies had been hiring young, inexperienced people with perky attitudes and a willingness to work sixty-hour weeks. But that was all right with her. It just made her all the more powerful, and all the richer. Someone who is inexperienced hardly notices an inflated estimate or two.

As the limo pulled up in front of the building, a little smile crept up the corners of her perfectly outlined mouth.

5

William Briggs was in Katherine's office, his large frame seated uncomfortably in a chair across from her. His gray hair was somewhat messy, and, although he was wearing a tie, it was too short and wide to be mistaken for stylish. He had been the vice president of research at Benson for twenty years, surviving the merger with his job firmly intact. He liked working for Michael Benson—much as he had liked working for his father before him. He was a congenial man— he got along well with his coworkers at Benson, and he was rewarded by their respect and loyalty. He offered stability to a company dedicated to growth. But the long hours his job demanded and the internal political struggles had recently begun to take a toll on him. Five years ago, he might have offered to update the new marketing director on the status of the research department over lunch or invited her home for one of his wife's famous Mexican dinners. But times were different. Now he would settle for a cup of coffee and a minimal amount of small talk.

He glanced at the woman in front of him. She couldn't be any older than his youngest daughter. Yet here she was, in charge of vitalizing and perhaps saving his division. Unlike his daughter, who never asked him any questions about his job, Katherine had been asking him questions for the past hour and showed no sign of slowing down. Her enthusiasm and energy, although refreshing at first, were beginning to irritate him.

Katherine had big plans for him. She had chosen William to be the star of the advertising campaign for his division. And he wasn't sure he wanted the job.

"You see, it's a consumer campaign," Katherine said, smiling. "We want people to associate you with the division. We're giving the division a name and a personality."

"People aren't buying these engines," he stated matter-of-factly.

"No, but they're the end users. We want them to be aware that the capability is there for commuter flights to reduce their travel time. We want people asking for these engines."

William Briggs leaned back in his chair. "I want to discuss this with Michael."

"You should. Michael is aware of this campaign. He likes it. And I'm hopeful you will, too. Once you have time to think about it."

"Excuse me, Katherine." The interruption came not from William Briggs but from the intercom on Katherine's phone. "Carly Wentworth is here for her appointment. Should I tell her to wait?" Louise asked.

William Briggs stood up. "I really have to get back downstairs. If you have any questions, just give me a call."

"Thank you for stopping by," Katherine replied with a smile. "I'd love to come down a little later for a tour of the research division, if I could. And I'm going to have the advertising agency mock up some ads to show you what we have in mind."

"Please do," he said, shaking her hand. "Again, welcome aboard." He opened the office door.

Carly stood outside. "Hello, Bill."

William stiffened. He preferred to be called William, as everyone knew. Especially Carly, who had

46

been corrected several times. This time, however, he would let it slide. He had more important things to deal with.

"Carly." He gave her a curt nod as he passed by.

Carly turned toward Katherine. She smiled wide as she approached with her hand outstretched. "Carly Wentworth. You must be Katherine Wells. It's so nice to meet you. I've heard so many pleasant things about you."

"Thanks," Katherine replied. She was aware of a sudden tension in the room. "I certainly appreciate you coming to meet with me on such short notice."

"Not at all." Carly smiled coldly. "Why, just the other night, Michael asked me to stop in and say hello. After all, we'll be a team."

Katherine glanced at the woman cautiously. *Just the other night . . .* Obviously, Carly was trying to make a point. She was either threatened by Katherine because she was the new marketing director, or she was threatened by her because she was a young woman. In any case, she seemed intent on proving that she was close to Michael.

"So," Carly said, sitting down. She smoothed the wrinkles out of her short skirt. "I heard a rumor that Bill is going to be our new poster boy."

Katherine smiled. "Yes. I'll need your help developing that idea."

"Certainly. Michael has already given me some of the basics." Carly paused. "You've got him very excited," she added, flashing Katherine a smile that sent chills down her spine.

"Great. That's good to hear," Katherine said as casually as she could manage.

"Are there any questions I can help you answer?" Carly asked.

"Well, I've been going over a few of the marketing

materials around here, but I'd really like to see the boards of the last campaign you presented to Benson."

Carly laughed. "I wouldn't call it a campaign. Several ads and a few brochures and catalogs don't amount to a campaign."

"I'm aware that Benson spent five million dollars on advertising materials. I'd like to see what they did, that's all."

"Didn't Roy leave you any notebooks or samples around here?" Carly asked, still smiling.

Katherine hesitated. She didn't like the way Carly was treating her. As an account executive, she was supposed to be helpful, not antagonistic. After all, *she* worked for *Katherine*. When Katherine was an account executive, she never would have dreamed of treating a new client like this.

"Perhaps I could go to your office tomorrow and review the materials?" Katherine asked.

"Certainly. Michael has also warned me that you're going to need my help over the next few weeks for your Florida presentation. You can count on me. I've always bent over backwards to be of service to Benson."

Katherine glanced away. From the way she kept using Michael's name, she didn't doubt the last statement at all.

She realized that if this woman was a close "friend" of Michael's, she should probably be careful, but she still couldn't help asserting her position. "Carly, since we will be working closely together, I'd just like to give you an idea of how I like to work. Although I like to get the job done, I also believe in having fun."

"Yes, I'm sure you do," Carly replied, tossing back her shoulder-length frosted blond hair. She eyed Katherine suspiciously. "I like to have fun, too. Speaking of which, I'd love to take you and your husband out to dinner." Carly was fishing for information.

"I'm not married."

"Well, then, just the two of us." Carly forced a smile and glanced at her watch. "Would you look at the time! I promised Michael I'd stop by his office. He left his calculator at my house the other night. The poor man is lost without it."

Katherine stared at Carly in disbelief. She found her behavior unnatural and unprofessional. Obviously, she was trying to intimidate her. Well, Katherine thought, she would have to do much more than drop Michael's name to achieve that.

"Oh, by the way," Katherine said, glancing down nonchalantly at the papers on her desk. "I know I have a stack of invoices to process here from your firm. Roy apparently didn't have time to get to them before he left. Since I'm not familiar with the jobs, I was wondering if you could provide backup." Carly's firm was on a retainer with Benson. The agreement was simple. They paid her a flat fee each month, and, in turn, they were only billed net for all production. But unless a company received a copy of the invoices, it was very easy for the advertising agency to mark things up.

Carly stared at her coldly. "Backup?"

"Right. It'll help me a great deal. Just to familiarize myself with the vendors. I hope it's not a problem. I'll pick them up tomorrow when I'm at your office." Katherine knew that, normally, asking for backup was not a good way to begin a relationship. But it basically boiled down to trust. And her instinct told her not to trust this woman. Even if Michael Benson felt differently.

Carly regained her control. "Certainly. I'll look forward to it." Carly opened the door and stepped out. "Ciao."

Katherine watched as Carly maneuvered around an awkward Louise, who, with her crutches, was slowly but surely making her way toward Katherine's office.

"What do you think of the viper?" Louise asked, stepping inside the office.

Katherine jumped up and shut the door as she put her fingers to her lips to quiet Louise. Carly was still in sight, waiting for the elevator.

"She might've heard you," Katherine said once the door was shut.

Louise laughed. "No way. She's too busy thinking of herself. So, did you survive your first meeting with the boss's girlfriend?"

"Girlfriend?" Katherine asked. She felt a twinge of jealousy in spite of herself.

"Well, that's what we call her."

"We?" Katherine asked curiously.

"People in the office. You know," Louise said, shrugging her shoulders. "Anyone can tell she's got the hots for Michael. At least, I can tell. But then again, I'm really perceptive that way," she said, sitting down on the couch. "My friends are always asking me about their relationships. Like, 'He didn't call me, what does that mean? Does he still like me?' You know, that kind of thing. Because I can tell. I'm very good at sensing things. And to tell you the truth, everyone knew that there was something going on between them. He always brought her to stuff. Like to last year's office Christmas party. But it's my guess, I mean, I sense she's not really his girlfriend anymore. But they still get together sometimes. You know how it goes."

"Louise?" Katherine interrupted. "Did you need me for something?" Although she was enjoying this little bit of information, she felt it necessary to discourage her assistant from gossiping—especially about her employer.

"What?" Louise replied, obviously daydreaming.

"Did you want something? Why did you come in?"

"Oh. Right," Louise said, struggling to get up. Katherine handed her the crutches. "You need to fill out some forms at personnel. Sometime today. At your convenience. Anything else?"

"No," Katherine said slowly. She still wasn't quite sure what to make of Louise. "Thanks."

She watched Louise leave the room and shut the door behind her. She needed a moment alone to gather her thoughts.

No wonder Carly wasn't bothered about providing backup for the invoices. Obviously, she and Michael had more than a business relationship. Especially if he was bringing her to company functions. But last night, he had acted as though he was definitely interested in her. If he was involved with Carly, why would he ask for her phone number? And his good-bye had not been a good-bye from someone who had a girlfriend. Unless, of course, he was just another guy on the make. In which case, it was no wonder Carly was so insecure.

And who really cared what their relationship was, anyway? It's not as though he and Katherine would ever be romantically involved.

It's not like she was jealous, she tried to convince herself. She was just . . . angry. He had made her feel so silly about her relationship with Ross. And here he was, involved with a vendor. That wasn't very professional. If, of course, he was still involved.

Katherine leaned back in her black leather chair. She had a feeling she was going to find out the truth soon.

6

Katherine navigated her red Mustang convertible along the slick highway overpass, barrelling down the road at a speed that was barely legal for the highway. She and Michael were taking one of the company's private planes to Miami and she was supposed to meet him in the Executive Terminal in only twenty minutes. That in itself might not have been a problem, considering she had already passed the main terminal. Unfortunately, however, she was lost. The executive terminal was across the runway from the main terminal, and she couldn't find the road she was supposed to turn on. Katherine glanced down at the crude directions she had distractedly scribbled on her notepad. She had gotten them from Millie yesterday, and she could tell by her lousy handwriting that she had been thinking of something else when she wrote them down.

She stopped at a red light at an unmarked road. Where were all the street signs? Her fingers tapped the steering wheel anxiously as she waited for the light to change. This was not how she liked to begin her day. Her mind raced to the unpleasant scene of boarding the aircraft late and facing an angry, impatient boss. To add fuel to her already fertile imagination, Millie had specifically instructed her to be there early, as Michael hated to wait.

The light turned green and Katherine sped off, slowing at the next unmarked road. She paused. It looked like a service entrance to the airport. With a shrug of her shoulders she swung her car into the drive. Oh well, she thought wryly, at the very worst she would end up on the runway, and she felt certain she could find Michael's plane from there. Her eyes focused on a sign that immediately made her feel better: Executive Terminal Parking. She pulled up to the parking gate and rolled down her window to speak with the attendant. "I'm Katherine Wells. I'm flying with Michael Benson of the Benson Corporation." The woman glanced down at her long notepad, looking for Katherine's name. She looked up at Katherine and nodded as the gate swung open.

Katherine pulled into the first available parking spot she could find. She grabbed the overstuffed carry-on bag that was on the seat next to her and jumped out of the car. She had packed hurriedly, trying to neatly pack her clothes, including a rather formal cocktail dress, into a bag that she could manage with her heavy briefcase and the huge, cumbersome portfolio. She had no intention of appearing like a helpless female, struggling with a heavy piece of luggage in front of her boss. She had appeared helpless in front of Michael once before, and she was no fan of repeat performances, especially ones that she hadn't enjoyed the first time around.

Katherine opened the back door and pulled her briefcase and the portfolio containing the presentation boards out of the backseat. With her briefcase swung over one shoulder, and her carry-on over the other, she stood and faced the terminal. With the resolute air of a general about to give his battle cry, she began to stride toward the entrance. As she carried her awkward load, a chilly wind whipped through the light coat she had worn. But she welcomed it. The heat had finally broken two weeks ago, and fall was finally beginning to take over the landscape. She loved the changing of the seasons, and fall was her favorite time of year. Although Baltimore was about a month behind Albion in terms of seasons, she had noticed that some of the trees outside her apartment building were already beginning to change colors.

Four weeks had passed since her first day at work. Each day she attempted to memorize all the names of the people she had met and each day her research for the proposal had seemed slightly more complicated than the last. At times she had felt as though she was underqualified for her position—at other times the haze surrounding the endless and intimidating research seemed to lift, leaving clear and distinct facts and solutions. Although few and far between, at those precious moments Katherine was hit by a rush so intense she felt she could climb Mt. Everest in a single day.

Her excitement for her job had survived the initial unpleasant incident with Michael and the long, lonely hours the job had already required. She had been working at least seventy hours a week, and her modern, chic apartment that she was so proud of was beginning to feel like a impersonal hotel suite. It was a place for her to change her clothes and sleep. She had gone out to dinner with Cyndi to celebrate her first day of work, but besides that she hadn't even thought about her social life.

Katherine entered the terminal and looked around. Because this was a terminal that serviced only the passengers of privately owned corporate planes, there were no ticket agents to direct her. The terminal, in fact, seemed almost empty. A few men in stylish suits stood talking in a corner, waiting for a lone food vendor to open her breakfast cart. The men stopped talking when they noticed Katherine. Katherine could feel herself blush in response to their admiring glances.

She immediately reprimanded herself for her foolish response as she busied herself by checking her watch. She was exactly on time. Was it possible that Michael was already on board? There was only one way to find out.

"Excuse me," she said, approaching the group of men. "I'm supposed to be on a private plane . . . right now. Can you tell me how I get out to where the private planes are?"

"What plane?" asked a man in a gray pin-striped suit.

"The Benson jet," she replied.

The woman behind the vendor cart spoke up. "Are you meeting Michael Benson?" she asked. Katherine nodded. "I haven't seen him this morning," the woman offered.

"Thanks," Katherine said. She flashed a quick, professional smile at the woman and the men before walking over to a cluster of hard plastic seats situated in front of a large window overlooking the tarmac. She set her luggage down and waited for the men to finish buying their coffee before she walked back to the vendor and bought herself a cup. Then, as if standing guard over her luggage, she planted herself in front of the window and sipped her coffee as she looked out at the planes. It was difficult to determine which jet was Michael's. She had half expected to see "BENSON" emblazoned on the side of it. From a personal perspective she was happy to see he had some modesty. From a marketing perspective, she didn't think it would be a bad idea to suggest that he do just that.

She glanced anxiously at her watch. She had never been on a private jet before, although she had heard stories at the office about how plush the company jets were. She almost wished they were traveling on a regular commercial plane. At least then there would be some distractions. She didn't like the idea of being stranded alone with Michael anywhere, especially hundreds of feet in the air. Fortunately, she would be flying back on Saturday alone. Michael's uncle, Alan Benson, lived in Miami and Michael had chosen to stay on and visit with his uncle and his family.

Katherine watched through the window as the group of executives she had seen earlier walked out on the tarmac. Their ties blew in the wind as they hustled up the steps of a small commuter plane.

She glanced behind her toward the door. Although the terminal was slowly filling with passengers, Michael was not one of them. Most of the people looked like well dressed executives leisurely waiting for their coworkers to arrive so that they could board their private planes together. Katherine looked around her. This terminal was very different from the main terminal. Granted, it was tiny, but it wasn't just its size that distinguished it from its larger counterpart. The atmosphere was different. It was exempt from the normal frenzy and excitement in commercial terminals. These people weren't going on vacations. They were traveling on business. And they all knew their planes were supposed to wait for them, not the other way around. She wondered what their lives were like—these expensively dressed individuals with their own sets of troubles and travails.

She sat down on the stiff, cheap chair and took another sip of her coffee before setting it on the ground. She knew she shouldn't drink any more. She loved coffee but too much caffeine made her anxious.

Katherine opened up her briefcase and pulled out her presentation, admiringly thumbing through the neat, white pages. She had gone over it twice yesterday and she felt it was some of her best work.

Although Carly had been helpful in pulling together the creative side of the presentation, their relationship had remained cold and impersonal. She had compiled the invoices that Katherine had requested, and Katherine had not asked her for backup again. But she had not yet processed the invoices. Katherine was determined to be pleasant with the woman. But if Carly wanted to get paid, she would have to provide backup.

Katherine would have loved to hire the advertising agency she had worked with at Aerotech, but Benson had a contract with Carly's firm. And Carly continued to remind Katherine of her personal friendship with Michael.

She checked her watch again. Michael was now twenty minutes late. She slipped her presentation back into her briefcase and looked restlessly around her. She was ready to get on the plane. She didn't like having so much time to think about things . . . specifically Michael. She took a deep breath.

It was a weak attempt at settling some of her anxiety, an anxiety that she knew had little to do with the amount of coffee she had consumed. The thought of traveling alone with Michael had given her a rise in adrenaline so potent, she doubted she would ever need to drink another cup of coffee again.

She picked up the newspaper that was lying beside her and brushed off someone else's donut crumbs. She found the Style section and pretended to read as her thoughts settled on Michael. She had been desperately attracted to him the first night they met, and the desires he had unwittingly tapped into were still raw and vulnerable. The more she told herself to forget it, the more she secretly desired him.

Not that Michael had not done anything to perpetuate her infatuation. In fact, he treated her in a rather cold, professional manner. At first she had thought that this meant he was displeased with her performance, but she remembered Diane's assurance that Michael treated everyone the same.

Despite Michael's seeming indifference to his employees, it was obvious that he had won their respect. Although he had never been married and was known for the long hours he kept, he emphasized that family came before work, and Benson's home-office day care was one of the first of its kind.

But Katherine knew that most people were still intimidated by him. At lunch earlier in the week, some of her female coworkers had been telling stories about what it was like to ride in the elevator alone with him. Apparently he didn't invite conversation. And as far as she could tell, he didn't fool around with employees. With the exception of Carly.

Katherine vividly remembered her impression of him as he had walked out of her apartment building the night she met him. He had seemed quiet, but he had also seemed sensitive and honest. Although he had certainly been aggressive with her attacker. She almost wished that she had never taken the job at Benson. Perhaps then she could have found out what this complicated, secretive man was like on a date. Her mind replayed the tape of his voice. "You're not in Oz anymore, Dorothy." Yet he had apologized. And he had seemed so gentle when he said good-bye.

If she hadn't worked for him, would he have been the man for her? Or was he still involved with Carly?

Katherine set the newspaper back down on the seat beside her. She crossed her arms impatiently as she bit her lower lip. She shouldn't even allow herself to think of Michael that way. She worked for him and that was that. He treated her like everyone else. In his mind—as it should be in hers, she was simply an employee going on a business trip with her boss. She was in charge of making conversation, and like anyone else in her shoes, she was not looking forward to it. She glanced at her watch again. She thought his tardiness was extremely rude. The least he could have done was to let her know he'd be late.

Her eyes darted over to the phones across from her. She would call Millie. Hopefully she would be able to tell Katherine what his plans were. She probably should've called Millie yesterday to confirm Michael's schedule, Katherine realized uneasily.

She was on her way to the phones when she spotted Michael marching into the terminal. She ran back to her things and gathered them together.

"Why aren't you on board, Wells?" he growled when he got closer.

As usual, she noted, he referred to her by her last name. "I was waiting for you!" Katherine said irately as Michael whipped past her.

He paused for a moment. "Give me this," he said, taking her heaviest piece of luggage away from her.

She grasped on to her briefcase and portfolio as she followed him out of the door that led to the tarmac. He walked toward one of the larger jets that Katherine had seen from the terminal window and climbed effortlessly up the jet's steps. Katherine's knuckles tightened around the handles of her briefcase as she hustled onto the plane behind him.

They were greeted at the door by a pretty woman with brown hair and large brown eyes. She was wearing a white blouse with a blue vest and blue pleated pants. The flight attendant, Katherine assumed. "Good morning, Michael," the woman said, smiling at him sweetly. "Anything to drink?"

"Morning, Lisa," he said, setting their luggage in the closet. "Perrier on the rocks."

"What about you?" the woman asked just as sweetly to Katherine. Katherine smiled while her eyes inadvertently focused on the woman's ring finger. She was married. "I'll have some orange juice," Katherine said, embarrassed that she would even care if Michael's pretty flight attendant was married or not.

Katherine glanced around her. The interior was

done in varying hues of blue and gray. The front part of the plane contained two groupings of large gray leather chairs, one on each side of the aisle. Each grouping consisted of a total of four chairs, with two on each side so that one could look into the eyes of the person one was talking to. The next area reminded her of Benson's small conference room. A shiny, narrow wooden table with several straight-backed chairs were placed in the center of the plane. On the other side of the table was a door which was partly open. Katherine leaned forward, peering down the aisle for a better look around the door. She was a little surprised with what she saw. The room appeared to be a small bedroom. Katherine could even make out the silky blue bedspread that covered a double bed.

She focused her attention back on Michael and watched as he sat in one of the gray leather chairs next to the window. Katherine stood still, unsure of where to sit. Did he want to sit next to her, across from her or away from her?

He looked up at her as if reading her mind. "Have a seat," he said, pointing to the chair across from him.

Katherine sat her bags down on the empty chair next to her. "Nice plane," she said, settling into the chair across from Michael. "I suppose all the furniture is nailed to the floor."

He nodded. "Bolted." He looked around. "This is the plane I seem to use the most." He motioned toward the back room. "I like it because it has a bed in it. Kind of nice when I'm traveling long distances . . . alone," he added quickly, emphasizing "alone."

"I bet," she stated a little too quickly.

If Michael heard her, he ignored her. He snapped open his briefcase and pulled out some documents. Katherine followed suit, opening her briefcase as well and pulling out a manila folder stuffed with clippings she'd been looking forward to catching up on. Two could play at his game. She would just pretend he wasn't there. But sooner or later, they would have to deal with each other. After all, Diane was not there to ease the tension.

The flight attendant came back carrying the drinks. Michael was immersed in his papers, deep in concentration.

Lisa looked at Katherine for help in getting Michael's attention. Katherine touched Michael's arm. He jumped slightly and looked at Katherine curiously.

"Your drink," she said, motioning toward Lisa. The woman passed the Perrier to Michael and handed Katherine her orange juice.

"Thanks," he said with a quick nod.

He and Katherine sat across from each other, their knees bumping up against each other as the plane lifted off the ground. Once airborne, Katherine started to speak several times, but stopped herself. She was a little surprised. She had expected the trip to be awkward, but this was ridiculous. After all, she had been working with the man for the past several weeks. It wasn't like they hadn't been speaking. But still, Katherine reminded herself, this was the first time they'd been alone.

"I haven't really had a chance to talk to you since you started," Michael said, breaking the ice. "How are things going for you?"

"Oh, fine," Katherine replied reassuringly.

"You like your job so far?"

"Oh, yeah . . . yes," she said.

"Office?"

"It's great," she replied.

They both paused.

"It's too bad Diane couldn't make it," Katherine said, half under her breath.

"Why do you say that?" Michael asked, curious. He glanced down as Katherine crossed her long legs. Her short skirt hadn't escaped his attention, as much as he tried to ignore it. He didn't like sitting so close to her like this. Close enough to detect the intoxicating smell of her perfume. Close enough to reach out and touch her hand.

"She has so much experience in public speaking. I would've liked to see her in action," Katherine replied.

"She is great," he said, focusing back on business. "And the board is usually pretty receptive to her. But they've known her for a long time. I should warn you that a lot of the board are, well," he said uncomfortably, "a little intimidating. Just remember. I'll be right beside you. I'm not going to let them get too rough."

"I can hold my own, Michael. I didn't mean to insinuate otherwise," Katherine replied testily.

Michael grinned. "Good," he said. He turned and faced the window, staring out at the line of thick white clouds beneath them.

Katherine leaned back uncomfortably in her seat as she pulled her coat over her legs. It was clear her boss wanted her to be quiet now. His brief attempt at polite behavior had obviously exhausted him.

A quiet, uncomfortable hour later, they landed in Miami.

As they stepped into the terminal, they were hit by a blast of air-conditioning so cool Katherine was glad she still had her coat on. But even the powerful air-conditioning couldn't mask the heat as they made their way toward the revolving door that led outside.

Katherine stepped into the Miami heat and paused. It was close to ninety degrees, and the humidity wasn't helping. Even the palm trees, scattered throughout the airport's asphalt oasis, sagged as though begging for relief. Katherine struggled to take off her coat as Michael arranged for a cab.

"Ready?" he asked as he picked up her suitcase and threw it into the back of the cab.

Katherine gave her coat a final yank and pulled it off. She slid into the cab.

"To the Four Seasons," he said, jumping in beside her. He glanced at Katherine as he straightened his tie. "The show is about to begin."

The show turned out to be just that: a show. And Katherine was the female lead. Out of the twenty or more board members and corporate representatives at the meeting, she was the only woman. Babs Douglass, a key shareholder, had been unable to catch the Concorde back from Europe and refused to travel overseas on regular commercial planes. Carolyn French, the other woman on the board, was a professor of economics at Harvard and was out of the country on sabbatical. The most powerful board member in attendance was Michael's uncle, Alan Benson.

Katherine performed well, remaining confident and calm, even though the question-and-answer period seemed more like an interrogation. More than once, she was asked to recite her credentials: a degree in journalism from the University of Michigan and a master's degree in advertising from Northwestern. Her first job after college had been with a small business that manufactured greeting cards. The business had been teetering on the edge of bankruptcy for almost two years. Katherine had devised low-budget ways of increasing customer awareness. As soon as business picked up, she had persuaded the owner to reinvest the profits in commercial and print advertising. When she left two years later to work at an advertising agency, the greeting card company had an increase in revenues of twenty percent.

Katherine was not insulted that she had been asked to recite her résumé. In fact, she had expected it. She knew most of the board members were from the old school. Many had trouble believing anything a woman might say. The fact that she was an attractive woman under thirty didn't help. But she knew she had developed a strong proposal. Increasing revenue was her forte. And when Alan Benson had rejected her first two suggestions outright, Katherine had coolly presented additional plans until he found one he liked. They then spent the rest of the day shaping and re-shaping the remainder of her proposal. Michael, as he had promised, had been at Katherine's side during the meeting, her obvious ally. He had firmly—almost proudly—congratulated her for her fine work at the end of her presentation.

Katherine had arrived back in her room two hours earlier, leaving Michael to go out to dinner with his uncle alone. After a sandwich and a quick hot bath, she was just beginning to unwind. Exhausted from the stress and the pace of the day, she changed into a long, cream-colored satin nightgown with matching robe. She stood on her balcony, admiring the beautiful view of the ocean under the full moon. Rows of perfect palm trees lined the sandy path to the beach. The searing sun had set, and the night's peaceful, warm breezes gently blew her long hair back from her face. She leaned on the railing and closed her eyes, relaxing to the soothing sounds of the ocean waves lapping at the shore.

"Good evening, Wells."

Katherine's eyes flew open. Michael stood on the balcony next to hers.

"Nice night, isn't it?" he said, staring out over the water.

"Michael!" Katherine exclaimed. She crossed her arms modestly in front of her. "How long have you been standing there?"

"No more . . . than a few minutes," he said mischievously.

"You have the room next to mine?" She was unaware that the brightness of the moon had turned her satin garment into a nearly transparent sheath, illuminating her svelte figure. Michael's eyes inadvertently wandered toward the delicate curve of her breast, following the shadows to the smooth indentation of her firm, flat stomach. He glanced away.

"I thought you were in a room upstairs," she added quickly. She sat down in one of the two wicker chairs on her terrace and set her glass of ice water on the small round table between the chairs.

"I thought so too," he said, avoiding her eyes. "But I found it already occupied by some unsuspecting fellow. In any case, they switched me."

"Oh," Katherine said awkwardly. She couldn't help but notice how handsome he looked at that moment. His shirtsleeves were rolled up casually, and his tie hung loose around his partially unbuttoned shirt. His thick black hair had the rumpled look of someone who had a nervous habit of running his hands through it.

"Still working?" she asked.

"Unfortunately, yes," he said, casually putting his hands in his pockets. He looked up at the moon. "I'm a little stuck on something."

"Do you want someone to bounce ideas off of?" she asked, cautiously aware of the effect she was having on him.

"Help would be . . . nice," he said finally.

"Okay," Katherine said.

"I'll, uh, meet you . . ."

"Downstairs," Katherine said, completing the sentence. She eased back into her room. Michael watched her, enjoying her discomfort at her predicament.

She shut the sliding glass door and glimpsed herself in the mirror. She was struck by just how revealing her light attire was. Normally, she would never venture outside in an outfit like that, but when she had opened the balcony door, the evening had been so appealing, she had found it impossible to resist.

Embarrassed, she quickly changed back into her suit, ran a brush through her silky hair, and pinned it back in a barrette.

She stepped out of her room and pushed the elevator button just as Michael walked out of his room, briefcase in hand. So, she thought silently, she was about to experience the dreaded elevator ride alone with the boss.

Michael walked up to the elevator as the doors opened. "Good timing," he said, holding the doors and motioning for her to enter.

"Yes," Katherine replied with a silly, nervous laugh. She cursed her giddiness as she stepped into the tiny mirrored space. She bit her lower lip as she hugged her briefcase close to her body, backing up against the wall of the empty elevator. Michael followed close behind, pressing the lobby button and standing silently beside her. Katherine watched the doors close, desperately searching for potential topics for small talk. But just as quickly as she'd think of something, she would reject it as being silly, stupid or irrelevant.

The buttons illuminating the floor numbers lit up silently as the elevator slowly inched its way toward the lobby. Michael watched them closely, scrutinizing them as a scientist might look at a germ under a microscope.

"How was your meeting with Alan?" Katherine asked.

"Fine," he replied.

"You got back early," she said, trying to stretch out the conversation.

"Not really," he replied.

Katherine gave up. She joined him in staring at the elevator buttons. What seemed like an eternity later, the elevator doors opened. Katherine slowly let the anxious air expel from her body. She would have preferred to be upstairs, lounging in her soft, silky outfit, watching cable rather than standing in the smoky lobby, heading toward a smoky lounge and wearing the same, slightly rumpled suit she had worn all day. On top of all that, her panty hose were beginning to itch.

"How's this?" Michael asked, pulling out a chair in the middle of the room. Katherine managed a pleasant smile as she sat down across from him.

"So . . ." Katherine said after their drink order had been taken.

"So," Michael said. "Here we are."

"Right," Katherine replied nervously. This seemingly innocent meeting was feeling like an uncomfortable first date.

The waitress set her drink down in front of her. Michael had ordered a scotch, and Katherine, although she normally didn't drink hard liquor, had followed his lead.

"Good," he said. "Well, here's to your proposal." He raised his glass. "Congratulations on a job well done."

"Thank you." Katherine swallowed the golden liquid. She felt a ball of fire roll down her throat and into her belly, warming and relaxing her.

"Do you always do that?" she asked.

"Do what?" he replied, picking up his briefcase.

"Make a toast." Katherine set her drink down, suddenly horrified that she had referred to their first encounter in the bar.

"Sometimes," he said. His eyes sparkled as he looked at her mischievously, his mind focused on the last minutes of their first meeting. "So, tell me. Has any man ever been successful in persuading you to give him your phone number?" he asked, referring to their first exchange.

Katherine laughed and sipped her fiery drink. "No." She glanced at him. "Well, maybe." She smiled. "I guess I just didn't think you were trustworthy."

"Was it me you didn't trust . . . or was it yourself?"

"I thought we agreed never to mention our . . . initial meeting," she said, throwing his own directive back at him.

He set his drink down and leaned forward. He gazed at her beautiful, clear eyes. He found her every bit as bewitching as he had that first night. He had never encountered a woman who could appear so vulnerable and capable at the same time. He swallowed, as though gulping back his libido. Fortunately, at the office, he had been able to restrict his meetings with her, not yet trusting his own orders to keep their affair strictly platonic and professional.

"You're right. I'm sorry," he said quietly.

Katherine swallowed a large gulp of the potent liquid in front of her. Why did she remind him of their agreement never to mention how they met? She wanted to continue the conversation. "I don't know why I wouldn't give you my number," she said suddenly. "I've never been in that situation before. I mean, I wanted to see you again . . ." Her voice drifted off.

Michael leaned back in his chair, quickly losing all

previous intensity. He picked up his drink and shook the glass slightly and intentionally, rattling the ice cubes. He had the bored manner of a country gentleman at high tea.

"And besides," Katherine added indignantly, "it turned out my instincts were correct. You weren't really honest with me."

"Honest?" he asked nonchalantly, looking over his shoulder at the table behind them.

"About who you were. And pretending that car was yours." Michael drove a Range Rover. A black one, to be exact. She had seen it parked in the parking garage at work.

Michael's head snapped back in attention. "That car belongs to a guy who works for me . . . in my home," he said defensively. "I borrowed his car because mine was in the shop. And, anyway, what difference did the car make? Would a Range Rover have given me away?"

Katherine shrugged her shoulders stubbornly.

"As far as lying about who I was," Michael continued, "I didn't claim to be anyone else. So how did I deceive you?"

Katherine looked away. Okay, maybe it wasn't anything he said, but . . .

"Look," he said gently. "I didn't announce who I was because it didn't come up. Hell, I didn't even get your name until right before I left." He sighed. "Although I did enjoy my brief anonymity. Sometimes I do wonder what it would be like not to have money or fame."

"Well, I can tell you," Katherine snapped, her eyes flashing brilliantly. "It's just like anything else. You get used to it."

Michael hesitated, feeling the bite of her stinging words. He crossed his arms, setting up an imaginary barrier between them. "I'm sorry. That didn't come out right. I do know what it's like . . . not to have money—or fame, for that matter. I've been there. It's just that my situation has changed in the past few years, and sometimes you can't tell who your real friends are. Am I making any sense?" he asked, frustrated by his own inability to express himself.

"Yes," Katherine replied, reaching for her drink. She was a little stunned by her bold behavior. What had gotten into her?

"When did you realize who I was?" he asked.

"You wrote your name above your phone number."

Michael smiled slightly. "Old habits die hard. I forgot to use the old alibi," he joked. "So you knew you were going to have to see me the next day."

Katherine nodded uncomfortably.

"So . . . do you have any family still in Michigan?" he asked, abruptly changing the subject. He could still talk to her. Just as he would talk to any coworker.

"No," Katherine replied. "I was an only child, and my father died when I was young. My mom died last year."

"I'm sorry," Michael said tenderly.

"What about you?" Katherine asked, as if she didn't know. She already knew quite a bit about his background from the news weeklies.

"My mother died about ten years ago. It was right after my father lost his bid for the presidency—and all of his money."

"I remember reading about it," Katherine said.

"It was a . . . tough time for both of us," Michael said carefully. "I was always close to my mom, but my dad had been so busy, I never got a chance to know him. When she was gone, I found my buffer had disappeared. It was just me and him."

"No brothers or sisters?"

"I'm an only child too."

Katherine looked into the eyes that were staring off

into the distance, lost back in time. She felt an urge to put her hand over his. To comfort him.

"It sounds tough," she said instead.

"I didn't really like my father much at the time. I guess I blamed him for . . ." He stopped abruptly. "I shouldn't be talking like this," he said.

"Anything else?" the waitress asked, picking up Michael's empty glass.

"The check," Michael said. He glanced up at Katherine. What was it about her that made him want to open his soul to her? He had to be professional. He was her employer, for God's sake. What if she went blabbing around the office . . .

Katherine swallowed. "So what was it . . . you mentioned on the balcony you were having trouble with something?"

But it was too late. Michael had reprimanded himself already. He could not allow himself to indulge in intimate conversation with her. And he himself could not be trusted to follow his own rules. "Nothing," he said, checking his watch as he signed the check. "Look, it's getting late. I won't keep you any longer, Wells." He snapped open his briefcase. "I'll see you tomorrow," he added, dismissing her.

Katherine looked at him. "What about the work we were supposed to do?" she asked.

"It's too late now," he said accusingly, as though she had purposely led him off track. "And we have an early-morning meeting tomorrow with my uncle." He glanced at her coldly, like a king dismissing a tedious and aggravating subject.

"All right," she replied, standing up proudly.

Michael pulled out a thick folder. "Oh, Wells. One more thing. I know you've had a lot on your plate, but I hear we're getting a little delinquent with some of our bills. That's not acceptable."

So, Carly had been complaining. Katherine could

feel anger rise in her throat. "I'm not delinquent. I haven't paid those invoices intentionally. If you don't get backup from an advertising agency, it's very easy for them to mark things up."

Michael looked up from his briefcase. "You realize, of course, that in asking for backup, something we have never done in the past, you're insinuating that you don't trust Carly. That's a rather antagonistic way to begin a professional working arrangement, don't you think?"

"It has nothing to do with Carly," she lied. "I think it's poor business not to ask for backup."

Michael leaned back in his chair. "Let me put it to you this way," he said in a quiet, firm tone. "We have a contract with Bresser and Tenner. We have a unique relationship with them. They work very closely with us. They basically function as our marketing department, which has saved me quite a bit of money over the years. Do you think they're going to be more helpful if you insult them, or if you're nice to them?"

Katherine stared at Michael coldly. She didn't think it was necessary for him to use such a patronizing tone.

"I appreciate your diligence," he continued. "But I've known Carly for a long time."

So I hear, Katherine felt like saying. *So I hear.*

Michael hesitated, avoiding Katherine's eyes and glancing back to his briefcase. "In business, you need to choose your battles carefully. This one isn't worth fighting," he said. He paused. "Just pay the damn invoices," he added, opening a folder.

There was to be no discussion. The conversation was over.

Katherine turned and walked away from the table. Obviously, she had made an error. He was acting like a stupid, naive schoolboy. Or was he? Obviously, he not only knew Carly well, he trusted her. Perhaps even loved her. And Katherine had stupidly insulted her. Her new boss's girlfriend, or whatever Carly was.

But, Katherine thought, allowing herself to dwell on the subject, even if Michael and Carly were romantically involved, there had to be trouble. After all, he had wanted to ask her out. And there was still something there, between them. An awkwardness, an attraction. She could feel it.

Katherine pressed the elevator button and nodded politely at an elderly couple strolling past. Usually, she loved seeing old, happy couples. She imagined them married for decades, having shared joys and sorrows, facing the adventure of life together. But tonight, a small sigh of discontent escaped her lips. She was beginning to wonder if she would ever find a man she could grow old with.

The *ding* of the arriving elevator snapped her back to the present. She gracefully stepped inside and steadily reached a slender hand toward the panel of floor buttons. At least there wouldn't be any more uncomfortable elevator rides tonight.

8

Katherine awoke to the shrill ring of her phone. She fumbled for it groggily.

"Yes," she mumbled, assuming it was her wake-up call.

"Sorry to wake you so early, Wells," announced Michael without a tinge of remorse. "In all the excitement of last night"—he paused, allowing some of the sarcasm to sink in—"I forgot to mention that my uncle wants to meet us on his boat today, instead of at the hotel."

"But," Katherine said nervously, suddenly awake, "I didn't bring any casual clothes. I didn't even bring a bathing suit."

Michael grinned. Katherine was the ultimate professional, ready for anything. It hadn't occurred to him that she might not have brought anything appropriate for a day on a boat. But why would she? It had not been on the itinerary. He couldn't resist an opportunity to tease her about an oversight that was beyond her control. "You'll have to make do. Next time, I suggest you come a little more prepared," he said, as sternly as he could manage.

Katherine rolled her eyes.

"I'll meet you downstairs in half an hour," Michael said. He put down the phone, chuckling softly to himself.

Katherine flew out of bed and over to her suitcase.

Business shirt, business shoes ... she had nothing that was even slightly appropriate for a business meeting on a boat! She grabbed a sweatshirt and held it up for inspection. It looked too messy and unprofessional, boat or no boat. She disgustedly threw it on top of her suitcase. She decided she would have to buy a T-shirt from the gift shop downstairs.

Katherine looked at the clock for the first time that morning. Six thirty-five A.M. They weren't supposed to meet until nine.

In any case, Katherine realized miserably, no gift store would be open this early. She took a long shower and dressed quickly, choosing tailored slacks, a white silk blouse and sweater, and black pumps from her limited wardrobe. In honor of the occasion, she would forgo panty hose.

She was sitting in the café, sipping her second cup of coffee, when Michael arrived. With his green Bermuda shorts, crisp white T-shirt, and windbreaker, he looked ideally dressed for a day on a boat. Katherine couldn't help noting that his outfit was completed with brown boating shoes.

"Good morning, Wells," he said cheerily. "Ready to go?" She nodded, signaling the waiter for her tab.

Michael and Katherine climbed into a cab, placing their briefcases strategically between them. Katherine stared out the window. At least it was a beautiful day, she consoled herself. It could be a lot worse. It was the end of September. Hurricane season.

The cab crossed over a bridge surrounded by crystal-clear blue ocean water on either side. Katherine sighed longingly. She wished she was on vacation with friends instead of here on an uncomfortable business trip.

The cab made a right off the bridge and took them down a little road along the bay.

"It's up here on the right," Michael said to the driver, pointing to a large white mansion. "That's

Alan's house. He keeps his boat docked in a slip right behind it."

Michael paid the cab driver. Katherine stepped out of the cab, impressed by the stature of the house.

"I'll wait outside," she said, her heels sinking in the soft ground.

"We're not going into the house," Michael said, looking at her sternly. "We're meeting him around back."

Katherine stepped carefully through the dewy grass to the back of the property.

Alan Benson was standing on a fifty-foot sailing yacht, busily untying the sails.

"Ahoy there!" he called out cheerily. "Welcome aboard!"

Michael hopped on easily. Katherine hesitated before taking off her shoes and jumping aboard. Alan took one look at her and shook his head.

"No boating clothes?" he said. Katherine shrugged her shoulders uncomfortably.

"Go beneath," he said, pointing to the cabin. "My wife's about your size. I think she's got a bathing suit down there."

Katherine looked at Michael. "What are you waiting for?" he asked gruffly.

Katherine climbed into the cabin. On a hook outside the bathroom door was a black bikini with a matching sarong to tie around her waist. Obviously, she thought, holding the suit up for inspection, Alan Benson's wife was a very sexy lady. As she changed in the cramped bathroom, she continued to weigh the pros and cons of wearing a bikini in a business meeting or being on a boat in the middle of the ocean on a hot, sunny day dressed in a business suit. She looked down at the bikini top. It seemed to cover everything important. She tied the sarong around her waist and crawled back up to face the lions.

The men were almost ready to begin sailing the boat when she stepped on deck. They both stopped talking immediately.

"Well, it certainly seems to fit," Alan Benson sputtered, staring at Katherine's long, slender form. His wife had an excellent figure, but she was about thirty years older than Katherine.

Michael felt a sting of jealousy as his uncle stared appreciatively at the luscious figure before him. He knew that his aunt and uncle had been happily married for almost forty years, but it was an obvious reminder of how attractive his marketing director was.

"Here, wear this," Michael said, quickly pulling off his windbreaker and handing it to her.

Katherine smiled. Was it possible he was jealous?

Michael paused, aware of the amusement in her eyes.

"You might get cold," he said simply.

Katherine took the jacket and put it on. She rolled up the sleeves and sat down on Alan's side of the bench.

Michael glanced at Alan. "Alan's just been telling me what he thought of our presentation yesterday. Go on, Alan."

"Michael, I don't think it's necessary for Katherine to hear . . ."

"I want her to know what the internal struggles are. She needs to know what she's up against."

"There are no internal struggles," he said to Michael. Michael raised his eyebrows. Alan hesitated a moment, then turned toward Katherine. "Toby Nat is a little concerned that too much money is being directed into research and development."

Michael stood up and jammed his hands into his pockets. "That's bullshit, Alan! If we don't do research and focus on developing new products, our company isn't going to be worth anything. You and I both know that if we get a great new product, our stock prices could double."

"If, Michael. If."

Michael sat back down. He took his hands out of his pockets. "Toby should have talked to me in person instead of asking you to do his dirty work."

"You know that's not the case, Michael."

"I know that the A-14 engine could revolution-ize—"

"Michael," Alan said reasonably. "The entire A-14 division lost money last year. New engine or not."

"A large part of that was due to lousy PR," Katherine interrupted. Both men turned and looked at her. "I'm sure you all know about the rumor. It snowballed with some bad press. I think we can change that."

Michael glanced back at Alan. The elder man was focused on the rudder of the boat. Michael paused a moment before speaking.

"What are you trying to tell me?" Michael asked Alan. "That you agree with Toby? Use profits for bigger dividends instead of more research?"

"I'm not saying you have to eliminate the division, Michael. But I think Toby has a point. It's too hard and too costly to stay on top of Japan. We're trying, and we haven't been able to. Let's just let them develop the new products. We'll simply improve them and sell them under our own name."

Michael shook his head. "That would go against my whole foundation, all the principles I built this company on."

"Calm down, Michael. You asked me what I thought. I think it's worth considering. But enough said," he announced, suddenly changing his tone of voice. "I think it's time for a swim. If you'll excuse me," he said, dropping the anchor, "I'm going to go downstairs and change into my suit."

Michael crossed his arms and stared out into the

choppy water as Alan slammed the door to the cabin. Katherine sat quietly for a moment, respectful of Michael's brooding silence.

"You didn't realize what you were getting yourself into, did you?" he asked suddenly. "You probably thought this would be a nice family outing."

"A lot of families are in business together," she said.

"Perhaps. But I'm not so sure it's a good idea. The corporate environment does not really encourage healthy family relationships."

Katherine crossed her long, slender legs as she stared out at the choppy water. Michael watched as the sarong fell open, allowing her right leg to slip out. He swallowed.

"I don't know," she continued, unaware of the effect her legs were having on Michael. "I do think Toby is mistaken, however. We can change people's perception. I have no doubt we can make the division profitable. We have a great product."

Michael glanced up from her legs. His steely blue eyes softened as he admired the fine details of her face. Katherine brushed a strand of hair away from her eyes.

"I appreciate your support," he said.

"We can increase sales. I don't have any doubt."

"Good," Michael replied, still staring at her. He wasn't sure he believed her, but her outfit was making it difficult for him to continue a business conversation. He was tempted to kiss her instead.

Katherine smiled uncomfortably, aware that Michael wasn't reacting to what she said. Was she boring him? Or was he just as uncomfortably warm as she was?

"You can take off the windbreaker, you know," Michael said with a smile. It was almost as if he had been reading her mind.

"I know," Katherine replied. Even though she had a bikini top on under the windbreaker, she felt like Michael was asking her to take her shirt off.

"You're hot, aren't you?"

Katherine shrugged her shoulders.

"Go ahead," he said, obviously enjoying her embarrassment. He leaned back and crossed his arms, as though daring her to undress in front of him.

Somewhat shyly, she stood up. She turned away from Michael and began to pull the jacket over her head. Suddenly, a large wave crashed into the boat, causing it to lurch precariously. Katherine lost her balance and fell toward the side of the boat.

Michael jumped up and caught her, pulling her in toward him. He yanked the jacket off Katherine's head and spun her around, still holding her tightly in his arms.

"Excuse me!" Alan said loudly, more amused than embarrassed. He was standing in the entrance to the hull.

Michael and Katherine clumsily broke away from each other.

"Anyone care to join me in a swim? It might help to cool off," he added, smiling at his own joke.

"We don't need any cooling off, thank you. Katherine almost fell into the water. I stopped her fall," Michael said angrily.

"Do what you wish!" Alan said cheerfully before jumping into the water.

"Damn!" Michael said softly under his breath. He glared at Katherine.

"I didn't ask you to stop me from falling!" she said defensively. She glanced at Alan swimming laps around the boat. He stopped and waved.

"Come on in!" he yelled. "Water's great."

Katherine smiled and waved back.

"I've got some work to do," Michael announced, disappearing into the cabin.

"Is there anything I can help you with?" Katherine asked matter-of-factly.

"You've done enough already," he replied, not looking back. Katherine glanced away, hurt. She looked at the cold, dark water. She had two options. She could either stay on the boat with Michael, or she could go for a plunge with the sharks. It only took her a second to decide.

Down below, Michael heard the splash of Katherine's lean body diving into the chilly water. He put down his pen.

It irritated him to think that his uncle had witnessed his desire for Katherine. He didn't need this added ... distraction right now. Especially with the internal political storm that was brewing. He needed to convince Toby that he knew what was best for the company. And how could he earn his respect if Toby thought Michael was fooling around with one of his new employees? He was confident Alan would not hesitate to share his thoughts about Michael and Katherine with the family. It was just a matter of time before word would get back to the board.

And to his father. Michael realized he would have to find a way to reassure his father that his feelings for Katherine were under control. His desires were not, nor would they ever be, a concern.

He had to do something drastic. He had no choice. He would talk to Katherine and explain his situation. Perhaps she could help him combat the rumors. And the sooner he spoke to her about it, the better. And he didn't have much time. His aunt and uncle had insisted he and Katherine attend a party at their country club tonight.

9

Katherine took her black cocktail dress out of the closet and checked it for wrinkles. She was not looking forward to the evening. It had been a long, uncomfortable ride back to shore, with Michael speaking only when necessary. Even when they were alone in the cab, Michael had avoided conversation by pretending to be immersed in a report. Not that Katherine had minded. She preferred to stare out the window at palm trees and blue water rather than subject herself to unpleasant conversation with unpleasant company.

Katherine pulled the dress over her head and clasped the button shut at the back of the neckline. Part of the reason she had chosen this dress was that it traveled so well. Part of the reason she almost didn't choose it, however, was that it was fairly short and fairly snug. But that was the style of the dress—form-fitting black crepe which from the distance almost made the dress look strapless. But sheer black netting made up the long sleeves and the scooped neckline, creating a sexy yet elegant appearance.

After a quick glance at her watch, she pinned her hair into a French twist. She was tired of trying to understand Michael. How could he be so nice one minute, so rude the next? Was it possible that he was responding to cues he was picking up from her? Was he aware of her infatuation? He must be, she realized miserably. On the boat, he had basically insinuated that she had thrown herself at him.

She put on her pearl drop earrings. Well, she thought indignantly, tonight she would stay as far away from him as possible. Even if she did have a silly little crush on him, that didn't mean she would act on it. No. She needed to assure him that she had no desire to become involved with him, she thought, slipping her high-heeled shoes over her sheer black panty hose.

Katherine stopped. She could hear someone closing a door. She grabbed her purse and stepped into the hall as Michael approached.

"Ready?" he asked, his eyes quickly taking in the lovely sight before him.

Katherine smiled. "Nice tux," she said, turning away. "Your tie is a little crooked, though," she added casually, walking toward the elevator.

Michael, still flustered from the effect of her beauty, hesitated. He glanced down awkwardly at his tie as he yanked it to the middle.

"Coming?" Katherine asked, holding the elevator doors open. Michael raised an eyebrow as he picked up his pace. Katherine seemed to be acting differently. It was almost as if she wasn't intimidated by him. Not that he wanted her to be intimidated. Of course not, he thought to himself, stepping into the crowded elevator.

The elevator stopped on the floor below, and the elderly couple Katherine had seen the night before got on. They smiled at Katherine in acknowledgment.

"Hello," Katherine said cheerfully.

"All dressed up tonight," the woman said.

"Yes," Katherine replied.

"Fancy dinner?"

Katherine laughed, glancing uncomfortably at Michael. "I guess so."

The woman grinned as though she suddenly understood. "What a beautiful couple you are. On your honeymoon?"

Katherine inhaled deeply. She was horrified. "N-no . . ." she stammered.

"Don't worry, sweetie. We're not married, either. Hey, it's the nineties," the lady said, squeezing her date's hand. Katherine forced a weak grin as she glanced quickly at Michael. He was staring down at her, but, fortunately, he looked more amused than embarrassed. Katherine focused her gaze on the floor numbers. She was beginning to understand why Michael chose not to talk in elevators.

Outside the hotel, Michael hailed a cab. He held the door open for her, and Katherine slid in. He sat beside her, staring at her curiously.

"Who the hell was that?"

"Who?" Katherine asked innocently.

Michael shook his head. "To the Epmeer Forest Country Club on Key Biscayne Boulevard" he said. The cab pulled out of the driveway.

"Katherine . . ." Michael began. He paused. He couldn't bring himself to talk to her yet. He needed to warm up first. "Ever been there before?" he asked.

"To the Epmeer Forest Country Club?"

Michael nodded.

"No. Why?"

"No reason," he replied, crossing his arms in front of him and staring moodily out the window. Katherine shrugged. She was not going to allow one crabby boss to distract her. She was determined to enjoy herself in spite of her stiff companion.

Michael and Katherine arrived at the club and were seated next to each other at a table for four. Across from them sat Michael's uncle Alan and aunt Theresa.

Dinner was served promptly at seven. The chicken Cordon Bleu was served on white china that had the

Epmeer Forest logo engraved in the center of each dish in royal blue. Every dish, every piece of silver, radiated wealth and prestige. Katherine knew the moment the cab had dropped them off under the blue-striped awning that this country club was going to be a little different from the Albion club she had waited tables at during the summers. This club had green manicured lawns that rolled down toward the ocean. The patio surrounding the pool bar was dotted with cherry-red cabanas for when the very wealthy members preferred to drink their scotch and sodas out of the sun. And the inside of the club was just as elaborate. Crystal chandeliers subtly lit the expansive dining room which was decorated in varying shades of blue. Candles on each table added a touch of romantic ambiance. The tables were arranged around a parquet dance floor, where a band was playing the big-band hits of the forties and fifties. The back of the room contained sliding glass doors which were completely open to a brick patio, leading to the beach.

Katherine took a sip of wine. If she concentrated, she could even hear the sound of the ocean over the band.

"A roll?" Theresa said, holding out the bread basket. Katherine accepted the basket. She nervously glanced at the bread plate on her left and then the bread plate on her right. Which was hers? At times like this, she wished she had paid attention to her mother's sporadic etiquette lessons. Rather than risk a faux pas, she passed the bread basket on to Michael without taking a roll.

Michael, who had been watching Katherine carefully and was fully aware of why she had declined to take one, took out a roll and put it on the small plate to her left. "You really should try these, they're excellent," he said.

"Now, Michael, maybe she doesn't want one," Theresa said. Theresa, though a lovely woman, was not quite the sex kitten Katherine had imagined. She was in her early sixties, and her white-blond hair was swept up in an elaborate style that only a professional hairdresser could have mastered. She wore a sequined gold dress which, Katherine suspected, had not been bought off the rack.

"No, really. It's all right."

"Michael's always like that. He always thinks he knows what's best," Theresa said, smiling at Michael knowingly. She focused her attention on Katherine. "So, Katherine, tell me," she said, leaning across the table. Katherine eyed the woman's diamond stud earrings. They appeared to be at least two carats each. If they were real, of course. And Katherine had a sneaky suspicion they were. "How long have you worked at Benson?"

Michael breathed a small sigh of relief. He loved his aunt dearly, but she was known for asking personal and inappropriate questions. They had been seated at the table now for almost thirty minutes, and so far, so good.

"Just about a month."

"Well, I'm sure you'll enjoy working for Michael. He's always been my favorite nephew. So sweet and kind."

"Only," Michael interrupted, "I think you mean I've always been your *only* nephew." He glanced at Alan and smiled.

"There he goes," she said, looking at him proudly. "Being modest."

Michael shook his head slightly, although he was trying to shake off some of Theresa's strangeness. Katherine grinned at Michael. It was apparent that although Theresa seemed to mean well, she had spent one too many years in the sun.

"I'm sure you'll find that he's every bit as attractive

inside as he is out," Theresa continued. "All of my girlfriends' daughters are crazy about him. Of course, he's broken more than one heart at this very club. Even Jenna Tyler, who's here tonight, as a matter of fact . . ."

"Katherine, would you care to dance?" Alan said, interrupting his wife in an attempt to rescue Katherine. He stood up and extended his hand to her.

Katherine glanced at the one other couple waltzing on the floor. "I'm afraid I'm not a very good dancer . . ."

"There's no such thing," he said, pulling out her chair.

"In that case," she replied graciously, "I would love to." Which was true. Except not at that moment. At that moment, she would have preferred to stay at the table and hear more about Jenna Tyler. Katherine wondered who she was. Was she carrying a torch for Michael?

Michael watched as Alan steered Katherine to the dance floor.

"She's a lovely girl," Theresa said, smiling at Michael.

"What? Oh, yes. I guess so," he replied nonchalantly. Theresa raised an eyebrow. His nonchalance did not fool her. It was obvious in the way he looked at Katherine that he was acutely aware of just how lovely she was.

"So, did I hear you mention that Jenna Tyler is here? It'll be great to see her again," Michael said, avoiding her eyes.

"Oh, really," Theresa said knowingly. "You never felt that way before." Michael shrugged.

"Come now, Michael. What exactly is going on with Katherine?"

"Nothing. She works for me."

"So what? I was Alan's secretary, remember? That's

how I met him. And we've been married for forty-two years this March.''

"It was different back then. Things are more complicated now. If he asked you out now, instead of saying yes, you'd probably sue him.''

"And would I have won?" she asked with a curious smile.

"Maybe.''

"And to think I thought I had to marry him to get his money . . .'' She laughed, shrugging her shoulders.

"Very funny," Michael said with a grin.

Theresa smiled sweetly. "You can reason away all you want, my dear, but coworkers, bosses, and marketing directors are still falling in love all over corporate America. Why, almost all the young people I know met their spouses through work. I think that's why my son is still single.''

Michael laughed as he shook his head. Her son, Kevin, was a playboy who had been living off his more than ample trust fund ever since he graduated from college.

"But anyway, it's obvious that you and Katherine like each other. Alan said he found you in each other's arms.''

"It was an accident.''

"There's no such thing as accidents," she said, putting her napkin on the table indignantly.

Michael raised his eyebrows. "If that's true, then how do you explain the large dent on your car's front bumper?''

Theresa frowned. "How did you know about that?''

"Alan told me.''

"Oh," she said, shaking her head. "That wasn't an accident. That was stupidity. The man in front of me never should've stopped. The light hadn't even turned yellow yet. And Alan promised me he wasn't going to tell anyone. Now, are you going to ask me to dance? Or, in these modern times, do I have to ask you?"

"I would love to. Thank you," Michael said, offering her a teasing smile as he stood and pulled out her chair.

She grinned as she accepted his arm. "You can be quite a charmer, Mr. Benson. But you can also be . . ."

"I call a truce," Michael said. "And to show you what a good sport I am, I'm going to sweep you off your feet."

Michael grabbed his petite aunt by her slender waist and waltzed across the floor. They had barely danced one dance before the band began its version of "Strangers in the Night."

"I absolutely love this song," Theresa exclaimed, looking across the room. Michael followed her gaze, focusing on Alan and Katherine. Katherine seemed to be dancing just fine, despite her earlier protests. Theresa took the lead, steering Michael over toward Katherine and Alan.

"Aunt Theresa. What are you up to?" Michael whispered in her ear.

Theresa smiled as she ignored him. "Alan," she said, calling out to her husband. "It's our song." She switched her focus to Katherine. "Do you mind if we switch partners?" she asked.

"Not at all. I'm ready to sit down," Katherine replied.

"Then I won't have it. Sorry, Theresa," Alan said with a twinkle in his eye. "I can't desert my partner."

Michael and Katherine shot a pained look at each other. It was obvious that neither Theresa nor Alan would dance with each other unless Michael and Katherine danced together as well. Michael sighed. He would humor them. After all, it was one dance. Michael dropped Theresa's arm and approached them.

"Mind if I cut in?" he asked, tapping his uncle on the shoulder.

"Not at all, my boy. Not at all. Theresa, my love . . ." Alan exclaimed, grabbing Theresa by the hand and twirling her around in a pirouette before pulling her in close.

Michael and Katherine awkwardly joined hands, and Michael pulled her in close to him. Katherine's head rested slightly against his cheek. Feeling nervous and awkward, she immediately stepped on his foot.

"I'm sorry," she said, breaking away. "Maybe this isn't such a good idea."

"You're doing fine," Michael replied, still holding on to her hands. "Just relax," he said, pulling her in close again.

Katherine tried to relax, promising herself that this was a simple, innocent dance, a dance with a boss who just happened to be attractive. But it was only a dance.

Michael breathed in the smell of her lightly perfumed hair as he held her, moving slowly to the music. He was surprised at how light she felt in his arms . . . how right.

"You're great," he said. "Are you sure you haven't taken dance lessons?"

"I'm more than positive," she said, pulling back far enough to look at him. "I think all little girls are either ballet students or piano students. I was a piano student."

"You can play piano?" Michael asked.

"I didn't say I could play. I said I took lessons," Katherine replied with a smile.

Michael smiled back. He focused on her lips as he instinctively grabbed her hand tighter. He boldly pulled her back in to him so that her slender frame was pressed up against him. Michael's left hand brushed behind her, resting casually on her lower back.

Katherine inhaled suddenly as an acute twinge of desire shot through her. The nearness of their bodies made it impossible to deny the attraction. She closed her eyes, allowing herself to relax and enjoy the adrenaline pulsing through her. She let herself go as she fell into a natural rhythm, responding to his moves as if by reflex.

Michael could feel her relax in his arms, and that pleased him. He disregarded the inner voice reminding him that it probably wasn't proper to be seen practically hugging an employee on the dance floor as he continued to rest his cheek lightly against her hair. His eyes wandered down the back of her form-fitting dress as he admired her perfect proportions.

Both were so caught up in their own private world that it took them a moment to realize the song had ended. Michael was disappointed to see the band leaving the stage.

"I guess they're taking a break," Michael whispered in Katherine's ear, as if trying to wake her gently.

That was all she needed. Katherine snapped back to attention. "Thank you," she said politely, pulling back.

"The pleasure was mine," Michael said, still holding on to her hands.

Katherine blushed as she pulled her hands away. They walked back to the table. When they arrived, another woman was sitting in Katherine's seat talking to Theresa.

"Hello, Michael," the woman said quietly, not looking at him.

"Jenna. What a surprise," he said, obviously not pleased to see her. He turned toward Katherine. "Why don't you have a seat?" he said, pointing to his chair.

"No . . ." Katherine began.

"Oh, dear, did I take your seat?" Jenna asked, not showing any sign of moving.

"No, not at all. As a matter of fact, I was just going to ask you all to excuse me for a while. I'm a little warm from dancing. I was just going to take a short walk down to the water," Katherine said.

"Don't be long, dear," Theresa said. She shot Jenna a nasty look for Katherine's benefit. Katherine hid her smile as she turned away.

She made her way over to the patio and escaped outside. The tropical air had cooled significantly since sunset. She crossed her arms in front of her for warmth and walked down the steps toward the beach. The full moon lit up the sky, allowing her to admire the geraniums that bloomed in perfect rows on either side of the fence.

"Katherine?"

She turned, surprised to see Michael standing behind her. He had taken off his jacket and was holding it in front of him. "I thought you might need this," he said.

"No, I'm fine," she replied quickly. That was the second time that day that Michael had offered her his jacket.

"Go ahead, take it. It's getting cold," he said.

Katherine smiled. He looked so cute standing there with his suspenders and bow tie. The humidity had curled and tossed his brown hair. "Thanks," she said, taking his coat and drooping it around her shoulders.

"Do you mind if I join you?" he asked. Katherine shook her head. "Walking toward the beach?" Michael asked.

"I thought I'd take a look at the ocean."

"Great idea. It'll be nice to see something real after, well . . ." Michael said.

"What?" Katherine asked.

"Its just that, well, that," Michael said, pointing to the geraniums. He shrugged his shoulders. "Everything is just too . . ."

"Country clubbish?" Katherine asked, laughing.

"You got it," Michael said, putting his hands in his pockets.

"I'm surprised you were able to break away from . . . your family," Katherine said, loosening up a bit. Michael was being so charming.

"They're a little strange, aren't they? I'm sorry they keep trying to throw us together."

"That's all right," Katherine replied, a little too quickly. They had reached the last step. The beach was in front of them.

Michael sat on the step. "Care to join me?" he said, patting the spot next to him. Katherine sat down. The step was small, and she couldn't avoiding touching him.

"Katherine, I followed you out here for a reason. I just wanted to tell you that, well, if I seem gruff sometimes, it's just because . . . I, well, I'm human."

"What are you trying to say?"

That I want to kiss you, Michael thought silently. *That I can't be alone with you without wanting to take you in my arms.* "Nothing," he said quickly. "I have a lot on my mind. I sometimes have difficulty remembering to praise my employees when they've done well. And you have been doing extremely well."

Katherine paused. "Is that why you followed me out here?" she asked. She turned toward him. The breeze blew the wisps of hair that had fallen out of her twist away from her face. Michael paused, staring into her big green eyes.

Katherine could feel her breath began to quicken as Michael leaned in closer. His eyes gazed tenderly into hers.

"No," Michael said. Katherine waited patiently. "I . . ." He hesitated. He couldn't bring himself to talk about the potential rumors regarding their involvement. Especially when he himself was doing nothing to discourage them. "I wanted to tell you that you should take a cab back to the hotel tonight by yourself," he said quickly, his demeanor changing as he glanced back toward the club. "I have to stay here and talk to my uncle. I didn't want you to have to hang around and wait for me."

"I don't mind waiting," Katherine said.

"Thanks, but I need to talk to him alone."

"Of course," Katherine said. She doubted that he needed to talk to his uncle at all. He probably wanted her to leave so he could be alone with Jenna Tyler. He was afraid that if Katherine saw him with her, she would gossip about them back at the office. She handed him back his coat. She certainly was not going to stand in the way of his rendezvous with an old flame. "In that case, I'll say my good-byes and go."

Michael stood still, continuing to look at her.

"Shall we head back?" Katherine asked cheerfully as she began to walk away. It took all of Michael's self-control not to reach out and grab her, to stop her . . .

"That's a good idea. You're sure you don't mind taking a cab by yourself?" Michael asked.

"I'll be fine," she said. "I'll be fine." It sounded more convincing the first time.

10

Katherine worked in the dark of night, her desk illuminated by a single lamp. She sipped her coffee and made a face. Already cold. She glanced at the clock in front of her. No wonder it was cold. She had poured it at eight, more than two hours ago. She stretched her arms out in front of her, pausing when she heard her neck crack from the built-up tension. She looked at the document in front of her with pride. It was Benson's new marketing plan, and it was almost finished. Since her return from Miami two weeks ago, she had worked on little else. Surprisingly, she had had little exposure to Michael during this time.

But she didn't need to see him to be reminded of him. She had found herself dreaming about him—seductive, romantic dreams so vivid that the next day she found herself blushing at the mere thought of him. She found herself thinking of Jenna Tyler, of Carly. She realized with dismay that she was jealous.

She told herself that she was suffering from a simple schoolgirl crush. After all, any single woman who was working for a man like Michael would feel some attraction. Louise had even told her that almost all of the women in the office had a crush on him.

But that fact had not made Katherine feel any better. Instead, it annoyed her to no end. She liked to think that she was above all that. That she had more self-control and dignity than to allow herself to be swept up in a dreamy infatuation with her employer.

The shrill ring of the phone distracted her.

"What are you doing there so late?" Cyndi's cheerful voice bellowed out of the receiver.

Katherine smiled. It was nice to hear a friendly voice.

"I've got a meeting with Michael tomorrow. He wants me to show his father the outline for the marketing plan," Katherine said officially. She had never told anyone, not even Cyndi, about what happened between her and Michael that first night.

"Great," Cyndi said. "After you're done, I've got a perfect way for us to celebrate tomorrow night."

Katherine could sense the mischief in the air.

"Involving what . . . or whom, may I ask?" she said suspiciously.

"Well," Cyndi said, "as you know, I went out with that great-looking guy last weekend. He was perfect. The lawyer, remember?"

"Yeah . . ." Katherine said hesitantly.

"Well, it just so happens that he has a rich, successful, handsome friend named Christopher . . ."

"No!" Katherine said sternly. "You know how I feel about blind dates."

"Even if those blind dates have tickets to the ballet at Kennedy Center?"

Katherine paused. Cyndi knew full well she was crazy about ballet. She had been scanning the entertainment section of the newspapers since her arrival here, following the program offerings religiously.

"Come on, Katherine. It will do you good to get out!" Cyndi exclaimed. "They're also taking us to one of the best restaurants in Washington afterward. The Occidental."

"I don't know," Katherine replied. "I don't know if I'll feel like going all the way to Washington after work." Washington was only about forty-five minutes from Baltimore, but Katherine didn't like the idea of spending an hour and a half stranded in the backseat of a car with a blind date.

"C'mon, Katherine. It's not that far away. You make it sound like it's on the other side of the planet or something."

"The ballet is expensive. Not to mention the Occidental. That's a lot of money to spend on someone without expecting anything in return," she said cautiously.

"Loosen up," Cyndi commanded. "These are rich, handsome, *nice guys*. Got it?"

Katherine flipped a coin on her desk. It came up heads.

"All right. I'll go," she said, admitting defeat.

Michael sat behind his desk, staring at the document in front of him. His father would be walking into his office any minute. And Michael was nervous.

He stood up and checked his watch. He blamed Millie for his predicament, even though he knew it wasn't her fault. She had scheduled their meeting with Katherine as the first order of business when his father arrived. Apparently, his father had called Millie yesterday and asked her to schedule the appointment with Katherine as soon as he arrived.

Michael shrugged. He knew it didn't really make any difference whether the meeting with Katherine was the first order of business or the last. He had known all along that his father wanted to meet with her. Word had been circulating in the industry about the new marketing wunderkind at Benson. But why was it necessary to meet with her as soon as he arrived? Had he heard a rumor about Michael's supposed involvement with her?

Michael sighed. His father had always been so perceptive. He would take one look at his son with Katherine and know something strange was going on. His dad seemed to possess an uncanny ability to read Michael like a book.

But Michael was going to try to make it difficult for him. Over the past week, he had purposely prevented himself from being alone with Katherine so that they would appear awkward and unfamiliar with each other in front of his father. And when Millie had set up the meeting, Katherine had been told only that Michael wanted her to present what she had on the marketing campaign. Millie had not mentioned that Michael's father would be present.

To make matters even stickier, Diane had sent Michael a memo stating that Katherine had progressed very quickly in her job. Diane was impressed and had recommended that Katherine report directly to him. Michael had decided to tell Katherine the news at the meeting with his father. He wanted his father to see that he did not have a "secret" relationship with Katherine. Everything was out in the open. As everything really was.

Michael checked his watch one more time before jamming his hands in his pockets. If his relationship with Katherine was so innocent, why was he standing there feeling so guilty?

He sighed as he sank into his chair. He knew the answer. He had fantasized many times about throwing caution to the wind and asking her out. In fact, his feelings for Katherine were so strong that he always found himself overcompensating for them by acting distant and cold toward her. But it was only because his mind, his heart, was feeling anything but professional. He was beginning to think he would sell the company for one night alone with her.

Michael paused. If he was thinking about selling the company, now was the time. He was tired and frustrated. The A-14 engine had been a terrible disappointment for him. He had expected the industry to be excited, to be curious, but he had not expected the reaction he had received. Everyone seemed to be rejecting it. Without a real reason.

He had heard the rumors about the A-14, specifically that his own company had falsified data. Michael glanced down at the research papers scattered about his desk. His initial reaction had been to demand even more safety tests—but what would more tests mean if their validity was being questioned? Which was obviously the case. Because even when confronted with more data, the industry expressed little interest in the engine. Why? He knew the answer would lie with the discovery of who was behind the rumors. If he didn't know better, he would think that someone was out to sabotage the entire A-14 project. Was it possible that someone had a vendetta against him personally?

If so, if this was all a personal vendetta, the man or woman behind it must surely be satisfied. Because the A-14 engine predicament had begun to snowball. Research and development had always been Michael's main focus. It was a focus that had contributed to the company's rapid growth and expansion. Millions and millions of dollars had been funneled into the A-14 engine, but the A-14 fiasco had forced the stockholders to reevaluate the company's priorities. The entire research and development division was beginning to be viewed as an expensive white elephant that was dragging down the rest of the company. The stockholders' patience was wearing thin, and investors were beginning to question Michael's judgment in placing so much emphasis on research and development. Michael knew that was an ominous sign. Soon they would question his ability to run the company. If they weren't already.

He wasn't quite sure whom to trust. Toby Nat had

made his feelings clear about the direction Michael was leading the company, although Michael had a difficult time believing that he was out to sabotage him. And his uncle had expressed his disapproval of the A-14, but Michael and his uncle had clashed before. Despite their professional differences, they were family. They had always managed to maintain a cordial personal relationship. Still, he thought, the only people he felt sure about these days were his father and ... Katherine. She was the one who had been able to pin down the problem with sales to the A-14 rumors. And she was the one who was trying to come up with a solution to the problem.

Michael hesitated. That was why he knew he was doing the right thing by keeping their relationship strictly business. If he were to become romantically involved with her, the results could be disastrous. People in the industry might stop taking her seriously, thinking of her as Michael's girlfriend rather than the marketing guru who might just turn the Benson Corporation's luck around. Or worse, their romantic entanglement might sour, thereby alienating the one person who was trying to help him. The one person he trusted.

No. He had no choice but to play the distant, uninvolved boss. As best and as long as he could.

"Michael?" Millie's voice emanated through the intercom. "Your father is here." Michael cleared his throat as he stood up. His toughest audience had arrived.

Minutes later, Katherine was organizing her notes in the conference room when Michael walked in. He was followed by an older, handsome and distinguished-looking man.

"Katherine," he said professionally. "I would like

you to meet the founder of the Benson Corporation, my father, Leslie Benson."

Katherine smiled and said hello as she shook his hand. She was a bit curious about why Michael hadn't told her his father would be present.

"It's nice to meet you," the older man said, smiling. "I've heard quite a bit about you."

Katherine blushed. So Michael had been talking about her.

"From Diane," he added. Katherine glanced down toward the table, embarrassed. Diane, not Michael. Of course. Why would Michael mention her to his father? He only noticed her when he had to.

She looked at Michael, waiting for his cue to begin. He sat at the head of the table, obviously organizing his notes. If he was uncomfortable at all, he didn't show it.

Michael glanced up at his father and Katherine. "Well, shall we? I've got another meeting after this," he said authoritatively, checking his watch. He knew his voice must not betray his attraction toward Katherine.

"Where's Diane?" Katherine asked.

"Diane's daughter is sick today. She's at home taking care of her. Besides, she thinks you're ready to handle this job by yourself. And my father agrees. From now on, you report directly to me."

But did Michael agree? Katherine looked at him, waiting for a vote of confidence. Michael shuffled the papers in front of him, not even looking at her. He had seemed so preoccupied since their trip to Florida. She was beginning to worry. Perhaps she had done something to irritate him. Or perhaps he just didn't have confidence in her professional ability.

Katherine smiled at Leslie Benson. She could do this. She would prove to Michael that she was ready and capable of handling the pressure.

She stood up confidently and walked to the front of

the room. In a clear, strong voice, she went over her proposal, using the blackboard to illustrate points when necessary. While presenting the information, Katherine lost herself in the world of facts and marketing, the business world she reveled in. At the end of the presentation, she stopped speaking and spent an hour answering questions from both Michael and his father.

At the end of the meeting, Michael's father smiled warmly.

"Very good, Katherine. And thanks for all of your hard work. You've definitely given us something to think about."

Katherine looked at Michael. He was checking his watch again.

"Dad, we've got to run if you're going to make that meeting," Michael announced, pushing back his chair and standing. "We'll talk tomorrow, Wells," he added offhandedly, dismissing her.

"Nice to have you on board, Katherine," his father said, almost as if he was attempting to compensate for his son's rude behavior. He stood up and shook her hand warmly. "I look forward to meeting with you again soon."

He followed his son out of the room. He glanced at Michael as they approached the staircase. "You were a little harsh with her, weren't you?"

Michael shook his head, surprised. "I didn't think so. I thought I was pleasant and professional."

"Hmmm" was all his father said. "Shall we head back to your office?"

Michael frowned. When Michael misbehaved as a child, his father would dish out his punishment by saying, quite cordially, "Shall we go to your room?" Once in his room, his father would outline what he had done wrong and what his punishment would be. Michael suspected that he was in for more of the same now.

The only difference was that his room was in an office instead of a house, and he, not his father, was the proprietor.

Michael and his father walked the steps back up to his office in silence.

"I thought Katherine was very impressive," his father said, shutting the door behind him.

Michael put his papers down on his desk and shuffled them busily. Sometimes, in dealing with his father, ignorance was bliss. "What? Oh, yes. She's very thorough. Very research-oriented in her approach."

"Like you," Leslie said, settling into the chair facing Michael's desk.

Michael glanced up. "And you," he said.

"She's a very smart woman," Leslie continued. "Very beautiful as well."

"Dad, please. She's an employee. I'd rather not think of her that way," Michael replied casually.

"What way? As an employee or as a beautiful woman?"

Michael sighed. He never was a very good actor. "What are you getting at, Dad?"

Leslie Benson spoke quietly. "It was quite a performance, Michael, but the tension between you two is so thick I could've cut it with a butter knife. Now, I'm not sure what's going on . . ."

"Nothing is going on," Michael stated adamantly.

"What you do is your business," his father continued. "It's just that right now, Toby Nat is looking for any excuse to try to prove to the board that you're out of control. A loose cannon . . ."

"Dad," Michael said, "trust me."

Leslie Benson crossed his arms in front of him, still staring at Michael, evaluating him. Michael continued making eye contact, sure that to look away would be to concede defeat. "All right," Leslie Benson said, shrugging his shoulders. He respected his son a great deal. He had watched with pride as Michael fought successfully over the years to win back the family honor and fortune that he himself had lost. And both father and son were aware of Leslie's limitations. He was Michael's adviser and counselor, but there was no doubt that, despite their age and roles, Michael was in charge. "Let's get back to discussing her presentation. I was impressed by what she had to say. As a matter of fact, I think she might be helpful in convincing the board that we're on the right track."

"What are you suggesting?"

"Bring her to the board meeting. But only if you're sure she will not be a distraction to you."

Michael paused. This was to be his punishment? "Bring her to Sun Valley?"

"Why not?" the elder man said. "William's been attending these things for years."

"William owns stock in the company," Michael said "But he's not on the board."

"He's the head of research and development."

"A department that an increasing amount of the board would like to see terminated."

"I don't think that's true," Michael said defensively.

"If you don't want her there, then so be it. But I hope your decision is based solely on her professional capabilities." He paused. He trusted his son to make the right decision. Michael looked away, considering his father's proposal. "I think she can help you, Michael . . . help you present your case to continue funding research. That's all." Leslie Benson glanced at his watch. "I've got to get going."

Michael stood up. "Let me think about this until tomorrow."

Leslie Benson nodded. He smiled encouragingly at Michael. He realized his son was in a difficult situation, and he felt for him. He knew how hard it was for Michael to meet women who could match his intelligence and his stubborn enthusiasm for life. He also knew that few women could compete with Michael's fierce love for his company. He often worried that Michael spent too much time working and not enough time socializing. He had tried to talk to Michael several times about his concerns, but Michael had a hard time accepting advice from him. Michael remembered all too well how Leslie had put his wife and son on the back burner while he traveled across the country, always putting his career before his family. And Michael had made it clear that he was determined not to make the same mistake. In fact, he was so determined that Leslie was beginning to think that Michael might never marry. Michael didn't want to hurt a woman as he felt Leslie had hurt his wife, Michael's mother.

Leslie sighed resignedly. He stood up and walked toward the door. At any other time, he would have encouraged him to pursue his interest in Katherine. But not now. It was too dangerous.

He turned back before leaving. "I'll see you tomorrow. Are you working late tonight?"

"As a matter of fact," said Michael, looking him in the eye, "I have a date."

Katherine waited until Michael and his father had left the room before she began gathering her papers. She knew she had been thorough and prepared. Why hadn't Michael acknowledged her—or her hard work? Perhaps he didn't like her proposal.

She walked slowly back to her office and threw her notebook on the desk. She was exhausted. All the late nights and early mornings spent at the office had been catching up with her. She looked at her calendar.

"Double date with Cyndi" was written in small letters. She collapsed into her chair. What she needed was to go home and get some rest. She just hoped she could stay awake.

11

The buzzer rang in Katherine's apartment promptly at seven. She finished putting on her lipstick. This was the only time she could remember Cyndi being on time for anything.

"Cyndi?" she asked into the intercom on the wall.

"It's Christopher Longley . . . I'm here to pick you up," a voice said hesitantly.

"Oh," she said, trying to hide her surprise and dismay. Cyndi had promised that she would pick Katherine up at her apartment herself. She had also promised she would never leave Katherine stranded alone with her blind date.

"I'll be right down," Katherine said politely. She walked to her closet and yanked out her coat.

She buttoned her coat slowly. She had no doubt that this guy was going to be terribly boring and awful. Why else would he need to have his friend arrange a date for him?

She stepped off the elevator and looked down the long hallway. Two men stood in the small waiting area. One was standing with his back toward her, the other was sitting on the bench. The man standing up had blond hair and an athletic build. The one sitting down had thinning brown hair and a portly belly. She didn't even have to inquire which one was her date.

She opened the door, and, with as big a smile as she

could muster, she turned toward the man sitting on the bench. "You must be Christopher. I'm Katherine."

"Hello, Katherine," said the man who was already standing. Katherine turned to face him. His tall, well-built frame towered in front of her. Katherine's eyes narrowed. This guy didn't look like he needed to be fixed up. With his sandy blond hair and soft green eyes, he looked like he would feel right at home on a beach.

"I'm Christopher. Cyndi and Howard are waiting in the car," he said, holding the door open for her. Katherine stepped out into the brisk night air.

"We're going to have to squeeze in," he said, pointing to a VW Rabbit. Cyndi and Howard were chatting happily in the front seat. "I hope you don't mind. I know it's a long ride," he added, flashing her a friendly smile. "It should be a nice drive, though. All the leaves are changing colors. Fall is my favorite time of the year."

Katherine smiled at him. Perhaps this wouldn't be so bad after all.

The confines of the car forced Christopher and Katherine to sit snugly side by side as they attempted to make small talk. Cyndi, deep in her own conversation with Howard, made no effort to ease the tension.

"Where do you live?" Katherine asked Christopher after an awkward silence.

"In Chicago," he replied.

"Chicago? I thought you worked here."

"Not really. My firm has an office in Baltimore, so I'm in town about once a month or so. I've thought about transferring, but I still haven't decided yet," he said.

She was slightly relieved that he currently lived hundreds of miles away. It took a lot of the pressure off. She smiled at him. She could relax now. He was a handsome and charming date for one night only. To the ballet, no less. She looked out the window. She was beginning to enjoy herself.

She changed her mind when they pulled up in front of the theater. She recognized the Range Rover parked in front of them immediately, as well as the man taking the ticket from the valet. Michael! She had hardly expected to run into Michael at the ballet in Washington.

She watched as a lovely, tall blond gracefully stepped out of the passenger side of the Range Rover. It was Carly.

She turned back quickly to Christopher as Michael and Carly disappeared into the theater.

"Ready?" he asked, smiling and holding out his arm.

"Thank you," she said sweetly. She tried to ignore the wave of nausea that threatened to choke her. Why should she be surprised to see Michael out with Carly? Carly had all but told her they were an item.

Christopher opened the theater door for Katherine. She stepped inside, carefully glancing around the lobby for Michael.

"Come on, you guys," Cyndi said excitedly, leading the way. "We're through there," she said, pointing to a doorway on the right.

Katherine and Christopher followed Cyndi and Howard to their seats. They sat down just to the right of front-row center. Some of the best seats in the house.

"I hope these will be okay," Christopher said considerately. "We only called yesterday, and they were the best we could do."

Katherine turned her head to answer him. As she did, she noticed Michael and Carly stepping into the row behind them. She realized with terror that she would have to acknowledge them.

"Hello," she said cordially to Michael as he got closer.

Michael glanced toward Katherine, seeing her for the first time. He was stunned. "Wells," he said. He quickly glanced at Christopher.

"Katherine! What a pleasant surprise," Carly said, looping her arm through Michael's. Her words rang with sarcasm. She glanced at Christopher. "I'm Carly Wentworth," she said before Katherine had a chance to introduce her.

"And I'm Christopher Longley," Katherine's date said politely. "And you are . . . ?" he said, looking at Michael.

"Michael Benson," Michael managed, looking back toward Katherine.

"Nice to meet you," Christopher said, offering Michael his hand.

Michael shook it firmly. He gave him another once-over with his eyes, as though sizing up his competition.

"These are twenty and twenty-two," Carly said, pointing at the seats directly behind Katherine and Christopher.

Katherine looked with dismay at the seats and then at Michael, who was staring at Christopher.

"How convenient," Michael said, sitting down stiffly. He had never felt like this before. What was wrong with him? Michael glanced sideways at Carly. He hadn't see her socially since . . . since Katherine came to work for him. But with his father in town, he had decided it would be best to dispel any rumors about his involvement with an employee by making a public appearance with Carly and stirring up gossip about their ongoing friendship.

He stared at Katherine's back, admiring her slender, sexy shoulders. His father had not exaggerated. Katherine was a beautiful woman. Of course, she would be dating. He knew she wouldn't stay single in this town for long. Beauty. Brains. A seductive Midwestern innocence.

"Would you like to move?" Christopher whispered in Katherine's ear. He could tell she was bothered and preoccupied. Why wouldn't she be, with her boss sitting directly behind them? That would unnerve anyone. Especially if that boss was the powerful Michael Benson.

Katherine smiled and shook her head. That would be too obvious, she thought. Better just to sit there and try to ignore the fact that Michael was seated behind her.

Michael felt an uncontrollable wave of possessiveness as he watched Christopher whisper to Katherine. He was vaguely aware of Carly rambling on about some inane topic. He wished he had told her he was busy when she had asked him out. As a matter of fact, he reminded himself, he *had* told her he was busy. But she had persisted, and he had finally acquiesced, realizing that a date with Carly while his father was in town might be enough to throw his father off Katherine's track.

Michael ignored Carly, bending forward and tapping Katherine on the shoulder.

"My father was impressed with you . . . your presentation," he said like an awkward schoolboy.

"Good," Katherine replied uncomfortably, looking at the empty stage in front of her.

"There's a couple of things we still need to discuss. Now, if we enter the new markets . . ."

"Darling," Carly interrupted, furious that Michael was unable to ignore Katherine. "I'm sure Katherine doesn't want to talk about work right now." Carly smiled. "But while we're on the subject, thank you so much for processing those invoices, Katherine. I appreciate you making it a priority." She placed her hand on top of Michael's.

Katherine grinned uncomfortably as the lights dimmed. She focused on the dancers entering the stage. If she had any doubt about the status of Michael's relationship with Carly, it had been clarified.

At intermission, Katherine managed to follow Christopher into the lobby without so much as a glance at either Michael or Carly. She had decided that for the remainder of the evening, she would focus on her date.

Christopher paid for her champagne and handed her the glass.

"To your undeniable beauty," he said, raising his glass, not noticing Michael behind him. Katherine smiled sweetly and raised the glass to her lips, gulping down the bubbly liquid. Michael glared as he walked past, closely followed by Carly.

Katherine and Christopher were in their seats watching the second act of the performance when Katherine realized that Michael and Carly were not coming back.

The chandelier dropped elegantly from the ecru-colored ceiling. Katherine smiled. She loved ornate, expensive restaurants that bordered on gaudy.

The maitre d' took out four menus. Katherine attempted to follow him but was greeted by a wave of champagne dizziness that caused her to trip back slightly. Christopher reached out and steadied her.

"Are you all right?" he asked gently.

"I haven't really had much to eat today. I think the champagne was too much. Not to mention I've had an exhausting week at work," she said, embarrassed.

"I know how that goes," he said.

"Isn't that your boss again?" Cyndi asked quietly, nodding across the room. Michael was gallantly pulling Carly's chair back from the table. It looked as if they had just finished with their meal.

Katherine turned away quickly. Why couldn't they have gone someplace else? Her bad luck was truly amazing. This could only happen to her.

Michael was helping Carly on with her coat when he noticed Christopher and Katherine sitting down. He, too, felt a chill of dismay. He glanced at his watch. It was already ten-thirty. It was a little late for dinner, he thought jealously as he noticed Christopher's arm casually perched on the back of Katherine's chair.

He steered Carly over to their table.

"Hello again," he said sternly to Katherine. Carly flashed another toothy smile at the table. "I hope you enjoyed the ballet." Michael stared at Christopher as though he was declaring a duel.

"Very much," Christopher replied, smiling. "But not nearly as much as the company," he added, looking fondly at Katherine. She smiled weakly back at him.

Michael glared at Christopher. "I'll see you at seven-thirty tomorrow morning, Wells," he commanded, abruptly turning to leave.

Katherine looked at him, stunned. Seven-thirty? What was he talking about? She didn't have a meeting scheduled with him.

"Do we have a meeting?" she called out impulsively. Carly raised an inquisitive eyebrow at Michael.

"Didn't Millie call you?" he asked, glancing back. Katherine shook her head.

"She must have missed you, then. We have a meeting tomorrow morning. My office. Bright and early," he added, emphasizing the *early*.

Michael turned and whisked Carly out of the restaurant. He handed the doorman the ticket for his car and impatiently jammed his fists inside his coat pockets.

Carly glanced up at her date. He seemed even more preoccupied than usual. She knew Michael well, and she could tell by his jealous behavior that her instinct had been correct. There was a little more between Michael and Katherine than he was admitting.

"Should I go back to your house with you?" she asked, smiling seductively. Michael glanced in her direction. He found her completely undesirable. Ever since he had first laid eyes on Katherine, he had found it impossible to be with another woman. He was leading a monkish existence. But he couldn't help himself.

"I don't think so," he said. "As you just heard me remind my marketing director, I've got an early meeting tomorrow."

12

Want some coffee?" Michael asked in a monotone. He poured himself a cup.

Katherine glanced at her watch. It wasn't even seven-thirty yet. She had arrived at the office early so that she could have a few minutes to gather any materials she might need for the meeting. But she didn't have a chance. Michael had buzzed her office impatiently at seven-fifteen.

"Yes, thanks," Katherine said, taking the cup from him. "I didn't get much sleep last night." Because of the late dinner and long drive back to Baltimore, she hadn't gone to bed until two in the morning.

He stopped pouring to give her a dirty look.

"I didn't ask you about your personal life, did I?" he snarled.

Katherine sat down in the chair wearily. She was in no mood to argue with this temperamental man.

"It was quite a coincidence running into you and Carly like that," she said, ignoring his comment while sipping her coffee carefully. "I didn't realize you two were dating." She was baiting him. She wanted more information.

"She's a friend." He looked her over as he swallowed the hot coffee, waiting for some disclosure from her in return. "But I have other friends as well."

Katherine's blood ran cold. Of course. He was not the type to get tied down to one woman. He played the field. And he wanted her to know it. She should be happy that she worked for him. Otherwise, she too may have been just another one of his conquests.

"Did you enjoy yourself last night?" he asked, raising his eyebrow inquisitively.

"I thought the ballet was beautiful."

"Oh," he said. Damn her. She was purposely teasing him, mentioning how tired she was, then refusing to say why.

"What did you want to see me about, Michael?" she asked wearily.

He put down his coffee and looked at the calendar in front of him. He knew that he needed to ease up on her. He had no reason to play the jealous boyfriend. It wasn't her fault that she was all he thought about. She certainly had not done anything to perpetuate his feelings. In fact, she had been nothing but professional and polite with him. He should be thanking her for ignoring his rudeness, not berating her for going on a date.

"My father was very impressed with your proposal," he said congenially, trying a different tactic. "So was I. We want you to give a presentation at our annual board meeting next month, basically restating what you told us yesterday."

"Really?" she asked, flattered. It wasn't often a novice employee got to attend the closed board meeting. Usually, only board members were allowed.

"It's going to be held the second week in November in Sun Valley, Idaho. It will last about two days— Thursday and Friday. As a perk for all of the long hours you've been putting in, we'll pay for your room and board through the weekend as well."

Katherine's eyes opened wide. "Great!"

Michael leaned back in his chair and smiled at her enthusiasm.

"Do you ski?"

"Yes," she said. "But I haven't been in quite a while."

"Well, it's a great place to go skiing. It's beautiful out there. My family has vacationed there for years."

Katherine nodded her head, momentarily forgetting the anguish of the previous night.

"I have decided to add some factors to your proposal, however. Because the board meeting is coming up, I wanted to give you as much time as possible to work on them."

"Right," she said, opening her notebook and dating the top of the page.

Michael pulled out the paper on which he had scratched down his father's comments. He read them off point by point, feeling more and more comfortable as he watched Katherine write frantically, attempting to keep up with him.

He finished giving her the information only a few minutes after Millie had buzzed in on the intercom to let him know she had arrived.

"I think I've got it," Katherine said, standing to leave.

"If you have any questions, any questions at all, come and see me," he responded, smiling at her. Katherine looked at him, taken off guard by this sudden display of warmth.

"Thanks," she said, hesitating before turning to leave. Michael was staring at the documents in front of him, already appearing to be deep in concentration. Katherine opened the door.

"Oh, Katherine," he said, stopping her before she left. He looked up from his papers as she turned back toward him. "Why don't you take the rest of the day off? You look like you could use some sleep."

She mustered up a smile before exiting his office, shutting the door behind her. She paused to glance at Millie, aware that the older woman had heard what Michael had instructed her to do.

"Miracles never cease," Millie said in her usual monotone, shrugging her shoulders.

Balancing her briefcase, grocery bag, and mail, Katherine awkwardly struggled to open the door to her apartment. As the door swung open, she smiled. Her apartment was nice and clean. Just the way she liked it, but not the way she'd left it. On the advice of Cyndi, she had decided to treat herself by hiring someone to clean for her twice a month. She had initially felt a little guilty about the extravagance, but her grueling schedule left her little time to sleep, never mind clean.

She walked across the plush, cream-colored carpeting and set her briefcase down on the glass table facing the gas fireplace. She was lucky to have found this apartment. She had worked with a rental agent, instructing her to find an apartment in her price range that was safe, attractive, conveniently located, and furnished. She had rented the apartment on a month-to-month lease, sight unseen. Fortunately, she liked the modern furnishings. The color scheme was cream, white, and tan, muted colors that worked well with the magnificent views the apartment commanded. Floor-to-ceiling windows ran the length of the entire apartment, giving her a stellar view of the harbor and the entire downtown area. She could even see the Benson Building from her bedroom window, a fact that was not conducive to sleep.

Even though it was only two o'clock in the afternoon, the day was overcast and cold, making it seem like evening was imminent. She turned on the gas in the fireplace and watched as the flames automatically shot up. Although she had not left work after her meeting with Michael, she had taken him up on his offer to leave early. She had used the opportunity to invite Cyndi over for a late lunch, after which she planned on curling up in front of the fire and attacking some of the papers crammed in her briefcase.

Katherine quickly changed into an oversize turtle-neck sweater and a pair of jeans. She had just finished placing the deli cold cuts on a plate when Cyndi knocked on the door.

She opened the door and greeted her friend with a hug.

"I was so happy you called," Cyndi said. Cyndi was a freelance graphic artist who worked out of her apartment. She often complained of feeling isolated. "I was dying to get out." She took a couple of steps and smiled. "This place is gorgeous, Katherine. And to think that not too long ago, we were both crammed into a room half this size."

"Don't remind me," Katherine called out from the kitchen. She came out carrying a plate loaded with food and set it down on the coffee table. "Dig in. Do you want some tea?"

"Tea would be more than tremendous," Cyndi said. "It's been a while since I've seen this place in the daytime. I almost forgot what an incredible view of the water you have."

"Thanks," Katherine said, filling the tea-kettle. "I don't often get to see this place in the daytime, either."

Cyndi walked to the kitchen and stood in the doorway, leaning up against the frame. "So what's the deal?" Cyndi asked, crossing her arms casually. "Playing hooky this afternoon?"

"Michael gave me the day off."

"Why?"

Katherine turned on the stove. "I don't really know. He said I looked tired. I think he thought I had a big night last night. And he was a little rude to me this morning. Maybe he felt bad. I think he realizes how much overtime I've been putting in."

"Humph," Cyndi said, raising an eyebrow.

"What's that supposed to mean?" Katherine asked.

Cyndi glanced at her. "I saw the way he looked at you last night."

"What?" Katherine asked with a hint of irritation.

"He looked like he was jealous, that's what," Cyndi replied.

"Oh, please," Katherine said, not very convincingly.

Cyndi stared at Katherine suspiciously. Katherine hurried around the kitchen as though the physical acts of pulling mugs out of the cupboard and opening a box of teabags required every ounce of concentration. She poured the boiling water into the mugs.

"Don't tell me," Cyndi said, shaking her head.

"Don't tell you what?" Katherine said curtly, handing her the steaming mug as she walked past her and into the living room.

"Nothing. It's just that I thought you learned your lesson with Ross," Cyndi said, following her.

"There isn't anything going on," Katherine said defensively.

"Then how come you look so guilty?" Cyndi questioned. Katherine was silent. Cyndi shook her head.

"No wonder he seemed jealous. When did all this happen?"

"Do you really think he seemed jealous?" Katherine asked, trying not to sound hopeful. "You're imagining things."

Cyndi just raised her eyebrows and shrugged her shoulders. Katherine rolled her eyes. She recognized Cyndi's look. The look meant that she didn't believe Katherine, but she wasn't going to argue about it. Katherine knew she couldn't leave it at that.

"Cyndi, nothing has happened. I swear to you. It's just that Michael and I had an awkward beginning," she blurted out.

"I'm listening," Cyndi said.

"We met that night at the Tavern when I was supposed to meet you. He started talking to me, and after a few minutes I left, by myself, and began to look for a cab. This creep from the bar followed me out and started, well, basically assaulting me. Michael . . . rescued me."

"And then you took him home with you. And you both went to work together the next morning. How convenient."

"For God's sake, no." Katherine paused. "Nothing happened. He dropped me off. And then, later, I realized who he was."

"Not even a kiss when he dropped you off?" Cyndi asked suspiciously.

"No."

Cyndi hesitated. She leaned back against the couch and hugged her knees to her chest. "I don't understand. No kiss. Nothing. What's the big deal?"

"It's just . . . there was an attraction. You know. Then, when we were in Florida . . ."

"You slept together."

"No!"

"You tried to resist his charms, but before you realized what was happening, he had pulled you into the bedroom on his private plane. . ." she continued, teasing her.

"Very funny," Katherine replied.

"Tell me what happened," Cyndi said excitedly.

Katherine paused. "Nothing like you think. As a matter of fact, just the opposite. We had to go to a dinner at his uncle's country club, and he all but pushed me out the door because there was a woman there he was interested in."

Cyndi looked at Katherine as though she was trying to read her expression. Katherine had never lied to her before, and she doubted she would start now. "Oh," Cyndi said. "So he's not as nice a guy as the media likes to think?"

"Well." Katherine shrugged her shoulders. "I think he can be. He certainly seemed sweet the first night I met him. But he's under a lot of pressure with work, and I think it takes a toll on his personality."

Cyndi looked at Katherine. She had known her for ten years. Long enough to recognize that her friend was falling in love. "I just don't want to see you get hurt," Cyndi said. "You've got a lot more to lose in a fling gone awry than he has. The woman always does, especially when the man owns the company, like Michael Benson." Cyndi sighed. "But he certainly is gorgeous, isn't he? Last night was the first time I've seen him in person, but I see his picture in the paper all the time. The lady who writes the gossip column absolutely loves him. She's always writing about him. Baltimore's golden boy, as she puts it. She's always trying to link him up with different women."

Katherine felt a pang of jealousy run through her before she had a chance to stop it. She took a sip of her tea. She had to proceed very carefully if she wanted any information out of Cyndi.

"Oh, really?" she said nonchalantly. "Have you

heard anything about the woman he was with last night, Carly . . ."

"Wentworth? She gets her mug in the paper a lot too. I can't remember what the deal is with her. I think I read they were supposed to be just friends or something. They grew up together, something like that."

"Hmmm," Katherine said, bringing the cup to her lips.

"Oh, no," Cyndi said, shaking her head. "You can't fool me." She set down her mug. "Don't try to tame him, Katherine. He's too formidable an opponent. Look how messed up everything got with Ross." Katherine looked into her tea. Cyndi paused. She realized she was being harsh, but she wanted to spare her friend some pain if she could. "I'm sorry, Katherine. I'm not helping matters any, am I?"

Katherine shrugged her shoulders. "I understand why you're concerned. But there really is nothing going on between us. So you can just relax, okay? He doesn't see me in a romantic light."

Unlike you see him, Cyndi felt like saying. Instead, she shrugged her shoulders. "Okay. Let's talk about Christopher. Does he stand a chance?"

"He lives far away."

"In other words, no," Cyndi said.

"What about Howard?" Katherine asked. "You both seemed lost in your own world."

Cyndi smiled. "He's just what I need right now. Good-looking, funny, smart, rich, and crazy about me. I think this might just be it."

Katherine opened her mouth to speak but stopped herself. She was just about to remind her friend that as long as Katherine had known Cyndi, she had possessed an uncanny ability to fall in and out of love as often as some people grocery shop.

Each new man Cyndi met was always *"perfect,"* an

adjective that was usually used for a month. After that, the new man would suddenly tumble from grace, and the word *perfect* was discarded from Cyndi's vocabulary like old trash. Until the next new man came around. But, Katherine reminded herself, she was not Cyndi's mother. It was not her job to pass judgment. "That's great," she said simply, commending herself on her restraint.

Cyndi smiled. "I'll say. So . . . do you think you'll see Christopher again?"

"Maybe. But I've been on my last date for a while. I'm going to be practically living at work until the board meeting."

"Just make sure you stay out of the boys' dorm," Cyndi said, half under her breath.

13

Good morning, Louise, Katherine," Carly said, standing up from the conference table to shake their hands. "I can't believe I haven't seen you for weeks . . . since the ballet," she said to Katherine. Louise glanced at Katherine. She had never mentioned running into Carly outside work.

Carly turned toward Louise. "I could hardly believe it. Michael and I go to the ballet, and who are we sitting behind? None other than Katherine and her friends."

"Really?" Louise said, looking at Katherine. She wondered why Katherine hadn't mentioned it. Katherine found Louise's obvious interest in her private life a little disconcerting. Even though Louise's curiosity was only natural, she began doubting her judgment in allowing her assistant to sit in on her meeting with Carly. Because she was understaffed, Katherine had found herself relying on Louise to perform more of an executive role in the marketing department.

"And then, later, we end up at the same restaurant," Carly continued, focusing back on Katherine.

"Small world," Louise stated.

"Did you enjoy it?" Carly asked.

"The ballet? Yes, thank you," Katherine replied politely.

"It was so funny running into you like that," Carly continued.

Katherine smiled slightly. She checked her watch. She didn't have time for chitchat. Especially when Michael was concerned. The board presentation was less than two weeks away, and she hadn't even seen a rough of the advertising boards for the presentation yet. "Shall we?" Katherine said, motioning toward the table.

"Well, ladies," Carly began once Katherine and Louise were seated across from her. "As you know, we've been very busy at Bresser and Tenner preparing for the board meeting," she said, opening her briefcase. "I've got the presentation boards right here." She pointed inside her briefcase with her long red nails. "I think you'll be pleased, Katherine. We took your concept, and we added to it, just as you suggested." She pulled three boards out and laid them in front of Katherine.

Katherine stared down at the mocked-up ads in front of her with disbelief. Carly had either misunderstood her or ignored her instructions. Although the ads in front of her were directed at the consumer, they emphasized the speed of the A–14 engine, not safety. She looked back at Carly.

Carly flashed Katherine a sugary, phony smile. "Well?" she asked.

Katherine leaned back in her chair as she glanced sideways at Louise. Louise gave her a quick shake of the head, indicating her displeasure as well.

"Carly," Katherine began, "these ads are very clever consumer ads. Unfortunately, they're not relevant."

"I beg your pardon?" Carly said, the smile still plastered on her face.

"I wanted a campaign that emphasized safety. Using William Briggs as the icon."

Carly raised an eyebrow as her smile vanished. She leaned forward on the table. "Katherine, we are your advertising agency," she said with a patronizing tone. "Michael pays us to do his advertising. He does this because we are professionals. All we do, every day, is create campaigns and ads."

"What's your point?" Katherine asked. She was getting irritated.

"The consumers are interested in speed. That is the major selling point. Not safety."

Katherine stood up. She was beginning to realize that Carly had intentionally disregarded her instructions.

"Carly, as a former account executive, I know how advertising agencies work. I also know that you cannot just throw some ads in a client's face and say that they will work because you know what you're doing. If you're so convinced that speed is the way to go, convince me. Tell me facts and figures."

"Excuse me?"

"I gave you my agenda, and I backed it up with substantial research. I didn't come up with the idea to promote safety off the top of my head. I did primary research by talking to division heads at airlines. I did secondary research by reading everything I could find about previous airline campaigns."

She stopped. Carly sat still, silently glaring at her.

"Why did you ignore all of my research and emphasize speed?" Katherine asked.

"Everyone knows . . ." Carly began angrily, her nostrils flaring.

"You'll have to do better than that," Katherine replied calmly, interrupting her. Louise cleared her throat. Both Carly and Katherine glanced at her. Louise looked around uncomfortably.

Katherine thought for a moment. She stood up. "Unless you have research to show me, I think this meeting is over." Louise followed Katherine to the door, almost bumping into her when Katherine stopped suddenly and turned toward Carly again. "We don't have much time," Katherine said. "I want you to create new ads featuring the campaign I developed. I know it's not a lot of fun for the creative people to work with someone else's concept, but we're too short on time to argue. The meeting is in two weeks. If you can't help me create something to show the board, then I'll do it myself."

Carly stood up. "You are making a mistake."

Katherine shook her head. "I don't think so. But let's get one thing clear. Even if you do feel that way, I am the marketing director. It is my mistake to make."

Katherine walked out of the room. Carly looked down at the ads scattered on the table. She had expected Katherine to be a pushover. She hadn't expected to be asked to justify the campaign she had developed. Katherine was a rookie, an inexperienced, egotistical rookie who was ill equipped to direct Benson's new marketing campaign. Michael had been a fool to allow Diane to hire her. And an even bigger fool to allow himself to become enamored with her.

Unless Carly helped him, his obvious infatuation with Katherine was going to cost him millions of dollars.

Carly shoved the boards into her briefcase. She would try to convince Michael of the mistake he was making before it was too late. And she wasn't thinking about the campaign.

Carly knocked on Michael's door before poking her head in.

"Am I coming at a bad time?" she asked.

Michael furrowed his brow. "Hi. What brings you here?" he asked. He glanced at his watch. "That's right, you had a meeting with Katherine. How did it go?"

Carly sat down in the chair facing his desk. She sighed as though she was absolutely exhausted. "Well, actually, that's why I'm here." She sat up straight and smiled sweetly. She crossed her long legs. "This is a rather delicate situation." She paused for effect. "I'm not going to beat around the bush, Michael. There's a problem."

Michael glanced up. He crossed his arms in front of him. "And the problem is?"

"Katherine." Carly paused, waiting for the right moment to continue. She attempted to look as distressed as possible. She must pretend that coming to Michael was a last resort. "Quite frankly, Michael, I'm doing all I can to help her, but she's just not up to the job. She doesn't have enough experience. She keeps telling us to create ridiculous campaigns that change daily depending on her mood. I know there's a learning curve, and I'm trying to be patient, I really am, but . . ."

"But?"

"You've got to talk to her. She's so . . . stubborn. Tell her she needs to let me do my job. Tell her to let me help her."

"I see." Michael glanced at her briefcase. "Do you have the campaign you developed with you?"

Carly smiled. "I thought you'd like to see it." She reached down and unsnapped her briefcase. She pulled the boards out. "Speed. After all, this is a consumer campaign directed at the people who use the airlines the most: the frequent flyers. And speed is what they care about. See," she said, pointing to the words underneath a picture of man wedged tightly in a cramped airplane seat. *" 'You could be home right now.'* It's great. And we'll run these in all the in-flight magazines. It will make a tremendous impact. We're all excited about it at the agency."

Michael thumbed through the boards and set them down. "And Katherine didn't like these?"

"No," Carly replied, opening her eyes and shrugging her shoulders incredulously.

"Did she give you a reason?"

"Not a substantial one."

"Perhaps an insubstantial one, such as that all of the research, which, by the way, she gave me a copy of, points toward safety as the driving issue?"

Carly glanced away.

"Look, Carly," Michael continued. "Katherine has a lot of experience dealing with this industry. You're going to have to trust her ... and respect her wishes."

"She's making a mistake, Michael. As someone who has done business with you for quite a while, and as a friend," she said, emphasizing the word *friend,* "I would hope you would listen to me. Katherine is making an extremely dangerous tactical error simply because she is in over her head." She paused. Michael was staring at her coldly. "Don't let her do this to you, Michael," she said, almost desperately.

Michael hesitated before glancing down at the boards. He stacked them in a pile and handed them to her. "I have a lot of work to do, Carly. If you'll excuse me."

Carly stood up and took the boards away from him. She would not allow Katherine to defeat her that easily. "I understand," she said resolutely, putting the boards back in her briefcase and snapping it shut. She turned to leave. She paused. She glanced back toward Michael. "Michael, I know that I shouldn't repeat nasty gossip. But word has it that you and Katherine have been getting ... well, close. I hope you won't let your feelings affect your good business sense."

And with that, Carly left the room. As she closed the door behind her, she raised an eyebrow and pursed her lips together. The battle may have been lost, but the war was far from over.

It was night. The office halls had cleared out almost three hours ago. At almost nine o'clock, Katherine was just beginning to think about going home. She sat immersed in a report, her office dark with the exception of the Tiffany lamp on her desk. She heard footsteps outside her door, causing her to stop her work and glance up toward her closed office door. The security man usually checked her floor around nine, but his footsteps always made her a little nervous until she confirmed it was him. Katherine walked to the door in her stocking feet and opened it. Michael stood before her, his briefcase tucked under his arm. His trench coat hung open, and he had loosened the tie around his neck. He looked every bit the part of a tired corporate chief.

"Michael." She glanced around the room, looking for her shoes. Where had she left them? "Come in!"

"Working late?" he said, walking in. He glanced around before sitting on the couch

"There's a lot to do before the meeting next week," Katherine replied. She gave up the search for her shoes and instead decided to hide her feet by sitting behind her desk.

Michael leaned forward uncomfortably and pulled a black leather pump out from underneath him. "Did you lose something?" he asked mischievously.

Katherine shrugged her shoulders, embarrassed. She stood up and accepted the shoe. "There's not another one in there, is there?"

Michael stood up. Katherine spotted the other shoe half hidden under a pillow and swiped it. She slipped them both on her feet. "I do a lot of reading on the couch. Especially at night."

"I see," he said, attempting to hold back a smile. "So," he said resolutely, "how is everything going?"

Katherine sat back behind her desk. Michael's visit was not a surprise. She had expected to hear from him, although she had thought it would have been earlier in the day. Louise had told her that Carly had stormed up to his office directly after their meeting.

"Fine," she replied nonchalantly. She was not going to volunteer any information. As far as she was concerned, she had handled the situation with Carly. If he disagreed with how she handled it, it was his job to tell her. She wasn't going to allow herself to be in a situation where she was stooping to Carly's level.

"Everything's fine?" he asked, baiting her.

"Everything is fine," she replied.

Michael nodded. "How's the campaign coming along?" he asked, studying her reaction.

"As far as I know, it's coming along fine as well. Unless . . ."

"Unless?"

"Unless you're here to tell me otherwise."

Michael smiled. She had spirit, and he liked that. Obviously, she knew that Carly had gone to see him after their meeting. And she had probably assumed that Carly had complained about her. Yet she had done nothing to try to defend herself. She was waiting to see how he would respond. "You're doing a great job, Wells," he said, standing up. "Let me know if you have any more problems."

Katherine watched him walk toward the door. Had he changed his mind about talking to her? Or had he already made up his mind?

"What do you mean, if I have any *more* problems?" Katherine asked. "I wasn't aware I had *one.*"

Michael glanced back toward her. A half-smile formed on his lips. "You don't."

Katherine breathed a sigh of relief as Michael shut the door. "Thank you," she whispered.

14

Katherine stifled a yawn as she threw the last pair of pants into her suitcase. It was getting late, and she had an early flight the next day. Because of the time delay, she was able to leave Baltimore at six in the morning and still arrive in Sun Valley in time for a ten-thirty meeting. She needed to attend a meeting the following day as well, but Friday through Sunday were vacation.

Katherine smiled in anticipation. It had been several years since she had taken a "real" vacation—"real" meaning to a locale that was not a home in the suburbs owned by relatives. A week ago, Millie had sent her a memo that stated she would be given a daily stipend just for food and expenses, even on the days she wasn't working. The hotel had been paid for in advance.

Katherine's suitcase was packed so full, she had to sit on it in order to be able to close it. She knew she'd probably overpacked, but she had learned her lesson in Florida. She'd rather have too much than not enough.

She struggled with her suitcase zipper, tugging it around the border of the case. She succeeded in snapping it shut and quickly changed into her nightgown, not even bothering to wash her face before she climbed into bed. She picked up the brochure lying on her bedside table.

The glossy photos displayed the magnificence of the four-star hotel where they would be staying. The hotel had been built in the early 1900s, and the decor reflected its historic roots. The rooms were furnished in antiques, yet they possessed all the modern conveniences one could desire. Each was equipped with a large marble bathtub and a dazzling view of the mountains. There was even a photo of people drinking champagne in a large outdoor Jacuzzi on the side of a mountain.

Katherine sighed softly to herself. What a great, romantic place to go. She set the brochures back on her nightstand and turned off the light.

At five-fifteen the next morning, Katherine was climbing into the backseat of a taxi. She had decided to forgo the aggravation of driving herself to the airport. Instead of driving like a maniac and arriving flustered, she would sit back and read her newspaper while someone else navigated the roads. She pulled a large stack of newspapers out of her briefcase as the taxi pulled out of the apartment driveway. Baltimore offered home delivery of four papers, the *Washington Post,* the *Baltimore Sun,* the *New York Times,* and the *Wall Street Journal.* Katherine glanced through all four, but it was a large black-and-white photo on the front page of the Style section of the *Washington Post* that caught her eye. It was a picture of Michael in what appeared to be a rather amusing tête-à-tête with a prominent senator. Carly was in the picture as well, casually hanging on to Michael's arm as she smiled into the camera.

Katherine quickly scanned the small print under the photo:

"The local stars were out last night for a benefit for the Red Cross. Pictured are Senator Ryan Jeffrey and aeronautics magnate Michael Benson with longtime companion Carly Wentworth."

Katherine put the paper down and took a deep breath. So Carly was officially his "longtime companion."

"Don't be upset," she ordered herself. "He is your boss, nothing else," she chanted softly, as if trying to convince herself. Considering his romantic involvement with Carly, she was surprised that he had allowed Katherine to develop the campaign she had wanted. Especially when Carly was so opposed to it.

"Hey, lady, you talking to me?" asked the cab driver.

"Yes," Katherine responded quickly. "Take Martin Luther King Boulevard to 295. It's quicker than going through downtown." She didn't have time to waste. She had a plane to catch.

Katherine arrived at the airport and boarded the plane without hesitation. She felt no need to wait for her boss. She was aware that Millie had arranged for them to sit together so they would be able to discuss business, but at this point she had no desire to see him.

Katherine stepped through the doors of the Executive terminal feeling much more relaxed and refreshed than she had the last time she had traveled on business. She walked through the small terminal as if she had been there a million times before and made her way directly toward the door that led to the tarmac. Unlike the last time she traveled with Michael, she had no intention of politely waiting for her boss before boarding the plane.

As she walked across the tarmac, she couldn't help reflecting on the status of Michael's relationship with Carly. It was obvious that they had been an "item" for quite a while. But it was just as obvious that he was not very loyal to his "long-term companion." Still, Katherine admitted, over the past few weeks she had noticed that Michael had grown even more distant. Perhaps it was an indication he had renewed his commitment to Carly.

Lisa was waiting for her in the plane. "Good morning," she said cheerily. Katherine smiled. At least one person on the plane was in good spirits. After Lisa had taken her drink order, Katherine settled into the same seat she had sat in before. She looked out the small window of the plane. The sun was just beginning to rise. She could see the main terminal in the distance. Uniformed men scurried around planes, loading the baggage into luggage compartments and readying them for takeoff. She focused her attention on several executives climbing up the stairs to a commuter plane nearby. They were laughing and talking amongst themselves. It was a cold November morning, and their breath was frosty white against the background of the clear blue sky.

Katherine glanced at her watch. The plane was scheduled for departure in only five minutes.

She had just finished fastening her seat belt, when Michael entered the short yet spacious aisle. He threw his leather bag into the overhead compartment and plopped down across from her without so much as a nod in her direction.

"Good morning, Michael," she said professionally.

"Wells," he acknowledged gruffly as he flagged down Lisa from the back of the plane. As soon as Lisa saw him she came scurrying forward.

"Could I have some coffee, please?" he asked. "Want some, Wells?" he said, looking at her for the first time.

"No thanks," she said, glancing back out the window.

"One coffee," he stated simply.

"Late night?" Katherine asked as Lisa hurried away to get his drink.

"Not especially. Why?" he asked, looking at her suspiciously.

"There's a picture of you and Carly in the *Post* today," she replied in a biting tone. "It looks like there was quite a benefit last night," she said, pulling the stack of newspapers out of her briefcase.

"Good God," Michael said, eyeing the stack. "Do you think you have enough to read? Or are you planning on lighting a bonfire?"

"I like to keep up with what's going on," Katherine replied.

"How do you have time for anything else?" he asked.

"I have to stay informed," she said defensively. "Anyway, did you see the photo?" she asked, flipping the paper open to the Style section.

Michael glanced over her shoulder. "Oh, that," he replied nonchalantly. "It was too boring to be legitimately referred to as a party. Those pictures always try and jazz it up," he added, accepting a steaming cup from Lisa.

Frustrated, Katherine folded up her paper. He certainly didn't seem to feel the need to offer any explanation for why Carly had been hanging on him in the picture. She sat the stack of papers down on the chair next to her and plucked a *Time* magazine out of her briefcase. She thumbed through the magazine half-heartedly, her mind obsessing about Michael's relationship with Carly. How could he be involved with that woman? Despite the fact that Carly had been extremely polite to Katherine since their heated meeting two weeks ago, it was obvious she was doing what Katherine wished only because Michael wanted her to. Katherine wondered what Michael had said to her. Had he supported Katherine? The night he stopped by her office, he had seemed to be on her side. And Carly had eventually delivered the advertising campaign that Katherine requested. Yet, according to the newspaper, he was still seeing Carly socially. Perhaps he and Carly were both able to separate business from pleasure.

She glanced toward Michael. He appeared oblivious to her discomfort as he sipped his coffee and read the *Wall Street Journal.*

Katherine focused her attention back on her magazine, browsing the "People in the News" section. In the center of the page there was a small picture of Michael. The blurb to the side mentioned that he might soon be considering a run for the Senate.

"You're in *Time,* Michael," she said, pointing to the article. Michael leaned forward. His face was so close to her she could smell the aroma of coffee on his breath.

"Oh, yeah. I've already seen it," he said simply, turning back to his paper. She looked at him curiously.

"Is it true?" she asked.

"At this point, no," he said, avoiding her eyes. She looked away. She could tell by his reaction that he was seriously considering it. She couldn't help wondering what the repercussions would be for the company if he took a leave of absence for years. She reminded herself that a failed Presidential bid had forced his father to sell the company.

Katherine closed the magazine and distractedly tucked it back into her briefcase. She couldn't believe Michael would ever allow the company to slip away from him. Yet, she thought, her mind wandering back to the *Washington Post* picture of him with Carly, he did seem to be positioning himself for a campaign.

"Do you want to go over my presentation?" Katherine asked suddenly, forcing herself to think about business. She pulled her briefcase onto her lap.

Michael glanced at Katherine. Was it his imagination, or was she bothered by the picture of him with Carly in the paper? He longed to reassure her that he had no romantic interest in Carly, but he knew that it would be inappropriate. He had to confine himself to a professional relationship with her. He didn't even have any evidence that Katherine desired anything to the contrary.

"Michael?" Katherine repeated.

"Ready," he responded quickly after clearing his throat. He reached for his briefcase as Katherine began to speak.

15

The cab driver pulled in front of the opulent hotel just as a soft and steady snow was beginning to fall. The bellman dashed to their service and loaded their luggage onto the cart while Michael paid the cab driver. Katherine, excited, entered the hotel, not bothering to wait for Michael.

Despite the reputation the hotel had for attracting Hollywood celebrities, Katherine was happy to see it was every bit as lovely and understated as the brochure had indicated. A fire blazed in a stone hearth so large it took up an entire wall. Several guests sat sipping coffee in the red velvet chairs and couches in front of the fire.

Katherine spotted Alan Benson at the reservation desk.

"Alan?" Katherine said warmly, approaching him. She hadn't seen him since Florida.

"Katherine," he said, smiling. "It's so good to see you again," he added, shaking her hand.

"Alan," Michael announced unenthusiastically, catching up to Katherine.

"Michael," Alan replied, nodding his head coldly to Michael.

Katherine watched the interaction between the two men suspiciously. The tension between them was obvious.

"I'll see you in an hour," Alan said, giving Katherine a quick nod good-bye.

"What was that all about?" Katherine asked when Alan was out of earshot.

"I'd rather not discuss it . . . for now," Michael said evasively. He finished with the clerk and handed Katherine the key to her room.

"Your room is in the east wing of the hotel. I'm staying in the west wing, so we might as well each go to our room and drop off our luggage. I'll meet you in the conference room," he said, dismissing her.

Katherine arranged for a porter to carry her bags and followed him up to her room. She tipped the man generously before shutting her door and surveying her room. The furnishings made her feel she had stepped back in time one hundred years. A colorful handmade quilt covered an antique wooden four-poster bed. Large, fluffy down pillows beckoned invitingly. An Oriental rug lay on a polished wood floor. The only reminder of modern times was the large picture window. Katherine moved closer for a better look. The ski slopes were in the distance, a couple hundred yards off to the right. Fashionably outfitted skiers were crowded around the lifts.

Her vision shifted back in front of her. A majestic and serene mountain seemed to reach into the clouds, lending a peaceful contrast to the hectic ski scene. It was strange to see snow on the ground. It was only the second week of November, yet here in the mountains, the snow seemed firm and deep, as though it had been winter for months.

Katherine stepped away from the window. She had been surprised yesterday when she learned that Michael would be staying at the hotel rather than at his family's Sun Valley house. When she asked Millie abut it, Millie had explained that when Michael went to a board meeting, he liked to stay in the hotel where it was held.

She turned back toward her bulging suitcase. She felt no need to go over her notes again before the meeting. She was ready.

Katherine laid a conservative blue suit, a silk blouse, and a single strand of pearls on the bed. She washed her face, put on a dab of mascara, and pulled her hair back in a chignon off her face before changing into them. *Brava,* she thought, admiring her reflection in the mirror. She looked every bit as corporate and professional as she intended to behave.

The hotel had two conference rooms. One was so large it also functioned as a ballroom. The other was more intimate. Only twenty-five people could be seated comfortably around the large wood conference table. There was an expansive window opposite the door which was draped with very heavy, expensive-looking burgundy curtains.

Katherine was the first to arrive. She was more prepared than she had been in Florida. After all, she was basically presenting the same campaign that she had designed for her interview. And this was the third time she had presented it. A couple of the board members had already seen it in Florida, including Alan. But the remaining eleven had not. And she had a sample television spot that no one, other than Michael, had seen yet.

Katherine was excited. She liked public speaking, she knew her material, and she was ready for tough questions.

Katherine took the boards and the video cassette out of the portfolio. She picked up the tape and popped it into the VCR. She wanted to make sure it was working.

"Need any help?"

Katherine turned around. It was William Briggs.

"Hi, William. I think I can handle this." She smiled. "When did you get in?"

"Last night." He put his hands in his pockets. Although Katherine didn't know him very well, she thought he appeared nervous. "I wanted to get a good night's sleep for today. So . . . are you speaking?" he asked, glancing at her boards.

"Yes. I'm presenting the rest of the campaign."

"Oh, yes."

"We're planning on shooting you in front of the planes next week. Provided there are no objections today, of course," she said.

"Of course. I'm sure they'll love it," he replied automatically, not sounding at all convinced.

"Do you like it?" Katherine asked, looking at him intently. It was important that he did. He was the star, and she was counting on him for support.

"It's not a question of like. It's a question of effectiveness. And . . ." He shrugged his shoulders, as if he wasn't sure he was going to continue.

Katherine leaned forward. "Yes?"

"I'm not sure advertising like this is the cure-all. We're in research. We can't go broadcasting our secrets."

Katherine tried to remain cool. She couldn't believe that William was expressing doubts about the campaign moments before her presentation. His support was crucial. She had spoken with Michael about William, and he had assured her that William was excited about the campaign.

"I'm not suggesting that," she said evenly. "I'm just trying to help sell what we've developed. You know what the industry's saying about this, the rumors that are . . ."

Katherine stopped. They were no longer alone. A man with thinning white hair stood in the doorway. His face was darkly lined, and his skin had the leathery look of someone who has had a tan for most of his life.

"Who are you?" he asked curiously.

Katherine stood up. "I'm Katherine Wells."

"Ah, yes," he said, entering the room. "Our new marketing director. The whiz kid." He extended his hand. "I'm Toby Nat. It's a pleasure."

Katherine shook his hand. Although they had never met, Katherine knew who he was. Toby Nat. A career military man who had risen quickly through the ranks. After retiring from the military several years ago, he joined the boards of several companies, including Benson.

Toby glanced at William. "Good morning, William. What's all this about the rumors?"

"I was just discussing the problem we had in launching the A-14 engine," Katherine said quickly.

"And you think the problem lies within the industry?"

"Yes. Yes, I do," Katherine replied. Toby smiled, and then, slowly, he began to laugh. A long, patronizing laugh.

"As you know, she's not alone in thinking that," Michael said. He had entered the room silently and stood in the doorway, directly behind Toby.

Toby glanced behind him. "Can she—or you—back that up?"

"She'll address any questions at the end of her presentation." And with that, Michael took a seat at the head of the table. He opened his briefcase and motioned for Katherine to take a seat next to him.

Katherine sat down to his right. William Briggs took a seat next to Katherine. And Toby distanced himself, sitting at the far end of the table. William glanced at Toby, then, despite his earlier pessimism, smiled at her in support.

The sides were already being drawn.

16

Katherine turned the lights back on. People were smiling. They liked it.

"Keep in mind, the commercial you just saw is a rough," she said. "It's just to give you an idea of the direction we plan on going."

Katherine stood facing the table. Twenty people looked at her expectantly. She still needed to deliver. She glanced down at her notes.

"So, William Briggs, a real man who works as an engineer at Benson, is the icon of this campaign." She motioned to William. He smiled modestly and squirmed uncomfortably in his seat. He stared at the ad behind Katherine. In it, a white-haired man, a professional model, smiled at the camera. Katherine had not wanted to bother William for a shoot until she was sure the campaign was approved. So Bresser and Tenner had mocked up the ad using stock photos. The man in the ad looked intelligent, professional, yet kind. He was wearing a business suit and standing in front of a plane with his arms crossed. He looked like he was in charge.

"So this is essentially a real people campaign?" The question came from a smartly dressed woman in her fifties sitting on the other side of Michael. Katherine knew she was Babs Douglass, the woman who refused to travel on commercial jets yet was on the board of Benson. She had married into money, and when her elderly husband died, she had taken his place on the board.

"Real person. We'll only be focusing in on one individual. William."

"Isn't that dangerous? I mean, no offense to William here, but what if he gets involved with something that we don't want to be associated with? You know, picked up for drunk driving or something?" Babs asked. There was laughter.

"I think you should all talk to William and Michael about this before you make a final decision," Katherine said. "I would add, however, that your point is well taken. I think there is an element of risk with any action that's worth taking. The easy way doesn't often produce results." Katherine caught Leslie Benson's eye. He smiled at her reassuringly. She continued. "We have an opportunity to do something different here," she said. *Don't say "I think,"* she reminded herself. Her professors had drilled that into her head. She had to act as though she knew what she was talking about. She needed people to view her as a marketing expert. "At least in the aeronautics industry. The car manufacturers have used a similar approach for years, and they've been extremely successful. I have the data for you on page thirty of your marketing proposal."

"But cars are bought at the dealer. A-14 engines are bought by the airlines, not by the consumers," Alan Benson said.

"That's right. But we're hoping to pull through the consumers. Air safety is a major issue right now. We have an engine that's exceedingly safe and technologically sound—not to mention faster than any other commercial engine for small planes. It's more expensive than the other engines of it's type, but it's worth it. We not only want the consumers to be aware of it, we want them to want it."

"How much?" This time, the question was directed by a man in a three-piece suit sitting in the middle of the table. His reading glasses slid down on his nose. Katherine recognized him from Florida. And he had asked the same question then. "How much is this thing going to cost?". he repeated.

"If you'll all turn to the last page of your proposal, I've got the breakdown for you. Not including a staff."

"A staff? You do have an assistant," said Alan.

"Yes. Louise Trehorn. But I need more than one assistant."

"You realize that this figure is equal to your entire advertising budget for the year," Toby said. "And your salary is included in that."

"Yes. But my salary only accounts for two million," Katherine replied with a smile.

Laughter emanated from around the room.

"All kidding aside," Katherine said, getting back to business, "in the past, the problem has been that the money was spread too thin. We tried to do too much with too little. And because there really was no marketing department to speak of, things were done a little haphazardly. I don't mean any offense toward my predecessor. I think he did a tremendous job with the resources he had. However, these are different times. We have a different problem. We need a campaign where we get some consistent exposure on the networks and cable. Cable comes cheap, but the networks don't. This campaign will not only brand us as the leaders in the industry, it can also work as a general awareness campaign. Everyone knows Boeing. It's a reputable name. Let's do the same for Benson. We have an outstanding product, one that we have developed, one that we invented ourselves. Let's use it."

The room was quiet.

"Impressive," Toby Nat said. He glanced at Michael before continuing. "However, I see one fatal flaw. You base your entire campaign on an assumption. An assumption that a quote-unquote rumor is floating around out there that has tainted the industry toward the A-14 engine. As I asked you before this meeting, can you back this up?"

Katherine smiled. The question she was waiting for.

"Actually, I can. I had some primary research done. We questioned thirty-five heads of industries, heads being defined as primary buyers or presidents. I've made copies of the questions and their responses for you all." She took a leather folder out of her briefcase and pulled out a neat stack of Xeroxed questionnaires. She passed them around the table.

"As you can see, each person remembers hearing that the engine was unsafe, but no one remembers where he heard it. Perhaps they just weren't willing to say. And although we released research that showed how safe the engine was, no one was even willing to test it. They were convinced that it was unsafe."

"All this because of a rumor?" Alan said, unbelieving.

"Perhaps it was more than a rumor," Michael said. Up until now, he had been quiet.

"What do you mean? Are you insinuating there's some sort of conspiracy?" Toby Nat asked, laughing as though he had just heard a funny joke.

Michael waited until his laughter died down. "Perhaps they didn't just hear this from some faceless source. Perhaps they were told the engine was unsafe by an insider at Benson."

Alan raised an eyebrow. "That is a very serious accusation. I assume this is speculation on your part."

"It would explain things, wouldn't it?"

Alan sat back in his chair.

"Interesting," Babs Douglass said. "I suggest we tighten security and investigate this matter more thoroughly."

"I second the motion," Leslie Benson said.

Michael glanced at Katherine. He nodded. It was her cue to wrap it up.

"If there are any more questions, I'd be happy to answer them. Otherwise . . ." She paused. People were thumbing through their questionnaires, obviously disturbed by the suggestion of corporate espionage.

Michael looked up at her and smiled. "That's all, Katherine. Thank you."

About half of the board members offered some polite applause.

17

The morning sunlight streamed through the crack in the drapes. Katherine groggily rubbed her legs together for warmth. She slowly realized that she wasn't even under her covers. She sat up in bed and glanced down at her outfit. No wonder she was uncomfortable. She was still in the same suit she had worn all day yesterday. She hadn't even bothered to take off her panty hose.

Katherine sat up on the edge of the bed and stretched her arms. She had been exhausted after her presentation yet had sat through the rest of the meeting. When she finally did return to her room, the bed had been so inviting, she couldn't resist lying down and closing her eyes for what she had planned on being a few minutes.

Even now, after a sound night's rest, she was half

tempted to put on her nightgown and sleep for a couple more hours. After all, she reminded herself, she didn't have to report in today. She had covered all of her issues yesterday. It had made a long day even longer, but it did give her an extra day of vacation.

And after yesterday, she needed some rest. The preparation leading up to the meeting was grueling, and the meeting itself had been intense. Although she had been prepared, and she was able to answer the questions satisfactorily, she left with a feeling of malaise, rather than the normal enthusiasm and relief that she usually felt after a major pitch. And although she was on the client side, her presentation had all the elements of a pitch. She had to persuade the board to buy it. And when she finished her presentation, she wasn't sure she had succeeded. Not because of what she said or what she didn't say but because everyone had been distracted by what Michael had said. Or, rather, suggested.

Corporate espionage.

Was it really? There *was* a nasty rumor. There was also some bad press. It was more like corporate destruction. Someone did not want the engine to succeed. People might pay for information, but they would want proof that the information was correct. They would need research to back it up. And there was no research that indicated the A-14 was unsafe.

Or was there?

Katherine sat up. She couldn't believe Michael would withhold data like that. But, she reminded herself, he was under fire right now from certain members of the board to prove that it was worthwhile to commit money toward research. Perhaps he had overlooked data that would have been detrimental to the A–14. And someone had taken it elsewhere. If so, who? William?

Katherine got out of bed and opened the drapes.

Snow was falling lightly in the early dawn. The slopes had not yet opened, and Katherine reveled in the quiet and stunning beauty of the day. Her mind focused back on Benson. She had to stop herself. She was getting carried away. She had read too many Raymond Chandler books. This was the real world, not some mystery novel.

She opened the window and breathed in the clear mountain air. This was her vacation, her first in years, and she was going to enjoy herself.

After a hot shower, she changed into a warm turtleneck and a comfortable pair of old jeans. She had a large breakfast in the hotel dining room consisting of coffee, orange juice, a cheese omelet, toast, and hash browns. She was happy and relieved not to run into any of the Benson board of directors.

Katherine decided to complement her early meal with a long walk in the fresh, cold mountain air. The snow crunched beneath her boots as she trudged out of the hotel's circular driveway and toward the main road. The desk clerk had said it was about a mile to town.

It was only seven o'clock in the morning, and she knew the stores wouldn't be open yet, but she was looking forward to window shopping. She laughed as she realized that this was probably an ideal time for her to shop—it certainly would prevent her from buying anything even if she was tempted.

The town was a charming strip of old-fashioned stores featuring modern, high-priced items. Katherine looked in a window and admired a beautiful long wool coat. Although it was still more than a month away from Christmas, many of the stores already had their holiday decorations up.

She browsed the store windows for an hour before heading back to the hotel. Nearly two hours had passed since she left the hotel, and the slopes would be open by the time she returned.

Katherine arrived back at the hotel, invigorated by her long walk. She returned to her room and changed into her long underwear, layering on some additional sweaters before putting on her ski suit. She stepped out of her room cautiously. Her clothing had padded her svelte figure, making her feel like a chubby four-year-old in a snow suit. She didn't want to run into anyone from Benson.

The elevator doors opened, and Katherine waddled out. She had pulled her scarf up so that it was covering the lower half of her face.

Katherine's heart stopped as she spotted Michael and his father in the center of the lobby. She quickly turned, attempting to head out the side door and avoid them, but Michael was too quick for her.

"Hey, Wells, wait a minute," he said, interrupting his conversation with his father to walk over to her.

"Great job yesterday," he said, uncharacteristically enthusiastic. Katherine pulled her scarf away from her mouth so she could speak.

"Thanks," she responded shyly, surprising herself. "I wasn't sure. I was a little confused by the way my presentation ended."

Michael nodded his head. "Oh, that. Well, I'm sorry that it happened while you were up there, but it was something that needed to be said. So," he said, switching the subject, "going skiing?"

"Yeah," she replied, aware that his father was waiting for him and anxious to break away.

"Be careful. You said you skied before, right?"

"Oh, sure," she said, somewhat unconvincingly.

"The snow out west is different, you know. It's powder. Be careful," he added, repeating himself.

"Good luck in the meeting," she said, heading for the door.

Michael was oblivious to his father's perceptive glance. He was too busy watching Katherine walk through the lobby. He'd do anything to be able to join her. But he wouldn't. He would be on his best behavior. And to guarantee that, there was Carly. Her parents had a place near his family's ski lodge, and she had informed him she was going to be out there this weekend. He had made tentative plans to get together—if he had time. It was the perfect screen.

Katherine walked around the back to the lodge, where she rented skis, boots, and poles. A ski patrolman gallantly helped her put on her skis and pointed her to the chair lift. She stood in line, nervously watching the machine sweep people off their feet and carry them up the mountain. She had heard that it was necessary to take several chair lifts up to the top. The ski patrolman had told her that sometimes it would take people hours to get back down. Fortunately, he had said, there was a halfway house on the mountain that served hot drinks and sandwiches. She looked at her watch. It was already ten o'clock. She figured she'd be there by noon.

It was almost her turn for the chair lift when she heard someone crying out, "Any singles?"

"Single!" she yelled.

She turned and saw a handsome man skillfully pull into place alongside her. Together, they jumped in front of the lift and awkwardly slid into a seat as the chair swung by.

"Great day," he said, raising his goggles and smiling at her.

"Yeah," she responded nervously as the chair began to lift them up in the air.

"What's the matter?" he asked sympathetically.

"Nothing," she whispered, her eyes still focused on the ground below. He smiled.

"Is this your first time skiing out west?" he asked gently.

"Yes," she admitted, somewhat embarrassed. "And you?"

"My family has a place here."

"It's beautiful," she said. "I probably never would've come here, though, if it wasn't for work."

"Do you have a convention here or something?"

"No, a board meeting."

"Where do you work?" he asked, somewhat suspiciously.

"An aeronautics company called Benson," she replied, looking with terror at the ground below.

The man beside her started laughing. "Don't tell me you work for cousin Mikey?" he asked. Katherine's eyes widened in dismay as she looked at his face carefully. She could detect a faint family resemblance.

"Let me guess," she said slowly. "You are . . ."

"Kevin Benson. Alan Benson's son. Michael is my cousin."

She stared at him awkwardly, cursing the coincidence. She had not wanted to run into *anyone* connected or even related to work—particularly Michael.

"Why aren't you in the meeting right now?" he asked.

"I finished my portion of the meeting yesterday. The rest of the weekend I'm on my own."

Kevin smiled at her good-naturedly. He would be staying in town for another two weeks. He knew that Michael thought he was a lazy bum who liked nothing better than to date women and play on the beaches and ski slopes. It was sure to make him angry if he knew that he was fraternizing with a member of his staff.

Unfortunately, he couldn't tell what she looked like under her scarf and hat. He'd hate to think his time in Sun Valley would be even partially monopolized by someone who was not very attractive or wealthy. But the thought of making Michael angry was too tempting to resist.

"Great!" he said enthusiastically. "So we can hang out."

Katherine hesitated. "Sure. I mean, maybe," she said rather weakly. The last thing she wanted was to be surrounded by Michael's family. But then again, she thought to herself, it might be nice to have someone to eat dinner with.

"Get ready," he said as the chair began to drop closer to the ground. Katherine surprised herself by landing easily on her feet and skiing away from the chair.

Thirty minutes and three chair lifts later, Katherine was standing on top of the mountain.

She looked down at the magnificent slopes, but, instead of appreciating the beauty, she was astounded by how high up she was and feeling a little queasy as a result. This mountain didn't resemble the well-worn hills of northern Michigan. The snow was so deep and light, it looked as though the skiers would sink right into it.

"Come on," Kevin said enthusiastically. Katherine watched her new friend skillfully bound off down the mountain. Even though they appeared to be close to the same age, she felt much older than he. He had almost bragged about how he had attended several different colleges, managing to be thrown out of two of them and dropping out of the third two credits short of graduation. From what she could discern from their conversation, he basically did odds and ends for his father when he needed extra money. Otherwise, he lived off his modest but ample trust fund.

She had a sneaking suspicion that he and Michael were not very close. She had never heard Michael or anyone at the office talk much about him. She wondered what Michael would think of her spending the day with him. He probably wouldn't like it very much, she realized with a certain amount of satisfaction.

She scooted toward the edge of the mogul-dotted mountain. Kevin was covering the slope skillfully and quickly. *He makes it look easy,* she thought to herself. She glanced at the black diamond warning sign posted by the chair lift. For advanced skiers only.

Katherine was exhausted by the time they reached the halfway house. Despite her inexperience, she had held her own on the mountain, only suffering a small tumble that hurt her pride more than anything else.

"How long have you worked at Benson?" Kevin asked, setting down a tray laden with sandwiches. Before Katherine could answer, he had taken a large bite out of a hamburger.

"About five months," she replied.

"What do you do there?" he asked between bites.

"Marketing director," she said.

"Wow," he said, putting down his sandwich. "I didn't think you were much older than me."

"How old are you?" she asked, sipping her coffee.

"I'll be twenty-nine this spring," he said.

"I'll be twenty-nine in April," she said, smiling. He grinned.

"So you're not older than me at all. No offense. It's just hard to tell what people look like underneath all this skiing gear."

"No offense taken."

"So you're pretty high up there, huh? I'm sure you know all about the recent feud between my father and Michael."

Katherine set down her mug. She knew this was probably sensitive material not meant for her ears, but she couldn't help asking him about it.

"What do you mean?" she asked, pretending naïveté.

"They got in a big fight in Florida. Made quite a scene."

"Just recently?"

Kevin nodded.

"I was in Florida for a meeting with some of the board. I was with Michael most of the time. When did they get in a fight?"

"So you're the one my mother keeps talking about."

"Your mother is very sweet," Katherine replied modestly. "So, about Florida," Katherine said, returning to the subject at hand. "When did they get in a fight? It must've been after I left." Or, Katherine thought, perhaps Michael had been telling the truth the night at the club. Perhaps he had wanted to talk to his uncle.

"I don't know when it happened. But it was a big argument. They were at the club. My mom said it wasn't pretty. My dad was telling Michael how some people are unhappy with the direction Michael has been taking the company in. Michael got pissed and took it from there."

"How are they unhappy?" Katherine asked.

"They're complaining that the company's not his priority anymore. He's always been involved in politics, and I guess they think he's interested in following in his father's footsteps. Selling the company and moving on."

"I see," she said softly.

"My father approached Michael about buying the company back from him, but Michael turned him down. I guess Michael wanted more money or something . . ." He noticed her fallen face and silently cursed himself for bringing the subject up.

"No wonder there's so much tension between them," Katherine said.

"That's part of it. That and the fact that Michael's said some pretty nasty things to my dad in the past few weeks. He accused him of starting some terrible rumor so that stock would fall and he could get a better price for the company."

Katherine looked away, alarmed. So that was it. Yesterday was just for show. It was for the benefit of the spectators. Their confrontation had already occurred, and it was much uglier than yesterday's performance.

Kevin looked at Katherine. "But, hey, what do I know?" he added cheerfully. "Maybe I misinterpreted things. Maybe I just assumed that he'd be getting married soon and running for office or something."

She looked at him sadly. "Married?" she asked. "And you know all of this because your father has confided in you?"

Kevin finished chewing. "Not really," he said, not very convincingly. "But Michael's on pretty thin ground." Kevin knew he should keep quiet, but he couldn't resist getting his digs in about his cousin. It was obvious that Katherine was impressed by Michael. He was just trying to enlighten her. "I've heard a rumor floating around the family that my father and Toby Nat might just combine shares and take over the company by force."

"Could they do that? Push Michael out of his own company?"

"Not exactly. He'd still be major stockholder. He just wouldn't control it anymore. He wouldn't be chairman of the board anymore, but he could still be president of the company. Although I doubt they would allow that."

"But I thought your father and Michael were pretty close. They seemed to get along well."

"They do like each other. But this is business."

Katherine looked him in the eye. "Is there more to this story than just rumor?" she asked sternly.

Kevin smiled. He could sense her involvement with

his cousin was more than professional. She wasn't the only woman unable to resist his cousin. And she was becoming more appealing all the time. He liked a solid conquest.

"I can assure you, my father doesn't confide in me. It's all just family gossip. I probably shouldn't even have said anything. Listen," he said enthusiastically, "why don't you come to the family homestead with me tonight? We can hang out and roast marshmallows, build a snowman . . . you name it."

She smiled back at him. "I don't think so," she said. She felt all of her earlier spirit had been drained from her. So Michael wanted to sell the company. And get married. She wasn't sure which upset her more. She knew she couldn't afford to be unemployed right now. But she also didn't like the thought of losing Michael. She cared about him, as a person, as a boss. But why should she? They weren't romantically involved. Nor would they ever be. He had someone else. And even if he didn't, he had made it clear that he didn't want to be involved with her. At least, not while she was working for him. If ever.

Katherine looked at the man sitting across from her. Perhaps she should take him up on his offer. He was handsome, like Michael. He was a terrific athlete, and he seemed to be intelligent, although a touch reckless and immature.

"Come on," he cajoled. "It'll be fun. I promise." She looked at him suspiciously.

"I won't lay a finger on you," he said, flashing her his best pretty-boy smile.

She couldn't stop herself from laughing. She might as well go. After all, it was difficult to vacation alone with no work to mask her loneliness.

"What time?" she asked.

He leaned back in his chair and grinned.

* * *

By the time she and Kevin made it down the rest of the mountain, it was close to five. She said good-bye outside the ski lodge after promising to meet him in the hotel lobby at seven. She had offered to take a cab to his family's house, but he had insisted that he would pick her up in his jeep.

She returned her skis and was in the lobby waiting for the elevator when she noticed Michael walking toward her.

"Are you just getting back now?" he asked, quickly checking his watch.

"Uh-huh," she replied, nodding her head. "The slopes are incredible," she added, trying to sound like a pro skier.

"Oh, yeah?" he said, smiling as he realized she was covered in snow. It looked like she had suffered more than one tumble. "Well, I'm glad you're having a good time."

"A great time," she said, privately wishing the elevator would hurry up.

"If you want to meet for a drink later on, I can update you on what happened today," he said right before the elevator doors opened.

Katherine stepped inside the elevator and pressed her floor number.

"Thanks, but I have plans," she replied, smiling sweetly as the doors closed on Michael's stunned face.

As soon as Katherine got back to her room, she threw off her wet clothes and ran a hot bath. She sat soaking in the tub, cautiously going over her options with the company and her motive for spending time with Kevin. Perhaps going out with him this evening would get her mind off Michael. Kevin was more her age and, more importantly, in her league. Michael was simply too important and powerful to be interested in a small-town girl like her.

She slipped out of the tub and wrapped a large

fuzzy towel around her slender body. She brushed her long brown hair and lay down on her bed. Part of her wished she could just stay in the room and go to sleep.

She ordered some hot tea from room service. She decided she would rest until it arrived, then she would sip her tea while she dressed for her evening with Kevin.

18

Two hours later, Katherine appeared downstairs refreshed and ready for a relaxing evening. Her snug sweater was tucked into black jeans. Her long winter coat hung casually over her shoulders.

The lobby appeared to be lit by candles. Although there was dim electric track lighting, the majority of light came from the huge blazing fire and the candles flickering on the coffee tables. The intimate arrangement of the fat, overstuffed chairs encouraged cozy gatherings where people leaned in toward each other as they spoke in hushed tones.

In the far corner, her date for the evening sat apart from the crowd. Across from him, appearing stiff and uneasy, was none other than Michael himself. Katherine took a deep breath. She was not going to allow herself to feel uncomfortable just because Michael was there.

"Hello," she said calmly.

"Hello," they both responded, almost in unison.

"Katherine, I'd like you to meet my cousin, Kevin

Benson," Michael said, standing up. Michael had changed out of his conservative work attire and into a black turtleneck, jeans, and cowboy boots. Even in casual dress, this handsome man was a powerful force to reckon with.

Katherine forced herself to turn away from Michael and smile at Kevin. She couldn't help but compare the two. Unlike his cousin, Kevin was dressed sloppily in an untucked white flannel button-down shirt over a pair of faded, torn jeans. He looked more like a rebellious college student than a man nearing thirty.

"We've met," she said.

Kevin's eyes opened wide.

"Katherine?" he asked, astonished. She looked sleek and beautiful. Not like the tomboy he had spent the afternoon with.

"You two know each other?" Michael said, suspiciously looking from Katherine to Kevin.

"I guess we do," Kevin said happily as he half-heartedly attempted to tuck in his shirt. He was suddenly painfully aware of his messy appearance. "You look beautiful," he added, staring appreciatively at Katherine.

"Thank you," she replied. She glanced quickly at Michael as she attempted to gauge his reaction.

"We met on the slopes this afternoon," Kevin said, turning back toward his cousin. "I'm happy to say this lady has agreed to be my date tonight."

"Really," Michael stated, dismayed. He should have known his reckless bum of a cousin would zero in on the most beautiful woman he could find.

"I thought I'd take her to the house and show her around," Kevin added, putting his arm loosely around Katherine.

"What a coincidence," Michael said through clenched teeth.

"What do you mean?" Kevin asked apprehensively.

"I was planning to go there, too. You don't mind if I catch a ride with you," Michael added, attempting a casual smile.

Katherine grimaced. Just her luck. She had hoped to forget about Michael, at least temporarily. That would be a little difficult to do if she was in his company all evening.

Kevin looked at Michael, frustrated that his sudden hope for a romantic evening was so quickly derailed. "Uh, sure," he said slowly, dropping his arm from around Katherine's waist. "But we're ready to go right now."

"Perfect," Michael replied, hoping they would escape before his dinner date, Toby Nat, arrived in the lobby to meet him. He realized that it was a poor business decision to stand up Toby, but he figured he had till tomorrow to think of a good excuse. Besides, his father was still in town. He'd be more than happy to go to dinner with Toby.

"Let's go," Kevin said, giving Michael a dirty look before turning toward the door.

"After you," Michael said politely. He motioned for Katherine to follow Kevin.

The trio walked outside and into the lot where Kevin had parked the Jeep. The snow was falling steadily and in heavy clumps, drastically diminishing visibility.

"Did you check the weather?" Michael asked. Katherine pulled her coat tightly around her.

"Didn't have a chance," Kevin said, obviously not concerned. "It's too early in the season for a bad storm. You're not afraid of a little snow, are you, cuz? If so, you could always stay here ..."

Michael glared at Kevin, quieting the younger man. Kevin held the passenger door open for Katherine while Michael climbed into the back.

Kevin jumped in and started the Jeep. The vehicle

rolled out of the icy driveway and onto the snow-covered streets.

"This is the type of weather a Jeep loves," he said, revving the engine as he picked up speed on the empty highway. Katherine peered out the window. Although she knew that they must be in town, the snow made it difficult to see the stores.

The Jeep plowed speedily through the deserted streets. The only sounds were the windshield wipers moving back and forth across the glass.

"Do you mind slowing down?" Michael asked in a commanding voice. "I don't think it's smart to be driving so fast when you can barely see five feet in front of you."

Kevin laughed as though he had no intention of slowing the vehicle, but Katherine couldn't help notice the speedometer dropping.

Kevin was having a tough time staying on the road. At one point, the Jeep slipped off the road and lurched precariously.

"For God's sake, Kevin, watch it!" Michael yelled. He looked over protectively to Katherine, checking to make sure she was wearing her seat belt.

"I've got it under control," Kevin shouted back unconvincingly.

"Do you want me to drive?" Michael asked arrogantly from the backseat.

"No!" Kevin responded angrily.

Katherine stared out the window into the blizzard. Why did Michael have to be so nasty to Kevin? He certainly wasn't helping to ease the tension of the situation. Perhaps it had been a little irresponsible for Kevin to suggest that they drive out to the country without checking the weather reports, but no one asked Michael to come along.

Katherine glanced back at Michael. His dark,

brooding face was clouded with concern over their immediate situation.

Suddenly, a deer appeared in the road. The wild animal seemed paralyzed by the glare of the head-lights. Before Katherine had a chance to scream, Kevin jerked the wheel to the right. The Jeep hit a patch of ice and swerved off the road, ramming into the embankment.

"Kevin!" Michael yelled, too late. He jumped forward and wrapped his arms protectively around Katherine's shoulders in a successful attempt to keep her grounded to her seat. But he couldn't stop her head from knocking into her window.

"Everybody okay?" Kevin asked after the vehicle came to an abrupt stop.

Michael was already outside the car. He opened Katherine's door. "Are you all right, Katherine?"

"Yes," she said, holding her head. She glanced at her window. "I'm surprised I didn't break it."

Michael kneeled beside her and gently moved her hand away. A small red bump was already appearing.

"Is Katherine okay?" Kevin asked.

"No, she isn't," Michael said. "She could have a concussion."

"Katherine's fine," she said, looking up at him. "Let's just get out of here."

"How many fingers am I holding up?" Kevin said, waving two fingers in front of her face.

"Kevin!" Michael ordered. "Katherine's right. We should get her someplace warm." Michael rolled a small snowball and handed it to Katherine. "Hold this where your head hurts. It'll help the swelling." Michael turned and walked quickly to the front of the Jeep, where he surveyed the damage. Despite the speed they had been traveling, it didn't look that bad. "Can you back out of here?" he yelled to Kevin over the roar of the wind.

Kevin tried the car. A weak rattle emanated from the engine.

"Okay," Michael said, taking charge. "Turn it off." He walked around and leaned in Kevin's window. "We're going to have to flag down a car to take us back to town. You and Katherine stay in the car until I get some help."

Kevin sat beside Katherine, staring morosely in front of him, embarrassed by the whole incident. Still holding the snowball to her head, Katherine watched Michael walk to the side of the road, his back partially illuminated by the headlights of their Jeep.

After only a few minutes, Michael had succeeded in his mission. He reappeared at Kevin's door.

"Okay, Kevin. They only have room for one. You go with them back into town. Katherine and I will try and get a car to take us either to the house or back to town from here."

"But if there's only room for one, shouldn't Katherine be the one to go?"

"It's a car full of rough-looking mountain men. I don't think so," he replied sarcastically. "She'll be safe here with me. Now, go!"

Kevin reluctantly climbed out of the jeep. "Why don't you go?" he whined.

"Kevin, *get going!*" Michael ordered.

"Mountain men. My luck. They're probably hungry ones at that," Kevin muttered to himself. "See you later, Katherine. Be careful," he added, speaking to Katherine but looking sternly at his cousin.

Michael walked Kevin to the other car, and, after saying a few words to the driver, he slammed the door. He came back and, without saying a word to Katherine, tried the Jeep once more. After listening carefully to the hollow sound of the engine, he jumped out and walked around to the front of the Jeep, unlatching and opening the hood.

While Michael tinkered around under the hood, Katherine threw the remains of the snowball out the window and pulled her knees to her chest, hugging them tightly in an attempt to keep warm. Though her head ached, and she was aware of how precarious their situation was out there in the wilderness, she somehow felt safe and protected. She had no doubt that Michael would make sure they got out of there in one piece.

A few minutes later, her intuition was confirmed. Michael slammed the hood and jumped back in beside her. The Jeep fired up with a healthy roar. He pressed the accelerator and yanked them out of the embankment.

"What did you do to it?" Katherine asked, sitting up in her seat.

"The choke was jammed shut. I just opened it," he said, driving back onto the road. She noticed he was driving in the direction they were originally headed— away from town.

"Put your seat belt back on," he ordered as he skillfully maneuvered the car through the snow.

"Where are we going?" Katherine asked, tightening the belt around her.

"To the house," he said, not taking his eyes off the road.

"But in a snowstorm like this, wouldn't it be best for us just to go back to town?"

"We're closer to the house at this point," he said, keeping his eyes on the road.

She had to admit that she agreed with his decision. After their frightening ride, she wanted to be out of the car as soon as possible, even if it meant being stranded out in the middle of nowhere with her boss.

The Jeep plowed slowly along the deserted road. Michael stared into the blind fury swarming in front of him, deftly steering clear of the ditch along the side of the road.

Katherine looked sideways at the man sitting beside

her. She had worked for him now for almost five months, yet she really didn't know him at all. And even though she had diligently attempted to ignore her physical desire for him, his cool, professional treatment of her had only served to exacerbate her longing.

She had to admit there were times, like after her date with Christopher and tonight with Kevin, where it almost seemed as though Michael was jealous that other men found her attractive. It was as though he was afraid that if she developed a personal relationship with someone else, it might distract her from her work at Benson.

She knew she had every reason to harbor animosity toward the man who had ignited the lust that had lain dormant inside her. Her life would be much more pleasant if she didn't have to continuously remind herself that the man she desired was not only off-limits because of their professional relationship, but that he was very much taken by a certain blonde named Carly Wentworth.

Regardless of his relationship status, Katherine thought as she focused her eyes straight ahead of her, she had to confess she was more than a little excited by the idea of being stuck with Michael in the middle of nowhere during a raging blizzard.

Michael turned off the road onto what looked like a clearing in the snow-covered woods.

"Believe it or not, this is the driveway," he said, stopping the car. He pulled the keys out of the ignition and looked at Katherine.

"I'm afraid we're going to have to walk from here. The driveway's not plowed, and we'd never make it down," he said.

"But we're here, aren't we?" Katherine said, her eyes wistfully searching for a house. "I mean, this is the driveway, isn't it?" she added somewhat hopefully.

"Unfortunately," he said, opening his door, "we

have a rather long driveway." He leaped out of the Jeep.

Katherine opened the door, clutching her coat against her as she felt the blast of cold air. Michael walked over to her side to help her down.

"How long is long?" Katherine asked as she jumped into the snow.

"A mile or so," he said, grabbing her hand. "Follow me," he added, pulling her into the darkness.

They plodded silently through the snow. Even though Katherine was wearing boots, she could feel her toes becoming seeped in cold wetness.

She was feeling weaker by the moment, and her thoughts were becoming tangled and confused. Her head was hurting her. She'd never had a migraine before, but she imagined that the pain she was experiencing must be similar. The pain began to fade into dizziness, making it difficult for her to walk. If she could only rest for just a moment . . . her hand slipped from his as she fell into a soft, warm oblivion.

19

Katherine was faintly aware of someone tugging on her feet. She looked down. Michael was kneeling beside her, pulling her off her boots.

"Hey," she said in a hoarse greeting.

"How're you feeling?" he asked, still tugging on her boots.

"All right," she said quietly. She looked around her.

She was in small room with oak paneling and a cold, empty fireplace. "What happened?" she asked, slowly attempting to sit up.

"You passed out about a quarter of a mile from here."

She attempted to shake her head. "How embarrassing. I've never done that before." She rubbed her frozen hands together weakly.

"There's nothing to be embarrassed about." Michael pulled off her socks and rubbed her freezing feet gently.

"How did I get back here?" she asked, bewildered.

"I carried you," he said, using the back of his arm to wipe off the snow that was beginning to drip from his face.

Katherine rolled her eyes. It was worse than she thought. She was never going to live this down.

"Now, let's see that bump of yours," he said, eyeing it closely. "I'll get an ice pack for it."

"No more ice," Katherine said. "But I will take some aspirin."

"I'll get you some ice too, just in case you change your mind."

Michael left the room. Within moments, he was back carrying a small ice bag, aspirin, and water.

As Katherine swallowed the aspirin, he grabbed some kindling from a basket at the side of the fireplace. He picked up some logs that were stacked outside the room and carefully placed them on the grate, crumpling up an old newspaper and tucking it in between the wood.

"Unfortunately, this is all the heat we're going to have for now. The storm knocked out the electricity," he said, picking up the matchbook on top of the fireplace. He lit the match on the first strike and threw it at the wood. Katherine watched the fire blaze upward as she held the ice bag to her head. She crept closer to it as Michael dropped down beside her.

"You look exhausted," she said sympathetically. Michael shrugged his shoulders. "I'm sorry I passed out. You probably wouldn't be so tired if you hadn't had to carry me back here," she said apologetically, shivering in her wet clothes.

He looked at her, a smile barely visible. "I didn't mind carrying you at all." He suddenly realized that she was cold and wet. "I'm going to look for some dry clothes for us," he said, standing up slowly. "I'll be back in a minute."

"Here," she said, handing him the ice.

"You're finished?"

Katherine nodded as she attempted to smile gratefully. Michael grinned and left the room. Katherine held her hands up to the fire to warm them.

She glanced around her, slowly digesting her surroundings. The room was casually decorated with comfortable, livable furniture—a couple of easy chairs and a plump, well-worn couch with a blanket thrown over the side. Family photos framed the dark, wood-paneled walls.

The door creaked open behind her.

"Here are some sweats and some sweaters," Michael said. "Throw on whatever you want." He set the clothes on the couch. "I'll give you some privacy."

Katherine waited until he shut the door. She stood up stiffly. She picked up the large, soft crewneck sweater he had left for her and touched it to her face. Cashmere. With great effort, she took off her turtleneck and sweater. Her bra, she realized with dismay, was soaking wet and would have to go, too. She reached behind her and undid the hook. She pulled it off and, using an extra sweatshirt as a towel, gingerly dried herself off. She pulled the cashmere sweater over her head, relishing the soft, luxurious warmth against her bare breasts. She undid her wet and heavy jeans and pulled them off too. She hesitated as she looked at her underwear. She decided she would have to wear whoever's sweatpants these were without underwear, at least until hers dried.

She carefully laid her clothes down by the fire and grabbed the blanket from the couch. She settled into the comfortable, plump chair, wrapping the blanket protectively around her. Michael came in a few minutes later. He, too, had dried off and was wearing a sweatshirt and faded jeans. He held a package of crackers and a block of cheese. Under his right arm was a bottle of whiskey.

"I brought dinner," he said, smiling and setting the crackers down on the coffee table. "I also thought we could use something to help warm us up." He unscrewed the cap of the whiskey and handed the bottle to Katherine.

"Glasses?" she asked.

"Just take a swig," he responded, plopping down on the couch. She gulped a large swallow of the liquid and immediately began to cough. She passed the bottle back to him.

"Careful there," he said, grinning. "This is pretty strong stuff."

"I'm fine," Katherine said indignantly, her coughing beginning to subside.

"Okay," he said cheerfully. "Back to business. I've got some good news and some bad news," he said, swinging his legs up onto the couch. "Which do you want to hear first?"

"The bad," Katherine groaned.

"The bad news is the phone's out," he said. "The good news is I was just checking the supplies in the kitchen. We're pretty well set on food if we're stuck here for a while. And we've got plenty of wood," he added, looking toward the fire.

Katherine glanced at him nervously.

"What do you mean, 'stuck here for a while'?" she asked.

"We're in the middle of a bad storm," he replied. "It's going to take them time to clear the roads and get us out of here."

Katherine looked down at her lap. She wasn't sure how she should feel about being stranded with Michael.

"I suggest, at least for tonight, we stay in this room with the door shut. That way, we'll preserve as much heat as possible. I'll look for sleeping bags for us. You can sleep wherever you want—on the couch, in the chair, or on the floor." He stood up. "I'll be back in a minute," he said.

Katherine leaned back and rested her damp head against the back of the chair as she pondered her situation. She realized she had gotten herself into quite a mess. If word got around the office that she had spent the night alone with Michael at his family's house in the wilderness, it could damage her professional reputation. She didn't want people thinking that she was just another notch in Michael's belt.

Of course, she realized guiltily, if she hadn't agreed to go out with Kevin in the first place, none of this would have happened.

"Here are some blankets," Michael said, entering the room and setting them down on the couch. "Are you comfortable there?"

Katherine nodded her head. He picked up the whiskey and took a swig before handing it back to Katherine. Katherine leaned forward to take the bottle, and for a split second their eyes locked as their hands brushed against each other.

"So this is your family's house?" Katherine asked, desperately trying to make conversation as she broke their stare.

"I own it now, but it's been in my family for generations. It belonged to my grandparents originally. They took their kids here when they wanted to get away from it all. My father and uncle spent a lot of their holidays and vacations here."

"Are you pretty close to your family? I mean, to your uncle?" she asked, remembering what Kevin had mentioned earlier that day.

"Alan?" he asked, stiffening slightly and setting the brandy back down. He bent down in front of the fire and threw another log in. "I let Alan and Kevin use the house whenever they want . . . as you know."

"Michael," she said, ignoring the dig and quickly deciding to repeat the family rumor about Alan Benson's plans for the company. "Earlier today, Kevin said that . . ."

"Enough about Kevin," he said. "Why did you bring him up? Are you wishing you were trapped here with him instead of me?"

"No. I just . . ."

A thunderous crash and the sound of breaking glass abruptly stopped all conversation. Before Katherine realized what she was doing, she was over on the floor by Michael, clutching his arm.

"Come on," he said, jumping up and pulling her to her feet.

They opened the door and were rudely greeted by a rush of frigid air. A tree branch had crashed through the window to the left of the front door, spraying the hallway with glass. Michael calmly walked through the glass and inspected the damage.

"I don't believe it," he said, looking outside through the broken window. A once magnificent oak tree in the front yard had split in half.

"Watch your step," he commanded as Katherine followed him through the glass. She shivered as a gust of snow blew in through the jagged glass.

"Let's get in the other room and keep warm," he ordered. "I'll do what I can to fix this in the morning."

Katherine gingerly stepped back toward the sanctity of their cozy room. She headed straight for the fire as Michael closed the door behind him. He grabbed a blanket off the couch and shoved it under the door.

"What are you doing?" Katherine asked, glancing back toward him.

"We need something to stop up the cracks under the door," he said. "It's already freezing in here."

Katherine turned back toward the fire and wrapped her arms around her.

Michael pulled another blanket off the couch and sat on the floor, leaning against the couch. "Remember in Florida? When I said I was stuck on something?"

Katherine nodded.

"Well, I still have the same problem. Maybe you can help me with it."

"Sure," Katherine said. She was relieved that Michael wanted to talk about work. That would sober them both up in no time.

"There's this friend of mine . . . Gary."

Katherine looked at him, confused. Was this a personal problem?

"Gary is the president of this aeronautics company," Michael continued. "Well, it seems that one night, Gary met a woman he really liked. A woman we'll call . . . Michelle. Well, as luck would have it, Michelle turns up at his company the next day, and he's embarrassed to find out that she is his new director of marketing. So now here he is, interested in one of his new employees. And that's a problem. Unfortunately, Gary does not have a great track record with relationships, and he's afraid if he gets involved with, er, Michelle, someone who works for him . . ."

"I assume that Michelle is interested in him as well?" Katherine asked, raising an eyebrow impishly as she emphasized the word *interested*.

Michael paused. "That is an excellent question," he said, standing up and stoking the fire. "I have to admit, Gary is a little ignorant when it comes to romance. Perhaps you can use your woman's intuition and tell me what you think. Is she interested in him as well?"

"Not knowing all the facts," she said, watching him, "I can only guess. Is Gary a nice guy?"

"Extremely. Maybe not at work," he added quickly. "But he tries to be a very nice guy."

"Is he funny? Smart?"

Michael glanced back at her. "Yes on both counts."

"Modest?"

He put down the fireplace poker and shook his head. "I'm afraid that would be a negative."

Katherine smiled. "Hmmm, that's what I thought. Is he handsome?"

"I don't know about that," he said, sitting down next to her. He twisted around so that he was almost leaning over her. "I'm not good at judging men. Only women. And I can tell you Michelle is extremely beautiful," he said, his blue eyes twinkling as he stared at her mischievously.

Katherine inhaled, staring back at him. "I think," she whispered as Michael drew his head closer, "she might be interested in him as well ..."

"Katherine," he said huskily, his lips brushing her ear. "There's more. To make matters even more complicated, Gary hasn't acted on his desires because he feels it's his responsibility to stay away from her."

"Because?"

"Because he's got his hands full dealing with his company and a difficult board. An office romance, especially one that sours, could be disastrous."

"Then I think Michelle would agree that your friend Gary is very wise," Katherine replied. Despite her soreness, she jumped up and brushed off her jeans. "If Michelle was my friend, I would advise her to stay away from Gary. It sounds like a bad idea all around." She held out her hand toward Michael. "Can I help you up?"

Michael accepted her hand. He rose to his feet, but he didn't let go of her hand. "I didn't finish," he said, steering her toward the couch. "He's never felt like this for anyone before. He's ready to throw caution to the wind. He's having a hard time focusing at work, all he can think about is her. Does that change your advice?"

Katherine stopped. She was backed up against the couch. She shrugged her shoulders. Michael reached out and touched her face. He slowly ran his finger along the outline of her chin. He leaned in and softly kissed her cheek. Keeping his cheek pressed to hers, he closed his eyes tightly, reveling in the closeness. "One word from you, and I'll back away," he whispered in her ear. "But I wouldn't recommend it. It's getting cold in here. We're going to need each other for body heat."

"So," Katherine managed. "In a sense, the situation is out of our control."

Michael smiled. He reached down and grabbed the blanket off the couch. He took her hand and gently pulled her down onto the floor, in front of the fire. He wrapped the blanket around them both. Katherine stared into the fire, trying to deny the excitement that was building inside her. The attraction she felt for him was overshadowing all of her other instincts.

Michael slipped his hand around her and began rubbing her arm to warm her.

He delicately kissed the bump on her forehead. Katherine pulled back. She knew that if she didn't resist him now, she would quickly lose her willpower.

"I can't," she said, turning her face away. "I work for you!"

Michael gently eased her face back toward him. His intoxicating desire mixed with the brandy had created an aching need that begged to be satisfied. He wanted her. Damn the consequences.

"All right," he replied with a sexy grin. "Have it your way. You're fired." He drowned her protest with a long, deep kiss.

Katherine found that she was responding in spite of herself.

Michael kissed her forehead gently, then both of her cheeks and her chin. Katherine held his head in her hands, her fingers buried in his soft, curly hair. Michael began to kiss her lips, slowly, delicately, like a fine wine that deserved to be savored. Just when Katherine thought she couldn't stand any more anticipation, Michael slipped his tongue inside her mouth. Katherine sighed as though she had never experienced such intimate pleasure. She responded in kind, allowing their tongues to meet and explore.

Michael's hands deftly reached underneath her sweater, finding her breast and tugging at her nipple gently with his fingertips. He pulled his hand out of her sweater and carefully pulled it over her head. He yanked his sweatshirt off and placed his strong, muscular arms on either side of her half-naked body. He slowly brought his bare chest down and rubbed it gently over her breasts, as he looked deep into her eyes.

"Oh, Michael," Katherine murmured.

"It feels so good to finally be close to you," Michael whispered gently into her ear.

He brought his head down on her chest, his tongue gently licking the dark, hard point of her breast. Katherine smiled as she closed her eyes and ran her fingers through his thick, curly black hair. He leaned over her, caressing her steadily with his experienced mouth and hands.

"Michael," she said, forcing herself to break away. "I'm not sure we should sleep together ..."

"Just close your eyes," he said tenderly. "And trust

me. We're not going to have sex. But I have every intention of making love to you."

Michael gently kissed her hand as though he was a gentleman from the royal court. As the fire burned and crackled, Michael held her in his arms, occasionally caressing her cheeks and hair, as though he had all the time in the world to admire her beauty. Katherine continued to stare into his eyes, hypnotized by the intense desire that had taken over her body.

When the need to feel his lips on hers was too much to bear, Katherine reached out and hungrily pulled him to her. She kissed him as she had never kissed before, as though the months of frustrated, unrequited longing had pushed her past the curtain of uninhibited passion. Michael responded in kind and, with his mouth still on hers, began a slow exploration of her body, beginning with her ears, and covering the territory with soft butterfly kisses.

Katherine began to breathe a little more quickly as Michael approached her bare stomach. As his tongue explored her belly button, he deftly slipped off her pants. She moaned softly as Michael nestled his head between her legs, his tongue exploring every crevice. Her body began to move instinctively, responding to his touch.

Moments later, she lay with her eyes tightly closed, only vaguely aware of the world around her. She felt a dampness on her cheek and realized that the vulnerability and intensity of the emotion she felt had caused uninhibited tears to flow.

Michael sat up and pulled her into his arms, embracing her tightly.

"Don't cry, love," he said, kissing her softly on her forehead and running his fingers through her soft brown hair.

Katherine could feel herself slowly turning back in to reality. She felt a brutal sting of embarrassment.

She realized that the man who now held her in his arms had seen her in her most vulnerable state.

She turned to face him, staring into his deep blue eyes. But this wasn't any man, she reminded herself. This was her ... this was Michael.

"What are you thinking about?" he asked quietly. Katherine turned away and looked into the fire. She was hit with the sudden reality of her love for him.

"Just hold me," Katherine said, looking up at him.

20

Katherine awoke slowly. She was lying on the cushions from the couch that had been placed on the floor. She realized she was naked under the blankets loosely thrown over her. She pulled the covers over her head as the memory of the night before came flooding back. How in the world could she possibly face Michael this morning?

"Good morning," said a deep, cheery voice. She pulled the covers down just enough to reveal her eyes.

"Ready for breakfast?" Michael asked, setting down a tray with some bread and juice on the coffee table. He sat on the edge of the couch, next to Katherine. "How's that bump of yours?" he asked, leaning over her as he studied her forehead.

Katherine pulled a hand out from underneath the covers and felt for the bump. It had gone down significantly from the previous night.

"It's almost gone," Michael said, confirming her

opinion. He smiled at her. "How are you feeling? All right?"

Katherine stared at him curiously. He was obviously a morning person. She'd never seen him so enthusiastic before.

She pulled down the covers to reveal her mouth. "Fine," she squeaked.

"Just fine?" he asked quietly. He flashed her a sexy grin. Katherine managed a nod.

"Good?" she asked. Perhaps he'd like that more.

And he did. "Good is better than fine. Definitely." He paused, aware that she was feeling uncomfortable. He didn't want her to feel embarrassed. He wanted her to feel happy. As happy as he was feeling. "It's a beautiful day outside," he said, glancing toward the window. "A real winter wonderland." He stood up and opened the curtains.

Katherine was suddenly aware that she hadn't brushed her hair or her teeth in longer than she cared to remember. She ran her fingers through her tousled hair.

"I think there's a toboggan in the shed," he said, still looking out the window. "I thought after breakfast we could go sledding. There's a great hill out back."

"Excuse me for a minute," Katherine said as she awkwardly stood up, careful to hide her nakedness by wrapping a blanket around her. She wanted to take a shower and put on some clothes.

"Sure," he said, looking at her and smiling warmly. "We still have hot water, and I put some towels out for you if you want to take a shower. I also found some additional clothes in a dresser upstairs. I set some out that I thought might fit you. They're by the sink in the bathroom."

Katherine smiled and mumbled thanks as she clumsily half walked, half tripped to the door.

"Wait a minute," Michael said, grabbing her boots

and handing them to her. "There's still glass out there from the window. I cleaned it up as well as I could, but I don't think you should be walking around in bare feet."

"Thanks," Katherine said, slipping the boots on. She was glad there was not a mirror in the room. What an awkward sight she must be, wearing only a blanket and boots. She opened the door.

"It's also freezing out there," he added, grabbing another blanket and looping it around her shoulders.

Katherine laughed. "Thanks," she said, trying not to look at him. She wasn't quite sure if they were supposed to kiss and talk about how wonderful the previous evening had been, or if they were supposed to apologize and talk about what a big mistake they had made.

"Let me help you around the glass," he said, taking her hand.

"I'm fine," Katherine said. "It's not going to go through my boots."

"Follow me," he said, ignoring her plea for independence. He led her around the glass in the foyer. "You know where you're going from here?" he asked.

Katherine nodded. He watched her walk down the hall, staring after her happily. He hadn't felt this carefree for years. He woke up this morning feeling a genuine childlike enthusiasm for the day ahead.

As soon as he could, he had to take care of things with Carly. He hadn't been fair to her or to himself. He needed to end their relationship. There really wasn't much to end, he reminded himself. They had never really been a couple. But in the past month, Carly had changed. She had started calling him more often, trying to arrange a way to see him. It was odd behavior for Carly. Usually, she asked him for nothing. One of the things he had found attractive about her was the fact that she was extremely independent.

But in the past month, she had begun to pressure him for a commitment.

The night after she showed up in his office to complain about Katherine, she had dropped by his house with a bottle of champagne. She said she had a "business" proposal for him. She said she knew he didn't love her now, but she didn't care. If he married her, he would find her to be an asset to his political and professional career. She offered to campaign for him and entertain for him. She told him that love would develop once they were married. In the meantime, she was willing to make allowances with him that, she had told him, no other wife would. For instance, she would allow him to be with other women if he promised to be discreet.

Michael had to admit that if he hadn't already met Katherine, he might have found Carly's offer appealing, if only for its sheer audacity. After all, he had long ago given up the notion that true love existed. He firmly believed there were only two kinds of romance: like and lust. He knew that he did care about Carly. Carly was a beautiful woman who was as tough and smart as anyone he had ever met. She was willing to put up a hell of a fight to get what she wanted. And he admired that. He had seen the difficulties she had faced being a single woman in a tough, male-dominated field. But admiration was not love.

His eyes wandered through the door that Katherine had just walked out of. He felt this woman was different from anyone he had ever met before. Last night, he had felt so at peace with her. It was as though he had finally found the woman he had always hoped existed but had long ago given up trying to find.

He stood up and walked toward the window. A cold, light wind blew over the top of the snow, causing it to swirl gently and fall. He found himself hoping that ice would form, making it more difficult for anyone to dig them out.

Katherine opened the door and slowly entered the room, trying to avoid looking at Michael. Although she felt much better after showering and putting on clean clothes, she was still embarrassed. She sat down on the couch and hungrily yet daintily pulled off a small hunk of bread.

"It's freezing out there," she said. Michael smiled.

"I know. I put a piece of fiberglass in the window where the branch broke it, but I'm afraid in these temperatures it doesn't do much good."

Katherine stared at the fire. "Do you think someone will come for us soon?" she asked.

Michael sat down next to her and looked at her intensely.

"Is that what you want?" he asked softly.

Katherine could feel his gaze melt the icy frost of professionalism she had tried to muster. She looked back toward him helplessly.

"What do you say we bundle up and head outside? Those hills haven't experienced a good sledding in quite a while," he said, his eyes twinkling.

Katherine smiled. She found his little-boy manner completely irresistible. "Why not!" she said enthusiastically.

Michael grabbed her hand and helped her up. They put on some extra sweaters, and after Katherine had again piled on enough layers to make her feel like the Pillsbury doughboy, they headed outdoors. Katherine inhaled at the sight of the white splendor before her. The snow had coated the mountains and the rolling hills with a fluffy, soft-looking powder, leaving the air crisp and clean. She followed Michael to the shed, being careful to step into his footprints. She patiently waited outside as she heard Michael clanging around inside searching for the toboggan. He came out of the darkness a few seconds later carrying an old-fashioned cushioned sled built for two.

"I don't think it's had much use lately," he said, blowing a layer of dust off it. He winked before picking up the sled and hoisting it over his head. He furrowed through the snow, hooting and hollering. Katherine giggled and jumped after him. Michael abruptly stopped at the top of a steep hill and set down the sled. Katherine caught up with him and anxiously stared down.

"I think it might be too steep," she said, somewhat unsure.

"No way," Michael said enthusiastically. "It'll be great. Hop on!"

Katherine sat down behind him, holding him close for protection. She felt excited not only by the danger of the moment but by their close physical proximity as well.

He wrapped Katherine's legs around him and pushed off. The sled picked up steam as it quickly slid through the snow. Katherine yelled as the sled hit a bump, sending her flying up into the air.

The snow broke her fall, and she rolled down the hill a few yards before coming to a stop.

"Katherine," Michael yelled. He was over to her in seconds. "Are you all right?"

Katherine's face lit up in a Cheshire-cat grin. "What a blast!" she said. "Let's try it again!"

Michael laughed as he lifted her out of the snow and into his arms. She wrapped her arms around him and planted her lips on his.

She realized he was carrying her away from the sled and back toward the house. "It's kind of cold out here," he said, his breath leaving a white cloud of smoke in the air. "What do you say we go back inside and warm up?" Katherine hopped out of his arms and onto the snow. Scooping up a ball of the white powder, she swung it at him playfully, barely missing him.

"Whatever you say," she said laughingly before taking off in a run, leaving a momentarily stunned Michael behind. He grinned and dashed off toward her.

Katherine yelled with pleasure as she ran to the house with Michael close behind. She opened the door and ran giggling inside, covered with snow. Carly Wentworth stood in front of her, glaring at her angrily.

21

Katherine's laughter stopped abruptly.

Kevin leaned casually against the wall behind Carly, providing her with silent reinforcement.

Michael bounded in.

"Hello, darling," Carly said icily to Michael. Carly looked cool and elegant, her slender shoulders wrapped inside a white fur coat. Her attractive face was delicately framed by a white fur cap that matched her coat. Her slim hands, fitted snugly inside a pair of expensive-looking white leather gloves, were clutching a small white bag in front of her. Kevin, in stark contrast to Carly, looked as though he had just rolled out of bed.

"Look who's here," Kevin said, motioning to Carly. He winked at Michael and smiled mischievously.

"What a . . . surprise," Michael said cautiously, pausing in the doorway.

"Yes, I can see that," Carly said, staring at Katherine. Katherine looked helplessly back at Carly, stunned by the wave of guilt that engulfed her. She quietly begged herself to try and maintain her sense of dignity. Why should she feel ashamed? After all, Michael had told her weeks ago that he and Carly were just friends.

Michael calmly pulled off his scarf as he walked toward Carly and gave her a quick kiss on the cheek.

"When did you get in?" he asked. "And how? I would have thought the airport was snowed in."

"I actually got in before the snow, last night. I had cocktails with my father before heading out to your hotel. When I got there, I was told I had just missed you. Kevin came in shortly after and said that you were stranded. I was frantic with worry that something might have happened to you ... and Katherine," she said, visually shooting Katherine with daggers as she mentioned her name. "I wouldn't want you both to freeze to death."

"Thanks for coming for us," Michael said. "We were beginning to wonder if we'd ever get out of here, isn't that right, Katherine?" He looked at Katherine casually, without revealing a flicker of their new-found intimacy.

Katherine surprised herself by managing a nod. Kevin looked at her and smiled. He was obviously thoroughly enjoying the situation. He glanced at her forehead. "How's that concussion?" he asked.

"Concussion?" Carly asked.

"It was nothing. A small bump. I feel fine," Katherine said.

"What a relief," Carly said without feeling. "And what about you, Michael? Were you injured?"

"Me? No, I'm fine."

"Yes," Carly said, brushing some snow off his back. "It certainly looks like you made out all right."

"I guess so," Michael said, pretending not to catch

her loaded meaning. "Considering we didn't have any heat or real food. Speaking of which, I'm starving. Let's get out of here and get something to eat," Michael said, stepping over the glass.

"Oh, by the way cuz," Kevin said, raising an eyebrow cockily. "I ran into Toby Nat and your dad last night. Seems you forgot you had a meeting with them or something. But I covered for you. I explained that we had been in an accident. Your dad and I were pretty concerned about you guys being stranded on the road like that. But the troopers told us my car must've started after I left, since it wasn't there anymore. Your dad and I figured that you and Katherine had gone up to the house by yourselves."

"Thanks, Kevin," Michael managed. He held his hand out to Carly. "Carly," he offered, "I'll help you around the glass."

"Funny thing, that car not starting when I was there," Kevin continued. "Oh, well," he said, shrugging his shoulders as he stared coldly at Michael. "As long as you're both okay."

"Katherine doesn't look like she's okay to me," Carly said, glaring at Katherine suspiciously.

"I'm fine," Katherine said quickly.

"On the contrary. You look like you've been through quite a shock. Last night was probably too much for you." Carly sighed dramatically as she glanced back at Michael. "I'm just happy that you're both in one piece," she said.

Katherine stared down at the floor, overcome by a sudden humiliation. Friends or no friends, Michael was certainly acting like the guilty boyfriend.

"Katherine," Michael said, extending his hand to Katherine to help her around the glass.

But Kevin was too quick. "Allow me," he said, taking Katherine's arm.

"I can manage," Katherine said, shrugging off his arm. "I have to change first. I'll be out in a minute."

"Change?" Carly asked.

"We'll wait outside," Michael said as he gave Carly's arm a little tug. "Kevin," he said, motioning for Kevin to follow him.

Katherine glared at Michael before turning back toward the living room. How romantic, she thought wryly. And how embarrassing. Katherine pulled off her snowy clothes and laid them in front of the fireplace. She quickly put her own clothes back on and headed back outside.

"Katherine, you and Kevin can drive back together in Kevin's Jeep. I'll take Carly back," Michael said as soon as Katherine appeared in the doorway. He helped Carly into the passenger side of the Ford Explorer.

Kevin smiled at Katherine. He felt his cousin had just given him a little gift. Obviously, he wasn't that enamored with Katherine. Otherwise, wouldn't he insist on driving her back?

"Whatever you say," Kevin said sarcastically.

"Get in," Michael said, holding the car door open. "I'll drive you both to your car."

Kevin climbed in the back, closely followed by Katherine.

Katherine rolled down her window for some fresh air. She felt sick about the cool way in which Michael had dismissed her. He was acting as though nothing more personal than a civilized "good night" had passed between them.

"Wells," Michael said professionally, looking at her in the rearview mirror as he backed up the Jeep. "When we get back to the hotel, I want you to outline some of the points I mentioned to you last night. It doesn't need to be a formal memo, just jot them down so we can discuss them in more detail back at the office."

Katherine got his message, loud and clear. To the world, she was still just his employee.

Carly looked at him with relief. "You discussed business . . . last night?"

Michael looked at her quizzically. "What do you think we did?"

Carly glanced back at Katherine with a hint of a smile. Katherine felt as though a knife had pierced her heart. Obviously, Michael intended everything to return to "normal."

Kevin slid over and put his arm around Katherine.

"Boy, was I worried about you," he said, giving her a little hug. Katherine turned away, trying to hide her disgust. Michael silently continued to maneuver the car, either unaware or not caring that his cousin was putting the moves on Katherine.

"I thought we could go out for a quiet dinner tonight, to celebrate your rescue," Kevin said.

"Maybe" she answered faintly.

Michael slammed on the brakes, causing the vehicle to slide to a stop next to Kevin's car. "There's your car," he said gruffly to Kevin. "Now, be careful. It's still a little icy. I'll follow you back to the hotel," he said, pulling Kevin's keys out of his pocket and throwing them to him.

"That's not necessary," Kevin said, opening his door.

"I want to make sure you get back safely," Michael said, glancing at Katherine. She was standing outside Kevin's car, waiting for him to unlock the doors.

"Why, cuz," Kevin said, flashing him a suspicious smile. "I didn't know you cared." He slammed the car door.

22

Katherine stood in the shower, the hot water force-fully beating upon her back. She scrubbed her body ferociously, almost as if she was trying to wipe away Michael's invisible fingerprints. She was frustrated and angry that she had naively allowed herself to be seduced by Michael. She had risked her dream job for an infatuation that would force her either to resign or be fired. She wasn't sure she could look Michael in the eye ever again without being reminded of the passion he had aroused in her.

She knew there was more to her dismay than just the issue of what last night may or may not have meant to Michael. After the way he had behaved this morning with Carly, she didn't think she could ever allow herself to be in a situation where she would have to respect him. It was obvious that he hadn't been honest with her about his true relationship with Carly. But that wasn't the only thing that had annoyed her. It was how he had acted when Carly and Kevin had walked in on them. He had been deceitful and dishonest. Carly was every bit as much of a victim as she was. Michael had used Katherine for his own enjoyment and lied to Carly for his own benefit. He was nothing more than a self-centered, cold-hearted, egotist.

She stepped out of the shower and dried off. But what exactly had he done so wrong? True, she thought, he hadn't proclaimed to everyone that they had spent the night in each other's arms, but was it really the time or place for a proclamation like that? It had been awkward for everyone involved. Perhaps, she thought, it was too soon to make a judgment call on Michael.

Katherine wrapped a white, fluffy hotel bathrobe around her. She looked at herself in the mirror. She looked tired. Tired and confused.

She was interrupted by a knock at the door. She looked at the clock next to the bed. She had told Kevin she would grab some lunch with him downstairs, but she wasn't due to meet him for another half hour.

"Just a minute," she said, walking toward the door. She had to pull herself together. No one must know what had happened between her and Michael last night. If she was to appear upset or bothered, she would only give herself away. She didn't want anyone thinking that she was just another one of his conquests.

She opened the door to find a nervous-looking Michael on the other side.

"Can I come in?" he asked sheepishly.

"I'm not dressed," Katherine said in a loud whisper as she tried to shut the door. Michael blocked it and held it open.

"Katherine," he pleaded softly.

Katherine walked away from the door, allowing Michael to enter. He shut the door and walked over to the window, looking out at the snowcapped mountain. Katherine clutched her bathrobe tightly to her chest, keenly aware of her nakedness underneath.

"I, uh, felt bad about the way things turned out. I just want you to know that . . . well, last night was not just another night for me. Neither was this morning, but it probably wasn't wise, either, you know?" He glanced at Katherine as he stumbled over his words.

"I understand," Katherine said coldly. "We work together. We have a professional relationship. That's all."

Michael took a few steps toward her but hesitated as Katherine backed away.

"I've wanted you ever since I first saw you that night at the Tavern. It's just that, well, we work closely together, and . . ."

"And you want us to stay friends, right?" Katherine said quietly.

"I need time to think, Katherine. This is a complicated situation. I want to do what's best for both of us. I'm just asking you to give me some time."

"Your reputation precedes you, Michael, giving a hollow tone to your words," she said dramatically.

Michael looked at her, helplessly caught in a web he had spun. He walked toward the door.

"It was just a game for you, wasn't it?" she asked, tearfully biting her lower lip.

Michael's hand was on the doorknob. He glanced back at her. "No. No, it wasn't."

Katherine glanced away. Michael walked out, closing the door behind him.

Katherine sat resignedly on the bed. She promised herself that the survival strengths that had helped her through so much pain in the past would soon kick into gear, taking control. Not only would she survive this humiliation, she would recover as a better person because of it.

Over the weekend, she would decide whether she would stay at the Benson Corporation or look for another job. She wouldn't think about that today. Her goal for today was to get through it.

Kevin was waiting patiently in the restaurant of the hotel. His eyes lit up with pleasure when he spotted Katherine stepping off the elevator.

"This is for you," he said somewhat bashfully as she got closer. He handed her a single white rose. "The other eleven will be delivered when I pick you up for dinner. It's my way of inducing you to join me this evening."

"Thanks for the rose," she replied sweetly, gracefully accepting the flower. She purposefully avoided responding to his invitation.

"Listen, Katherine," he mumbled. "Whatever happened between you and my cousin ... I just hope you don't feel bad about whatever happened ..."

"What are you talking about?" Katherine asked, embarrassed.

"Let's just say I know my cousin," he said. "Trapped with a beautiful woman, alone in the mountains ..."

"You may know your cousin, but you obviously don't know me," she responded quickly with a cool smile.

"Then there's nothing going on between you?" Kevin asked with relief.

"Don't be ridiculous," she said, smiling reassuringly. She wasn't lying, she thought silently, there was nothing going on any longer. "Michael is my boss. That's all there is between us and all there ever will be," she said, looking down at the lunch menu. "Now, what's good here?"

Katherine ate ravenously. She hadn't had anything substantial to eat in almost twenty-four hours. When she finished her meal, she felt satisfied and sleepy.

"Allow me," Kevin said, reaching for the check.

"No. I''m buying," Katherine said.

Kevin smiled. "I'll accept only if you let me buy you dinner tonight," he said. Katherine hesitated. She was feeling tired ... but she had all afternoon to sleep, she reasoned. And she didn't want to give herself too much time alone to focus on Michael.

"It would be my pleasure," she replied. Kevin grinned with satisfaction.

After the waiter had taken the check, Kevin graciously pulled Katherine's chair out for her and walked her to the elevator. Katherine was dismayed to see Michael waiting for it as well.

"Hey, cuz," Kevin said.

Katherine mustered up a strained hello.

Michael looked at them suspiciously. He couldn't help but notice the rose Katherine was carrying.

"What time are you going to the lodge?" Kevin asked, checking his watch.

"I'm not," Michael said.

"Carly told me that she made reservations for you both . . ." Kevin began.

"Something's come up," Michael said, interrupting Kevin as he looked directly at Katherine. "I'm returning to Baltimore immediately."

"Too bad," Kevin said. "There's a big party tonight at Jason's downtown. Katherine and I are planning on being there. If you were going to be around, I'd ask you to come with us," he added facetiously.

Michael shot Katherine a nasty look. She certainly wasn't having any problem moving on with her life.

Katherine glanced at Kevin. She had said yes to a dinner, but she hadn't agreed to go to a party. More importantly, she wondered, why was Michael canceling his weekend plans? Did last night have an effect on him after all?

"Is anything wrong? Did everything go all right with Toby?" she asked Michael cautiously.

"Toby heard about the accident last night. He was fine. After all, accidents happen," he said icily. The elevator doors opened, and Michael stepped inside. Katherine realized she would have to follow him.

"I'll see you at eight," Kevin said, giving her a quick peck on the cheek.

"Coming?" Michael growled impatiently.

Katherine hesitantly stepped inside. As the doors closed, she and Michael stood stiffly side by side, watching the light at the top of the elevator change floor numbers. Katherine swallowed.

"If you need me to work this weekend, I can change my plans and come back," she said.

"It's not necessary," Michael said in an unmistakable business tone. "Stay here and enjoy yourself," he added with some difficulty as the elevator doors opened on Katherine's floor. Katherine avoided his eyes as she left the elevator.

"See you next week," she said, stepping out quickly. Her voice was met with silence.

Katherine opened the door to her room. In the future, she would make a heroic effort to avoid being in situations where she was forced to be alone with him. From now on, she would take the stairs.

She flung herself on her bed and nestled her head into the down pillows.

Michael rode the elevator in silence, his mind wrestling with the thought of Katherine becoming involved with Kevin. He wondered if her relationship with Kevin was merely a ploy to make him envious and force him into taking action. Or perhaps he had been mistaken about Katherine's innocence and her feelings for him. Maybe he had been overly concerned about hurting her.

The elevator door opened just as the possibility dawned on Michael that perhaps, just perhaps, he, Michael Benson, was feeling jealous.

Damn her. She was definitely complicating his life. He preferred to keep his affairs simple and nonexclusive. Which is part of the reason why he had never been involved with woman who worked at Benson.

He couldn't help frowning as he opened the door.

Katherine was a forbidden love. He had broken his rule about dating employees, and now he was doomed to his own private hell. He silently cursed fate for bringing them together that first night. Who knows? If they hadn't met that night, perhaps he never would have viewed her as a . . . woman.

It seemed all of history was against them. Office affairs were known for being disastrous.

And he could see why. Temptation was at every corner, every working moment. He had already allowed himself to miss an important meeting last night simply to be with Katherine. His father had done his best to fill in for him, but the damage was unavoidable. He had little doubt that Toby Nat was aware that, accident or no accident, he had been stood up for a much more attractive dinner date. But the whole mess was his own fault. He realized from the moment he had announced that he was joining Katherine and Kevin that he was making a mistake. Toby was looking for reasons to distrust Michael. And standing him up hadn't helped any.

Michael walked toward his room, his lips pursed together in thought. He had never been like this before. He had always put business before pleasure, no matter how desirable the woman. But he seemed to lose all control with Katherine. It was obvious that he simply couldn't trust himself with her anymore. His desire was too strong. Better to return to Baltimore, where he could lock himself away for a while within the security of his office walls. Where he could think. He just needed some time to think.

Yes, he thought, it made sense that he should leave immediately.

But, he realized, slipping his key card through the lock on his door, that didn't mean he would.

23

Katherine walked into the lobby. She was hoping, as usual, that she wouldn't run into anyone she knew. She didn't want anyone from work to see her dressed the way she was. Her heavy winter coat hung loosely over her bathing suit. Her bare legs were partially covered by her snow boots.

Katherine paused and looked around the room inquisitively. The front desk had told her that one of the doors to the outside led to a Jacuzzi that nestled into the side of the mountain. The same Jacuzzi she had admired in the brochure.

Katherine opened the back door of the hotel and was welcomed by a cold blast of air. She couldn't help but shiver under her coat and wonder if perhaps this wasn't such a good idea after all.

Her apprehension dissolved when she spotted the Jacuzzi. The vision of warm, churning water at the base of a snowy mountain was irresistible. The heat from the water created so much steam it was nearly impossible to tell if there was anyone inside.

An outdoor bar was staffed with a waiter and a bartender, both wearing parkas over their uniforms. Katherine smiled. This was definitely luxury at its best.

As she got closer, the bartender and waiter stopped their banter to smile appreciatively at her. She nodded in their direction as she hesitantly surveyed the situation.

"Can I take your coat?" the waiter asked, stepping toward her. Katherine looked at him. She was suddenly having second thoughts about peeling off her protective layers.

"I'll hang it right over here," he said, pointing to the bar. "I'll bring you a towel and your coat as soon as you want to get out of the water," he said reassuringly.

Katherine peered into the thick mist in front of her.

"The water's great," the waiter added in an encouraging manner. Reassured, Katherine flashed him a grin as she bravely took off her coat and handed it to him. She wrapped her arms around herself in a weak attempt to cover her sleek bright blue swimsuit. She stepped into the warm water and smiled with pleasure.

"See?" the waiter said. "Now, what can I bring you to drink?" he asked flirtatiously. Embarrassed by his attention, Katherine sank her scantily clothed body deeper in the water so that only her head was above.

"White wine?" she said, pointing her toes and touching them together under water.

"I have a nice Chardonnay," he said.

"That sounds great. Thanks," she replied. The waiter disappeared into the fog. Katherine looked around her. She could hear the voices of an older couple who must have been not even ten feet away from her. The smoky vapor made it impossible to see their faces. She was tempted to move around in the pool, but she was afraid she might bump into someone.

The waiter returned with her drink. Katherine realized with embarrassment that she had no way of paying him.

"I'm sorry," she said. "My purse is in my room . . ."

"Don't worry," he said, holding the drink out in front of her. "We usually just bill it to your room."

"Usually?" she asked curiously.

"That's right," said the waiter, standing back up. "This drink was bought for you by the gentleman across from you."

Katherine turned toward the mist. A hazy figure was making his way over to her. Michael's tall, muscular, bare form took shape before her.

"Michael!" she said with surprise bordering on dismay. She sat up straight. The swimsuit clung to her firm wet breasts as though it was a second skin.

"Hello, Wells," he said, boldly taking a seat on the ledge next to her.

"I didn't see you there."

"I figured if you did, you probably wouldn't have come into the water." He stared at her as though he was removing her bathing suit with his eyes.

"I thought you were leaving . . . to go back to Baltimore," she said quickly, sipping her drink.

"I was. I changed my mind."

"What changed it?" she asked softly.

Michael looked straight ahead. "Not what, Katherine, but who. You changed it," he said, his professional manner completely slipping away.

She hesitated before responding. "Don't . . ." she pleaded emotionally. She paused and said abruptly, "I think you were right about what you said in my room. We need to put the past behind us and move forward."

"You're putting words in my mouth," he said, turning to face her. "I just said I needed time to think."

Katherine set her wine down on the cement patio surrounding the Jacuzzi. "I don't think an afternoon is quite enough time, do you?" she asked quickly. She signaled to the waiter to bring over a towel and began to lift herself out of the water. She wasn't about to be caught up in a romantic triangle with her boss and his girlfriend. He could find someone else to seek his thrills with.

"Katherine, listen to me," Michael pleaded.

"What?" she asked angrily.

"I want to explain. Carly and I . . . well, we have a kind of unique friendship. We have for years. I'm not in love with her. I never will be. But I know how she feels about me, and I know how vicious she can be toward someone she considers her rival. And I didn't want her broadcasting our relationship before it even began."

"I see. What you're trying to tell me is that you acted like a jerk this morning because you were being so protective toward me," she said sarcastically.

Their heated exchange was apologetically interrupted by the waiter.

"Did you want your towel?" he asked Katherine.

"Set it over there," Michael ordered, pointing to a chair nearby.

As the waiter walked away, Katherine sighed hopelessly, locking eyes with Michael. "What does it matter, anyway?" she asked quietly. "Even if what you say about Carly is true. We work together. The situation is futile."

"It's also irreversible."

Katherine turned away, rejecting his analysis. Michael grabbed her and roughly yanked her to him, drowning her intellect with a powerful kiss.

Katherine pulled away. "It's no use!" she said, lifting herself out of the water. "Do you understand me? I work for you. That's all there is and all there will ever be between us." She picked up her coat and threw it over her wet body. "Don't you see?" she asked him quietly. "Even if I didn't work for you, it would never work. We're from two different worlds," she said softly. "I'll never be a Carly Wentworth." *And I hope I never will be,* she felt like adding.

She picked up her boots. Not even bothering to put them on, she turned and ran through the snow in her bare feet toward the safety of the hotel. Michael easily lifted himself out of the water. The only reason he had let her go was that he wanted to continue this conversation in the privacy of her hotel room.

Minutes later, he was standing at the front desk in jeans and a flannel shirt that he hadn't even bothered to button.

"Excuse me," he said to the clerk. "I can't believe this, but I accidentally locked myself out of my room. Would you mind giving me another key?" he asked with a wet grin. The clerk recognized Michael immediately.

"Certainly, Mr. Benson," he said. "And you're in room . . . ?"

"Four-ten East," Michael said quickly. The clerk pulled out the key and gave it to Michael.

"There you go, sir," he said. Funny, he thought to himself as he watched Michael walk away. He could have sworn that Michael Benson was staying in the west wing. He shrugged his shoulders and went back to work.

Michael walked resolutely toward Katherine's room. He was a man obsessed. He wouldn't be able to focus on anything until he had a chance to talk to her.

He listened at her door. Silence. He opened the door quietly and heard the faint sound of running water. He entered the room, quickly realizing that she was taking a shower. He drew the heavy drapes closed and stood by the bed, calmly waiting for her.

Katherine turned off the shower and wrapped an oversized towel around her slender form. She picked her swimsuit up off the floor and stepped out of the bathroom.

Her eyes opened wide in terror as she stepped into the darkened room only to see a man's figure in the shadows. Michael stepped into the light.

"What are you doing?" Katherine asked, stunned

to realize that the man was Michael. She grasped the towel covering her body.

"I wasn't finished," he stated.

Katherine hesitated, as the immediate shock of finding Michael in her room began to wear off. "How dare you barge in here ..."

"I want you, Katherine. I want you to work with me, and I want to be with you. I want it all, and I think I've thought of a way to do it."

"I can't deal with this," Katherine said in a tired, worn-out voice.

"Can't or don't want to?" Michael asked, approaching her slowly.

Katherine shook her head. He stood in front of her. He put his hands around her face and gently lifted it toward him.

He leaned over and began softly kissing her long, delicate neck. His mouth moved toward her breast, and then away, as though he was teasing her intentionally.

Katherine found her body responding despite the protest resounding in her mind.

Michael put his hands on her shoulders. "I'm not going to force you to do anything," he said. "I'm tired of games." And he meant it. He was not turned on by feigned coyness. As much as he wanted her, he had no intention of seducing anyone who didn't want him.

Katherine turned back toward him. She could sense the change in him. He wanted her to take charge. But if she didn't, if she hesitated, he would leave her alone. It was up to her.

She didn't think twice. Taking the initiative, Katherine leaned forward and kissed him. That was all it took for Michael to respond. He wrapped his arms around her as Katherine nestled her head in his chest. Her whole body was alive with desire. He wanted her. No one and nothing else mattered.

Michael picked her up and carried her to the bed. Katherine wrapped her arms around his neck, kissing his cheeks and chin. Michael carefully laid her down on the bed. Katherine pushed herself up, so that she was kneeling with her legs open in front of him. She reached out and grabbed both sides of his shirt, pulling it off. Michael yanked the shirt off his wrists and leaned forward. Katherine smiled as he gently ran his fingers around the outline of her face.

"You're so beautiful," he said.

Still looking into his eyes, Katherine took his hand and massaged his index finger, slowly putting it in her mouth. She wrapped her tongue around it and bit down on it lightly. Michael pulled her in to him, softly kissing her face and neck.

"Tell me you want me," he whispered. She arched her back as she pulled his hand between her legs.

But he wanted her to do more than just show him. "Say it," he commanded softly.

She pulled back. She stared at him intently. She slowly leaned back on the bed, enjoying every second of the hold she had on him. He was in her power.

She opened the towel slowly, inviting him to come nearer.

Michael leaned over her as Katherine wrapped her arms around him.

"I want you."

Katherine blinked sleepily. She had been so comfortable in Michael's arms that she had fallen fast asleep. She cautiously glanced next to her, expecting to see Michael. Instead, there was a note lying on top of the empty pillow.

She leaned over and picked up the small piece of paper, resting her elbow on the linen, still warm from Michael.

"Katherine, I have some business I need to take

care of. Continue with your plans with Kevin as scheduled. I'll meet up with you at the party. I have a surprise for you. All my love—Michael."

Katherine studied the note quizzically before sitting up on the edge of the bed. Surprisingly enough, she didn't feel guilty or embarrassed by her intimacy with Michael. Instead, she was filled with a sense of peace and a calm inner joy.

She walked over to the closet and pulled out the sequined black dress she had borrowed from Cyndi. She had heard the party was going to be black tie, and she had every intention of looking ravishing for Michael.

24

The portly jeweler smiled knowingly at the dashing and familiar man before him.

"So," he said with a hint of a German accent. "You are finally going to give up your bachelorhood and become like the rest of us." He chuckled merrily, his hands on his round stomach.

Michael pulled back from the loupe he was using to study the diamond and smiled at the man.

"It is the largest that we have in stock," the jeweler said, shrugging his shoulders. "Of course, I could order you something larger if you like . . ."

"That won't be necessary," Michael interrupted. He was excited to show it to her. This was the first spontaneous thing he could remember doing, and he was really enjoying himself.

"It's a magnificent stone," the jeweler said, watching his expression. "Are you worried it's not big enough?" he asked, raising his eyebrows.

Michael reached for his wallet. "Will you take a check?"

The jeweler smiled with satisfaction.

"Of course, Mr. Benson," he said.

Kevin strolled lazily down the street, casually admiring the expensively dressed store windows. He glanced inside the jewelry store just in time to see Michael selecting a large, sparkling diamond engagement ring. Kevin grinned as he opened the door and stepped in from the cold.

"A little trinket for your lady?" he asked mischievously.

"Kevin!" Michael exclaimed. "How are you this fine afternoon?"

"You're certainly cheery," Kevin said, eyeing the ring. Obviously, Michael had made up with Carly. "I thought you were leaving town," Kevin added as Michael wrote out the check to the jeweler. "What happened? Did you have a sudden change of heart?"

"You could say that," Michael responded, thanking the jeweler as he took the box and slipped it into his pocket.

"Look, Kevin," he said quietly, changing his tone. "This isn't exactly what it looks like, so I'd appreciate it if you didn't say anything."

"You got it! Say no more, cuz," Kevin said, holding up his hands in mock protest. He reached over and opened the door, grinning at Michael as he politely motioned for him to go first.

Michael raised an eyebrow at the younger man as he walked out. Kevin had always been a mischievous, rambunctious child, and he had matured very little. Michael didn't trust him to keep quiet, but he knew he had no choice in the matter. He had to get back to the hotel so he could talk to Carly before the party.

Out on the busy street, Michael successfully hailed a cab.

"Want a lift?" he asked Kevin, holding the cab door open.

"No thanks," Kevin responded. "I've got a few more errands to run. I'll see you tonight."

Michael nodded in acknowledgment as he slammed the door.

Kevin watched the cab pull away from the curb. So, he thought happily as the traffic swallowed the cab, Michael was getting engaged to Carly. Katherine was all his.

He thrust his hands into his pockets and began whistling as he sauntered confidently down the street.

He picked up his pace as he recognized a package-laden Carly at the corner.

"Kevin!" said Carly.

"Hey, how's it going?" Kevin asked, not believing his good fortune. "Need some help?"

"Thanks," she said gratefully, handing him a few packages.

"Been doing a little shopping, I see," Kevin said. "Special occasion, perhaps?"

"Not really. Michael said he wanted to take me out to dinner tonight. I assume we'll be going to Jason's for the party later on, and all I brought were casual clothes. I had to rush out and get something appropriate to wear out in this town."

"Of course," Kevin said, smiling broadly.

Carly looked at him suspiciously. "What are you smiling like that for?"

"Oh, no reason," he said with fake innocence.

Carly stopped walking. "What do you know?" she asked him suspiciously.

He shrugged his shoulders and laughed.

"Kevin, don't tease me. Is there something going on between Katherine and Michael?"

"I'm sure they're just friends . . . like us," he added teasingly.

She looked at him coldly. She and Kevin had a brief affair several years ago, but he had promised her he would never mention it again.

"You're a bastard, Kevin Benson!" she replied angrily. She quickly turned and walked away for effect, leaving Kevin with some of her packages. Kevin hurried to catch up with her.

"Relax, Carly," he said, catching up to her and whispering seductively in her ear. "What would you say if I told you Michael is planning on proposing to you tonight?" he asked quietly.

Carly whipped around to face him. "What?"

"I just saw him at the jeweler's. Will a diamond rock convince you?"

Carly looked at him with surprise. "Are you sure?" she asked, trying to hide her fear.

"I'm positive. As a matter of fact, I was with him when he bought it—no more than a few minutes ago."

Carly was barely aware of the superficial grin that crept over her lips. She knew the ring was not for her. Michael had been distant and standoffish. They hadn't slept together in months. Her suspicions were confirmed. He was having an affair with his little office tramp.

She had to stop it. He was Michael Benson, not a stupid, infatuated schoolboy. And she had spent years waiting for him, patiently waiting. She wouldn't allow anyone to breeze in and steal him. Especially now.

She had been encouraged when Michael had made dinner plans with her tonight. But now she realized he had probably planned to dump her so that he could be free to propose to Katherine. And here was Kevin, poor stupid slob, congratulating her. But then again, if he thought the ring was for her, perhaps others would, too. After all, many people did think they were an item. And she knew how to work the media to her advantage. She'd made a living from it.

She checked her watch. She would have to work fast.

"Oh, Kevin," she said, laughing gaily. "You're on to us. Michael asked me to marry him this morning, but I told him I needed to see the ring first. Otherwise, I couldn't possibly believe that he was finally ready to settle down. But please, don't say anything to anyone yet. Now, would you mind hailing me a cab?"

Kevin shot his arm up, stopping a cab almost immediately. He planted a brotherly kiss on Carly's cheek before opening the cab door. "I guess this just goes to show you, if you work hard enough at something, it's possible to succeed," he said, winking deviously. "See you at the party."

Carly flashed him a convincing smile before slamming the door, barely giving Kevin a chance to jump out of the way. She had no time to waste. After all, she was already eight weeks pregnant.

25

Michael scanned the room numbers on the wall. He followed the arrow in the direction of Carly's room, stopping to pause outside her door and straighten his tie. He knocked three times as he quickly cleared his throat. He planned to address the issue at hand immediately.

Carly opened the door and smiled at him warmly. She leaned into him, giving him a whisper of a kiss on the cheek. Carly's parents stood up to welcome him.

"Hello, Michael," Mrs. Wentworth said, echoed by her husband.

"Mrs. Wentworth, Mr. Wentworth," Michael said, attempting to mask his dismay at seeing them there.

"Look who came by for a surprise visit!" Carly exclaimed, clapping her hands together. "You don't mind if they join us this evening, do you?" she asked, reaching for her coat.

"Well . . ." Michael muttered.

"If you're worried about our dinner reservation, don't be. I already called and changed it."

Michael felt as though he had no choice but to smile agreeably as he held Carly's coat for her. He knew he had to get her alone before they went to Jason's that night. After all, he had promised Katherine a surprise.

Katherine awkwardly zipped up the back of her dress.

She carefully applied a bit of mascara to her long black lashes and a touch of pink lipstick to her already full, lush lips, still a bit swollen from Michael's passionate kisses. She easily wrapped her long hair into a chignon twist and fastened it loosely. She picked up the cultured pearl drop earrings that her mother had worn the day she married her father. Katherine put them on and stood away from the mirror to study her reflection.

She calmly smoothed her dress. She was ready. For what, however, she was not sure.

Kevin checked his watch before knocking on the door. He had made it here in record time. Only an hour ago, he was still in his jeans, pulling out of the Rolls Royce dealership. He had been in such a good mood after running into Carly that he had rented the finest and flashiest car he could think of. An extravagance, no doubt, but he was willing to dip into his trust fund if it meant he had a better chance of scoring with the lovely lady on the other side of the door. Now, with Michael safely out of the way, he felt he could begin his game plan for seduction. He looked down at the bouquet of eleven white roses he had brought with him. Giving eleven together and one separately was his special trademark. It never failed to impress.

Katherine opened the door. She smiled at the sight of the flowers. Kevin stepped back, admiring her clean beauty. Katherine emanated class. He knew that even his family, who had blatantly rejected his other girlfriends, would approve of this intelligent and lovely creature. Hadn't his mother already told him how gorgeous she thought Katherine was?

"I brought you some roses," he said with a smile.

"How sweet of you," she said, ushering him in. He handed her the flowers as Katherine scanned the room for a makeshift vase.

"Unfortunately, I don't think I have anything to put them in."

"We could order a vase from room service, along with a bottle of champagne and two glasses," Kevin offered. "My father has generously given me his room for the weekend, so I insist on billing it to my room, of course."

Katherine eyed the empty sink. The thought of sipping champagne with Michael's cousin in a room in which she had made love with Michael only hours earlier was distinctly unappealing.

"I've got a better idea," she said, gently setting the flowers in the sink and running cool water over the stems. "I'll just leave them in here for the night. I'm starving. I'd kind of like to get to dinner ... and then on to Jason's," she added casually.

"Yes, I'm looking forward to arriving there myself," Kevin said mischievously. "It's my understanding that it's going to be quite a big night for Michael," he added, assisting her with the flowers.

"Really," she responded coyly, her heart skipping a beat.

"Well, it's time a man like Michael thought about settling down. If you know what I mean," he added with a wink. Katherine looked at Kevin with amazement. Marriage? Was Michael planning on asking her to marry him tonight? Her eyes widened with excitement. Surely Kevin was mistaken.

"You mean ... ?"

"C'mon," Kevin said, drying off his hands. "Let's get out of here and go to dinner. I've said too much already. Besides, there'll be plenty of reason to celebrate later," he said, playfully pushing Katherine toward the door.

Katherine felt as though she was in a dream. A thick, hazy, wonderful dream. She fought to regain her composure. In this state, she'd never make it through dinner. She analyzed Michael's note in her head, looking for clues. Could he possibly want her to marry him? She glanced at Kevin out of the corner of her eye. It was obvious that something was up. Yet why would Michael confide in Kevin? The two weren't even close, to say the least.

Michael sat next to Carly. Carly's parents sat across from them, studying him as though he was a plant specimen in a biology class. He was aware of a throbbing energy in the air—almost as if the Wentworths were as excited and nervous as he was.

He quickly scanned the wine list for an appropriate bottle.

"Don't you think we should get champagne, darling?" she asked, flashing him a sugary smile.

Michael glanced at her. He was becoming increasingly irritated at having to postpone his conversation with her because of the presence of her parents.

"Sure, whatever you like," he said. He leaned toward her and lowered his voice. "Do you think I could talk to you . . . alone?"

Carly beamed at him. "Whatever you have to say to me you can say in front of my parents," she responded, a little too loudly.

"Can I bring anyone a drink?" the waiter asked, suddenly appearing at the table.

"A bottle of your finest champagne," Carly said authoritatively.

"Carly, I have to speak with you. It's rather important . . . and private," Michael said.

"Well, Michael," Carly said loudly, looking at him hopefully. "What is it?"

Michael looked away guiltily, aware of the fact that all eyes at the table were on him.

"Speak up, boy," Mr. Wentworth said gruffly.

"Daddy!" admonished Carly.

"That's okay," Michael said quietly, backing down. "It can wait."

"That's right, dear, take your time. Don't let us rush you," Mrs. Wentworth said sweetly.

Michael looked at her curiously. What in the world was going on?

26

The Rolls Royce pulled up in front of the popular nightclub. A small sign outside notified guests that the party was "invitation only."

A uniformed man ran over and opened Katherine's door, graciously assisting her out of the car. Kevin took hold of Katherine's arm as he pulled the invitation out of his pocket and showed it to the doorman.

Katherine stepped inside. Her eyes adjusted to the darkness as Kevin helped her out of her coat. She was aware that the woman managing the coat check was staring at Kevin.

"Hello, Kevin," the woman said in a rather low, husky voice. Kevin handed her the coat, peering at her closely as though a better look might help him remember her.

"Oh, hi," he replied, vaguely recalling a drunken evening several weeks ago. He struggled to recollect her name. He had a memory for bodies, not names. He glanced at the ample bosom bulging through the tight, low-cut black uniform. Her body he remembered well. She was the striking brunette he had picked up here a few weeks ago.

"I'm still waiting for that phone call you promised," the woman hissed as she eyed Katherine jealously. Kevin glanced at Katherine, hoping that his date was unaware of the interaction. Katherine looked over and met the woman's frosty stare with a friendly smile.

"I'm going to go walk around," Katherine said pleasantly. She felt as though she should make it clear to the woman that although Kevin was arriving with her, they were just friends. "Why don't you stay here and talk? You can catch up with me later." She looked toward the sea of people in the ballroom. She didn't want anyone thinking that she was Kevin's date—including Kevin. The expensive dinner, the roses, not to mention the Rolls Royce in the parking lot, led her to believe he had either grossly misinterpreted their relationship, or . . . perhaps Michael had asked him to do all of those things.

Katherine left Kevin standing uncomfortably at the coat check and entered the huge ballroom. The size of it alone was breathtaking. The ceiling was two stories high. Huge chandeliers shed a small amount of diffused light on the people below. Heavy maroon velvet curtains framed the mirrored walls, and gigantic palm trees were scattered throughout the room, giving it the atmosphere of a slightly garish, ostentatious boudoir.

Katherine scanned the room for Michael. She quickly noticed the handsome couple sipping cocktails a few feet in front of her. She recognized them as the stars of a recent movie she had seen.

Katherine felt someone loosely touching her arm. She turned around with excitement, expecting to see Michael.

"Here I am," Kevin said. "Sorry about that. Just an old friend . . ."

"Don't be ridiculous, Kevin. You certainly don't owe me an explanation."

Kevin smiled gratefully. "Want a drink?" he asked, his eye catching a glimpse of the bar on the opposite side of the room.

"That would be lovely," she said.

Kevin looped his arm around Katherine and steered her through the crowd. The place was becoming crowded with the rich and beautiful, already famous and those on their way. Katherine couldn't help but feel slightly out of place as she admired all the stunning women. Michael could have any one of these women, she thought to herself. She felt like a country bumpkin at the inaugural ball.

Katherine glanced back at Kevin. He was smiling in recognition as he nodded to the famous couple she had spotted moments ago. It was obvious that he felt at home in this high-society world. And why wouldn't he? He had grown up in it.

Kevin smiled and turned to face her when they reached the bar.

"Two Kir Royales?" he asked Katherine.

"What is it?" Katherine asked with a smile. She certainly didn't have to hide her naïveté around Kevin.

"Champagne with a touch of creme-de-cassis."

"Thanks, but I think I'll just have a glass of sparkling water with a twist of lime," she said, secretly keeping an eye out for Michael.

Michael held out his hand as he assisted Carly out of the car.

He led her by her arm and paused, purposely allowing her parents to enter before them.

"Let's talk," he whispered sternly.

"Certainly, darling," she said. "Just let me take my coat off first," she added, stepping into the warmth of the club. It was almost time.

"Carly? Carly Wentworth?" said a high-pitched voice behind them. Carly turned and squealed when she recognized the beautiful, statuesque woman with short brown hair.

"Lauren!" She and the woman gave each other a small peck on the cheek. "It's so splendid to see you again. Michael, you remember me talking about Lauren, don't you?" she lied. "We roomed together at the Brownsly School."

Michael frowned. His plans were foiled for the moment. "Nice to meet you, Lauren," he said, shaking her hand. "Now, Carly . . ."

"Michael? Michael Benson?" Lauren said with a touch of a Southern accent. She turned back toward Carly and smiled in admiration. "Carly, I heard you two were dating. You lucky girl."

Carly smiled. Soon Lauren would see just how lucky she was. "Michael, be a doll and pick us up some champagne," Carly ordered. "Wouldn't some champagne be lovely, Lauren?" Carly took Lauren's arm. "We'll wait for you right there, darling." Carly pointing toward a crowded space at the end of the room.

"No, Carly. We need to talk *now*."

"He's so silly. He really hates to be away from me," Carly said to Lauren, ignoring Michael.

Michael watched in dismay as Carly disappeared into the crowd. At least now he had a chance to find Katherine.

He made his way toward the bar, keeping an eye out for Katherine.

Katherine stood under a palm tree at the edge of the bar, politely listening to Kevin. She caught her breath as she noticed Michael approaching. Kevin stopped talking as his eyes followed Katherine's to Michael.

Michael felt a current of electricity rip down his spine. Katherine looked more beautiful than he could have imagined. Her stylish black dress left little of her eye-catching body to the imagination. He quickly fought the impulse to take her in his arms and whisk her away from this place.

"Having fun?" he asked as their eyes locked. Katherine began to breathe softly, her body torched by excitement.

"Yes," Katherine managed to say as she blushed and looked away. Michael glanced at Kevin. He hoped Kevin had kept quiet about the ring. He didn't want anyone spoiling Katherine's surprise.

Michael turned back toward the bar. The sooner he got back to Carly, the sooner he could return to Katherine, permanently.

"Three glasses of champagne," he said to the bartender. Katherine looked at him. Was he ordering champagne for the three of them?

"Any news yet, cuz?" Kevin said, approaching Michael and whispering into his ear.

Michael looked at him warily. "Give me a minute," he said, his eyes back on Katherine. Katherine looked at the two men curiously. It was obvious that something was going on.

The bartender handed Michael the three glasses of champagne. "I'll be back," Michael said, looking at Katherine apologetically. Katherine looked after him, hurt and confused that the drinks he had ordered were not for them. He certainly had not been very intimate with her. Obviously, she had been greatly mistaken about a proposal. At this rate, she would be lucky to get a dance.

Carly glanced nervously over Lauren's shoulder. A tall, striking woman with bright red hair had just entered the room. She was Georgia Sun, the well-known newspaper gossip. Local but with contacts all over the country. Carly caught her eye and gave her a little wave. Georgia smiled as she began to walk toward her.

Carly glanced around anxiously for Michael. She had to find him. In order for her to pull this off, the timing needed to be perfect.

"Darling, there you are!" Carly said, spotting Michael walking briskly toward her, awkwardly holding the champagne glasses. It was time for her event. She grabbed his arm and quickly gave Lauren her champagne. As she took one for herself, she leaned forward, giving him a well-timed kiss on the cheek as a society photographer snapped their picture.

"Michael Benson, you finally came to your senses!" Georgia said in her high-pitched, distinctive voice.

Michael looked at the woman. "Hello, Georgia. What are you talking about?"

"Don't be so bashful. It's all over town. Congratulations on your engagement, you two!"

Carly looked at Michael. She feigned a reaction that mixed confusion, surprise, and pleasure.

Michael turned ashen white.

"I know you bought her the largest ring in the store," Georgia continued. "You lucky girl," she said, giving Carly a wink.

Carly threw her arms around Michael. "Oh, Michael! So that's why you've been dying to get me alone all night. And I had to go invite my parents to dinner. You poor darling!"

"Hold on, Carly . . ." Michael said.

"You don't know yet?" Georgia said to Carly, not even hearing Michael. "Good Lord," she said, glancing at Michael. "I'm sorry! My tip said you had already proposed . . ." Georgia rambled.

"I'm so happy!" Carly squealed. "We just got engaged," she called out to Lauren. "We're getting married!" she yelled.

No. He had to stop this before it went too far.

But it was too late. Lauren had already informed the bandleader.

"Ladies and gentlemen," the bandleader said, speaking into the microphone. "We've got some great news. It appears that Michael Benson has just proposed marriage to Carly Wentworth. And Carly," he said, smiling at her in the crowd, "did you accept?"

Carly smiled and nodded back to him, toasting him with her champagne.

"Let's have a hand for Carly Wentworth and Michael Benson! Or, rather, the future Mr. and Mrs. Michael Benson."

Katherine felt as though the world had suddenly exploded before her eyes.

"I ran into him at the jeweler's this afternoon," Kevin said, smiling. "I was the first person he told that he was going to ask Carly to marry him. You should see the diamond he bought her!"

This afternoon? He must have rolled out of bed with her and, racked with guilt, headed directly to the jeweler to buy a ring for Carly. The surprise he had intended for her was more cruel than she could ever have imagined.

"Apparently, he proposed to her this morning, and she told him she needed a ring before she would believe him."

"Kevin," she managed to whisper. "I'd like to leave now."

27

Katherine. Sweet Katherine had heard the announcement. He had to find her.

"Is there a ring?" he heard Lauren twang in his ear.

"Shhh. He hasn't had a chance to give it to me yet, have you, sweetheart?" Carly said, locking her arm though his. He reached inside his pocket, his fingers gently touching the engagement ring.

"Darling, don't you think it's time you gave me the ring you picked out today?" Carly asked sweetly.

Michael was distracted by a flash bulb going off in front of them.

"I'll be right back," he said, breaking away from Carly and pushing his way through the crowd. He was relieved when the band picked up its set again and music temporarily distracted everyone. He rushed over to the place where he had last seen Katherine and Kevin.

"Did you see the woman and man who were standing here a minute ago?" he asked the bartender.

"Yeah," the man replied, servicing a customer. "They just left. Looked like they were in some kind of hurry."

"Which way did they go?" Michael asked, alarmed.

"Out that door," the bartender replied, nodding to the right. "Hey, by the way, congratulations," he added. But Michael was already too far away to hear.

* * *

Kevin was assisting Katherine into the Rolls Royce when Michael appeared in the doorway of the club.

"Katherine, wait!" Michael yelled.

"Get out of here, Michael," Kevin said angrily, slamming Katherine's door and standing protectively in front of it. It was obvious to Kevin that Katherine was devastated by Michael's announcement. Her reaction only confirmed his earlier suspicion that Michael had seduced her the night before. Obviously, his last fling before he settled down.

"Kevin, please. I need to talk to her," Michael said, trying to remain calm.

"You couldn't leave her alone, could you?" Kevin asked wrathfully.

"Kevin! You don't understand," Michael replied angrily.

"I understand just fine," Kevin exclaimed. "You knew she would be here tonight. Did you have to propose to Carly in front of her?"

"No!" roared Michael. "You have no idea ..."

Katherine pushed open the door and stepped out of the car. She stood facing Michael, her green eyes focusing on him like frozen pools of water.

"I have nothing to say to you," she said calmly and remotely.

"Let me explain," Michael said, suddenly aware that Katherine and Kevin's attention had been diverted behind him.

"What's going on here?" Carly asked sternly. She was standing in the doorway of the club. Her mother stood behind her with a concerned expression on her face. Carly glanced at Katherine in the car.

Kevin examined Michael cursorily. "My cousin was just saying good-bye, weren't you, Michael?"

Katherine slipped silently into the car.

"Good-bye, Michael. Carly, Mrs. Wentworth," he

added, nodding curtly in their direction. "Oh ... and congratulations," he said with a smirk.

"I'm sorry, Kevin," Katherine said as Kevin pulled out of the parking lot. "I didn't mean to ruin your evening. Just put me in a cab on the corner, and you can go back and enjoy the party."

"That boring thing?" he asked, flashing her a bright smile. "No way. Besides, I'm a gentleman. I insist on escorting you back to the hotel."

A few moments later, Kevin handed the car keys to the valet. He wrapped a protective arm around Katherine's shoulders and gingerly led her into the hotel lobby.

"I don't want to go back to my room," she said abruptly, pausing before the elevator. She couldn't stand the thought of sleeping in the same bed she and Michael had made love in. Her room was ridden with memories of her afternoon with Michael.

"Come with me," he said, heading back toward the front desk clerk. Although this appeared to be an opportune time to take her to his room, even he hesitated to take advantage of her in the state she was in. "The lady would like to change rooms," he said authoritatively.

"Hmmm," the clerk said, furrowing his brow and pressing in some letters on his computer keyboard. He studied the screen. "I'm afraid that's impossible. We're completely booked."

Kevin glanced at Katherine's concerned face. "C'mon," he said, grabbing her arm.

"I'll just go to another hotel," Katherine said quietly.

"Don't be ridiculous. It's after midnight. Besides, you're not in any condition to be running around to hotels looking for a room. You can stay with me. In my room," he added.

Katherine stopped walking. "I don't want to . . . I can't," she muttered.

"Nothing is going to happen. You take the bed, and I'll take the chair." He took Katherine by the arm and walked her to the elevator. "Don't argue with me," he added sternly.

Katherine didn't want to go with Kevin, but she knew she couldn't face going back to her room. She wished that this afternoon had never happened. How could she continue working at Benson now? She had slept with him.

Kevin opened the door to his room and showed her inside. Although the maid had made the bed, Kevin's dirty clothes and ski equipment were scattered everywhere. Embarrassed, he began taking clothes off the bed and throwing them in the corner.

"Sorry it's a little messy," he said, flashing her a boyish smile.

Katherine sat down on the bed, exhausted. She was too tired to care where she was, never mind the state of the room. Kevin pulled a pair of flannel pajamas out of his suitcase.

"Wear these," he said. "They're clean. You can change in the bathroom."

Katherine accepted the pajamas. She silently stood up and walked to the bathroom, shutting the door behind her.

She stopped as she caught her reflection in the mirror. She looked as exhausted as she felt.

She scrubbed her porcelain complexion clean and changed into Kevin's pajamas.

She opened the door and smiled weakly yet bravely at Kevin.

Kevin swallowed hard at the sight of the beauty in the doorway of his bedroom.

He instinctively stood up, as though he planned on climbing into bed with her. Instead, he took off his tuxedo and plopped back down on the chair, using his jacket as a blanket. Katherine climbed into bed and turned off the light.

"Kevin . . . thank you," she said quietly in the darkness.

"Anytime," he responded quickly, squirming on the chair. It was going to be a long night.

Michael escorted Carly out of the party. He had not been able to talk to her all night. It had taken a considerable amount of self-control to calm down after the incident with Kevin and Katherine. He didn't want to take out his considerable fury on Carly. He felt Carly had made an honest mistake—one that he knew would prove humiliating for her. He steeled himself for a scene as he led her to the car.

"My parents took a taxi back to the hotel," Carly said. "I guess they wanted to give us some privacy." She hooked her arm through Michael's. "I'm so happy, darling," she added, playfully resting her head on his shoulder.

Michael opened her car door for her. He quickly walked around to his side and tipped the doorman before exiling himself into the confines of his car.

"We've got a problem," he said with a grimace.

"I know, darling. We've suddenly got so many problems! Where to get married . . . and when! And, well, darling, you haven't even given me the ring yet."

Michael put the key in the ignition and turned to face her. He took her hands gently in his.

"There isn't any ring, Carly," he said softly but clearly.

Carly looked at him, pretending not to understand.

"I don't have a ring for you," he repeated.

"Oh, Michael, quit teasing me." She looked at him, her eyes open wide.

"I don't know how to tell you this any other way. I did buy a ring. But it wasn't for you."

"What . . . what do you mean?" she asked, her face still caught in an eerie smile.

"I didn't plan on asking you to marry me tonight. I planned on breaking up with you."

"You can't be serious!" she said, her face contorting in fury. "But everyone knows now, everyone thinks . . ."

"I know. I'm sorry. I tried to tell you. I didn't want this to happen." Carly sat back, pretending to be stunned.

"Who is, who was the ring for?" she asked, staring straight ahead.

"I would rather not say at this point."

"Katherine. Don't tell me it's for her!"

Michael leaned back and crossed his arms defensively.

"Michael, please," Carly pleaded. "You've only known her for a couple of months."

"It doesn't matter. You and I were not going anywhere. You deserve someone who can love you. And, as you know, I've told you before I can never love you."

"You said you cared about me as much as you could. You said you didn't think you were capable of feeling real love."

Michael looked at her. He paused. "I was wrong."

Carly took a deep breath. "All right, Michael," she said, suddenly calm. "I understand. We'll call it off. But news of our engagement will be printed in the papers tomorrow. It would be terribly humiliating if people thought I made this whole proposal up in my mind. Let's just wait a month or so before calling it off. After a few weeks, we'll just say we both decided it wasn't a good idea."

Michael studied the woman beside him carefully as he pondered her request. He had known her for a long time. She had been a good friend to him through the years. The last thing he had wanted to do was publicly embarrass her.

"Please, Michael," she whispered, willing her eyes to tear.

"I need to talk to Katherine first, before I can make any promises," he said, turning the key in the ignition and firing up the car.

Carly took a silver tube of lipstick out of her purse and skillfully applied it in the dark. A tortured smile appeared at the corners of her carefully lined lips. If Katherine Wells wanted to be the future Mrs. Michael Benson, she was going to have to put up a hell of a fight.

Michael quietly inserted the key into Katherine's lock and opened the door. He had a lot of explaining to do, and he knew it. So much had happened since their afternoon together, and he was desperate to see her. In his hurry to avoid a confrontational scene with Carly moments ago at her doorstep, he had even agreed to a breakfast date with her tomorrow morning.

He was confident, however, that once he proposed to Katherine and gave her the ring, she would agree that they should protect Carly from any unnecessary humiliation.

"Katherine," he whispered into the darkness. His voice was met with silence. "Katherine," he said a little louder. Again, no answer. His hand felt for the light switch, and he flicked it on. The room was empty. His eyes scanned the room. He noticed the roses in the sink.

"That scoundrel," he said aloud, realizing they were from Kevin.

He was annoyed. If she wasn't here, she must still be out with him. He decided to wait for her in the room. If she arrived back with Kevin, all the better. He could straighten out the situation with both of them.

Michael sat down on the bed and rested his head on Katherine's pillow. He could smell her fragrance on the linen. He smiled as he closed his eyes.

Soon she would be lying beside him.

Kevin picked his wallet up off the dresser. He caught Katherine's eyes in the mirror and turned around.

"Good morning," he said with a smile. "I didn't wake you, did I?" he asked.

"No," she said, sitting up straight. She glanced over at the clock. It was already eight in the morning.

"I thought I'd go grab a cup of coffee and the Sunday paper," he said, tucking his wallet into his back pocket. "There's a towel for you in the bathroom if you want to take a shower. I'll be out of here so you can have some privacy." He grinned at the sight of Katherine sleepily blinking in bed. She looked like a frightened, wide-eyed doe.

"Want anything?" he asked, heading for the door. Katherine shook her head silently. "Okay, then. See you in a few," he added cheerfully, shutting the door behind him.

Katherine bounded out of bed as soon as the door was closed. She wanted to take a quick shower, return to her room just long enough to pack her bags, and catch the first plane out of there.

She was just stepping out of the tub when she heard someone banging on the door.

"Just a minute," she yelled over the racket. She assumed it was Kevin returning with his key. She looked around, frantic for something to cover her nakedness with. She grabbed the oversized bathrobe hanging on the hook inside the bathroom door and wrapped it around her. She pulled off the shower cap and threw it on the counter.

Katherine ran her fingers through her long, silky hair as she walked over to the door. She opened it slightly and peeked out. Her face dropped when she saw Michael standing before her.

"I hope I'm not interrupting anything," he announced angrily, pushing his way in. Katherine backed away from the door, speechless. She clutched the robe to her chest.

"What do you want?" she managed to whisper.

"I want to know what the hell is going on here!" he said. "Where's Kevin?"

"Right behind you," Kevin replied, standing in the open doorway. He had tucked the paper under his arm and held two steaming Styrofoam cups of coffee in his hands. He walked in and shut the door with his foot.

"You had no right ..." Michael said to Kevin in a low, threatening voice.

"To what? What this lady does shouldn't concern you anymore, should it, cuz?" Kevin stated calmly, setting the coffee down and crossing his arms defiantly. "Unless, of course, you've started a new policy that allows you to monitor your employees' behavior outside the office."

Michael stepped toward him threateningly, his fists clenched.

"Michael, no!" Katherine said.

Michael unclenched his fists and glared at Katherine. "How could you?" he murmured.

He turned and walked stiffly toward the door.

"Oh, by the way," Kevin said.

Michael glanced back. The sight of Katherine standing beside Kevin, wearing his robe, disgusted him.

Kevin flung open the paper. On the front page was a large photo of Carly kissing Michael. Under the picture was the bold caption "THEY'RE ENGAGED!"

"Nice picture," Kevin said with a smile. Michael grimaced and slammed the door behind him so forcefully, a picture fell off the wall.

"If I didn't know better, I'd say that man's in love with you, Katherine."

Carly and Michael sat in the breakfast room. They were barely speaking, despite Carly's almost heroic efforts to make conversation. Several people had already stopped by the table to wish them well.

"Why, look," Carly said, glancing over at the registration table. Katherine was checking out. Carly hoped Katherine would glance in her direction. After all, she had specifically chosen this table for its view of the lobby. She wanted everyone to see her having breakfast with Michael.

"There's Katherine." She glanced at Michael and smiled sweetly. "This must be very awkward for you," she added, feigning sympathy. "Would you like me to excuse myself to the ladies room so you can talk to her?"

Michael glanced up from his eggs. He saw Katherine checking out at the registration desk, her luggage beside her. He moodily grumbled, "That's not necessary," and went back to his eggs.

"How did things go last night? Did she agree to give me a month?"

Michael grunted a nonresponse just as Kevin

popped in the front door of the lobby. He grabbed Katherine's suitcase.

"I'm waiting out front," he yelled to Katherine.

"Good morning, Kevin!" Carly called out to him. She waved cheerfully.

"Carly!" Michael said angrily. But it was too late. Kevin approached the doorway of the restaurant.

"Hey, cuz! Hey, Carly. Congratulations again!" Kevin said sarcastically. "What a happy morning this is, eh?" He laughed and turned back toward Katherine.

Carly looked at Michael suspiciously. "What did he mean by that?"

Michael shrugged his shoulders, focusing back on his eggs. He was not in a mood for chatter.

"My God, it looks like they're leaving together," Carly said, leaning over toward Michael. Michael glanced up.

Katherine stepped away from the registration desk. She instinctively turned toward the dining room, just in time to catch Michael's eye. She glanced away quickly. She grabbed her briefcase and disappeared into the revolving doors leading outside.

Carly sipped her coffee. She had observed and analyzed every second of their wordless interaction. Obviously, she thought smugly, things had gone somewhat awry for Michael's beautiful new lover. If her instinct was correct, Michael was unhappy this morning because he had discovered that his faithful bride-to-be had turned to his playboy cousin in her time of need.

Perhaps this was going to be easier than she thought.

29

Katherine sat on the floor of her apartment, in front of the fire. She grabbed a piece of pizza. Cyndi sat cross-legged beside her, shaking her head.

"You should've gone for Christopher," Cyndi said, taking a large bite from her fifth slice. "He was crazy about you," she added with her mouth full. "He's a nice guy, from a nice family. Those Bensons are trouble. Too handsome and rich for their own good."

Katherine smiled sadly. She had called Cyndi the moment she returned. The Sun Valley ordeal had left her tired and feeling raw and vulnerable. She had needed the comfort of an old friend. Cyndi's lighthearted antics and joie de vivre always made her laugh.

"This has nothing to do with Christopher," Katherine said. She shut the pizza box and leaned back against the couch. "How am I going to face Michael tomorrow?" she asked wistfully.

Cyndi put down her half-eaten pizza and wiped her face with a paper napkin. "Don't go. Take a sick day."

Katherine sighed. "I'll have to deal with this sooner or later, anyway. I have to go back tomorrow. If I don't, it's just going to make it harder. I've got to prove to myself that I can still work with him."

"You're crazy!" Cyndi said. "You're not planning on keeping your job?"

"Believe me," Katherine said strongly, "I would

like nothing better than to quit, but I can't afford to. I've got rent and bills ..." Katherine's voice trailed off. "I *am* going to start looking for another job, however," she said resolutely.

Cyndi stood up and brushed the crumbs off her jeans. "So call Christopher. Maybe he can help you. That law firm he works for here in Baltimore is pretty big."

Katherine nodded. That was a good idea. She needed to network, and almost everyone she knew was connected with her job.

"Hey, listen," Cyndi said. "Before you quit your job, do you think you could introduce me to this Kevin guy? He sounds pretty cute."

Katherine looked at Cyndi and smiled. "I thought you said he was too rich and handsome for his own good?"

"I've had worse," she replied with a grin.

"What about Howard?"

"Ugh. I got the speech last week."

"The speech?"

"You know. The 'I really like you, and this has nothing to do with you, but I've got a lot going on right now, so let's be friends ... blah, blah, blah.' "

"Oh no!" Katherine said. She felt terrible. She had been so wrapped up in her own problems, she hadn't even given her friend a chance to share her troubles. "Cyn, I'm so sorry," she said.

Cyndi furrowed her brow. "You are? Well, that makes one of us."

"You're not upset?" Katherine asked suspiciously.

Cyndi smiled. "I've met someone else." She plopped down on the couch. "He's perfect!"

Katherine sighed as she braced herself for another round.

"He's got salt-and-pepper hair, he's tall, he's got beautiful blue eyes, he's got an exercycle in his bedroom, and he's normal. It's so nice to be in a normal relationship. I think he may be just the guy I've been waiting for."

"Normal? There's no such thing," Katherine said.

"Sure there is!"

Katherine tried not to roll her eyes. *"Normal* is a relative term."

"Okay, forget I ever used the word. He's just not a flashy kind of guy. He's an accountant. Very sweet. The kind who calls and sends flowers."

"See? Definitely not normal. Even if it is a relative term."

"You got a point," Cyndi agreed, laughing. "Do you prefer decent over normal?"

Katherine nodded. "Decent is always good."

"It's decided," Cyndi said, pounding her fist lightly on the table. "This guy is *decent.* So . . . what do you think?"

"Sounds great. Especially the part about the exercycle in his room," Katherine said with a hint of sarcasm. She grinned.

"You know how I love to work out," Cyndi said earnestly. "Howard was a slouch in the athletic department. I like a guy who can keep up."

Katherine laughed. "So, if Mr. Salt-and-Pepper is so terrific, why the interest in Kevin?"

"I like to keep my options open," Cyndi said with a teasing smile.

Katherine laughed. "I guess so. Well," she said, picking up their plates and carrying them into the kitchen, "if I ever talk to him again, I promise to put in a good word. You two may be suited for each other. Who knows?"

After she had ushered Cyndi out, Katherine walked over to her closet and opened the door. She wanted to look her best tomorrow. She intended to confront Michael first thing in the morning and request that they put their personal feelings behind them so they could continue working together until she found another job. Unless, of course, he fired her first.

Katherine swallowed as she forced herself to face the harsh reality that he, as president of the company, could easily terminate her at a moment's notice.

Millie was at her desk when Michael walked in. She did her best to smile. "Congratulations!" she said in her typical monotone. Michael glowered at her as he walked into his office, slamming the door behind him.

Katherine pressed the elevator button carefully, going over her words in her head. She would be calm, rational. They had gotten carried away by the romance of the snow. They had been working closely together. Affairs like this were bound to happen. They had to rise above it—at least, temporarily—until she found another job. She would even ask for his help in suggesting other companies she could work for. She was sure he would agree that it would be best if she left. Perhaps he knew people she could talk to about finding work.

"Good morning, Millie," she said as the elevator doors opened. "Is he in yet?" she asked professionally, ignoring her racing heart and the lump in her throat.

Michael was sitting at his desk, looking at the front page of the Style section. There was another damned article about him marrying Carly. He was interrupted by Millie's voice on the intercom announcing Katherine's arrival. The back of Michael's neck prickled at the mere mention of her name.

"Tell her to come in," he said calmly. He folded the paper and threw it out.

Katherine opened the door and stepped inside, shutting the door behind her.

"Michael," she managed to say with a slight nod of her head.

"Katherine," he said coldly. "What can I do for you this morning?"

"I had to see you."

Michael raised an eyebrow.

"I wanted to see you and tell you that . . . well," she stuttered. "I came here to ask for two things." Michael leaned back in his chair. Instead of being angry, he found he was amused by Katherine's obvious nervousness.

"Yes?" he said.

"One," Katherine said, looking away, "I'd like us to put our personal relationship behind us. And two, I obviously plan on resigning. I was wondering if you would help me look for another job."

Michael folded his arms in front of him as he digested her proposal. "I agree that we should put our, ah, personal relationship behind us, but . . . you're too good. I have no intention of letting you leave this company," he said matter-of-factly.

"I appreciate that, Michael," she said angrily, "but I plan on leaving the company as soon as I can find another job. I hope you understand." She stood to leave. Whatever his intentions were, he couldn't keep her there against her will.

"Just a minute," he said. "I've found that employees who are looking for another job don't usually have the ability to focus on their current one." Michael stood and walked around to the front of the desk. Katherine straightened her fingers against her side. Despite her anger, she was still aware of her animal-like attraction to this calculating man. Michael stopped not five inches away from her. "They usually find themselves fired. Without a recommendation."

"What do you want from me?" she asked, staring into his deep, ice-blue eyes.

"I want you to stop by Harvey's office today." Harvey was Harvey Doss, a lawyer and head of finances. "I'm having him draw up a contract for you to sign."

"A contract?"

"Actually, I should've had you sign something when you started here. It's standard. It just states that if you were to leave here for any reason, you couldn't work for a competitor for five years."

"For five years?" Most contracts prevented an employee from working for the competition for no more than a year.

"What's the matter? Doesn't that fit into your plans?"

Katherine stepped away. "And if I don't sign?"

He sighed. "Look, Katherine. I'm sure Kevin has told you about some of the . . . turmoil going on within my family and the company. I just need to know what side you're on. But, just for the record, I think it would be a mistake for you to leave at this point. There's too much potential for you here."

"I've already made the mistake," she said, avoiding his eyes.

He paused. "Is leaving what you really want?" he asked, leaning on the desk in front of her.

Millie's voice came from the intercom. "Carly's on line two."

"Katherine!" Michael exclaimed as Katherine dashed out of his office, slamming the door behind her.

He grabbed the phone. "What is it, Carly?" he asked angrily into the receiver.

"Hello, darling. Don't I even get a good morning?" she asked cheerfully.

"Look," said Michael, "don't call me darling. I don't like it."

"All right . . . Michael. I just called to remind you of Mommy and Daddy's party tonight."

Michael dropped into his chair. Of course, he realized, as her "fiancé," he was expected to attend. The charade was becoming too elaborate for his taste.

"Look, Carly, I don't know if I can go through with this."

"But Michael," she said icily, "it's just their annual anniversary party. You went to it last year, too. You don't have to stay long. Just make an appearance. It would look strange if you weren't there. It would be embarrassing for me. Oh—Michael hold on for one second. It's my other line," Carly said, putting him on hold.

Michael swiveled around in his chair so that he was facing the window as he took the moment to evaluate Carly's request. He had to push the thought of Katherine out of his mind. Even if he wasn't officially engaged to Carly, he wouldn't be with Katherine. Or would he? Until just a few moments ago, he had thought he could never forgive her for sleeping with his cousin. But now, after a moment's interaction, he found himself defending her. After all, what would he have done if he thought she had accepted a marriage proposal only hours after she had made love to him?

Michael shook his head. The whole idea was preposterous. If she had only trusted him, if she hadn't allowed herself to give in to human weakness, he could have explained everything to her that night. Michael looked toward the closed door. If only he hadn't gone out to dinner with Carly that night. If only he hadn't run into Kevin at the jewelry store . . . he would now be spending his nights with Katherine. But perhaps he had been wrong about her, he reasoned. Perhaps she had not felt any love for him in the first place. If she did, how could she have allowed herself to be with Kevin? Perhaps she had discovered that she was not as enamored with Michael as she had thought she was. Perhaps she even preferred Kevin over him.

Michael slammed his fist down on his desk. Damn her! He could not remember ever feeling so frustrated. So hurt. The thought of Kevin touching Katherine, running his hands over her creamy white breasts, kissing her soft red lips . . . his jealous nature could not stand that type of indiscretion.

"Michael?" Carly's voice rescued him from his own hell. "Sorry about that. Did you reach a decision?" she asked cheerfully.

"What time?" he asked in a defeated tone.

Katherine ran into her office just in time to pick up her ringing phone.

"Katherine?" said a familiar voice on the other end. She recognized it immediately.

"Hello, Christopher," she said, trying to muster some cheer in her voice.

"I hope I'm not calling at a bad time," he said.

"No," she lied. "Not at all."

"I was delighted to hear you were in town this week. I thought you were going to be away on business."

"I was for a short while . . . last week." she said.

"Listen, Katherine, I'm going to be in town tonight, and I'd love to see you. I'll take you anyplace you want to go."

"I don't know," she said. The only place she wanted to go was in search of a big rock to crawl under.

"C'mon," he urged persuasively. "We'll go out for a nice dinner, and I'll have you home by nine. Nine-thirty at the latest. I promise." Katherine laughed despite herself. She could see why he was such a successful attorney.

"It's a date," she said.

"I'll see you at seven."

Katherine sat back in her expensive leather chair and exhaled. It was hard to believe that the job she had viewed as her salvation was suddenly her prison. She knew that, with or without Michael's recommendation, she would find another job. She certainly wasn't going to let him keep her here against her will. Perhaps Christopher would have some job-hunting ideas for her.

Katherine found herself preoccupied with her situation for most of the day. She watched the clock, impatiently waiting for five-thirty to arrive, the earliest time she would allow herself to leave the office.

At five thirty-one, she had packed up her briefcase and was on her way out the door. She planned a long bubble bath before her date with Christopher.

She found herself wishing that Christopher had never called. She would greatly prefer a quiet night at home, but she was afraid if she canceled with Christopher, she would be so obsessed with thoughts of Michael she would only make herself and her situation more miserable.

Katherine stepped into the elevator, relieved that she had made it on unnoticed. She usually didn't leave work until seven or later, and she didn't want people thinking anything was wrong.

She put on her sunglasses. Somehow they made her feel more comfortable, almost as though she was traveling incognito. She stepped off the elevator, not noticing the woman standing in the lobby.

"Katherine? Is that you trying to sneak out of here early?"

Katherine turned toward the voice. Carly Wentworth stood in front of her. The last person Katherine had wanted to see.

"Hello, Carly," Katherine said politely. She found that she had trouble looking Carly in the eye.

"I am so sorry I haven't called you! I feel terrible

about us not spending any time together out west," she said, displaying her toothy smile. "Did you have fun? I know Kevin is crazy about you. I think you both make an adorable couple."

Katherine forced herself to answer. "Kevin and I are just friends," she said.

"That's not what he thinks," Carly said, her nostrils flaring. She was readying herself for the dig. "I called Kevin this morning. My parents are having a little party for Michael and me tonight," she lied. "And I was hoping he could make it ... and bring you, of course." She paused as she carefully noted the agony evident in Katherine's face before continuing. "He reminded me that my invitation was a little late, considering he's still on the West Coast." Carly laughed as though she found herself very funny. "Of course, you're still welcome, if you can make it. I know it's last minute. It's just a spontaneous, casual affair." Carly paused to smile. "I'm sure you know the type."

"No," Katherine responded, a little too quickly. "I mean, thanks, but I can't. I—I have other plans," she added nervously. "I have to go," she said, smiling politely in Carly's direction before turning and heading for the door.

"I'll call you to confirm the time for the photo shoot," Carly said. But if Katherine heard Carly, she didn't respond.

How rude, Carly thought with satisfaction as she watched Katherine walk out the door. Katherine hadn't even bothered to congratulate her on her recent engagement.

30

The waiter set a large plate of spaghetti and meatballs in front of Katherine.

"I love this place," Christopher said. "I discovered it once when I was completely lost in the country. I like it because it's so private. And the food," he said, watching Katherine take a bite, "is wonderful." He smiled. "The only reason it's not more crowded is that it's outside the Beltway."

Katherine swallowed. Her mind wasn't on the food. She knew she had to summon up the nerve to ask Christopher if he had any job leads for her.

"Is something wrong?" Christopher said, picking up his fork. "You seem so quiet."

Katherine looked away. "I'm under a lot of pressure at work right now," she said carefully.

Christopher studied her. "What happened out west?"

"There were some . . . complications," she said, staring at her lap. "Unfortunately, my situation at work is pretty bad. I'm thinking about looking for another job," she added, looking back at him as she reached for her wine.

He shot her a concerned look. "I thought you loved your job," he said. "What happened?"

Katherine shrugged her shoulders, unable to stop the tears from welling in her eyes.

Sensitive to her distress, he quickly retracted his

question. "I'm sorry. It's none of my business," he said, pouring her another glass of wine.

"No. It's quite all right," she replied, pausing before continuing. She attempted to twirl the spaghetti onto her spoon. She was suddenly surprised that she had ordered spaghetti in the first place. Everyone knew that spaghetti was not proper date food. It was too messy. And too difficult to eat. Especially when you were trying to look attractive. "There was a miscommunication between myself and Michael Benson. I feel because of it, I should look for another job," she said.

Christopher immediately realized what her statement implied. "I know this is a delicate situation," he said quietly. "But there are certain steps you can take legally if he has stepped out of line . . ."

The impact of his statement dawned on her. She slurped a lone rebellious noodle into her mouth and quickly dabbed her lips with a napkin.

"No. *No*," she repeated, swallowing quickly. Date rule number two: don't talk with your mouth full. "It's . . . it's nothing like that."

Christopher looked at her sympathetically. He knew how difficult it would be for Katherine to go up against a powerful and well-connected man like Michael Benson.

"It's just a . . . miscommunication," she said, shrugging her shoulders. "Which has led to my decision that I should look for work elsewhere. I was wondering if you knew anyone I could talk to. I'm kind of anxious to find another job," she managed to say.

Christopher glanced at her suspiciously as he remembered the tall, handsome man they had run into at the ballet. He had read about Michael's engagement in the paper this morning. He silently wondered if this "miscommunication" had anything to do with his marrying Carly Wentworth.

"I guess there's more to the problem than just a

miscommunication," Katherine said, reading his look. "Unfortunately, the job isn't what I thought it would be."

Christopher picked up his wine glass. "I've noticed that it certainly does keep you very busy," he said.

Katherine looked down at her plate. She had to be honest with Christopher. As Cyndi would say, he was a decent guy who deserved better. "Christopher, there's something I have to tell you. I'm . . ."

"Seeing someone else?" he interrupted.

Katherine was surprised. Either everybody knew about the spaghetti rule or Christopher was extremely perceptive. Or she was extremely obvious. She had the feeling it was the latter. The fact of the matter was, although she was not dating Michael, as long as she worked with him, she would still feel involved with him.

"There is . . . someone else." She looked at him. "I'm sorry."

He nodded. "It's serious, isn't it?"

"Am I that obvious?" she asked quickly.

"The spaghetti was a good sign," he said, nodding toward her plate.

Katherine looked at him, surprised. "You know about the spaghetti rule?"

He shrugged his shoulders as he grinned at her.

She shook her head. He was the type of guy who would make a great friend. "I'm sorry, Christopher."

Christopher shrugged his shoulders. Even though it was not what he wanted to hear, he appreciated her honesty. After all, she didn't owe him any explanation. He barely knew her. "About what? We've only gone out once. Besides, ever since I saw you with Michael on our first—and only, I may add—date, I had a feeling you were going to be . . . busy."

Embarrassed, Katherine attempted to focus on her spaghetti.

"Hey," he said cheerfully. "They're looking for a communications person at the law firm I do some consulting for in Baltimore—Bender and Ann. Perhaps I could talk to the director about you."

Katherine smiled at him appreciatively. "I would certainly be grateful to you," she said.

"I don't think it's quite as prestigious as the position you have now," he said.

"I don't care about prestige," she said. "I would just like to find another job as soon as possible." She lowered her voice as she noted with surprise the two men who were entering the restaurant.

Christopher followed her eyes. "What's wrong?" he asked. "Do you know them?"

"Not really," she said, stifling her surprise. "They're on the board of my company. That's Alan Benson and Toby Nat."

"I'd like to propose a toast," Carly's father said, clinking his champagne glass with a spoon. "To my daughter and her fiancé. Michael, it's nice to see you finally came to your senses!" the older man joked. The crowd laughed as Michael managed a half-smile. He painfully raised his glass to the toast and gulped down the champagne. He found the party more than he could endure. Despite the fact that the focus was supposed to be on Carly's parents, he was beginning to feel like he was at his own engagement party.

He scanned the crowd, searching the room for a familiar face. Unsuccessful, he walked over to the bar to get another drink as his thoughts drifted back to work. His relationship with his uncle had grown even more strained since Sun Valley. His uncle had all but accused him of attempting to sell the company behind his back, an accusation that was totally inaccurate. Referring back to the mention in *Time* about Michael's rumored plans to run for office, his rumored involvement with Katherine, and his supposed engagement to Carly, Alan had informed him that it was obvious that Michael's focus was not on the company. Michael had asked to meet with him, one on one, so that he could address his concerns in person, but his uncle had put him off, claiming that his schedule was too busy for him to allot any time to his nephew. Michael had also attempted to talk to Toby Nat, but he had not returned any of Michael's repeated phone calls. Michael's father had also been trying to calm the board's jittery nerves, but he had not been able to help any more than Michael.

His father. Michael sighed inwardly. His father was not pleased with Michael's current personal situation. Michael had explained his engagement to Carly as an unfortunate misunderstanding, a charade that would not last longer than a month. He had avoided explaining how the misunderstanding had occurred, although he was sure that his father suspected it had something to do with Katherine. After all, it was his father who had covered for him the evening he, Katherine, and Kevin were in the accident with the deer.

"Michael," said Carly, suddenly appearing beside him and tugging on his arm. "You're being so quiet. You've hardly said a word all night."

Michael managed a smile. "It's been a long day," he said, finishing his drink. "And I've got a long day ahead of me tomorrow," he added, setting the empty glass down on the bar.

"You're not leaving?" Carly asked. It was more of a command than a question. Michael kissed her on the cheek.

"I'll slip out the back," he said. "No one will even notice I'm gone."

"But, Michael," she pleaded.

"I'll talk to you tomorrow," he said as he turned and walked away, leaving an angry Carly behind.

He went through the kitchen and escaped out the back door like a convict leaving prison. Once outside, he paused to savor his freedom. He loosened his tie as he looked up at the clear, starlit sky. He had realized the moment he arrived that the evening would be difficult, but he hadn't expected it to be as disastrous as it was.

Michael walked back to his car as he reviewed the party. The entire evening had seemed almost surreal, as though everyone was just acting a part in some sort of dark comedy. The whole scenario was too ridiculous to be a tragedy.

He sighed, his breath leaving a frosty white trail in the night. What a farce. He didn't even like dark comedies. Yet he was smack dab in the middle of one he had created himself. But could he write the ending?

The only thing he was sure about anymore was his desire for a good night's sleep.

Katherine lay tossing in bed. She kept remembering something Kevin had said. At lunch the previous week, he had told her there was a rumor that Toby and Alan were going to combine shares and try to take over the company.

She wondered if Michael knew about the meeting they had last night. Would he care?

She put her pillow over her head in her frustration. What did she care, anyway? She was leaving the company. It was just a matter of time.

31

◦◦◦

Katherine walked briskly through the dark, cold morning. There were no birds to sing to her on her way to work this day. Most had already gone to a warmer climate, and the ones that were left were smart enough to still be huddled together in their cozy little nests, sound asleep.

Katherine entered the deserted office building and stepped into the elevator. She pressed her floor number, but the button remained dark. Katherine suddenly remembered the elevator would not open onto a floor unless the office manager had unlocked it first. Katherine groaned in frustration, pushing all the floors. If she could get onto any one of Benson's corporate levels, she could take the inside stairs to her floor.

Katherine smiled when her random button pushing lit up a number on the panel. Unfortunately, she realized, the floor that lit up was the tenth, where Michael had his office. That meant that either no one had locked it the night before, or someone had already unlocked it this morning.

Katherine checked her watch as the glass elevator began its ascent over the still, dark lobby. It was not yet seven. Surely he wouldn't be in yet.

Michael looked up from his desk at the sound of the elevator doors opening. Katherine stepped into the enormous lobby.

"Millie?" Michael's voice asked authoritatively.

Katherine swallowed as she eyed the nearby staircase. Perhaps she could make a run for it. "Hello, Michael," she managed to muster, walking quickly toward the stairs.

Surprised to hear Katherine's voice, Michael jumped up from his desk. He caught up to Katherine just as she was approaching the stairway.

"It's a little early, isn't it?" he asked.

"I—I have a lot of work," she muttered. He eyed her suspiciously.

"How was your party?" she asked suddenly. Michael frowned.

"It was fine, I guess," he said. "How did you hear about it?"

"I saw Carly yesterday. She told me about it." Michael nodded his head as they continued to stare awkwardly at each other. He rejected the vulnerability he could feel seeping through his tough exterior.

"I guess I'll talk to you later," he said gruffly, turning and walking back toward his office. Katherine took a step toward the stairs and hesitated. She was still bothered by seeing Toby and Alan last night. Why hadn't they been at Michael's party?

"Michael," she said, pausing on the stairs as she called out to him. Michael reappeared at the top of the stairs.

"Were Alan and Toby at your party last night?"

"What are you talking about? The party at the Wentworths'?"

Katherine nodded. "Yes."

A sudden shadow passed over Michael's face. "No. Why do you ask?" He began to walk down the stairs toward her.

"I saw them at the restaurant I was at last night. I assumed they were here for a meeting, but ..."

"What are you talking about?" Michael asked, alarmed. He stopped five steps away from her.

Katherine took a few steps toward him. "They were at dinner together. Last night."

Michael clenched the banister tightly. His uncle? He had spoken with him not two days before. He had not mentioned that he would be in Baltimore, even when Michael had specifically told him that he wanted to meet with Alan in person. Why would Alan fly all the way out here and meet with Toby instead? The answer was obvious.

"Did he see you?" he asked quietly.

"No. No, I don't think so," she said. She fought her urge to ask him if she could help. She needed to get back to her office and work on her résumé. Why should she care if his uncle took over the company? At least that way she might be able to keep her job. "Well, I've got to get to work," she said, beginning to walk down the stairs.

"What do you know about this, Katherine?" Michael commanded. Katherine stopped in her tracks. "What did Kevin tell you?" he asked.

Katherine turned back. Kevin? "Nothing," she replied angrily.

"C'mon, Katherine. Be honest with me," he said as though he was threatening her.

She thought back to the first time she met Kevin. "Nothing of substance. He just said there was a rumor floating around that Toby and Alan had spoken about combining their shares to take over control of the company. They thought you were planning on getting married and running for office—you weren't devoting as much energy to the company as you should be," she replied quickly.

"Another damn rumor? What the hell is this?"

He was sick of rumors. And this was not a rumor. This was a case of Alan making a stupid, careless mistake and confiding in his big-mouthed son.

"Why didn't you tell me this sooner?" he asked

coldly. "Or were you trying to protect Kevin?" he added, as though Kevin's mere name was acid on his tongue.

"No . . ." Katherine said, shaking her head. "No!"

Michael turned abruptly and forcefully walked up the steps. Katherine looked after him, shaken by their confrontation. How could he think she would do anything to damage his company? She slowly began walking back downstairs but stopped herself after only a few steps. How dare he accuse her like that! She felt like running after him and telling him that she hoped his uncle did take control.

Katherine looked desperately toward the tenth floor. Despite her anger, she still felt a strong thread of company loyalty. Michael may not have treated her well, but he certainly had the respect and devotion of the people who worked for him. What would happen to Diane, Louise, and everyone else if Michael lost the company?

Katherine turned and began to climb back up the stairs. She was still his employee, she reasoned. Her loyalty was to the company.

When she arrived at Michael's door, he was already on the phone. He quickly slammed down the receiver.

"Michael, please," Katherine said calmly. "I would never do anything to harm the company. I'll do what I can to help you."

Michael looked her in the eye.

"I told you about seeing Alan and Toby last night, didn't I?" she said, meeting his stare. Michael hesitated. He needed her support right now.

"I'm fairly convinced that what Kevin told you is true," he said slowly. "My uncle and Toby are planning to combine their stock and take control of my company. You see, I had suspected this before today, but until now . . . I guess I was waiting for some proof. I've been a little blind, not to mention ignorant. Their meeting may have been innocent, although I doubt it. Alan just assumed he could slip in and out of town unobtrusively."

"But why meet here?"

"Toby lives in Washington," Michael said quietly.

"What are you going to do?" Katherine asked.

"I don't think I have any choice. I already decided that if Alan joined forces with Toby, I would have to call an emergency stockholder meeting. I've got to convince them I'm firmly in control."

"But you own the controlling interest."

"I own twenty-five percent. But Toby owns five percent, and Alan is the chief stockholder, besides myself. He owns fifteen percent. That's too close for any comfort."

"What about your father?"

"Only three percent."

"What are you going to do?"

"I need to try at least temporarily to buy some stock from the rest of the board—unless, of course, Toby and Alan have already persuaded them to sell to them." Michael began to pace back and forth. "Alan's been attempting to make a case against me for years. If he finds out I'm calling board members asking for shares, he won't waste any time."

"What could he do?"

"He could call a board meeting himself. Probably a public one. He'll try to persuade them to vote me out." He turned back toward Katherine. "Alan can't find out. It's that simple. Katherine . . . are you—will you help me?"

Katherine nodded.

"Call William. You can trust him. Tell him what the situation is. Ask him to pull together some facts on the A-14 engine that might help us. We can put together a package that we'll deliver to the board later today."

32

William Briggs sat in the back of a black limousine in the dark, empty stadium parking lot. He passed a manila envelope to the man in the wool overcoat seated next to him.

"This is the package that went out today."

The man in the overcoat reached out a gloved hand and took it from him.

"Very good. When is he meeting with the board?"

William glanced out the tinted window. There had been a winter storm warning earlier in the day, but so far it was a still, quiet night. The only sign of trouble was the clouds hovering over the moon. Weather like this made it difficult to believe it was only November.

He turned back toward the man across from him. They had known each other for years, yet he felt fairly certain that neither had been involved in anything even close to corporate espionage before.

It was the fear that a hostile takeover was inevitable that had originally prompted William to take action. And the money had made it bearable. He needed to protect himself, protect his family. He couldn't afford to be looking for a job at his age, with his responsibilities. The money would allow him to retire and send his children to college. He had been promised a flat fee of two million dollars if the takeover attempt was successful.

But the money wasn't the only reason he had agreed to

participate. He had worked for a politically ambitious man before. He knew how terrible and seductive the desire for power could be. He had experienced Leslie Benson's campaign and the devastation it had wreaked on the company. If Michael sold the company before William was sixty, he wouldn't even qualify for early retirement. At least this way, if he invested the money wisely, he would be assured of an income. But to do so, he had to pay a very steep price. His honor.

"I don't know," he said tiredly.

The man sitting across from him sighed. He too was tired. "William, please. When does Michael want to meet with the board?"

William looked back toward the window. "He's trying to avoid it. He wants to meet with key members individually. He's trying to buy their stock."

He paused. "I see. I think it's time for us to call our own emergency board meeting. Except we're going to invite every single stockholder. We're going to ask for a vote. It's time to physically remove him. Before he does any more damage. In the meantime, I need your proxy."

"That's not part of the deal."

"William, I have been very generous with you. You will be compensated very well for your support during this . . . difficult time. It's too late to back out now."

William looked down at his hands guiltily.

"You are doing the right thing, William," the man said forcefully. "If you have any doubts, take a look at the stock."

The stock price had dropped five points over a period of two weeks last spring. And it hadn't recovered.

The man saw that his remark had the intended effect. He softened his approach. "How much more do you want for your proxy, William?"

"First answer me," William said, desperately clinging to the thread of strength he still possessed. "Did you falsify the data that I gave you on the A-14?"

"Don't be ridiculous. I just wanted the data so that I could see what was going on inside the company. I'm just trying to keep tabs on someone who's out of control. And that someone is Michael," he said impatiently. "Now tell me, how much do you want?"

William wanted to believe the man sitting next to him. And at this point, he had to.

He glanced out the window. He owned five percent of Benson. "One hundred thousand dollars per percent."

"You drive a hard bargain, William." He offered him his hand. "But I accept your terms. I may need your support in the meeting." He paused. "I know I can count on you. After all, we're partners."

"We're not partners."

"I realize how difficult this if for you," the man said sympathetically. "It's been hard on me as well. You know how I feel about Michael. Believe me, I want what's best for him too. And in the long run, this is what's best for him. He'll have more money. Along with the rest of us. Trust me. In the meantime, I'll see that Michael is taken care of. I won't allow him to be hurt . . . financially."

And with that, Alan Benson rolled down his window for some fresh, cold air.

33

The call requesting Michael's presence at the hastily called stockholders meeting came precisely at noon. It did not come from Alan or Toby but rather from a friendly camp. Leslie Benson had received a call asking him to attend, and he had called and informed his son immediately.

Michael picked up the phone and interrupted Katherine, who was in a monthly budget meeting with Diane. Within several minutes, she was standing in his doorway.

Michael stood up and walked over to her. He reached behind her and closed the door. "Who did you tell?"

"What?" Katherine looked confused.

"Who did you tell? Kevin? Did you tell Kevin?" he asked, his voice getting louder.

"What are you talking about?"

"They found out. Alan and his gang." Michael shook his head. "I don't know why I even trusted you with this."

"I didn't say anything to anyone, Michael. Only William. And that was per your instruction." Michael stared at her. "I haven't seen or even spoken to Kevin since he dropped me off at the airport." True, he had left several messages for her, but she hadn't bothered to return them.

Michael looked away. He wanted to believe her.

"Michael, I've worked so hard to pull everything together for you. Do you think I could sit here and work with you, then sneak away and inform Alan ... or Kevin?"

No. No, he didn't. And he couldn't afford to.

"Okay. I'm sorry," he admitted, shrugging his shoulders. "One of the board members must have talked."

"Unless it was William. He was acting a little strange at the board meeting."

"William always acts strange."

"It's possible, Michael."

Michael sat down behind his desk. He had known William for years. Alan was fighting for control so he could all but eliminate the research division. He couldn't imagine a reason why William would betray him. But, Michael reminded himself, William owned five percent of the company. If he gave Alan his proxy, Michael was in serious trouble.

"I'm sure it was one of the board members we contacted," Michael said mechanically. Katherine sat in the chair facing Michael's desk. "I want you working on nothing else besides this until we meet," he continued.

"When's the meeting?" Katherine asked.

"Next Tuesday. We have less than a week to gather all the information we need. I'll call the board members individually and ask them for their proxy. You continue your research. Speaking of which, any leads?"

"No. A lot of people heard the rumor, but they don't know or can't remember where they heard it first."

"Do you believe them?"

"So far, I do."

Michael glanced away. This wasn't going to be easy. He wanted to prove that Alan was behind the bad press. If he could do that, he would not only secure his position, he could vote him off the board.

"There's something else we need to address," Katherine announced. "We should deal with the possibility that the problems we had selling the A-14 engine were due to more than just a nasty rumor floating around the industry."

"What do you mean?"

"Why would these people believe a rumor? A lot of them are scientists. And we have the data to back up our claims. They know that. But they're not believing it. Why?" Katherine said.

"Bad press."

"Or false data."

Michael leaned back in his chair. He crossed his arms. "Keep going," he said

"It's possible that someone is feeding them false information. With proof to back it up." Katherine hesitated. "Or perhaps there really was some data that said the A-14 was unsafe. And someone released it."

Michael hesitated. He lowered his voice threateningly. "I'm not sure what you're insinuating, but I would never try to sell a product unless I was damn sure it worked."

Katherine looked away.

Michael leaned forward. "I don't like what you're accusing me of," he said coldly.

"I'm not accusing you of anything."

Michael shook his head in disbelief. "You've got to be kidding me. You think I would try and sell a product that was unsafe?"

"I think there's some false data floating around. Either it is safe and someone wants to make it look like it's not, or it isn't safe and someone tried to make it look like it is."

"So you're accusing William of falsifying information and selling it."

"Maybe not William. But I think someone in research, someone fairly high up, is involved."

Michael shook his head.

"Look at the facts, Michael."

Michael stood up and turned toward the window. He crossed his arms.

"Do you have any plans tonight?" he asked, still looking out the window.

Katherine looked at him curiously. "I have the photo shoot with William."

"Tonight?"

"We have to shoot in an airplane hangar at the airport. The only time they'd let us shoot was at night. They don't want us interfering with regular business."

"Can you get out of it?"

"I can't cancel it this late. At least, not without a good excuse. Everything is a go."

"Will Carly be there?"

"Yes, but . . ."

"Let her handle it."

"I have to be there, Michael. In a photo shoot like this, one that's this important, the client needs to be there. William is not some professional model. He needs direction."

Michael turned back toward her. "All right. What I need is going to take a little time to pull together anyway."

Michael pushed the intercom button. "Millie, get William Briggs on the line."

"What are you going to do?" Katherine asked.

Michael held up his index finger, motioning for Katherine to wait.

"William, I need your help. Something has come up. I want to see the data from every single test we've done on the A-14 engine. I want a copy of every study, any research that relates to it. On my desk tomorrow morning. Okay? Thanks."

He sat down in his chair. "There are volumes of information. I don't know how much is going to make sense to you, but I'd like you to help me sift through it. It's going to be pretty time-consuming."

"That's all right," Katherine said. "What did William say when you asked for it?"

"He seemed a little surprised, but I'm sure he'll do his best to get the information to me."

"Maybe." Katherine was not convinced.

"I want to look through it first. But I am going to have a talk with him. Before the board meeting."

Katherine picked up her notebook and tucked it under her arm. She stood up.

"Meet me here at noon tomorrow. In the meantime," he added nonchalantly, "don't mention this to anyone. Even Carly."

Katherine looked at him quizzically. Although she was flattered that Michael was confiding in her and not Carly, she thought it was rather strange.

"And if you have any plans for this weekend, you might want to cancel them. This is going to take a while. Oh, and good luck tonight," he said, without even looking at her as he picked up the phone. She couldn't help but wonder if he meant with Carly or the photo shoot.

34

William Briggs stood alone in front of a small twin-engine plane. He was uncomfortable, and it showed. His white shirt was beginning to show signs of perspiration.

"That's it . . . hold it." The photographer, Jim Garies, snapped a test shot. "Turn your head a little to the left . . . too much . . . there you go. Perfect!" He snapped again.

Eleven people stood watching him. Four assistants, a stylist, a makeup artist, William, Carly, Katherine, Louise, and a pilot whose sole purpose was to move the planes around the hangar. Katherine checked her watch. Although it was close to eleven and they had been here for a solid hour, they hadn't shot one photo yet. They had spent all of their time working on the lighting.

"Jim, can you turn down the music? It's giving me a headache," Carly said. Katherine glanced at Carly. All Carly had wanted to do since they arrived was discuss the wedding. Katherine wanted no part of it.

"I just haven't been feeling well at all lately." Carly paused, waiting for Katherine to inquire why. She didn't.

"Louise, did you bring the rough sketches of the ads?" Katherine asked. "I'd like to use them to keep track of shots."

"Good idea," Louise said, jumping up. "I've got them with me." Louise pranced over to her backpack and pulled out a large manila folder. Louise felt totally at home in the artistic, casual atmosphere of the shoot, and it showed. Her outfit contrasted sharply with the tailored suits Katherine and Carly were wearing. Louise was wearing a rather artsy combination that consisted of black spandex pants, what appeared to be ballet slippers, and a short white T-shirt. Katherine half expected Louise to fall into a somersault before she handed her the ads.

"Here you go," Louise said, beaming as she handed Katherine the folder. Katherine did appreciate her assistant's enthusiasm. She also appreciated the fact that Louise had offered to come to the shoot. She liked having a buffer with Carly.

Katherine pulled out the ads and studied them. Even if everything went perfectly, she figured the shoot would last another four hours.

"So, Katherine," Carly said, "you and I hardly ever get a chance to sit and talk. I feel so bad about that."

"Don't," Katherine said. "It's understandable. We're both always in a rush."

"True. But it looks like we'll have all night to catch up with each other, doesn't it?" she said.

"All night?" Louise asked.

"Don't worry. You don't have to," Katherine said reassuringly. But she would.

"How has everything been at work?" Carly asked, fishing for information.

Katherine shrugged her shoulders. Louise began nonchalantly to run through her various ballet postures, using the table as a ballet bar. "Busy. As usual," Katherine replied.

"I know how that goes," Carly said. "I can barely function now. I just don't know how I'm going to manage when the baby comes."

Louise stopped her pirouette in mid-spin. "Baby?" Louise asked, her hands still in the air. "You're ..."

"Pregnant?" Katherine interrupted.

"Isn't it wonderful? But please don't say anything to anyone. Especially Michael. He's thrilled, of course. But he wants to announce it after we're married." She paused. "At least he's making an honest woman out of me."

"Okay, what do you think?" the photographer interjected. He stuck the photo in front of Katherine. "We've got a shadow right there," he said, pointing to William's feet. "But we're taking care of it."

Katherine was having a difficult time spotting the shadow or anything else. Carly was pregnant. Carly was pregnant. Carly was ...

"Great. It looks much better," she heard herself say. She turned toward Carly. "Well, that's very ... exciting."

"Yes," Louise said, looking anxiously at Katherine. Katherine caught Louise's concerned glance. Was her pain so obvious?

"Michael and I were just talking about names that we liked for our children. He likes Michael, naturally," she said with a laugh. "And for a girl, perhaps Whitney."

Katherine paused. "Nice," she said simply, trying to maintain control. "Excuse me," she said, raising her voice as she called out to the photographer. She must focus. "Jim, are you getting the name of that other plane in the background?" Her relationship with Michael was over. Completely. There was no possibility of reconciliation. None.

Jim squinted through the camera. His assistants all gathered behind him. They leaned forward and made a square with their hands as if trying to block out the frame themselves.

"Good eye. We're going to have to move that plane." His assistants nodded in agreement. He pointed to the airline rep. "Can you move that to the right an inch or so?"

The rep looked at him and frowned. "An inch? I'll try."

Katherine's head ached. Was Carly's pregnancy the reason Michael had proposed? Katherine had to know. Of course, it didn't change anything, but still, it would help to explain quite a bit.

"How far along are you?" she asked.

Carly caught on instantly. "Oh, not far. We're usually so careful. I think it must have happened right before we went to Sun Valley. We had been talking about getting married, and we both want a large family. We just decided to throw caution to the wind. You know how it is."

Katherine took a step forward, attempting to hide her shock. The news was too much. She had been blind, stupid, and naive. She felt as though she might be ill. But she wasn't the only one. William Briggs was leaning over, wiping his forehead with a handkerchief.

"William," Katherine said, stepping forward. She must concentrate. "Are you all right?"

"Look, I'm sorry, Katherine, but I don't know . . . maybe a drink of water would help."

"Certainly." She called out to one of the assistants, "Can you get him a drink of water?"

"Are you going to be okay?" Louise asked worriedly, patting William on the back. Carly stepped forward and crossed her arms impatiently.

"Sure, I'll be fine. I just need a minute."

"Carly, your briefcase is ringing." An assistant laughed as he gave William his water.

Carly turned and ran toward her briefcase. She unzipped it and yanked out her portable phone.

"Hello? Hello, darling." She began to walk forward so that everyone could hear. "Well, it's coming. That's all I'll admit to right now." She smiled. "Tonight? I don't know. It will probably be pretty late . . ." She laughed. "It's never too late for that! Of course I'm feeling well enough. Okay. I love you, too." She hung up the phone.

"Whoo, Carly," the photographer teased. "Sounds like you've got a hot date. That wouldn't be with a certain Mr. Benson, now, would it?"

Carly giggled. "Please, don't embarrass me. Katherine and William work for him."

"Do you think you can continue?" Katherine asked William. She avoided looking at Carly. How could Michael have the nerve to call her here? To flaunt his romance in front of her?

"I'll be all right. I just need a few minutes."

"Well, the sooner we start, the sooner we can go home, or wherever," Carly said with a laugh. The phone call had its intended effect. Of course, Michael had not been on the other line. It was Carly's mother, who had been specifically instructed by Carly to call her at the shoot and ask if she was going to stop by afterward to make some wedding plans. She had been an unwitting participant in an elaborate performance. It had been staged and carried off perfectly.

Michael stood peering into his computer screen, his sleeves rolled up. A half-filled cup of cold coffee sat next to his computer. He ran his fingers through his hair.

Millie buzzed. "Michael, Katherine's here."

"Send her in."

The door opened, and Katherine walked in. She was wearing a gray Donna Karan suit. Her hair was pulled back in a sleek bun. She looked cool and elegant. She had had a sleepless night and a busy morning, but her appearance did not betray her.

Michael stood up. He tried to push her beauty out of his mind. He had more important matters to take care of. "Help me gather this stuff up," he said gruffly, motioning to the piles of paper stacked around his desk.

Katherine looked at it, surprised. "This is the research?"

"You got it. We'll have to make a couple of trips."

"Trips? Where to?"

"My car. I don't want to go over this stuff here, during working hours. I want to do this at my house. We can spread it out and leave it there. No one has to know what we're doing with it."

"What do you mean?"

"I've got people coming in and out of this office all day. I don't want them coming here and stepping over the both of us."

Katherine looked confused. "By the way," he continued, "you're not coming in to work tomorrow. You're going to call in sick."

"But I'm really going to be . . ." She paused, waiting for his cue.

"At my house, helping me."

Katherine looked at him curiously. She shook her head. The last person she wanted to be alone with right now was Michael. It was hard to believe that only a week ago, they had been together, sequestered away in his cabin. Katherine shuddered at the thought. He had made love to her knowing that another woman was carrying his child. A woman he planned to make his wife.

"Michael," she reasoned, "I should at least tell Diane and Louise what's going on. I can't just not show up. I'm in the middle of developing a campaign.

And anyway, perhaps you should be doing this with Carly."

"I don't want to involve Carly in this, and if I don't succeed, there won't be any campaign because there won't be any division," he said harshly.

"Why don't you want to involve Carly?" Katherine asked stubbornly. After all, she was going to be his wife. The mother of his child.

"This is a private business matter. Look, I like to keep my personal and professional life separate. I think we're both aware of what happens when they mix."

Katherine bit her lower lip.

Michael continued. "And anyway, you're already involved in this . . . so if you want an official invitation, you've got it. Will you help me?"

Katherine shook her head. "It's not that . . ." She hesitated.

"Or has too much happened between us?" he asked in a nonchalant tone.

"What will Carly say?" Katherine asked, her green eyes reflecting coldness.

"What do you mean?"

"I don't think she'll like the idea of me working at your house . . . alone with you."

"I'll deal with that. But you haven't answered my question."

Damn it! She couldn't say no. "I'll call Diane tomorrow," she said. "I feel a migraine coming on."

"Good." Michael smiled approvingly. "Grab a pile. We're taking it to my car."

"I have to get my coat, and briefcase."

"Okay," he said, suddenly impatient. "And meet me at my car. Parking garage, first level."

Katherine stood by Michael's Range Rover, waiting. She watched him walk out of the stairwell, his briefcase bulging with papers.

"Why don't you follow me back to my house?" he said. Katherine paused. He obviously thought that she had driven. She hadn't. She hadn't had any time for exercise lately, so she had been forcing herself to walk to and from work every day. It wasn't a lot, but it was better than nothing.

"I didn't drive," she said, shrugging her shoulders.

"Well, then, get in," he ordered, unlocking the door. Katherine climbed inside, secretly reveling in the luxurious smell of leather. She glanced sideways at Michael as he started the car.

"You can take a cab home later," he said.

Katherine simply shrugged her shoulders again.

Her eyes scanned the backseat. It was crammed with boxes packed full of papers from Michael's office.

Michael followed her eyes. "Millie took them down in a cart," he said, maneuvering the car out of the garage. "Did anyone ask you where you were going?" he asked, his eyes focused in front of him.

"No one," she said, looking at him. "I don't even think anyone saw me leave."

"Good," he muttered, his lips drawn tightly together. "By the way, how did it go last night?"

"Didn't Carly tell you?" she asked.

Michael glanced at her, irritated. "Tell me what?"

"Well, I just assumed she would've told you how it went."

"Well, she didn't."

Katherine paused, suddenly angry. *No,* she thought sarcastically, *of course she didn't.* Why would she waste precious time together discussing business? As he just reminded her, he didn't like to mix business and pleasure. "It went well," she said quietly. "William was acting a little strange, though."

"I've told you before. He always acts strange. Plus, he's not exactly an extrovert. It was probably difficult for him to be the center of attention like that."

"Maybe. But I think it was more than that. I think he was a nervous wreck. And I don't think the photo shoot had much to do with it."

"Well, detective, you'll be happy to know that I plan on talking to William. As soon as I'm finished catching up on my reading," he said, with a quick glance to the backseat.

A few minutes later, the Range Rover pulled up to the iron gate at the entrance of his estate. A cold drizzle had begun to fall, adding to the melancholy atmosphere of the day. Michael leaned over Katherine's lap and opened the glove compartment. He pulled out a remote control and pointed it at the gate. In a split second, the heavy iron doors swung open. Michael slipped the remote back into the glove box.

Katherine gazed at her immense yet eerie environs as Michael drove down the long, winding driveway. Thick, dense foliage surrounded the right side of the car. On the left was a perfectly manicured rolling lawn. A shadowy stone mansion loomed in the foreground.

Michael pulled into a four-car garage located behind the fortress. He parked the car between the sedan Katherine had originally seen him drive and a 1963 Corvette.

"Nice car," Katherine said, motioning toward the Corvette.

"Thanks. I like speed. To me, that's what that car represents. The beginning of an era."

"Interesting," Katherine said. "I like speed, too. But the only thing I have to show for it is a traffic ticket."

Michael grinned. "Grab as much as you can carry. I'll send Randy and Linda out to get the rest of it."

"Randy and Linda?" Katherine asked.

"They live here. They both work for me. Randy

takes care of the outside, and Linda takes care of the inside."

"Wow," Katherine said. "That's got to be nice," she said, grabbing a stack of papers. She couldn't imagine owning a house and not having to clean it or rake leaves.

"It is nice," Michael replied when they were both out of the car. "It would be impossible to take care of this place by myself," he said as Katherine followed him out through a side door in the garage. Although it was only five-thirty, the day was dark enough to merit the soft outdoor lights that lit up a landscaped garden walk. Off to the right, she could see an Olympic-size swimming pool.

"Actually," Michael said. "it was foolish of me to buy this huge house. But I lived here for a while as a kid. My father sold the house in the mid seventies. It happened to come on the market a few years ago, and I knew that if I ever had a family, I'd want them to live here one day too, so I bought it."

Katherine scanned the impressive structure in front of her. Up close, the house appeared even more gothic than it did from the road. It towered overhead as though promising a Victorian adventure.

Michael was right. It was a perfect house for a family.

Michael unlocked the door and held it open for her. "We're going in through the back door. I didn't think you'd mind," he said with a grin. Katherine smiled nervously as she stepped into a long, dark hallway.

"This way," he said, motioning for her to follow him. Michael walked past several closed doors before stopping at one near the middle of the hall.

He opened the door, and Katherine stepped inside, her whole body bathed in a soft, warm light. The room was furnished comfortably yet minimally. A black leather couch and marble coffee table sat facing a large stone fireplace in which a hearty fire was crackling. A brass liquor cabinet stood off to the right. The polished wood floor was partially covered by a thick, white lamb's-wool rug.

Unimpressed by the hazy glamour, Michael sat down on the couch and popped open his briefcase while Katherine stood there, admiring the room. She would have liked to see the rest of the mansion.

Michael raised an eyebrow. "We don't have much time."

Katherine snapped back into action. She set the stack of papers down on the floor. "What should I do with my coat?"

"Throw it anywhere." Michael jumped up and leaned out the door. "Randy! Linda!"

"Be there in a minute!" yelled a distant female voice. Katherine heard footsteps, and suddenly, a petite, plump woman of about forty with sandy blond hair appeared. She was barefoot, wearing jeans and a sweatshirt. She smiled when she saw Katherine.

"Hello, Michael. I didn't know you had company. I would've dressed."

"This is just Katherine," Michael said offhandedly. "She works for me."

Katherine rolled her eyes at Linda. Linda laughed.

"Thanks for making the distinction. Should I set another place for her at the dinner table, or will she be eating at your feet?"

Michael glanced at her. He was not in the mood for chatter. "Neither. We'll take trays in here. Katherine's going to be here for the next couple of days."

"Oh?" Linda said.

"Not staying here," Michael said, quickly correcting himself. "Just working here. She's helping me with a big . . . project. Where's Randy?"

"He's outside somewhere."

"When he comes in, would you ask him to bring in the rest of the papers from the back of the car?"

"Sure."

"And also, tell him that I don't want us to be disturbed. And everyone and anyone is a disturbance," he said.

"Got it," she said, taking Michael's coat. "I'll tell him to be very quiet."

"I'm not talking about you guys. No phone calls or visitors."

"Right. Dinner will be served around eight." She winked at Katherine as she took her coat.

"She seems nice," Katherine said after Linda had shut the door.

"Hmmm," Michael said, already totally ensconced in a paper.

Katherine picked up a fat-looking manuscript. She glanced over at Michael. She didn't feel like squeezing in next to him on the couch. She sat down awkwardly on the soft carpet, facing the fire. She leaned back against the couch. The room seemed smaller than when she had first laid eyes on it. And all the papers weren't even inside yet. She wondered why Michael chose this room to work in. Surely there were bigger, more appropriate rooms in the house. Katherine gazed into the fireplace.

"Wells, are you stuck on something?" Michael asked, staring at her impatiently.

Katherine cleared her throat. "No," she said, focusing on the intimidating manuscript in front of her. It looked like a detailed chemistry report.

It was going to be a long weekend.

36

Katherine looked at her watch. It was almost nine o'clock. They had been reading documents since eight in the morning. And the day before had been a seventeen-hour marathon. Katherine had driven home at midnight.

She looked at the papers scattered across the room. Some had been read by Michael, some by Katherine, some by both. There was primary research and secondary research, charts and figures from scientists and engineers around the world. So far, they had not found any data that suggested the engine was unsafe.

She glanced up at Michael. Over the past few days, he had been polite yet cold and distant. Despite the fact that they had spent hours in a tiny room, he treated her like an employee he didn't necessarily dislike or like, just a nonbeing he hadn't formed an opinion of yet.

Katherine glanced back into the fire, her mind wandering. She wondered how he could so easily dismiss their romance from his mind. She had found it impossible. But, for her, their romance had been much more than just a little fling. She had thought that she loved him. And she had mistakenly thought, at least for a while, that the feeling was mutual.

Katherine stood up.

Michael glanced at her.

"I'm going for a short walk," she said. "I just need to get some fresh air."

"Okay," Michael replied, setting down his papers. "I'll go with you."

Katherine hesitated. The only reason she was going for a walk was to get away from him.

"I'm only going for a short one. I'll be right back," she said.

"Great," Michael said, standing up. "I'll give you a brief tour of the grounds."

"Okay," Katherine replied somewhat hesitantly.

Michael stopped, aware of her reluctance. "Unless you wanted to be alone . . ."

"No. No, not at all," Katherine replied before she could stop herself.

"Then follow me," he said, grinning like a child at recess.

He led the way into the grand foyer. Katherine paused, admiring the magnificence of the entrance. The black-and-white marble floor was ten times the size of the room they had been packed into. There was a high ceiling from which hung an elaborate and delicate crystal chandelier. Off to the right was a large, sweeping circular staircase.

Michael opened the coat closet and handed her her coat. He grabbed an old, faded parka for himself.

"How beautiful," she said, her eyes resting on the carved wooden staircase.

"What?" he asked, distracted.

"The room."

"Oh. Hmmm." Michael looked around as though seeing it for the first time. "I don't usually come in here. I usually come in the back door and use the back staircase. I don't even keep my coats in here. We use it for guests. And Randy keeps some of his outdoor stuff in the closet."

"Oh," Katherine said.

Michael opened the front door. He glanced at his watch. "If we keep this short, I figure we'll be able to fit in a couple more hours tonight." He stopped. Something had just occurred to him. "Unless, of course, you have to go."

"No," Katherine replied, noticing his awkwardness, as she walked outside. It was obvious that he had something on his mind.

"I mean, I guess it is Saturday night. I wouldn't want to keep you from anything," he said, stepping out behind her and slamming the door. He began to walk toward the woods.

"I didn't make any plans for this weekend," Katherine said, attempting to keep up with him.

Michael slowed down his pace.

"What about you?" she asked carefully. "Do you and Carly have any plans later on?"

Michael jammed his hands in his pockets, suddenly irritated. "No."

Katherine glanced at him. She wondered why he was so bothered by her question. "I wasn't trying to be nosy . . ."

"Drop it," he said suddenly. Katherine stopped walking. She looked at him, hurt and angry. Michael walked a few paces by himself before stopping. He turned around and faced her abruptly. "I'm sorry," he said. "It's just that I don't really want to talk about it. Carly and I have a rather unusual relationship."

Katherine looked away. A snowflake drifted down lazily and landed on her nose. She wiped it off.

"It's starting to snow," Michael said, stretching out his hands. "This changes everything. I know where we should go. Where I always used to go as a child when it snowed." He seemed suddenly friendly. "Follow me." He motioned, picking up his pace. "There's a great view from the hill over there. You can see the lights of the city. It's where I used to build my snow forts."

Katherine entered the woods carefully. She edged her way up the hill, using tree limbs and scraggly bushes to help pull her up. Michael bounded ahead of her, as though the snow had taken fifteen years off his age.

He reached flat ground and turned around. "I haven't been back here since I bought the house," he called out. Katherine smiled receptively as she furrowed her brow in determination, still struggling to pull herself up. Michael, suddenly aware that Katherine was tiring, stepped down and offered her his hand for assistance. "Need help?"

Katherine shook her head. "No thanks. I'm right behind you."

Michael tried to keep from smiling. He admired her spirit.

Katherine finished climbing to the top. She stood beside Michael, staring at the twinkling city lights below them as she silently attempted to catch her breath.

"It's beautiful here," she said, as soon as she could manage.

"Yes," he replied, sitting on the frozen ground. "It makes you forget all of your troubles. At least, most of them," he added quickly.

"Michael," Katherine said, sitting down beside him. "I've been thinking. Why don't you call Alan and talk to him?"

Michael shook his head. "Not a chance."

"But it might help. Confront him one-on-one. He is your uncle, after all. In Florida, it seemed like he honestly cared about you."

Michael looked at her. He smiled patiently. "You think it's that easy? Just have a little talk, and we'll straighten this whole ugly mess out?"

"I think . . ."

"I know what you think. I believe I've told you this once before. You're not in Oz anymore, Dorothy."

Katherine stood up, insulted. "I think we better head back down."

Michael shook his head. He sighed and stood up. "I'm sorry, Wells. I know you're trying to help. And I do appreciate it. It's just that my family is related by blood only. The only person I have any type of close relationship with is my father, and it's even strained with him."

Katherine turned back toward him. She was surprised by the sudden revelation. "Was that because you never had a chance to get to know him?" she asked sympathetically.

"What?"

"When we were in Florida, you told me your dad was always either working or campaigning when you were growing up."

Michael shook his head. "There's more to it than that. After my dad lost the company and my mom died, I was so furious with him I didn't talk to him for years." He shrugged his shoulders. "I've never had a relationship with him," he said somewhat bitterly. "I've certainly tried. But the only relationship we've ever really had has been professional. Although sometimes I think I'm more like him than I care to admit," he said, thinking of the way his father was always able to read his mind.

Katherine hesitated. "Why didn't you talk to your dad after your mom died?"

"I guess," he said, shrugging his shoulders, "in a way, I blamed him for her death. My mother was not a very happy person. She tried, but she was in love with a man who didn't love her. At least, he didn't appear to. He never really treated her that well. She was by herself a lot. And when he wasn't running around campaigning or managing the company, he was having affairs. It wasn't until she was ill that he really realized how much he loved her."

"My dad was like that. A real womanizer. Except he never went through any catharsis. He died like that."

Michael glanced at her. He didn't tell her that he already knew that. He had taken the unusual step of running a background check on her, a practice that was usually only utilized when hiring high-level research staff. "I'm sorry," Michael said softly. "And I'm sorry about your mother. You've had a rough year, haven't you?"

Katherine shrugged her shoulders. She suddenly felt so emotional. She was afraid if she were to speak, she would start to cry.

Michael recognized her distress. He fought the urge to take her in his arms, to tell her everything would be all right.

She wanted to ask him if he, like her, was ever afraid of repeating his parents' mistakes. Perhaps it was his mother's unrequited love for his father that was responsible for his erratic behavior. Maybe he was just afraid of loving Carly too much. After an awkward, quiet moment, Katherine spoke. "Michael," she said, somewhat hesitantly. "Are you ever afraid of . . ." *Becoming your dad,* she wanted to ask. But she stopped herself.

"Afraid of what?" he asked gently.

Katherine shook her head. "Nothing."

"Katherine," he said, "I just want you to know that I appreciate all of your help. Really."

"Sure," she replied.

He looked at her, his tough veneer completely ripped away.

He took a step toward her. Katherine stared up at him. The silence of the snowy night hung over them, isolating them from the world. They were alone. All alone. Carly existed in another world, another time.

Michael took his gloved finger and gently traced the outline of her chin. He leaned forward and kissed her gently.

The spell was broken. Katherine pulled back.

"Don't, Michael. Please."

Michael sighed. He turned away. "You're right. I'm sorry. I just . . . well." He shrugged. "C'mon," he said quietly. He sounded tired. "Let's get back to the house." He paused, suddenly alert. His eyes were focused on the driveway.

"What is it? What's the matter?" Katherine asked, standing next to him. She followed his stare down the hill toward the house. It was not the driveway that had his attention but what was parked in it. Michael's attention was focused on the sleek white BMW that was now parked next to Katherine's red Mustang.

"That's Carly's car," he said.

37

Carly sat on the couch, comfortably settled into the room that Michael and Katherine had been working in. She wore a low-cut formal evening gown with a long slit up the side that allowed more than an ample view of her long legs.

"Darling," she said when she saw Michael. "I was getting ready to send out a search party. It seems like you two just drift away when it starts to snow."

"What are you doing here?" Michael asked coldly.

Carly stood up and kissed Michael on the cheek, ignoring his chilly reception.

Katherine stood in the hallway. If she hadn't left her purse inside the room, she wouldn't have dared come back in.

"Hi, Carly," Katherine said, embarrassed.

"I was in the neighborhood at a cocktail party, and I thought I'd drop in and see how your work was coming along," she said suspiciously. "I see you're both in the midst of things. I hope I'm not interrupting."

"No," Katherine said quickly. "As a matter of fact, I was just leaving." She picked up her purse.

"We're not finished yet," Michael insisted, looking at Katherine.

"Darling, perhaps Katherine has a date. After all, Kevin is in town."

"He is?" Michael asked.

Katherine winced. She had received a message on her answering machine from Kevin stating that he was flying in for the weekend, but she hadn't bothered to return it.

"As a matter of fact, he was at Evie's cocktail party. Looking very sad. He told me he flew all the way here just to see Katherine. And now here's poor Kevin with nothing to do, all because you're monopolizing her time."

Katherine stared at Carly. Her relationship with Kevin was no business of hers, and, besides that, she couldn't believe that Kevin had actually told her that.

Michael turned toward Katherine. "I certainly don't want to keep you," he said nonchalantly.

"No. No, you're not," Katherine stated.

Michael looked at Carly. "Well, my dear, thank you for stopping by. As you can see," he said, motioning around the room, "we're in the middle of things." He grabbed hold of her arm and began to steer her out of the room.

Carly held back. She glanced first at him and then at Katherine. She was not going to be rushed out so they could resume their lovemaking.

Carly leaned over and gracefully picked up her handbag. "I'm sure I'll see you soon, Katherine," she said, facing her. "By the way, I think it's so nice that you and Kevin have stayed in touch since Sun Valley. I don't know what you did to him, but you certainly made an impression. Kevin seems quite lovestruck. He said he had, and I quote, an amazing time with you that last night."

Carly paused, waiting for the impact of her words to sink in. She flipped her head casually back toward Michael. From the expression on Michael's face, she saw she had succeeded. "Will you see me out, darling?" She felt confident that it was now safe to leave them alone.

Michael glanced angrily at Katherine before following Carly out of the room.

Katherine sighed. She was angry that Carly had brought up Kevin. And even angrier at what she had been implying.

But, then again, she knew that Carly had every right to be distressed and jealous. After all, it wasn't as if she and Michael had been innocently working when she had arrived.

She looked up. Michael stood in the doorway, staring at her. Katherine's eyes locked with his. He seemed so strong, yet there was a definite vulnerability in his veneer.

"That was awkward," she said.

"Was it?" he asked.

He shut the door. "I didn't realize Kevin was in town. I've been very selfish."

"No," Katherine said, standing. "Speaking of Kevin, there's nothing . . ."

"I don't care to hear about it," he said definitively. "That's your own business."

Katherine swallowed. It was obvious that he was furious with her. Although he was the one who was engaged to be married. And to a woman who was pregnant with his child.

"You didn't have to ask Carly to leave. I should go, anyway," she said weakly.

"Anything the matter, Wells?" Michael inquired coldly, taking a step toward her.

"No. Why do you ask?" Katherine replied, as calmly as she could manage.

Michael took another step toward her. "You seem a little . . . nervous all of the sudden."

"You're mistaking fatigue for nervousness," she said, still avoiding his eyes.

"I think I know the difference. What's the matter, Wells? Are you worried I might suddenly mistake you for a . . . friend?" It was almost as though he was threatening her. Daring her.

Katherine responded in as cool a tone as she could manage. "Don't be ridiculous."

"I see," he said, aloof and distant. "As an employee, do you think you'd like a glass of brandy to toast the—loyalty you have displayed toward me?"

Katherine moved toward the door. She didn't like his tone of voice.

"Good-bye, Michael," she said.

"Let's have a drink," Michael said, stepping in front of her.

"You can't force me to stay," she said, digging her heels stubbornly into the carpet. She refused to let herself be intimidated by him.

Michael studied her carefully. He moved away from the door and began pouring two glasses of brandy.

"No. No, I can't. Nor do I want to. You're free to go, Wells. But I would like it very much if you would stay for a brandy," he said, softening his tone as he offered her the drink. Katherine hesitated before silently accepting it.

"To loyalty," he said, raising his glass. Katherine raised her glass and took a sip of the golden liquid. "Have a seat," he said, motioning to the couch.

Michael stood looking at her, leaning against the fireplace mantel. He smiled at her before gulping down the rest of his brandy.

Katherine followed his lead and swallowed the remainder of the brandy in her glass. She could feel the alcohol pushing her surging sexuality to the surface. She needed to get out of there. Fast.

"Thanks," she said, setting down her glass and standing up. Michael put his empty glass down on the mantel.

"For what?" he replied casually.

Katherine looked away from him and quickly walked toward the door.

Michael roughly grabbed her arm as she passed by him. He pulled her to him and breathed in the sweet smell of her hair.

"I think we need to talk," he said.

"I think I need to go," Katherine said, still facing the door. Michael took her by the shoulders and gently pulled her around to face him. He looked into her eyes searchingly.

"Why, Katherine?" he asked. "Why did you have to turn to Kevin, of all people? I knew you were hurting . . ."

Katherine broke away. "How dare you? You, you of all people, have no right to say anything."

Michael shook his head. She was beyond reach. It was hopeless.

"I know what I felt for you," he said softly.

Katherine stared at him. "A feeling so intense that you ran out and bought an engagement ring for someone else?" she asked.

"You don't understand," he said, his voice ringing with desperation as he grasped her shoulders.

Katherine broke away. "Get away from me," she said. "I don't want you touching me!"

Michael eyes reflected the frustration churning inside him.

Katherine backed away from him slowly.

"Michael, listen to me . . ." she tried to reason.

He stopped. "You're right. Forgive me." He turned and walked toward the door. "You were an excellent distraction, but I really need to start behaving myself. Sorry."

Katherine turned away from him, humiliated. Someone was knocking on the door.

"Michael?" said Linda.

Michael opened the door. "Carly is on the phone for you. Would you like to take it in here?"

"No. I'll take it upstairs. Tell her I'll be with her in a moment." He glanced back at Katherine. "Wait here. I'll be right back."

Katherine watched him leave the room, her face red with anger. He was treating her as though she was a common whore, someone he could take his pleasure with and then dismiss as if he was bored by her.

It dawned on her that this was his way of punishing her, of teaching her a lesson. Despite her assistance today, he still viewed her as a sex object. An employee he could use as he wished. His to use, his to discard.

Katherine shoved her purse in her briefcase. How could the man who had tenderly made love to her only a week before have changed so much? But he hadn't changed, she reminded herself. She had been a fool, imagining him to be someone he wasn't. And to think she had actually thought she was in love with him.

She picked up the crystal goblet she had carefully set on the coffee table and angrily whipped it into the fireplace. She slammed the door as the delicate crystal exploded into a million tiny pieces.

She grabbed her briefcase and pulled out her car keys. She wanted to get out of there before Michael discovered what she had done. After the way he had treated her tonight, she didn't want to have to see him ever again.

Michael hung up the phone. Carly had had nothing to say. She had obviously just called to distract him from Katherine. But it hadn't worked. Katherine was all he could· think about. He knew his behavior just now had been crass, but he couldn't forgive her for sleeping with Kevin. Nor could he understand it, no matter how hard he tried to rationalize her actions. He hadn't even been able to think of another woman since he first laid eyes on her.

Michael walked down the stairs. If she was anyone else, if she didn't work for him, he would be free of her. He wondered why he hadn't let her resign, as she told him she had planned on doing. At the time, he had reasoned that she was a highly valued employee. He had to admit that her behavior today had done nothing to prove otherwise. In fact, she had shown a cool head, keen understanding, and a unique sense about his business and predicament.

He reached the bottom of the stairway and looked toward the back door. He didn't remember leaving it open. He shut the door and leaned against it. He ran his fingers through his hair as he sighed deeply. He had to do something. He had never felt this way before. He found himself attracted to her intellectually as well as physically. Yet she had betrayed him. But had she really? In a moment of weakness, a moment when she thought he had betrayed her himself, she had turned to someone else for comfort. Was that so wrong?

Michael paused. He heard what sounded like the clinking of glass from his study. He began to walk back toward the room. He couldn't let her go. He wanted her too much. He needed her. His mind was made up. He would tell her the truth about Carly. He would ask for a new beginning.

He threw the door open, ready to confront Katherine again.

Instead, he saw Linda kneeling by the fireplace, picking up remnants of crystal.

"There appears to have been a slight accident," she said calmly.

Michael looked around the otherwise empty room. "Where's Katherine?" he asked gruffly.

"I don't have the slightest idea," Linda replied. "Randy and I were upstairs when I heard the smashing of glass. When I came downstairs, no one was here."

Michael picked up a shard of crystal. He could feel the fury begin to churn inside him. She had behaved in an immature manner for the last time. Not only by smashing the crystal but by running away as usual. He was no longer amused by her. Within seconds, he was in his car.

Katherine's Mustang sped along the slick, deserted highway. She had been so flustered she had missed her exit off the expressway and had been forced to turn around and backtrack, something that had only added to her frustration. She drove down the street across from her building slowly, swinging into the first open parking spot she could find. She stepped out of the car and onto the pavement. The snow had turned to slush, leaving the pavement cold and icy. Rather than open her umbrella, she decided to risk fate and made a dash for the door, clumsily sliding to a stop.

Katherine paused for a moment to gather her wits before she opened the door. Feeling slightly better, Katherine entered her apartment building, smiling pleasantly at the doorman. She took the elevator up to her floor while she silently outlined her agenda for the rest of the evening. She needed to de-stress. It had been a long three days and an even longer evening. She was ready to take a bath and make herself a steaming cup of chamomile tea.

Her key was in the lock when she was suddenly aware of a male presence behind her.

She whipped around to confront her intruder.

"What are you doing here?" she asked, stunned to see Michael standing before her.

"I'm getting a little tired of you running away from me," he spat.

"And I'm getting a little tired of you treating me like some . . . office tramp!"

"Maybe that would change if you stopped acting like one," he snarled.

"Get out of here," she ordered, holding her ground.

Michael stopped. He sighed. "Katherine, I didn't come here to argue with you," he said apologetically. "Can I come in for a minute? I need to talk to you."

"No," Katherine replied decisively.

"Katherine . . ."

"Look," she said, interrupting him. "I don't care why you came here. But this has to stop. And I'm going to stop it."

"What are you talking about?" Michael asked.

"I don't respect you," Katherine said evenly, meeting his eyes.

Michael paused, feeling the pain of her words slice through him. "You don't understand," he said.

"I'm afraid I do. All too well," she said coldly, turning away. She unlocked her door and pushed it open.

"No. No, you don't. This whole thing with Carly is a sham. It's all because ..."

"I know, Michael," Katherine said, shutting him up as she glanced back toward him.

"What?" he asked, disbelieving.

"I know the truth about Carly. She told me," she said, stepping inside the doorway and turning back to face him.

Michael paused. He couldn't believe what he was hearing. Katherine already knew about his arrangement with Carly? But why would Carly tell Katherine? Perhaps Carly was really looking after his best interests. Or at least trying to.

"And doesn't that make a difference to you? I wanted to tell you myself, in Sun Valley, the night of the party ..."

"The night of the party?" Katherine practically yelled. "Look, Michael," she began. She was dumbfounded. "This has nothing to do with Carly," she continued. "Even if you weren't with her, I could never be with anyone like you. And I never will." As painful as the whole situation was, at least she had discovered Michael's true nature before ... well, she consoled herself, better sooner than later.

Michael shook his head. "What? You're not making any sense. Only last week ..."

"Last week was a mistake. It never should've happened."

Michael paused, staring at her. He began to back away, shaking his head. "I don't know why I even bothered to come here," he said. Obviously, he had been wrong about Katherine. She was not the woman he had thought her to be. "By the way," he said, pausing briefly. "About what we talked about earlier. If you want to find another job, go ahead. I've changed my mind. I think it would be best if you left the company. Write up a recommendation for yourself, and I'll sign it."

"That's fine with me," Katherine said, slamming the door.

She would call Christopher tomorrow. She hadn't come all this way to let Michael defeat her.

38

Katherine sat at her desk, staring at her clock. Eight fifty-nine. She picked up the phone and dialed Christopher's number.

"Katherine!" Christopher said loudly into the receiver. "How have you been?" he asked, genuinely concerned.

"Fine," she replied quickly. "I just, I've been busy," she said.

"Yeah, yeah, yeah," he said teasingly. "Listen," he said. "I'm glad you called. I was going to call you myself. I arranged for you to meet with our personnel director. When's a good time?"

Katherine managed a tired smile. She knew she could count on him. "You're wonderful," she said. Suddenly, she remembered. The board meeting was tomorrow morning. And even though she knew she didn't have to go, she didn't think she'd be able to stay away. "I can come tomorrow afternoon."

"One o'clock?" he asked.

"Perfect. Christopher, thanks," she added simply.

"Anytime," he responded before hanging up the phone.

Katherine turned toward her computer and brought up her résumé on the screen. She had not gone back to Michael's house after the incident on Saturday night. Instead, she had spent Sunday updating her résumé. As far as she was concerned, Michael could fend for himself.

She reviewed her résumé again carefully. She knew she had some good experience, but the obvious flaw was that she hadn't been at Benson for even close to a year. What would she say when they asked her why she was leaving?

Katherine printed out a clean copy of her résumé. She had taken a stab at writing a letter of recommendation, but she wanted to think about it awhile before she finished it up. She put her résumé in her briefcase and grabbed her coat. The elevator doors opened. William Briggs was standing inside, briefcase in hand.

Small beads of perspiration lined his forehead.

"Hello, Katherine."

"William," Katherine acknowledged. She stepped inside the elevator. William pressed the close button. "I'm glad I ran into you. I wanted to set a time to show you the proofs from the other night."

"What?" William Briggs could not focus. He had just heard that Michael was waiting for him in his office. He had a premonition it was bad news. He was a thief, and he had been discovered. He was sure of it.

"They turned out really well," Katherine continued. She glanced at him. "I think the division could really take off with this campaign—literally." She made an attempt at laughter.

William was looking straight ahead. He hadn't even heard her.

The elevator doors opened at the lobby.

"Good-bye," he said, holding the door for her. A gentleman to the end. A gentleman thief.

"I've got a few minutes," Katherine announced. "I'll go with you to your office. I've got the prints right here. I can show them to you," she said, motioning to her briefcase.

He furrowed his brow. "Now's not a good time," he said quickly.

"It will only take a second," she said, looking at him suspiciously. She didn't trust him. Especially not the way he was acting. "You don't seem well. Are you nervous about tomorrow?"

"Tomorrow? Why would I be?"

"The board meeting. After all, if they vote Michael out, there could be some restructuring around here. It's no secret how Alan feels about the A-14 . . ." Katherine stopped. The elevator doors had opened. They were on the research division level. And Michael was standing in front of them. His tired, pale-faced lawyer, Harvey Doss, stood behind him, briefcase in hand.

Michael's voice was clear and cold. "Hello, William. We've been waiting for you."

39

Michael sat at his desk. The past few hours had drained him of whatever energy he still possessed after his marathon weekend of research. He wasn't sure what had taken more concentration, understanding the minute details in the papers William had given him or ignoring the distraction that had sat by the fire through most of the weekend. He ran his fingers through his hair. He had lost control. Every aspect of his life was being destroyed. He had been betrayed by people he thought he could trust. The most recent perpetrator was William.

Michael had hired a private detective soon after Katherine had shared her suspicions with him. He couldn't afford to take chances. Nor could he afford to wait. He was lucky he moved when he did. It had taken the detective less than forty-eight hours to come up with a laundry list of suspicious activity.

William had been careless. And obvious. He had even had the audacity to fax Alan from the office.

Michael slammed his fists on his desk. He stood up and began to pace angrily. William had admitted he sold his proxy to Alan. Although he swore he had not falsified any data, it was obvious that he was on Alan and Toby's side.

The outcome was inevitable. Toby Nat had succeeded. He had won over not only Alan but William as well. There would be no escape.

Michael was distracted by a knock on the door. He glanced toward it angrily. He had told Millie he did not want to be disturbed. By anyone.

"Yes!" he barked.

"Michael?" Katherine pushed the door open hesitantly. Michael stood in the corner, his face in the late-afternoon shadows.

"I'm sorry to bother you. I just, well, I saw the interaction downstairs." Katherine shut the door behind her and leaned up against it.

"And you were just curious if you had been right about William."

"Well . . ."

"Well, you were. Anything else?"

Katherine stepped back, embarrassed. "I'm sorry I bothered you."

Michael shook his head. He hadn't meant to take

his frustrations out on her. "Wait. I'm sorry." He stepped out of the shadows. His hair was tousled, and dark circles outlined his eyes.

Katherine shrugged her shoulders. "That's all right. You've got a lot on your mind." She paused. She felt a little guilty for being so harsh with him the night before. After all, perhaps he had really cared about her. Perhaps he was marrying Carly simply because it was the old-fashioned, honorable thing to do. Katherine had just had the misfortune of being his last fling. "How is it looking for tomorrow?"

"Not good. I had been counting on William to help me out of this mess. I wanted him to convince the stockholders that we were making strides."

"Was he falsifying data?"

"No. No, it's strange."

"I don't understand. William knew how Alan felt about research. Why would he want him to take over?"

"Because William is convinced that I don't really care about the company anymore. He said he knew that Alan wanted to take over the company, and he didn't think I was in a strong enough position right now to maintain control. He was trying to protect himself."

"I still don't understand. Alan wants to get rid of his division. He won't have a job if Alan is successful."

"I know," Michael said, deep in thought.

"It's just ridiculous," Katherine said quickly.

"I thought so, too. But apparently, Alan—or Toby—put a lot of work into this. And they succeeded. William admitted to selling Alan his proxy."

Katherine shook her head. "Can't you do anything?"

"I can't prove anything. Besides, a scandal would destroy this company. And I'm trying to save it. And I have less than twenty-four hours."

"If you need any help, let me know."

"I'm beyond help at this point."

Katherine glanced at him. "By the way, I'm sorry about breaking the glass. It's just that, quite frankly, I was upset about everything that happened. And confused."

"I appreciate the apology, but I've got a few things on my mind right now, so . . ." He motioned toward the door. She nodded. He was finished with her.

"Right." She walked over to the door, embarrassed. She hesitated. "I'm sorry about what I said last night. I was upset after Carly stopped by. I mean, here she is, pregnant, and I'm . . ."

Michael glanced up at her. "What?" he asked, irritated.

Katherine looked at him curiously. "I know Carly is pregnant. She told all of us at the photo shoot."

Michael leaned back in his chair. He was stunned. So that was what Katherine had meant when she said that Carly had already told her. He calmly spread his fingers on the desk.

"Us?" he asked.

"Louise and me."

"I see," he replied quietly. He needed time to think. "If you'll excuse me, Katherine," he said, using her first name, "I have a lot of work to do."

40

Michael sat in his den. The fire had died down hours ago, but the embers still smoked underneath the grate. The house was still with the ominous quiet of early dawn.

Michael had been sitting in the same position for hours, slowly reliving the tide of events that had turned his life upside down.

He was in love with a woman who had been so hurt by innuendo and rumors about him that she now wanted nothing to do with him. Even if she did learn the truth, would it make any difference? Michael shook his head. He had moved too quickly with Katherine, giving in to a passion that he had never experienced before. He, who had always shied away from marriage, was willing to propose to a woman he had known only three months. His actions with her had been spontaneous and ill thought, and he had paid dearly for them.

His mind drifted back to Sun Valley, to the events that unfolded only a week before. Their timing could not have been worse. Too many people had come between them. His mind focused on Carly. Kevin had obviously told her that Michael had purchased an engagement ring. But had she believed that ring was for her? Or had he allowed the woman who had been his friend and business associate for years to maneuver him into a fake engagement because she was pregnant? Pregnant with a child that could not possibly be his. He and Carly had not slept together for at least six months or more. But perhaps she wasn't even pregnant. Perhaps she had just told Katherine that to scare her away from Michael.

Michael picked up the same glass of brandy he had been nursing since nine the night before.

His professional life, so entwined with his personal life, was just as complicated. He was on the verge of losing the company he had fought so hard to build. He had been betrayed by his uncle, by Toby Nat, and even by William Briggs, a man who had just as much to lose if Toby and Alan took over the company as he did.

Had he been victimized by them all? Or did he play a part as well? His ego and inability to trust certainly had not helped. Nor had his inability to recognize the truth when he saw it.

He paused. There had to be a way to stop Toby. He was a former military man, a family man who was a no-nonsense steamroller when it came to business. Toby had made it clear that funneling money into research and development would enventually wreak havoc and devastation on the company. And he had persuaded several key players in the company to go along with him, most notably Alan and William.

Michael paused. He had to face the truth. He picked up the phone. He may not be able to solve his personal problems, but perhaps he could still salvage his company.

He dialed a number.

"It's Michael," he said. "I need to see you immediately."

41

Katherine arrived at the Hyatt ten minutes before the meeting was called to order. The grand ballroom was crowded with anxious-looking stockholders. Reporters hustled in the doorways, getting quotes from anyone who would spare the time. Katherine weaved her way through the onlookers. She flashed a pass and entered the room.

A single podium was placed strategically at center stage. On each side of the podium were eight chairs, one for each member of the board.

Katherine took a seat near the back of the room. She looked around. A group of five board members stood near the front of the room, talking animatedly among themselves. Katherine recognized some from Florida, others from the annual report. Two were women, Babs Douglass and Carolyn French. Of the other three men, she knew two, Tim Windsor and Brian Beltzer. Both were in their early seventies and had held high-level positions in the aeronautics industry. The remaining man in the group, Dan Klein, she knew by picture only. He was the parliamentarian, the man responsible for running the board meeting.

Dan Klein checked his watch. He said something to the people he was talking to and walked up onstage. He tapped the microphone to make sure it was working. He leaned over and spoke into it. "Attention, everyone. This meeting will be called to order momentarily. Please take your seats."

A quiet hum emanated from the audience as people began checking for available seats. The board of directors slowly began appearing onstage.

Safely anonymous from a distance, Katherine was free to focus on Michael. He was in deep conversation with his father.

Michael nodded cordially to Toby and Alan, who had just appeared onstage. William stood directly behind them, as if they were supposed to shield him from Michael's wrath.

Michael had not been successful in getting the board members to give him their proxy. Only two, his father and Babs Douglass, had agreed to his terms. But Michael did not look like an angry man. Instead, he appeared calm, almost confident. As though he was determined to accept his fate with grace. Katherine wondered what he would do if he lost. Would he still pursue a career in politics?

"Attention," the parliamentarian said when all of the directors were seated. "This meeting is now called to order."

"We are here today to discuss the rate of the dividends and the direction that has been taken by the president and CEO of the Benson Corporation, Michael Benson.

"Stockholders, as you probably know, you are allowed to vote on the issue of a dividend increase only. Only the board of directors may vote on the president.

"Okay. We're going to ask everyone to listen to the presentations and then vote yes or no." He held up a small card resembling an index card. "Drop the card in one of the boxes in the back. The computer will tabulate the results while the board votes on the remaining issue, and we will reconvene to announce the results."

Katherine squirmed. The room was crowded and warm.

"Okay. Michael Benson will begin."

Katherine slowly inhaled. Despite all that had happened between them, she was rooting for him.

"Good morning, everyone." Michael paused and glanced down at his notes. "The past few weeks have been, well, very interesting, to say the least." Nervous laughter emanated from the crowd.

"I think I've always made it pretty clear what my philosophy was. I've tried to be pretty public and vocal about it. Any of you who've been unfortunate enough to be caught alone with me have probably heard me ramble on more than you cared to listen." More laughter. Katherine exhaled.

"So here we are." He paused.

"I built this company on a philosophy. A philosophy that is directly tied into what I believe in, in both my personal and professional life. I believe that the only way to grow, the only way to triumph and succeed, is to take risks—and work hard."

He stared into the crowd in front of him. "The risks I suggest are calculated, and the payoffs are tremendous."

He glanced down at his notes. *Keep going,* Katherine whispered silently. *Make eye contact. You can do this.*

"As you all know, the A-14 division was created to break new ground. I believe we've already succeeded. But research takes time and money. Even so," he said, looking up, "within ten years, we've already designed an engine that can increase the speed of small commercial planes by almost twenty-five percent.

"And we're just beginning. So if everything is going along according to plan, what's the problem? That's easy." He paused and stepped in front of the podium.

"The problem is me."

People began to react, whispering among themselves quietly. Katherine sat up straight in her seat. What was he doing? Resigning? She wanted to run up and pull him off the stage. She had to help him.

"Just a minute," he said, motioning for everyone to be quiet. "Please. Let me finish."

He glanced around the audience.

"Lately. I've begun to realize how important it is to communicate. It sounds so simple, yet I would not be standing here if I had communicated to everyone what the facts are.

"I am so convinced that research and development is the core of this company, that if it is voted that the money should be taken out of research and development and put back into dividends, I will resign as president, sell my stock, and relinquish my position as chairman of the board."

An audible murmur of surprise rose from the audience. Toby and Alan glanced at each other.

"If you vote to put the money back into dividends, you will see a short-term increase. But in a period of years, or even months, you will see your investment stagnate. I know this is true, because it has happened before. To this company. My father and uncle were witness to that. And now, my uncle, if given the power, will do it again."

He shrugged his shoulders. It was over. "That's all I have to say."

Katherine shook her head. His presentation was disappointing. It was not enough. He needed to convince his audience with facts and figures, not a lecture on his philosophy of life.

Dan Klein stood up. "Thanks, Michael. Next, we'll hear from Alan Benson. Alan?"

Alan Benson stood up. He smiled congenially as he

walked to the podium. He glanced around the room as though the audience was filled with close personal friends.

"I think everyone can appreciate what a difficult position I'm in right now. Michael Benson is my nephew. And I happen to know he's an honorable guy. And he's a likable guy. But this isn't a personality contest," he said easily. He was comfortable in the limelight, and it showed.

"It's a business decision. One that will have an immediate impact on your finances.

"Let's look at the facts. Michael's premise that the stock will rise based on outstanding inventions depends on one thing: the quality of the research.

"He loves to talk about the A-14 engine. But the A-14 engine was introduced last year, and stock prices have fallen, not risen.

"This isn't the eighties anymore. This is the lean, mean nineties. We can't afford to have flat, bloated, tired divisions that don't produce. Especially when it comes to research and development. We're barking at the heels of Japan. They've been ahead of us every step of the way. Let's accept it and adapt. Let's become lean and mean so we can spring ahead. Let's let them waste their money in research. Take their products that work and adapt them to this market. That's where the growth is. That's where the money is."

He paused. "But don't just take my word for it. I'd like to call someone else up to share his opinion. The head of research and a fellow director and stockholder, William Briggs."

From her seat in the distance, Katherine watched as William Briggs rose and walked to center stage. This was much worse than she had expected.

Michael sat in his chair, his face revealing nothing. No anger, surprise, or indignation. His steely blue eyes were focused politely on William, as though he was merely a luncheon speaker.

William stood behind the podium. He glanced around the room nervously.

"I believe . . ." He hesitated. "I believe that the research we've done . . ." He paused again.

Katherine wanted to scream. He couldn't do this to Michael. It made no sense.

"We are on the verge of a technological revolution. We've had a couple of bad breaks, true," he said, his voice slowly becoming louder and stronger. "But we have a real possibility here of not only participating in this revolution but leading it."

There was a hum of confusion in the audience. William was representing Alan, yet he was supporting Michael.

"But," William continued, "it's not going to happen without belief, patience, and trust. Michael Benson took this company out of sure bankruptcy and shaped it into the international corporation it is today because he believed in his vision of the future. Unfortunately, I'm talking to you today not to praise our successes but to ask forgiveness for failures. For my own personal failure. You see, I made the mistake of believing gossip and innuendo . . ."

Katherine smiled. Michael had done it. He had succeeded. William was on his side.

Toby Nat jumped up. "Enough! What has he promised you?" He turned toward the crowd. "This man was ready to denounce Michael Benson yesterday."

The parliamentarian jumped up. "Mr. Nat! Please! Take your seat, sir!"

William turned back toward the audience. "He's right, you know. Due to some false information I received about Michael, I lost faith. I was scared. I was selfishly ready to trade in everything I believed in, everything I had spent my life working for, for money in the bank.

"I made the mistake of selling my proxy to Alan. But I'm selling my shares in the company to Michael.

"On that note, I regretfully offer the board my resignation. Effective immediately."

42

Katherine stood outside the hotel. The votes had been tabulated. Michael was staying on as chairman of the board and president of the Benson Corporation.

She had been surprised by William's sudden confession and resignation. She knew that Michael had confronted him yesterday, but she hadn't expected such a dramatic turnaround.

She walked past the limousine that was waiting to whisk Michael away and stepped up to the curb.

Despite the victory, Katherine was not happy. As it did for William, this meeting marked the end of her brief tenure with the company. Michael was free to move on with his life and his plans. He didn't need her anymore. He had won the approval and support of his A-14 division without an expensive advertising campaign.

Not that it mattered. Her campaign was ruined anyway. William had seen to that.

"Cab?" the bellboy asked.

"Yes," Katherine replied quickly. She didn't have time for conversation. She had an interview to go to.

"Katherine! Katherine, wait!" Kevin came bounding out of the hotel. He dashed up to her and gave her a kiss on the cheek.

"Hi," she said, moving toward the cab. "I'd love to talk to you, but I'm really in a rush right now."

"Sure," he said. "We'll catch up later." He opened the cab door for her. After she had climbed inside, he leaned into the cab.

"You're having dinner with me tonight."

"I'm sorry, Kevin. I can't. Now, if you'll excuse me," she said, attempting to shut the door. Kevin swung the door open and jumped inside next to her.

"Kevin!"

"Where to?" the driver asked calmly.

"Around the block for now," Kevin said, giving the man a twenty.

"Kevin, I'm running late!"

"So promise to have dinner with me, and I'll let you go."

"Kevin . . ."

"Make that twice around the block, driver."

"All right," Katherine said as the car headed out of the driveway.

Kevin smiled and leaned forward to talk to the cab driver. "You can drop me off around the back of the hotel. That will give this lovely lady a chance to tell me where she lives."

So distracted was Katherine by Kevin's antics, she didn't notice the crowd that had gathered behind the cab. Michael Benson had come out of the hotel and stood facing a swarm of reporters who were hanging on his every word. But his attention was not focused on them. He was focused on the taxi that was pulling out of the driveway. The taxi carrying Katherine and Kevin.

43

It was almost four-thirty. Katherine stood in front of
Millie's desk. She had been waiting to see Michael for
fifteen minutes.

"How much longer do you think he'll be?"

Millie shrugged her shoulders. Not only did she not
know, she didn't care. "No idea."

Katherine sat down. She was restless. She wanted
to resign and leave.

Her mind wandered back to her interview at Bender
and Ann. The interview had been short, but she felt
it had gone well. Although she was currently working
as a director and was applying for a job as a manager,
she had assured the director of personnel that she was
not overqualified for the position because of the limited amount of time she had spent at Benson. When
the personnel director had asked her why she was
leaving after only three months, Katherine had responded simply, if not honestly, indicating that the
political struggles within the organization were pre-
venting her from properly focusing on her job.

Suddenly, loud, angry voices resonated from behind
the closed door.

Katherine looked at Millie curiously.

"He's got his cousin in there," Millie said. "It's usually like this. I can tell they're wrapping it up. He'll
be available any minute now."

Katherine could feel her heart skip a beat. She

looked toward the door helplessly. Could their argument have anything to do with her?

Almost immediately, the door opened, and Kevin stormed out. He was so enraged that he walked right past her without noticing her and bounded down the stairs.

Katherine looked toward Millie for reassurance. Millie ignored her, focusing instead on the simple typing job in front of her.

Katherine paused as she eyed the empty staircase. Perhaps this wasn't the best time to speak with Michael.

"Michael!" Millie yelled. "Katherine Wells has been waiting."

Katherine rolled her eyes. So much for an escape.

Michael stood in his office doorway, glowering at her. "I'm sorry to keep you waiting, Wells," he said with a hint of a smirk. "Why don't you come in?"

Katherine followed him into his office as though she was venturing toward the guillotine.

"Shut the door," he commanded.

Katherine shut the door.

"Have a seat," he said, pointing to a chair.

"I'll stand," she replied calmly. "I'll only be a minute. Congratulations on today."

"Thank you," Michael said, leaning back in his chair. He wasn't in any hurry. He was in control again.

"I'm curious," Katherine said. "What made William change his mind?"

"I had a little talk with him early this morning," Michael said.

"What did you say?"

"I told him that I knew that he had been feeding Alan sensitive information. I just reminded him that not only is that illegal, but he had a fiduciary responsibility to the stockholders which he neglected."

"And what did he say?" she asked.

"He admitted it. He said he only did it because he was ill and financially pressed. He was worried that Alan would take the company over and dismiss him. When Alan offered him two million for his support, William agreed."

"And Alan? Was he falsifying data?"

"I don't think he had to. I mean, the A-14 engine is extremely safe, but the product we ended up developing took years. Alan could've circulated some of the early data, some of the tests that the early versions of the engine failed."

"But that's illegal, isn't it?"

"Illegal and unethical. It could also be viewed as manipulation of the press, which, in turn, caused the stock to decrease in value."

Katherine sighed. "Oh my God. What are you going to do?"

"Alan and Toby have both resigned their positions on the board and are selling me their shares. Needless to say, I'm getting a hell of a deal." Michael shrugged. "I'm not going to prosecute. A scandal of that nature would hurt this company more than it's worth. I'd just end up hurting myself."

"You're just going to let them go?" Katherine asked, almost disappointed.

"William has a heart condition. I can't help but feel badly for him. He really is a decent man, he's just a poor businessman."

"You're letting him stay?"

"No. But I paid a fair price for his stock in the company, and he's retiring. With pension."

"And Alan? Is this going to tear your family apart?"

"Hardly. My family is getting pretty used to this type of thing. Remember, I took the company away from Alan once. We'll get over it. And this whole thing has apparently taken a lot out of him. I spoke with my aunt Theresa this afternoon. Alan's decided to slow down a bit. He's talking about starting some sort of boating company." Michael stared at her intently.

Katherine looked away.

Michael asked softly, "Why did you come here, Katherine?"

She hesitated. It was time. The sooner she did it, the sooner she could get on with her life. "I came to submit my resignation," she said, laying it on his desk. "I'd also like you to sign a letter of recommendation," she added rapidly, setting it down beside her resignation.

"I see," he said nonchalantly. "When do you plan on leaving?"

"Immediately," she replied, her eyes meeting his. "I've decided that it would not be in my best interests to continue working here," she said.

"Of course," he said, his voice rising slightly. "Especially when you're considering an offer from my uncle to come and work for him."

Katherine looked at him, surprised. "What are you talking about?" she said.

He smiled, as though he believed Katherine was attempting to involve him in a game of deceit. "Kevin just told me that you're going to work for his father. He said you're meeting with him tonight to discuss the terms."

"Michael, that's not true . . ." Katherine responded.

"So you're not seeing him tonight?" he asked suspiciously.

"Yes . . . I mean, no. I am, but it's not what you think," Katherine mumbled.

Michael leaned forward and looked at the papers she had set on his desk. "I'll sign these so you can be on your way." He looked at his watch. "You've only got fifteen minutes to get it to personnel before the office closes," he said, holding up her resignation. Michael scanned the papers quickly before signing them. "I'd wish you luck, but you seem pretty capable of looking out for yourself," he said, angrily handing the papers back to her.

Katherine accepted her resignation and recommendation silently. So this was it? There were not going to be any apologies, any good wishes, however false? But then, of course, what did she expect? This was Michael. Cold, rude, inconsiderate. "Right." She walked over to the door. There was nothing left to say. It was over. She turned and quietly left the office.

Carly was waiting outside Michael's office. "Well, hello," Carly said.

"Hi," Katherine managed. She wondered if Carly had been eavesdropping on her altercation with Michael.

Carly Wentworth smiled smugly as she watched Katherine walk toward the staircase. From her demeanor, Carly would have to assume things were proceeding perfectly. She pushed open the door to Michael's office, not giving him even a moment to recuperate from Katherine's visit.

"Hello, Michael," Carly said, plopping into the chair. She smoothed her skirt and swung one long, slender leg over the other. She pulled on the pinkie of her small black leather glove. "I got your message. What's so urgent?"

"I wanted to see you," he said. He hesitated. He was tempted to run after Katherine. To stop her. Perhaps, if she knew the truth about Carly, she might forgive him. But could he forgive her indiscretion?

He checked his watch. He couldn't leave. He had one last important matter yet to deal with. And the timing was right. The confrontation had to happen now. Harvey was waiting.

He forced himself to look at the woman in front of

him. Poor Carly. He was in no mood to play games. Nor did he feel like allowing anyone to manipulate him.

"Carly, I want to officially break off the engagement," he abruptly informed her.

"What?" she asked. "You promised a month ..."

"Unfortunately, I did so foolishly. I should have realized that the longer we wait, the more difficult it will be."

Carly's nostrils flared with anger.

"Also, I've heard a rumor that you're pregnant," he continued, as if discussing a business proposal. "Is this true?"

She paused for effect. If he wanted to play nasty, then so would she. She smiled. "Yes," she said confidently. She had assumed Katherine would tell him sooner or later. "I'm pregnant with your child," she added indignantly.

Michael's voice dropped threateningly. "How far along are you?"

"Far enough."

Michael paused. He had to be careful. "You and I both know this child is not mine. We haven't been together in more than six months."

"Come now, Michael. No one will believe this baby is not yours."

"That's not true. *Someone* will. And more people will after the DNA tests come back."

"You can't do tests until the baby is born. And by then, I'll have created a huge scandal. It won't matter anymore what the tests say. You can kiss your political dreams good-bye."

Michael hesitated.

Carly smiled. She was winning. "It won't be so bad," she said. "I think you'll find me to be an extremely understanding wife."

Michael shook his head. "It's over, Carly," he said

softly. "I don't care what you do. I want you out of my life. I think . . . I hope that you'll handle this wisely."

"Does this have anything to do with Katherine?" she asked coldly.

"Leave her out of this," he said quietly.

"It does, doesn't it?" she said angrily. "You're going to publicly humiliate me just so that you don't hurt the feelings of this . . . office girl."

"That's enough," Michael said. "You're the one who concocted this whole bizarre engagement. You knew I had no intention of marrying you. You're the one who called Georgia."

Carly wasn't listening. "I'll tell everyone that you threw me aside, your pregnant fiancée, because you were sleeping with your trashy employee. Katherine won't be able to get any respect in this company, or any company ever again . . ."

"Enough!" Michael pounded his hand on the table. "Katherine has nothing to do with my not wanting to marry you. And as far as my professional relationship with Katherine is concerned, you might as well be the first to know that her employment has been terminated."

"You fired her?" Carly asked in disbelief.

"She just resigned."

"I see," Carly said, nodding her head and smiling bitterly. "And you're going to try and get her to come back by announcing you're single again."

Michael stood up and turned toward the window. "Do you want me to call the newspapers and make the announcement, or do you want to handle it?" he asked, refusing her bait.

"Michael," Carly pleaded, standing up and walking behind him. "Please reconsider. If you don't want a baby that's not yours, I understand. I'll get rid of it. It's not too late. We can make our own child."

Michael turned back toward her. He shook his head. "My God," he said simply.

The door opened. Harvey Doss walked into the room. "We've got enough."

Carly looked confused. "What?"

Michael glanced at her. "I recorded the whole thing. On video." He pointed to a camera hidden in the corner of the office. He paused. "The charade is over, Carly. If you so much as breathe a word of bullshit, I will send this to every news and gossip program in the country. Got it?"

"You wouldn't dare," she said.

"Don't bet on it."

"You'd be destroying yourself as well," she threatened. "Destroying the entire Benson Corporation."

"I'm not sure I care anymore," Michael said, exhausted.

Millie interrupted on the intercom. "Excuse me, Michael," she said. "Julie Major from Bender and Ann is on the phone. She said it's regarding Katherine."

Carly stood up. "You make me sick."

"One more thing," Michael said. Carly turned. "I'm firing you and your agency. In accordance with the contract, you've got thirty days."

"You can't do that. On what grounds?"

"Overbilling."

Carly gave Harvey an eerie look. Without a word, she turned and walked proudly out of the office, slamming the door behind her.

Michael leaned back in his chair. "Thanks, Harvey." Michael pushed the button on his phone to communicate with Millie.

He breathed a deep sigh of relief. He was facing every nemesis. "I'll take it," he said into the intercom.

44

Katherine put the disk containing her résumé into her briefcase, on top of the letter of recommendation that Michael had signed. She looked around the room carefully. She didn't want to have to return because she had forgotten something.

She turned. Louise was standing in the doorway in her multicolored fluorescent minidress and hot-pink tights. She had been crying. Katherine sighed.

"I don't understand why you have to leave like this," Louise said. Katherine had informed her just an hour ago of her decision to resign.

"It's complicated," Katherine said.

"It has to do with Michael, doesn't it?" Louise said. Katherine shook her head but refused to say anything.

"I won't tell anyone. You two were involved, and he dumped you for Carly. Because she was pregnant."

"Ouch," Katherine replied.

"Well?" Louise asked.

"Please," Katherine said, suddenly overcome with emotion. "I can't really think about it."

"I hate him," Louise said.

"No, you don't," Katherine said, reprimanding her as she would a child. "Don't let my leaving affect your relationship with Michael."

"How could he be so stupid? Carly over you? He's got to be crazy . . ."

"Louise." Katherine paused. She would miss her assistant. She had had a lot of fun working with her. But she couldn't confide in her. She couldn't bear the thought of her personal mistakes becoming fodder for the office gossip mill. "Please."

Louise paused. She sat on Katherine's desk as though she owned it, her legs swinging over the side. "Do you have another job?"

Katherine shook her head. "No. I'm moving to Chicago."

"Chicago," Louise said, surprised. "It's freezing there."

Katherine nodded. She didn't like long good-byes. She was ready to go.

And Louise could sense it. Louise jumped off the desk and picked up Katherine's briefcase. As she handed it to her, she gave her a little hug, whimpered good-bye, and ran out of the room. Katherine watched her go. Somehow the fact that she was returning to the Midwest, that she was not staying in Baltimore, made leaving much more bearable.

It was the job offer from Julie Major at Bender and Ann that had changed her mind about staying. She had offered Katherine another chance, another opportunity to start again. But Katherine knew as soon as Julie called that she had to leave the city. Just getting another job would not be enough. She could not stand to read about Michael in the papers and run into him at the ballet.

Katherine dropped off a note on Diane's desk. She would have liked to have said good-bye in person, but she didn't want to have to explain why she was leaving. It was better just to escape.

She took the back stairs and exited through the side door, merging quickly into the rush-hour crowd scurrying home. She glanced at her watch. She had to be at the car dealer in half an hour. She was selling her car. The money from the sale would help support her until she could find another job. Another job far away.

She felt a cool sense of resolve as she picked up her pace.

Katherine stepped into the warmth of her apartment building and looked around at the high ceiling and mirrored hall. Selling her car had been more painful than she had expected. When she stepped into a taxi to take her home from the dealer, she had felt sad, as though she was leaving behind an old friend. And even though she hadn't lived in her apartment very long, she knew it would also be difficult to give up her glamorous surroundings.

"Excuse me," said the doorman. "This came for you." He pulled a long box tied with a red ribbon from behind his desk.

Katherine curiously accepted the box. She waited until she was in her apartment to look at the card: "Looking forward to tonight—Kevin."

Katherine opened the box. Eleven perfect long-stemmed yellow roses were delicately placed inside.

Katherine sighed at the thought of Kevin. She knew he meant well, but she found him an incredible nuisance.

She changed out of her suit and into a pair of jeans

and a loose-fitting sweatshirt. She was determined that she would not go anywhere with another member of the Benson family. She was fed up and disgusted with the whole bunch.

Katherine opened the phone book and thumbed through it, stopping at the advertisement for Amtrak. She wanted to leave tonight, and a last-minute one-way plane ticket was too expensive for a woman without a job. Instead of flying, she would take the train.

Katherine made her reservations and hung up. Her train left this evening and arrived in Chicago around lunchtime tomorrow.

When she got into town, she would get a hotel room and begin calling her old friends from school. She felt sure she could stay with them if she needed to. But she hoped that wouldn't be necessary. Thanks to her trusty car and her savings, she had enough money to support herself comfortably for a while. And she could always wait tables or work as a temporary while she was looking for work.

Katherine shook her head. After years of a nice paycheck, it was going to be a rude awakening.

But she didn't have to worry about that now. She had a long train ride to relax and consider her options. Some time to plan her attack.

A few hours later, her suitcases were packed full. She moved around her apartment in a dissociated daze, her mind carefully going over all the details. She had to leave her keys with the doorman when she left.

Katherine came out of her trance long enough to hear someone knocking on the door. She finished zipping up her last suitcase before answering it.

"Hey, beautiful," Kevin said, leaning in for a kiss as he handed her a single rose. "That makes a dozen," he said, in case she had forgotten about the earlier bunch. Katherine turned her head so that Kevin's lips landed firmly on her cheek. He stepped in cheerfully, undaunted by the rebuff.

"Thanks for the flower," she said, "but I think you should keep it. I don't have anyplace to put it. And you should keep these as well," she said, handing him the box of flowers.

Dumbfounded, Kevin accepted the box. This was the first time he had reversed the process of sending a single rose before the eleven. Obviously, he should have stuck with what worked. He brought himself bad luck.

"Going somewhere?" he asked, nodding toward the suitcases that lined the foyer.

"I'm leaving," she replied, standing firmly in front of him.

Kevin furrowed his brow. "Business or personal?"

"Both."

"What do you mean?" Kevin asked, his suspicion quickly turning into alarm.

"I'm going to Chi—away," she said. "Tonight." Kevin stared at her with dismay.

"What are you talking about? You make it sound so ominous. Like you're getting the hell out of Dodge."

"That's exactly what I'm telling you."

"Why?" He looked at her suspiciously. "Because of Michael . . . because some guy dumped you? You're moving?"

"Honestly, Kevin!"

"C'mon, Katherine. If I had to move away from every girl who's ever dumped me, I don't think I could live in the States anymore. I would have to move to Europe or something . . . or maybe Wyoming. Wyoming and Alabama are still safe." He smiled. "Besides, you haven't even heard me out yet. I have an offer for you. A serious one."

"I have no intention of working for your father,

Kevin," she said. "There was never, nor will there ever be, any question of that."

Kevin hesitated. "I was hoping to do this over a quiet dinner, but I guess it can't wait. My father really wants you on staff. He'll give you twenty-five percent more than you're earning right now," he added quickly.

Katherine laughed. "You must be anxious to make Michael angry. Or do you think I could do some espionage work for you? My knowledge about Michael's company must certainly be valuable to you."

Kevin looked at her. "This is a great opportunity for you," he said.

Katherine shook her head slowly. "I've had enough of great opportunities." She hesitated. "You shouldn't have told Michael I was planning on meeting you to discuss this. If you hadn't done that, I would have gone out to dinner with you. Considering the circumstances, I have to decline."

Kevin looked at her angrily. "So that's that, huh? Adios, good-bye, I'll never see you again?" he asked.

"I prefer to think of it as a simple good-bye and good luck," she replied, holding the door open for him. "Oh," she said, pulling a piece of paper out of her pocket. "This is the number of a beautiful, fun woman who made me promise to mention her to you."

Kevin stared down at the number. "You mentioned me to her?" he asked, flattered.

"She's a friend of mine. But, quite frankly, I'd be more than relieved if you didn't take her number."

Kevin snatched it away.

"Oh, well," she said, opening the door. Kevin shoved the number into his pocket. Despite his jokes to the contrary, this was the first woman who had given him the brushoff. Not to mention another woman's phone number. He hoped she was the last.

He walked out of her apartment silently.

Katherine closed the door and turned back to survey the status of her apartment. She was right on schedule.

Kevin drifted aimlessly down the street. He laid the roses ceremoniously beside a trash can and pitifully pondered his lack of company. Regardless of his romantic situation, or lack of it, he still had to eat. Kevin turned down an alley and headed for the Tavern. He pulled the piece of paper with Cyndi's name on it out of his pocket. Who knows, he thought, his spirits picking up, perhaps he might even find a little dessert.

Michael was sitting at the bar when the bartender motioned for him to look toward the door. Michael felt the tension in his stiff neck intensify. He had come here because he knew Kevin frequented the Tavern when he was in town. And he thought his cousin might just bring Katherine here. But now that the bartender had signaled that they had arrived, he was having second thoughts. Why couldn't he just let it end?

But Kevin was alone. Michael watched as Kevin took a seat at the opposite end of the bar, not noticing Michael. Michael picked up his beer and walked toward him.

"Hey, Kevin. Expecting someone?" Michael asked.

Kevin glanced at him nonchalantly. "Michael," he said. "I wish I could say I'm surprised. You just here by chance? Or perhaps you were hoping to run into a . . . neighbor?" He turned back toward the bar.

"Is she coming?" Michael asked, as calmly as he could manage.

Kevin glanced at him out of the corner of his eye. "Not exactly," he said.

"Too bad," Michael said. "I would've enjoyed helping her negotiate her contract with you boys."

Kevin studied the menu. Michael sat down on the stool next to him.

"Did she stand you up because she decided to take the job at Bender and Ann?"

Kevin turned back toward him. "What are you talking about?" he said.

"She's going to work for a law firm in town. I got a call this afternoon," Michael said.

Kevin laughed out loud. "I don't think so. If that's true, she's going to have a hell of a commute."

Michael looked at him curiously. "What do you mean?" he asked.

"She's not going to work for that firm," he replied.

"She's going to work for you and your father?" Michael asked angrily.

"No. Although we offered her a lot of money to do just that. She wouldn't even listen to me." He looked at Michael as he continued, raising his voice. "You've pushed her too far this time, cuz. She's leaving town. Tonight."

"You mean . . ." Michael began, not quite understanding.

"I mean she's leaving. Packing up and moving on," Kevin responded. "I just left her. She said she didn't even have time to talk to me. Her suitcases were already packed."

Michael sat back down, stunned.

Kevin sighed. "That woman is too in love with you to stay in town and watch you marry someone else," he said. "She's a nice person, Mikey. She's not willing to be anyone's mistress. Not even yours."

"Or yours?" Michael spat.

Kevin laughed at him. "I wish." He looked away from Michael and stared at the liquor bottles lined up against the back of the bar. "Look, I don't know why I'm telling you this, but nothing happened the night that Katherine slept in my room."

"What are you talking about?" Michael replied belligerently. "I was in her room all night. I know she didn't come back."

"She was upset. She didn't want to return to her

room—she didn't give me any explanation, and I didn't ask for one, but I assume it had something to do with you. She tried to find another room, but the hotel was full."

"So you graciously invited her back to your room," Michael interrupted.

"I never even touched her," Kevin said, looking Michael in the eye. "I slept on the chair, and, believe me, I had the stiff neck to prove it."

Michael stared back at Kevin, stunned by the ring of truth to his story.

Kevin looked away before continuing. "I guess she never told you about what really happened between us—or, rather, what didn't happen—because she felt you probably wouldn't believe her. Or maybe she wanted you to think that something had happened because she was upset about your engagement, and it wasn't any of your business anymore. I don't know," he said, picking up his beer. "And frankly, I don't give a damn," he added dramatically, turning back toward Michael. But he was speaking to an empty chair. Michael had already left.

Michael's car screeched to a halt outside Katherine's apartment building. He jumped out and within seconds had discovered that Katherine had already left for the train station. He screeched out of the apartment building driveway as he reached for his cellular phone. He wasn't about to let her get away.

46

Katherine walked quickly toward her gate. Although she wasn't cold, she wrapped her coat around her shivering form. She felt physically weak from the emotional stress of the past week. She knew that if she allowed herself to cry, she probably wouldn't be able to stop until she arrived in Chicago, and she had no desire to draw attention to her plight.

She realized she had to numb her emotions if she was going to survive the long night ahead of her. It was a fourteen-hour train ride, which meant that if she was going to sleep, she would have to do it sitting up in her seat. A plane ride in good weather conditions would have taken only a couple of hours, but for the price of a one-way ticket at the last minute, she could stay in the Hyatt for a week.

As soon as Katherine arrived at the gate, the train began boarding. Fortunately, it was almost empty. Katherine picked a seat near the window and set her bag down beside her. She leaned back in the seat and carefully went over her fragmented plan. Once she arrived in Chicago, she would take a cab to the same artsy, inexpensive hotel that she and her mother had stayed at during one of their visits to the city.

She would start over. In a city where no one knew or cared who Michael Benson was. Michael . . . why did her every thought seem to drift back to him? Their cold, impersonal good-bye was representative of their entire relationship. But he was not to blame.

She had chosen him. *She* had allowed herself to be used and discarded.

"Ticket?" The conductor stared down at her. Katherine handed him the ticket, uncomfortably realizing that she had anxiously folded it into a little square. How long had she been daydreaming?

The man took the ticket and ripped off her receipt, sticking it onto the overhead bin above her. Almost immediately, she felt a little jolt as the train began to move away from the station.

Katherine closed her eyes in an attempt to suppress the wave of sadness enveloping her. She reminded herself that she had to leave the city. She wasn't really running away. She was taking responsibility for her actions and moving on. That was all.

Katherine stared outside the tinted window as the train methodically wound its way out of the tunnel and past the old, discarded hotels and factories dispersed along the tracks.

She glanced back at the aisle and the conductor who was making his way toward her. He looked at the ticket above her and then back down at her. "All the way to Chicago, huh? You've got a long ride ahead of you. We've got an empty sleeper cabin if you're interested."

Katherine hesitated. "How much more is it?"

"No extra charge. It's kind of like an airplane upgrade. We have the space, so you can use it. If we were full, you'd have to stay right here."

Katherine smiled. "Thank you. That would be great." She picked up her bag and followed him through several cabins, finally arriving at a long row of closed doors. The conductor opened the last door on the left and motioned for Katherine to enter. She thanked him again as she walked into a small, cramped room. The compartment contained a small couch next to the window. Above the couch was an overhead bin that folded down into a bed. There was a tiny bathroom off to the side. It wasn't glamorous, but at least she would be able to lie down comfortably in her own private space.

She went into the bathroom and splashed water on her face. She reached for the towel and wiped her face dry. As she glanced into the mirror, her heart skipped a beat. Michael stood behind her.

"Michael," Katherine managed, talking to his reflection. She turned around.

"I was hoping I'd get here before you," he replied.

"But what . . . you arranged this?"

"Sit down, Katherine." Katherine continued to stand, still too surprised to move. "Please."

Katherine hesitated. "What are you doing here? How did you find me?" she asked angrily.

"I ran into Kevin. He told me you were leaving, and I've been working the phones ever since to find you . . . with some help from Millie. I felt sure you were returning to Michigan."

"I'm going to Chicago."

"Well, then, it's a fortunate break for me that this train stops in Michigan."

"This private room . . . this wasn't any upgrade, was it?" She paused. He stood immobile in front of her, his blue-gray eyes bearing down on her intensely. Of course, she realized. Many rich, powerful men had mistresses. Why not him?

"Look," Michael continued. "I went to a lot of trouble to see you tonight. I've called in more than a few favors to get them to hold the damn train until I got there . . . not to mention a speeding ticket," he added mischievously.

Katherine looked at him coldly. His charm was not going to affect her. "Save it, Michael. I don't work for you anymore. You have no hold on me. Got it? I don't know what type of game you're playing, but if you want a mistress, I'm sure there are a lot of women who'll want the job. I quit, remember?"

Michael looked at her searchingly. "Hear me out, Katherine. That's all I ask." Katherine backed up against the window, still refusing to sit down. Michael stared at her. This wasn't going according to plan. "I'm not engaged. I never was. It was a sham. The whole engagement. It was ... something Carly invented in her own mind."

"Oh, please, Michael," Katherine interrupted angrily. "You announced it right in front of me. Right after ..."

"*She* announced it. Kevin told her he saw me buying an engagement ring, and she assumed it was for her. But it wasn't." Michael looked at her carefully. "It was for you. I never even gave it to her."

Katherine looked at him, stunned. "But Carly's pregnant."

"Not with my child."

"What?" Katherine asked incredulously.

"She may be pregnant, but it's not mine. And she knows it." He paused. "I didn't even know that she was pregnant until you told me."

Katherine stared at him.

"I haven't been with any woman since I first laid eyes on you. You have to believe me. Look. The only reason I didn't interrupt Carly when she announced our supposed engagement at that damn party was because I was caught off guard. As soon as the words were out of her mouth, all I could think of was finding you. To explain. To leave that stupid party. Then you wouldn't talk to me ... well, as soon as you and Kevin left, I told her the truth. I dropped her off and went straight to your room. Again, to explain. When you never came back that night, I assumed that you and Kevin ..."

"Michael. Nothing happened that night."

Michael nodded his head. "I know. The whole situation was a mess. It was my fault."

Katherine glanced away. So many pieces to the puzzle. "But you were engaged," she said. "You even had an engagement party. At her parents'. The night I saw Toby and Alan."

"What? There wasn't any engagement party. Her parents had an anniversary party. We were never really engaged," he repeated, walking around and facing her. "Like I said, Kevin saw me buying the ring and told her about it. She panicked. She planned the whole thing ... and I bought it. After you left the party at Jason's, I told her the ring was not meant for her, and she pretended to be mortified. She asked that I keep my mouth shut for a month, at which point she would announce that we were not engaged."

"A month?"

"She said if we announced it immediately, it would look like, well, like how it really was. She felt if we were engaged for at least a little while, she would be able to preserve some dignity. But I told her I wouldn't agree to anything until I talked to you. Which I planned to do that night."

"This is unbelievable."

"I know, but it's true. I don't think she figured out exactly what happened between us after I left her that night, but she knew I never spoke to you, and I think she realized it was because you were with Kevin. I think she was hoping that I would proceed with the engagement just to spite you. And when my back was turned, she would announce she was pregnant. With my child."

Katherine shook her head slightly. "I just can't

believe it. And even if this is true, it doesn't change the way you treated me. You made me feel used, and ..."

"I know. I'm sorry. Seeing you every day, and wanting you the way I do." He hesitated. "After I found you with Kevin, I was angry. At myself and at you for making me love you. I've never felt this way about anyone before ... and when things got complicated, I didn't handle them very well."

Katherine looked away. "I appreciate you taking the time and effort to go to all this trouble to explain the situation to me ..."

"Please, Katherine, listen to what I'm saying ... this is too important."

"But, as you just said, the situation is a mess," Katherine continued, trying not to listen to him. "And I think the best way is for us to say good-bye. I'm moving to Chicago. I don't even have a job anymore, remember? I don't even have a car anymore."

"What happened to your car?" he asked.

"I sold it. I needed the money. For Chicago."

Michael shook his head. "Oh, Katherine," he said sadly. "It's not too late. Look," he said encouragingly. "I'll call from the train and buy it back for you. And you have your job. Minus Carly. I fired her agency. You can hire your own agency, your own staff if you want. In the meantime, we'll go to Chicago together. We'll make a long weekend out of it. Just the two of us. We'll go out to dinner, to the museums ... and then you'll come back to Baltimore with me. Back to your job."

"You can't buy me, Michael. And I won't go back to my job. I can't."

"Then come back for me. I don't want to buy you, Katherine. I want to love you."

Katherine was on the verge of tears. Why was he telling her this now? It was too late for her to believe in fairy tales. "Forget it, Michael. You said yourself that a corporation was not a great place for families."

"There are exceptions to every rule. And you are my exception, in every sense of the word," he said.

"Good-bye, Michael." Katherine grabbed her bag and made a dash for the door. Michael's arm shot up in front of her, blocking her path.

"Look at me when you say good-bye."

"Get out of my way," Katherine said. "Please."

Michael dropped his arm and moved toward her. "Katherine . . ."

Katherine made a quick dash for the door. Michael grabbed her and spun her around to face him, clutching her slender shoulders. His eyes bore deeply into hers, looking for a sign of warmth, a sign of hesitation. "Tell me you don't love me, and I'll let you go."

"It's not a question of that, it's just . . ." Katherine protested.

Michael put his index finger on her lips to quiet her. He reached inside his pocket and pulled out a small ring box. "This was meant for you." He opened it up. The diamond ring sparkled enchantingly before her. She looked at Michael curiously. "You don't have to answer right now."

"Michael," Katherine whispered. "You can't be serious."

"Stay with me, Katherine," he replied. He took the ring and slipped it on her finger. "Will you marry me?"

"I . . . I don't know what to say."

"Say yes," he said decisively.

"You still want to get married? After everything?"

"I've been single a long time, Katherine. I know how I feel. I love you. I love you like I've never loved anyone before. I want to be with you. Always." He paused. "But, of course, if you don't love me ..."

Katherine couldn't stop the smile forming on her lips. "Oh, Michael," she murmured happily. "I love you. I just thought ..."

"No more thoughts," he whispered, pulling her in close. "Only fantasies."